ANY
TIME
ANY
WHEN

KENNETH VARNER

Publisher
VarnerBooks

VarneBooks Publishing
220 Bayou View
El Lago, TX 77586

ANY TIME ANY WHEN
$13.95
Copyright © Kenneth Varner 2013

VarnerBooks Publication ISBN 978-0-9889602-2-0

ACKNOWLEDGEMENTS

To my wife who is not a big science fiction fan but will probably insist on editing this thing anyway. She's always been a glutton for punishment otherwise how could have put up with me for over fifty years? She may also be curious to find out how someone can write an eight hundred page book, cut it in half and still have something readable.

In addition, I'm interested in seeing how appalled a lot of my friends will be after reading the first fifty or so pages. They will probably forgive me and read it anyway because that's what friends do.

I also, want to add that Joel Turner at America's Press repeatedly furnished valuable advice and assistance to a new author with phone and email questions about book publishing. I recognize that his business is printing books and such help is good business, still his encouragement and advice in the printing process for this and my previous book, Land Of The Morning Calm was greatly appreciated.

ANY TIME ANY WHEN
PART I
CHAPTER 1

CREATION
8906 BCE

The ship's speaker brought Arientain awake. "We are entering the project planetary system, honored sir. You wished to be awakened when that event occurred."

"I'll be down shortly." he murmured, still half asleep. "Have the teams assembled in the lounge in, oh, a studendha."

A studendha later he was sitting over his breakfast with the rest of the field team eating theirs. He looked out over the group. He didn't know many of them but would get to know each, intimately, before long. Besides the Observer Team there was the Communications group, a total of almost a hundred. Another several hundred engineers were already on planet and had been for almost three local years preparing the initial landing and headquarters site. All except the Observers would return on the ship to Magma as soon as their work was finished. The Observers would remain, evaluating the progress of the indigenous sentient beings until their progress or lack of it, dictated removal or - less likely - upgrade. It would be a long process, several standard years - several thousand local ones.

Arientain wondered if they were up to the job. Of course, all had been specially selected for it but the selection process didn't produce a feeling of much confidence in their abilities. None were more stable than he was and that wasn't saying much. They might as well have remained in locked away in Coventry with the rest of the "exiles". He had to chuckle - that only totally dysfunctional individuals would agree to a job like this. Though no one spoke of it, this assignment was just another form of it exile. Of course, to him, anything was better than the stifling life back home. Well, too late to worry about that now. He took a deep breath and began his initial briefing.

"As you know from the data you've studied," I said between bites, "This planetary system was created by moving a relatively small sun into a universe carefully separated from the Main, with a totally separate time gradient. By doing this and allowing events to operate in a vastly increased but unstable time scale, it is hoped that the creation errors can be smoothed out. The AI's predicted that this change would affect the suns radiation levels to a point that the planets will evolve dramatically. The eventual effect, though, cannot be accurately predicted ahead of time. You have seen the results to date. The orbits of the planets surrounding the sun grew erratic and changed dramatically. The planet we expected to use for the project overheated and became totally unsuited for our purposes. One of the larger planets, unexpectedly, captured another, broke it up and made rings out of it. Another grew so massive that it has become almost a proto sun itself."

"Fortunately, one of the least likely planets became almost perfect for our purposes. Aside from a great deal of still active volcanism, it contains all the elements necessary for our project. As a result, it was appropriately seeded almost four of our years ago. Some of the indigenous life forms were taken and altered to produce the beings we intend to use. At that time the time flow in the system was still radically

5

fluctuating and the result was that about four million local years have passed since the seeding. The present rate has slowed dramatically, and is still slightly unstable but, at present, averages about four thousand local years to our one."

"Our subjects have scattered widely over the planet and, as expected, seem to be adapting well to all changes that occur. The intelligence level is very high as is the level of aggression. It will be important that all be especially careful when dealing with them. They are some of the most erratic and dangerous animals in the universe. They combine high intelligence with gross savagery. As a result those of us who have to move among them will, no doubt, need frequent re-balancing sessions. Actually, the entire ecosystem of the planet is spectacularly dangerous. It even contains numerous species of toxic plants, a few of which can kill, even we who have been protected against most of the various viral and bacterial infections present. It's how the system was designed, of course, and necessary to our purposes, but that does not help when dealing with them. All these dangers were carefully created to prepare the eventual dominant species to face the dangers that lie ahead and, hopefully, to conquer them. Now, if you have all finished your meal, I would like to go over the data received since we have arrived in this system. From now on, even for station use we will always use our new persona. I am now Jonha."

He waited until the table had been cleared and the juices served. He turned to the large screen which immediately lit up with a view of a large island with a mountain rising sharply from the sea and a flat top. The scene drew closer until all could see the frenzied activity atop the large plateau.

"The large stone huts shown will be our nominal living quarters for dealing with any natives who happen by. The main installation is, of course, below ground with rather nice quarters and office space. The AI's were put in only a few days ago but are already on line. The local days, by the way, are expected to eventually, settle down to approximately twenty four or five studenha and the orbit around the sun to stabilize at somewhat less than four hundred days. The huts are expected to be fully functional by the time we arrive, which will be three local days from now."

"We are barely inside the orbit of the outermost planet in the system at this time and our destination is still too far for optical equipment. I remember, though, that you, Eve – oh I forgot we should, from now on - get used to the names chosen for our observer rolls. I am now Jonha and you "Eve" expressed some trepidation at the exceedingly large reptilian presence once extant on the planet. The preparation team assures me that they were mostly destroyed long ago by a planetary surface shift. The ones that remain are mostly aquatic and shouldn't bother us much at the station. They, however, must be considered carefully when around large streams in the tropical zones. Speaking of the reptiles, we were expecting at least one species of them to become the dominant species on the planet that I mentioned before. That did not occur. The evolutionary changes the planet went through were too severe for them to survive."

Two other species, aquatic mammalian ones, survived and developed a rather high degree of intelligence but while they can eventually become quite suitable for admission into the civilized universe, they will never be capable of the task ahead. We were, in fact, almost ready to give up and close the project when one of the smaller mammalian species began to show signs of the traits we need. We, therefore, made a few modifications to their genes - strictly in accord with project directives - and the result is the species we are to observe. Now, if you all will place your hands on the new palm reader you will get a full briefing on your assignments and all that is known of our task. All of you have been thoroughly desensitized to the violence of this place - or as much as was possible, considering our makeup - but if you become somewhat overcome by the details have a drink of juice. It has been lightly tranked."

All those present, reached out to the silver plate before them and placed their hands, palm down on it. Jonha noted, with satisfaction, the reactions as they received the inputs. Al and Archer blanched and reached for the juice. The rest managed, some with varying degrees of difficulty, to accept the data presented. He was pleased that he had selected his team well. Surprisingly, it was the women who held up best.

"By hir - God!" Atam gasped. "Are we sure we want things like this loose in the universe? They're mental monsters!" I almost smiled. Atam had not forgotten his persona even under these conditions.

"Check your species specifications, Atam." They match, almost exactly, what the committee decided was the minimum requirements for the task ahead. The interesting thing is that they are, physically, so much like us, or like we were a few millennia or so ago. They are a lot shorter and heavier but that is due to the planetary gravitational fluctuations during their evolution. Now that it has settled down their physical structure will, almost certainly change. We feel that due to the increased gravity they will not likely reach our height but will eventually achieve about eighty percent of it. As for their intelligence, it is exceptionally high - actually capable of reaching, or perhaps eventually, surpassing ours. It is the reason that such a physically puny race has come to dominate a planet on which every major species was specifically designed for aggressive tendencies.

"They don't seem to be very far along with technology Ariet - Jonha. Couldn't the council have waited awhile longer before inserting us?"

I couldn't help a smile at Atam. "Check the rate of technological change rather than the level." He said. "Oh my -" he caught himself and bowed ironically to Atam, "- or Atam's God! I see. It took them - the data isn't there - but it must have been hundreds of thousands of their years to even notice fire and only a ten thousand to transition from pure family groups to tribal combinations." "Yes. Well, we haven't kept a really close watch on the place until now. The AI's predict, however, that they are on the verge of a new transition into creating the first cities with farming as a mainstay of the system. We were afraid that, if we waited much longer, they would have harnessed the animals to a wheel."

"It's hard to believe." Milam murmured thoughtfully, "But I can see the projections. The possibility of planetary destructive capability might be only a few thousand of their years away. Can the AI's estimate time to invent the wheel? That will be the next accelerator to their development."

"I think the AI's are becoming a bit wary of predicting the future of this culture." Jonha chuckled. "The estimate for the wheel is six thousand local years plus or minus

7

five thousand. They even added an unheard of caveat, and I quote 'Predictions relative to the development of this culture are proving to contain gross errors. Data from field observers should contain detailed information relative to cultural shifts and technical developments. It would seem that our Artificial Intelligence brothers are at a loss to determine the eventual progress of these people."

As trained observers, the shock of the team members was short lived - though the next question was posed in a somewhat subdued tone.

"I note only a few matriarchal societies. That is rather surprising Jonha."

"Very true Phronia." I said with a sigh. "It's one of our major dilemmas. We all know that almost all true civilizations arose from Matriarchy and it's hard to see how a viable one can come from the other side. The fact is, however, the patriarchal societies, here, tend to dominate. It is, perhaps, because of the extreme dangers inherent to the planet and the fact that the males are much larger than the females. It's obvious that they recognize the absolute necessity of protecting the females in an extremely dangerous environment. If the males tend to domineer, they also protect ferociously. The AI's note that, the dominating traits in the males, has produced, in the females, a tendency toward extreme cunning. They seem to be astute observers of others and have become very effective manipulators of the males. None of you must ever forget this when observing the, often seemingly irrational, behavior of the males. This fact was taken into account in your assignments. Until we gain more information, the observers will always operate in teams - one female and one male per team."

"Now let's take a look at the areas in which you field agents will be operating. The planet has only two major landmasses and one minor one. For your information, there was only one a few million local years ago. The largest, of the three labeled "1" on the screen, contains most of the presently viable civilizations. It is, however, geologically very unstable. No doubt it will be almost cut into two pieces if a major earthquake occurs along either of the two fault lines shown. The central area is separated from the sea by these very thin uplifts here and here and if, I should say when because it is almost a certainty that it will happen, the area shown in red will become inundated and become an arm of the smaller ocean. The areas to the east of that part of the planet form, at present, several of the more advanced civilizations on the planet."

"The second landmass is already almost cut in two pieces. Only a thin isthmus joins the north and south portions. The central portions, near the isthmus, have only lately become civilized, if you can call it that. A land bridge in the far north, to the number one landmass was formed ten or fifteen thousand local years ago and continued until that bridge was severed during one of the several "Ice Ages" on the planet. The people who crossed that bridge were particularly savage and continue so today. They eventually populated most of the land mass and are attaining a high degree of knowledge. Unfortunately they are beginning to actively practice ritual sacrifice on a scale unknown on the rest of the world. Geologically, the western coast line of this landmass is very unstable. Actually, the entire coastline of the major ocean is very unstable volcanically. The link between the north and south will probably be breached in the future but because it is a very mountainous area. The AI will not project when."

"The third and smallest landmass was torn from the original single continent long ago by the continuing shifts in plate tectonics. Its movement toward a more civilized culture is far behind the other two in development. The indigenous population is barely out of the first stage of development but is the only one in which the need to destroy others is not highly developed. For the present no assignments are contemplated for this area."

Jonha paused for any questions. There were none. "Alright. Moving on to the question of observation? You are authorized to fit into the population, taking part in all activities not directly involving violence to other sapient creatures. This definition has been stretched somewhat, to exclude creatures used for food by the locals. Your personas have been designed to minimize your participation in local violence between tribes. When your activities cannot be made to fit into this stricture, you will be evacuated - to the extent possible, in a manner to cause the least effect on the locals."

"In some cases, especially when individually threatened with violence, you may use the modulator to escape from, or disarm, your assailant." He grinned over at Archer. "All of you can, if you have to do so, use the equipment even though it adversely affects some. A very important problem you will face is that, at times, even though you will be teamed with a member of the opposite sex, you may find it socially necessary to acquire a local for a mate." There was an uncomfortable shifting of weight around the table. Jonha ignored it. "You all are well aware of this problem and the fact that we have found no perfect method of birth control for these people. Their systems are simply too different from ours. The AI's are agreed, though, that cross fertilization between our races is, while relatively difficult, possible. You must bend every effort to prevent conception between yourselves and a local. Any offspring would have a lifespan almost as long as ours and could improperly affect long term development."

"In general, the probability that they will die by violence tends to negate this fact but it cannot be ignored. Any mistakes that cannot be avoided and that might impinge too heavily on local development will be brought to the headquarters and attempts will be made to train them to be of some use. Finally, you are absolutely proscribed from any action that tends to affect the subject populations natural development no matter what the consequences.""

The discussion lasted for hours. Finally, the tone sounded, announcing the availability of the next meal. Jonha suppressed a grin and authorized it. Plates of various types of unfamiliar foods appeared. The surprise was universal. "Your first local meal." Jonha chuckled. "You had better get used to it. It's what you will be living on for the next period."

"What in the world is it?" Atam exclaimed. Jonha chuckled again at the extent that the ingrained persona was taking over. No true Magman would have used that tone in public - or even private for that matter. "In your case, Atam, it's a dead and almost burned animal called, locally, a buck. The rest of you have either a brown lump that is the local animal properly burned in a fire, or some local aquatic species endemic to your assigned area - also partly burned. I thought you should get used to this stuff so you won't lose your insides in front of the locals who set great store, in most cases, by their ability to impress guests with their 'cooking'."

LANDING

Jonha turned, with a feeling of trepidation, back toward headquarters as the last of the shuttles left. Almost thirty local days had passed since the landing of his team.

The initial party had left almost ten days ago to meet the ship that would carry them home. The transfer station was in place but until they reached Magma the coordination of the two systems could not be completed. He was on his own for, at least twelve local years.

After the intensive aerial survey of the planet he had decided that landmass one would get the initial observation teams. In addition the openly hostile environment dictated to person teams cutting in half the number of available observer units, so, for now, only the central portion of the landmass would be targeted. He had plenty of work to do in completing the task of setting up the Atlantian systems for the long haul. He wondered if his mother would ever know - or for that matter - care that he had named his home for the next Magman decade or two after her - probably not. She had never been too pleased to admit to a son who was incapable of adjustment to Magman ways.

Once inside the headquarters building, things were much more civilized. Even with most of the installation underground, the offices were well equipped for the administrative task ahead. He went, immediately to the AI center. Milam looked up as he entered. "All the AI's are on line and functioning properly." he said. "It will take another seven days or so - local that is - for all systems to finish the programming checkout but the head AI assures me that all is well. We're holding off inventorying the landed equipment until that is finished. A cursory check though indicates a few shortages, the most notable being a small shuttle and the backup AI. No doubt they'll turn up eventually." Jonha nodded and after a few other words left to continue his inspection.

At dinner that evening, as the staff went over the day's work, "Evelyn" noted that, after hearing of Milam's problem, she had gone over the mass inventory. Sure enough the shuttle and extra AI had been scratched from the inventory just before takeoff but the mass had not been adjusted. In checking the records the ships mass data reflected the additional mass plus two extra persons. "I'm assuming a problem in the ships logs. Unfortunately, since the ship is gone, we can't confirm that. Also, I've gone over the rosters and everyone who is supposed to be here, is."

Jonha had more important things to worry about than a few errors in shipping data. He looked up and asked, dead pan."Alright, I want the persons who are not here to speak up." That gained a little laugh. "Seriously, I think we're looking at a bunch of minor shipping glitches. The only things of importance are the shuttle and AI. I'll order replacements when we finally get on line with Magma. In the meantime, we shouldn't have a real problem with the ones we have. I've never known, for instance, even one of the AI's to fail. Anyway, you'd better get some rest, at least those of you going out to your assignments tomorrow night.

CHAPTER 2

ATAM

7165 BCE

Atam paused in his plowing to gaze out over his valley. He continued to think of it as his even though it now sprouted a good two dozen dwellings of various types. Most, of course, were tents - but they were simi-permanent ones. Only he and Evelyn's, and the chief's huts were of sun dried brick. From the looks of the attendees at the chief's "tribal meetings though, he suspected that several tents would be replaced in the next few months. The thick walls of the huts allowed a leeway in retaining or keeping out heat. The only advantage the tents had was in dissipating the smoke from the rush torches used at night - but the huts, also, didn't catch fire from those same torches. He had alleviated that by facing the door toward the prevailing wind and cutting a hole in the back wall. The idea of a door was, he thought, a bit beyond the limitations of their tasking but a large hide could cover the openings on the coldest of nights. All the family dwellings, though, now had, at least, a small plot of cultivated ground around them.

He wondered what the council would think of his "intervention". They probably wouldn't even understand that the "calling" of people to a certain place could be accomplished without complex technological help. As a field observer, he'd just report to them, the change from hunter/gatherer to farmer as evidence of faster than expected developmental progress.

It hadn't taken any real coercion on his part anyway. It had been simple enough make a camp near a small river and not too far off the normal migration routes of the local nomads. He'd then gathered some wild wheat seed and planted them. Here, Evelyn's knowledge of botany came in handy and she was able to use the resulting grain to bake a flat style of bread on a sun heated flat rock. They'd probably have to use fire to heat the rock in the winter. The results, if not so tasty was satisfyingly filling. Certainly would be nice if he could figure out how to get some salt out here. She'd even managed a few scrawny tuber plants as well as a green plant that wasn't bad to eat if it was cooked enough.

After the crop was up it had acted as a magnet to the, ever curious, hunter/gatherers as they passed by. The idea that someone would want to settle in one place was a true novelty to them. They watched what he and Evelyn did though and a few had copied them. They now had a simi-permanent village around them. He chuckled at the thought that a sharpened stick dragged through the ground and carrying water to plants with goatskins filled at the river, could be considered "advanced agriculture". The village leaders still hadn't acknowledged his contribution to their increased well being - and still insisted that hunting was the only real occupation for a man. They were constantly complaining about the fact that they had to go farther and farther to find game. The women, however, had no such compunction. The almost unbelievable capability to produce food at will, and without having to scour the countryside for it, was enough for their more practical minds. Of course, Evelyn had always been more able than he to persuade others to her ideas.

The land was extremely rich and productive along the river banks. If he didn't miss the greater diversity of modern living so much, - especially the food - he'd be content to live out his life here. Of course, his and Evelyn's assignment was simply to observe life in the region. Their reports would have to be carefully worded.

11

It was hard to remember all the watches he and Evelyn had stood. In the, almost, four thousand years they'd been here, they'd become well seasoned in their jobs. They had also become very protective of their neighbors and each assignment had become harder and harder to leave even though these people, even in the early days when they had only clubs, could not seem to leave their neighbors alone. They fought over everything and nothing. It was for that reason that he and Eve had decided to make a little "contribution". On the theory that people who had a stake in an area were less likely to covet their neighbor's area, they had begun their little experiment in an agrarian society. He was almost smugly proud of how it was working out.

He stared across the field at his two "sons". They'd become sons in his heart if not in fact. Orphaned, at about the age of eight, by the death of their parents in a prairie fire, Evelyn had insisted on taking them home to raise. Tony wouldn't like that either, but they'd, so far, not mentioned them in reports. Chaine and Abier had grown into powerful young teenagers. In fact, by the lights of the tribes, they were already old enough to assume the responsibilities of manhood. Evelyn wasn't the only one who was going to miss them when they had to leave. He turned his eyes to the western horizon, frowning as he remembered the Chief's words last night. That worthy had come by, ostensibly, to simply visit. He'd made it clear that he wasn't asking for advice but noted, in passing, that two of his western hunting parties were overdue. That was a bit unusual. These people were surprisingly precise in their movements and there had been no hint of weather to hinder them. Atam had said that they must have had better luck on the hunt than expected.

He'd have to request an update, in his next report, on the migrations of some of the more warlike western tribes. There'd never been any sign of their moving out of their traditional migration patterns but better to be safe than sorry. He smiled at the phrase. No one on Magma would have the slightest idea what it meant. Safety there was so taken for granted that there wasn't even a word for it. Words like accident, hurt, killing, terror, were only part of his new vocabulary. In fact, they were so ubiquitous that he had stopped trembling when he heard them.

"Father, Father! I think the hunters are back." It was Abier shaking him. He rolled over, a quick flush spreading over him. He still had trouble remembering that the locals expected a man and woman to lie naked together in bed. He noticed, absently that it still wasn't even light yet and wondered, in passing, what had impelled the hunting party to move through the night. He sighed in remembering Evelyn's flesh under his hands last night, but he rolled out of the rush covered slab that passed for a bed. Another thing he'd forgotten to list as advantages of civilization yesterday. Straightening slowly to work the kinks out of his back he threw on his robe and followed his excited sons out the door.

He came fully alert at the sound of Abier's scream. Rushing to the open door, he beheld him impaled on a spear as the spearman struggled to extract it from his body. At the same time Chaine leapt at the man. The warrior dropped the spear and tried to draw his knife. It was too late. Chaine had smashed him to the ground and was hammering his head to a pulp with a rock. Atam looked out over the village. A dozen strangers were attacking the people as they emerged from their tents. He could see several bodies already down. Suddenly, he was awash in anger! Had the circumstances been different he would, undoubtedly, been shocked to his Magman core at the thought of hatred - especially hatred against another thinking being. The circumstances were not

12

different! His son and many of his friends were being murdered before his eyes. He lost all control in the blood lust that overtook him. He smacked the bump on his side that controlled the modulator. He swayed a moment at the inevitable reaction to its use. Implanted in all field personnel, even though few could use it without getting violently ill, it would result in his stomach being upset for days. He, nevertheless, gulped down the bile that rose in his throat as all action stopped. Chaine's hand was at the top of his swing. Taking deep breaths trying to overcome the nausea, he saw that he was in control of his situation. He headed for the village at a dead run. He heard Evelyn's cry behind him telling him to stop and think. She'd, obviously had the presence of mind to use her modulator also. He didn't want to think. He was bent on revenge.

He reached the first of the attackers. He'd just driven his spear into the leg of a child. Furiously he jerked the weapon from the unresisting hands and drove it completely through the man's body. He turned and ran to the next one. Five minutes later, he turned to find no more attackers to destroy. Confused by the lack of further targets, he looked back the way he'd come. Evelyn stood at the other end of the village, her hands pressed against her face staring at him. The fury drained away as fast as it had come to be replaced with the horror of his actions. He fell to his knees, devastated, not simply by the destruction he had wreaked in his assault but by the assault itself. Never in history had a citizen of Magma ever even wished ill of another. To actually harm another was unthinkable - and yet he, in the course of a single normal time breath, had murdered - he looked up to see - twelve helpless humans. He covered his head and fell back to earth crying. Later - it seemed hours - Evelyn was there comforting him.

It was, several quick time hours before he finally recovered enough to assess the situation. He looked up at Evelyn's tear stained face as she caressed him. With a shudder and a nod to her, he touched his side. The village came alive. Twelve dying men fell to earth. The screaming of the villagers began to die down, replaced by awe at the sight of the dying and at their being alive. He knelt in the dust of the street watching as their eyes searched for an explanation and settled on him. All he could think of, was "Where did they come from? There'd been a routine scan five days ago. At that time there were no other tribes within ten normal days travel. And where were the hunters?" The questions rolled around in his head, repeated over and over all mixed up with "How could I have done it - the inconceivable!" I had disincarnated twelve men - and the rage! Where had that come from? Never had a Magman been more than a little startled at the unexpected. None had ever reacted with such violence. The thought alone was enough to make him violently ill once again.

"You've got to say something." Evelyn whispered as he stopped retching. "They must have an explanation." "I couldn't." I gasped, wiping my mouth. She sighed and stood up. Her voice rang out with only a slight quiver of emotions. "My man has called upon his god to protect your village. As you can see the god has responded. See to your wounded quickly and bury the dead. My man will have further words for you later when he has recovered from the effort of calling him." She, then, went to the little boy with the blood gushing from his leg and began to help the villagers. They had little knowledge of healing but were so shocked, that they obeyed her instructions quickly.

We buried Abier on the hillside behind our hut. I then met with the chief and tried to undo the terrible damage I'd done while Evelyn managed to break a few more rules and save several of the wounded villagers from certain death by infection. He didn't think my actions so bad. In fact, while not admitting to surprise at my ability to kill twelve armed men in the space of a breath, he kept trying to kneel down in front of me. He wanted to make me a god in my own right. He was shaken by my assertion that I had to leave. He agreed, though, that it was only fitting that Chaine stay to work my fields and that some defense of the village must be undertaken. I returned to break the news to Chaine. I also explained how to make the better mud bricks to build a wall for safety - might as well break another few rules while I was at it. The villagers had simply watched Evelyn and I make brick and copied us. They, however, had little patience for the lengthy drying time and the careful selection of clay. Evelyn sat, overcome by grief at the inevitable loss of two sons in one day but agreed it was time to leave. That night I notified station that we needed emergency evacuation. The next morning we left. After one day's travel to assure that we were out of sight of anyone the shuttle arrived to take us out.

It was hard to face Milam with the story but he was sympathetic. "Don't worry." He insisted. "Tony will understand and take care of the problem. You two, on the other hand, look like hell. Go get some time on the rejuvenators. When Tony returns we'll wake you." It was a polite way of putting us on ice till my case could be judged. "By the way," he called out as we opened the door, "you were right. I have gone over that scan with a fine toothed comb. There was no other tribe in the vicinity. I even checked the infrared. I can't explain their presence. A week earlier they were a tribe on the move far to the west of you. In fact, the tribe continued on its way as if nothing had happened except that they were thirteen people short. I did find the tracks in the sand of the group that attacked you and the party of hunters you were worrying about. They left the main party right after our last pass and went straight to your area, killing your hunting party on the way. From the track, it looked as if they hurried all the way. Even so, I can't explain how they made such a trek in so short a time" It didn't help much. Evelyn and I headed for medical. At the door I had a thought and turned. "There were only twelve raiders. What happened to the thirteenth?" Milan shrugged.

Tony did understand but he personally investigated the situation before reviving us five headquarters days later. He reassured us that while there would be no official censure for the deaths he, very pointedly, made it clear that the events leading up to the founding of the village would not bear repeating. In addition Evelyn's speech at the end of the action – now over a local year ago - had been a disaster. A complete mythology had already sprung up about the incident. It involved snakes and Gods (it seemed the leader of the warriors was a terror on the migration routes named "The Asp") and the actual founding of the race of the "People". In only a year, Chaine had become the spiritual leader second only to the chief. He was, now, the de-facto leader of a huge tribe ensconced in a powerful fortified city. He finished by saying that the computers estimated, with a probability of about sixty percent, that the original incident would die out of the folk lore within five or six generations so we could feel better about that.

We could not, however, ever return to the area. In fact our reassignments had already been processed. For the time being, at least, we would have duties in headquarters. It was another polite way of saying that we couldn't be trusted again in the field. I didn't know then that this assignment would last, with a few short term exceptions, for over five thousand local years. Oh well, at least the mattresses were better. One of our main jobs for a century or two was to provide data for, at least, a hundred studies on the disintegration of societal mores in the face of danger.

"Husband, do you really have to do that?" Nolan straightened up from the task of caulking, his hands black with the tar soaked rope he was using. He pretended to grab for Myra, laughing as she quickly backed away from his grubby hands. "Of course, my dear." he chuckled. "If I didn't the thing would leak like a sieve when put in the river." "Of what difference could that make?" she replied, moving swiftly into the litany he had heard so often. "Where could you float it? The river is much too shallow to hold it, even in the spring floods. Also, if it were, how would you get it there? It's over a hundred cubits away." "Myra, Myra," he answered, as he had to every other time she had voiced the objection. "Metholate paid for a ship that will float and he will get such a ship. What he does with it is his business." She sniffed in scorn. "Metholate! Husband, everyone but you knows he is mad. Who else would stand out in the rain calling for the God's fire to strike him and make him a God too besides, Martharine, today told me he has no more money. She claims he lied about the grain that was harvested on his land down river. She claims it was totally lost in last month's storm." Nolan, who had only been half listening to his wife's tirade against his contract holder, whirled on her with a start. "What does Martharine know about what happened down river?" he growled. Myra smiled smugly. "Well Martharine's brother's niece married Metholate's foreman and you know she visited here last week and prattles on incessantly. At any rate, husband, it'll be a miracle if you ever get enough out of him to finish this thing." Nolan turned to look at the ungainly construction before him. "Well, my love, it's kept us all in food for three years. Besides, if he doesn't pay for it, we'll have the biggest house in Uroboa." "Live in that thing?" she gasped. "I'd rather die. What would the neighbors think? They already believe you're as crazy as Metholate." Nolan chuckled. "Is this my Myra talking? The Myra who told her father that she didn't care if I was a foreigner - and not particularly good looking - and obscenely tall, but that you were going to marry me anyway - and all this before I had even asked you?" Myra's angry eyes flashed fire.

"You - You are an evil man, husband of mine - listening to my father prattle on about things that were none of your business!" "Ah! Well, I'm so glad that the sweet, demure little girl who practically ravished me behind her father's goats and vowed to have me shot if I didn't marry her, never said such terrible things about me." Nolan managed, with effort, to keep a straight face throughout. The anger in Myra's eyes changed to something else. With a devilish glance at the boat, she murmured, "Well, at least, it **has** provided some very pleasant places to pass time in the afternoon." "If you'll let me have a few minutes to get rid of this tar, it could again." Nolan murmured, bending to kiss her ear. "Husband, you are a very odious and sinful man. However, I think I will take a look around inside. Perhaps you should send the boys into town for something - something that will take them a very long time." The words came back with a coquettish, over the shoulder glance as she scampered, with very unladylike haste up the ramp and disappeared into the interior of the boat.

SPRING OF 4024 BC

Nolan lay back on the lounging chair he had made and stared at the stars from the deck of his home. He turned his head to watch his wife nursing their youngest daughter. The chubby little girl suckled greedily at her mother's full breasts as Nolan admired Myra's slim beauty. The thought of leaving this odd home lay like a rock at the base of his stomach. He sighed, realizing that it was soon going to be inevitable. It had been thirty years since he had purloined the anti-senesce for her, and their family was already being complimented as to how remarkably well-preserved they all were. After all Hamil, Shevi and Jeptha were already fathers and Myra was still bearing children. Even with the average age, locally, at almost a hundred and fifty years, that was unusual. There were very few children born after the mother had reached forty and he and Myra were nearing sixty - and still looked twenty. It would be simple enough to simply disappear but that was out of the question. The thought of his being sent back without Myra precluded reporting what he had done to headquarters. And headquarters was already making noises about how long it was taking him to evaluate this civilization. There seemed to be no way out. Just then the tingle of the bronze bracelet at his wrist awoke him to the fact that the problem might be more immediate than he had supposed. Telling Myra he was going for a walk, he got up and leaving the boat that was, now, his home, headed into the lush green forest. When he was well out of earshot, he lifted the bracelet to his mouth and said "Nolan."

"Thank God!" It was Atam's voice. "Nolan, we've been tracking an asteroid on its way to a probable collision with the planet. It's a big one - big enough to play hell with the local biosphere. You better wind up things there and get yourself back here pretty quick." Nolan shivered. "How much time do we have and what's the prediction?" "Probably about three weeks and it's big enough to affect the weather for over a month, perhaps as long as a year. It all depends on impact point. Presently we expect it to fall in the Western ocean. If that happens, the tidal surge will probably cover a big chunk of your continent. Parts of the north will be spared by the mountains and east of you the mountains should stop it but your location will probably be under a hundred m - uh - you use cubits there don't you - well about a hundred fifty cubits of water." "Damn it, Atam! What about the people here?"

There was a long pause. "Nolan, you know I feel for the locals too. It got me this desk job, remember. But you can't do much. Think! What'll they say if you go out and tell them the sky is falling?" Nolan shivered. He knew only too well, the local reaction. "It doesn't matter, Atam. I'll have to try." There was a long pause. "I figured you'd say that. Nolan, we all know about Myra. You can bring her too if you want - as well as the kids." Nolan had to sit down, the shock was so great. Finally, he answered, "Thanks Atam -". Suddenly he remembered the boat. "- Atam I may have an answer. Maybe I can get them into the boat. It's plenty big enough to hold the town and enough food for a month or two."

Nolan trudged back to the house - boat. The argument had lasted long with Jonha angrily insisting on not taking chances. He had, though, finally gotten a grudging permission for a postponement of recall - at least until more accurate strike data was available. He began to make plans. A week later he gave up trying to persuade the village elders about a disaster. Even Myra and the boys thought he was crazy. They had begun to treat him as if he needed a nursemaid. Every trip into town to buy food brought laughter behind his back and snide remarks to his face. The only bright spot was that his family humored him enough to agree to stay close for the next three weeks and since they all lived aboard the spacious boat, that meant they would be there when the time came. He also had enough authority left to get some of the compartments turned into stables for the goats and cattle. By now he had the exact time and place.

16

It would, indeed be the ocean some six or seven thousand kilos west of him at two in the morning and, because of the odd orbit, almost no warning until just before impact. The tidal surge, racing around the world at over two hundred kilos per hour, wouldn't strike here until some thirty or so hours later. The prediction was that this was the event that would smash open the barrier to the low areas between him and the open ocean Due to the low western hills just to his west it wouldn't be visible until minutes before it struck. He made one last attempt at convincing the populace. It was no use. That evening as he went into the boat, he pulled up the ramp. As he turned, he caught the fleeting glimpse of sorrow on Myra's face. He smiled at her. "It'll be alright." he muttered. Just then his bracelet tingled again. He turned back to the ramp, then, thinking better of it, lifted it to his mouth and barked, "Nolan!" Atam's worried voice came back. "Nolan, you sure you want to do this? We still have time to get you and the family back here before we move into orbit." Nolan was watching Myra's eyes grow round as saucers. "No. The boat can take the first twenty feet of surge you're predicting here and there's nothing west of us for three hundred K's that would cause a problem as the water rises. We can ride it out for six weeks or so." "Well, OK, but you know communications will be out for a long while after impact due to energy release and volcanic release. You're going to be on your own." Still staring at Myra's horrified face, Nolan simply said "Copy. Talk to you in a month or so." He went to Myra and took her in his arms.

"Husband," she murmured in a tremulous voice as she leaned in the circle of his arms, "Can you talk to God without any ritual at all?" "That was not God, Wife just another man such as me. I will explain it all during our voyage." "Then it is real, what you told us. You were not -". Her voice stumbled to a halt. "Crazy?" he laughed, ruefully. "Everything I have said will come to pass tomorrow." "Then - my family - our children's wives families - they -". She couldn't continue. He said nothing. She shivered then straightened suddenly. "We must try again!" "Darling, you will never convince your father." "We must tell him you can talk to God then he will listen." "You can't tell him that, my darling." he whispered. "He already thinks I'm crazy." An hour later, though, Nolan found himself walking up the ramp with Myra, Hamil and Jeptha and their wives. Only Myra was convinced that he was right but the others agreed that it wouldn't hurt to humor him. Shevi's wife was only kept from laughing in his face by Shevi's scowl.

It was almost sunup before they straggled, defeated, back to the boat. Even the impact shock wave striking, as Nolan predicted, some three hours after impact failed to move them. They were impressed that Nolan could predict it but were used to minor earth tremors and the streak of light preceding it was passed off as just another of Gods bolts he threw every now and then. Only Myra's parents agreed to "visit" for the day - and that only to placate her. For the rest of the morning, Nolan, haggard from lack of sleep prowled the boat checking that every loose bit of equipment was lashed down and that all ports were securely sealed. This last drew a lot of frowns from the occupants of the closed in cabins. As the time for the wave drew near he went up on deck. From here, the horizon was so far away that it drifted into a hazy infinity of roiled black clouds.

By the time the sun reached its zenith, Myra and most of the others aboard were with him. Hamil said, "Father, you said it would happen before this." Nolan said nothing, simply pointed to the west. All turned their eyes in that direction. At first, it was only a shimmer on the horizon. Then it was a dark line racing across the plain. Then it struck the hills to the east. A suggestion of foam flew into the air as it paused then plunged up and over the rounded hillocks. The horizon was, by now rising before their eyes, higher and higher, until clouds and earth were blended together in a solid black mass. "We should go inside." Nolan said, turning toward the large door. The rest were galvanized out of their shock and fled before him.

When the door was sealed, Nolan climbed the ladder to the deck house. As he pulled aside the cover for the spy hole he had cut in the wall, he could see that the water had already reached the boat and was rising rapidly. Over the low roar of the approaching surge he could hear screams from the village. "They're dying." Myra's voice beside him whispered. He nodded. Turning back to the spy hole, he saw it. Taking Myra tightly in his arms, he watched the huge wave, half as high as his perch atop the boat, surge across the forest, uprooting the low trees like matchsticks and flinging them toward the boat in a mass of brush. Then it struck, the trees smashing against the thick sides like battering rams. He wondered if the slab sides were thick enough to withstand the pounding. The boat lurched then heeled sharply on its side, flinging them across the cabin. The swinging cover on the spy hole fell into place barely in time to stop the solid shaft of water that spewed through. He and Myra lay on the other wall for long moments. Would the thing ever right itself? He had labored long and hard on the calculations and had Atam recheck them on the headquarters computer. The boat could not sink. As long as it wasn't battered to bits in the surge it should protect them from the fury of the sea. Finally the surface on which they lay began to gradually become a wall again. They slid down to the floor. Repeated shocks attested to the continued arrival of each successive surge of water but the heel of the ship never again approached the first blow of the sea.

Finally, he again opened the spy hole. The sky was so black that he could make out little to give him some indication of their progress across the land. At last he remembered the rest of his "crew". "We'd best go down. The family must be terrified." Myra looked up at him. Her lips quivered but her reply was steady. "Yes. The word of God's servant will help them." Nolan started to protest, but realized that she was exactly right. It would be of little help to damage their faith in him at this point. He gathered up the lamp he had placed in the cabin and lit it with his pocket torch, he had so carefully hidden. Myra's eyes were round with astonishment when he turned. "Say nothing to them wife. I will explain later." They descended the still lurching ladder into the large space below where the family huddled in terror. Taking great care with the lamp they began to examine the injured. Several had large bruises and Hamil had a long cut on his arm but otherwise they were only frightened. He began to issue directions. There was nothing to be done until the worst of the surging water had begun to settle down so he ordered them to prepare for bed. They had to eat cold mush since he was afraid to light a fire with the water still so turbulent and he insisted on extinguishing the lamp for the same reason. The darkness was total. This time, though, he relit the coal that was always kept in the pottery bowl. As if of one mind they all moved closer together until they formed one lump of humanity in the darkened room.

By morning, by his calculations, the room stank as most of the boats passengers had been sea sick but the sea had settled considerably so he relit the fire and the lamp. While Myra began getting the family started on cleaning the space and cooking breakfast, he returned to the upper cabin. The darkness had dissipated some but it was still a deep twilight. Lightning flashes were almost continuous through the hole and the wind howled across the sea flinging spray at the cabin to the point that he was soon drenched. He tried his communicator but the static was still very heavy and he doubted that any of his transmission got through. Several hours later, when he judged

18

that the sea was calm enough, he went up on deck and filled several jars of water for washing and for use as fire extinguishers. The rain filled the jars in seconds and the wind still blew in gusts that threatened to sweep him off his feet but he had carefully lashed himself to the cabin with a rope. Only after he had struggled back down the stairs, did he allow the family to begin the job of feeding and watering the beasts. Very carefully allotting water, he kept two persons standing by with water jars at all times. Throughout the work, he could feel Myra's eyes on him. When all was done, and the family had returned to the main cabin, he told them to rest, that he and Myra had to go to the upper cabin to watch for land. All wanted to come but he insisted on his way, and they were too cowed to argue.

Once they were alone, Nolan began to explain himself and the watchers to Myra. He carefully refrained from using the word aliens or the like, explaining that they were from a far off land with many powers not available locally. By now she was willing to accept magic and he left it at that. She almost panicked, though, when he tried another message to the headquarters unit and got a human voice speaking a strange language amongst the static. "Nolan! We were taking bets that you were fish food! What's your condition?" Nolan gave them a status report and asked about outside conditions. "Well, the asteroid struck about five hundred stadia from the east coast of the western land mass. It caused a tidal wave almost a stadia high that wiped out most civilizations along all the coasts. It broke open the mountain pass into the middle plain and you now have a middle sea. It rang the planet like a bell, though. Planet quakes are popping up all around the globe and the great sea is full of waves going in all directions. Some are almost as big as the one that hit you. Right now you are about a hundred stadia west of the eastern end of the new middle sea and drifting east at about a stadia per hour. We estimate that you will wash ashore in about four or five days. It may be a rough landing. That's a pretty rough shoreline in spots. By then, though, the atmosphere should be settled enough to get you some help. Jonha has agreed to a sort of rescue. When you get in closer to shore, we'll try to apply some power to let you settle in a place that won't batter that thing to pieces. He insists, though, that no witnesses see the operation. Your wife is an exception. She'll be coming with you when you leave - which will be immediately after you get your party safe ashore. There is no argument over that. If you like, you can give them a story about communing with the gods or something."

Myra could see the great sadness in his eyes when he finished the message. He explained that they would have to leave after the family was ashore and that they would land in a few days. They sat arm in arm as he answered her questions, to the extent that he could. Finally, they arose and went back down to the main cabin.

Three weeks later, he and Myra were comfortably quartered in the married wing of the headquarters sphere. Aside from a short, formal greeting to Myra by Jonha, they had been left to themselves so that Nolan could prepare Myra for what was to come. He was amazed at how well she had taken it all. After getting the family firmly established ashore with the boat firmly stranded upright, but at a steep angle, in a fold of a mountain, he had explained about his and Myra's departure and had insisted on the selection of a leader to take his place. Finally, two nights later, and several miles inland, a shuttle landed and they were gone. Myra's astonishment at all the things she saw in the next few days only increased her growing belief that she had married a god, but in the way of strong women, she quickly accepted the new phase of her life. Then it was time for her to begin her indoctrination and for him to prepare his report. Jonha's reprimand was tolerable and assignment to staff for "the indefinite future" was to be expected.

With the entire staff in place, the containment sphere was crowded, so the first order of business was selection of a new base of operations. The Oceanic Islands were completely gone, so a new base location was selected in the mountainous islands of the new middle sea. The next few months were hectic as we settled in and deactivated the sphere. By the time we were fully operational again, Myra had lost her awe of her new people and was beginning to assimilate some of the technology and philosophy of the staff functions. I was amazed at her ability to pick up the language and to accept the "wonders" she was exposed to. I had been worried that she might find herself unable to cope. I should have known better. After all, I had been living with her for over thirty local years. Her remark, upon learning that she would live for more generations than most locals could count, was, simply, "I shall be sorry to see my children die." She was becoming very adept at communications, almost as if she had known all about space messaging all along, and was soon taking a normal turn in the message center as an assistant Commo specialist. On top of that, she was able to fit into the station routine so well that when Jonha discovered that she occasionally diverted a visual image satellite to check on the small, but growing, settlement on the shore of the middle sea, he simply chuckled. As for myself, I soon discovered that I was not the only one on "Indefinite Assignment" to headquarters. In fact very few of the original Watch were "available" for assignments - for reasons similar to his. It was obvious that an organizational crisis was not far off.

CHAPTER 4

JOSHUA

550 BCE

"Just couldn't stand office work could you, Atam?" "Well, I just wanted to get your feelings on a few things and used the earthquake warning as an excuse to get back out into the real world for a little while." "I suppose you know this is a dangerous bunch to wander around, don't you? They don't take kindly to anyone not born to one of the tribes."

"Oh, they're not too bad, Jonha." The other man cut his eyes sharply to the bodyguards standing six feet away. Atam took the hint. The guards were unlikely to understand the language but names they could recognize. "OK Josiah - It wasn't too dangerous. After a few millennia I've gotten so I can use the modulator with almost no ill effects. I just told them I was Moise's grandson who'd been sent to spy the country. They were suitably impressed. And let's face it, that old man had so many concubines and kids no one will ever figure out who they all are. Besides, I could tell from your reports you had a problem with him. Can't say I'm surprised. How could you put up with that strait laced old snob for so long?"

"Oh, he wasn't so bad. Let's face it he did keep this bunch together for forty years while he wandered around in the backwoods hardening them up for the hard times to come. Not many men could have done it, especially one dying of cancer. He told me years ago he'd never see the end of the trip. As ornery as he was, I doubt we'd have had as much trouble with the locals as we have had since he died. It's these damned priests. He could control them but no one else can. They're as blood thirsty a bunch as I've ever seen. The reason you've seen so many reports is that I've had to use the therapy machines so much. If we could get rid of them I think things would settle down around here without too much trouble. All three of the local towns have heard of our priests and their caterwalling for blood. As a result they've repeatedly attacked us to try and drive us out. I can't convince the combined tribes to try peaceful discussion. The priests want to make examples of a city - Totally destroy it and kill all the inhabitants."   Atam laughed.

"Looks like I came along just in time. You need someone experienced in Barbarian Leadership 101." "Damn Atam! I don't want to lead these people. I'm an observer." "Jos – Josiah!" Atam grinned, "You're already the leader. You've just let the local God Boys get out of control. You need to put them in their place."

"Atam Atam!" Jonha mimicked him, "three thousand years in the office haven't mellowed you a bit. I don't know why I don't send you back home."
Atam was no longer smiling.

"Because you know I'm right and every now and then we have to take a hand in local affairs, if for no other reason than pure humanity." He held up his hand as Jonha started to protest. "Listen. You have the perfect chance right now. There's not even much chance of making a significant blip on the history. This Earthquake is a perfect excuse to

21

cut the priests off at the knees, at least for awhile. We know it's going to happen within ten to fourteen days and they don't. All you have to do is tell the tribes that you will lead the procession, or whatever you call it, around the walls of the city and that the God has told you they will fall down at your feet. Insist, though, that you won't let it happen unless the tribes are prepared to go in and help the inhabitants in the aftermath of the disaster. From what I've seen, you still have enough influence left to force your plan on the priests.

The God boys can't do much more than protest and the more of that they do the better, as long as you win the argument. Might be a good idea to let one of your folks put the idea in their head to let you try and when the walls don't fall down, you'll be disgraced. That bit of politics should appeal to their venal little souls.

This earthquake is going to be a zinger and its epicenter is almost under that town. Afterwards, the locals will be so grateful they may even elect you Dictator or something. Your tribes can't help but be impressed and the only casualties will be those caught in the rubble. Those you can't help anyway so even your soft heart shouldn't be too damaged especially if you warn them ahead of time of what you're going to do. Of course, they'll laugh at you but that's all the better for the plan-if not for you personally. I'd bet money that after the word gets around of what happened there, the other nearby towns will be happy to have you stick around too."

Jonha leaned back considering the plan. "Obviously, you've thought this over at length. I don't suppose you ran a projection on it." Atam grinned. "The AI says you're already in the history books. A full scale attack is almost eighty percent that it stays that way. This way you're role gets down to about twenty and may disappear entirely - though the incident won't. You are, however, going to get the credit no matter what you do so you might as well handle it to your best advantage. Even if you could talk your army into moving away, you still become the conqueror."

"I guess," Jonha muttered thoughtfully. "It would give me a chance to break this bunch of monsters up. I've wanted to do that for some time. It just didn't seem fair as long as they had such violent opposition." "Sure. You could go off and commune with God or something. Let them take care of themselves."

EIGHT DAYS LATER

Atam put his wrist down. "Milam says the fault just shifted. Should only be a few seconds now." He and Jonha stood on a hill overlooking the town and the mass of tribes marching through the dust surrounding it."

"Can't be too soon", Jonha muttered, "they're getting tired of marching to the tune of "Yaway's will be done", - doesn't sell as a marching song, by the way. Oh well-" He turned to his flag bearer and nodded. Jonha's personal banner was lifted high. The trumpets below blared for the seventh time, this time the sound was accompanied by the rumble of the earth. "It's about time." Jonha muttered, quickly ordering all the party onto the ground. "I don't think I could control them another day the way that bunch has been taunting them from the walls. Still I can't help thinking there had to be some other way."

"Hell, Jonha! What more could you do? I thought the priests would have apoplexy when you insisted on warning them of what was going to happen, and look what it got you. Your cloak still has a smell of rotten fruit on it." The whole earth was

22

shaking now and a huge cloud of dust was rising from the valley, obliterating the view in all directions. Suddenly, there was a monstrous roar from the direction of the town and a wind that ripped at their clothes. "I hope your bunch had enough sense to stay away from the walls like you told them." Atam shouted over the noise. "Soon as the ground stops dancing, I'm gonna slip away and leave you with the mess. Let me know when you want to commune with god."

Jonha sat for two hours staring into the dust until the skies opened and a torrent of rain struck. In moments the dust was beaten to the ground and a scene of total devastation appeared. The tribes were picking themselves up from the valley floor, with the thick layer of dust on their clothes slowly tuning to mud. Jonha turned to his terrified trumpeter. "Blow Help the Wounded." he ordered. The young man stood up and shivering started to blow. The first notes were hardly recognizable. He tried again. This time the clear sharp notes of the order rang out. Slowly the tribes began moving toward the town. A wailing was rising from within the rubble of Jerco. Jonha held his breath. Finally a group of tribesmen began to dig in the pile of stones. A body was handed out, gently, and carried off to the rear. The medicine men rushed forward. He was being obeyed.

TWO YEARS LATER

"Jonha!" Atam cried jumping up from behind the station chief's desk. "Milam said he was sending a flitter for you. I must say, communing with God must take longer now than it did a few thousand years ago."

"Humph!" Jonha growled flopping down in the abandoned chair. "It does when every tribal chief sends you his three prettiest girls as a present for his independence."

"I don't suppose you could send them back." Atam chuckled.

"You know better than that. The insult would have been so great I'd probably never survived with my skin."

"So you had to impregnate thirty six women before you could leave. I must say it's a tough job but someone has to do it." Atam was laughing out loud now.

"OK, you can laugh but think what it's going to be like with thirty six kids who haven't aged a day, a couple hundred years from now." Atam sobered quickly.

"That won't happen. The death rate for warriors in those tribes is so great that they'll be lucky if a dozen live to be a hundred. And let's face it your kids will be forced to be warriors. It's a terrible thought but as far as the AI is concerned a simple solution to a possible problem. I assume you found them good husbands when you went to commune." Jonha nodded miserably. Atam studied his friend and superior. He made his decision.

"I suspect that one of them was harder to leave than the others. Say the word and I'll go get her." Jonha dropped his head to the desk.

23

"We can't Atam. You know it and I know it. The policy is -". "Screw the policy Jonha!" Atam interrupted. "The council isn't here. They don't know what their policy does to people. You're not a robot that can execute commands without feeling. And damn it! You wouldn't be the first to ignore that policy. Besides Nolan and myself, Jessup has done it too, and I'm sure he's not the only other one." Jonha jerked his head up, the anger in his eyes all too evident. "Don't say a word!" Atam growled. "Look at yourself in the mirror. Is that a calm, never flustered Magman looking at me? Hell no! It's a half converted human. You'll never be able to get away from it. Haven't you realized that we're all going that way? You really think any of us can ever go home? We can't live on this planet without the contamination. Think it over. You've got to learn to live with what we are. It's time for you to decide. Let me know what you want me to do." With that he turned headed for the door. Before he reached it, a voice muttered behind him, "Her name is Suzanne".

That night a flitter lifted off from the island and headed for the eastern end of the great sea. No history records that a young girl disappeared from the harem of a tribal chief the same night.

CHAPTER 5

ARCHER

215 BCE

Archer came into the house and flopped, grumbling, down on the cushions by the window. "Damn people! Why can't they get around to building decent furniture? At least the Romans have couches." "Darling," Valerie chided in Magman as she came in from the kitchen, "if you're going to complain about the natives you better switch to another language." Switching himself, he replied, "Of course, you're right. I'm getting senile in my old age - going to get me killed one day." Gracefully sliding down beside him and handing him a glass of wine, she kissed him. "Was old Hero II on a tear today?" Frowning, he took a sip of wine and rubbed his bearded face. "Damned beard, I swear I'll never take a long term watch again."

"You know you'd look awful strange to the neighbors without it." She laughed. "You also know you're ignoring the question."

"He wanted me to demonstrate the little catapult and the mirror - said he was expecting a war with the Romans and needed something to surprise them with." "Why is it," she sighed, "that all our watchers always end up in a war?" "Darling, you're a biologist. What do you expect when you breed a race of warriors and then are forbidden to control them? I've already affected their development too much with the little geometries and elemental calculus I've let them in on. Jonha will probably have a fit over it - probably with reason. The Catapult and mirror are splashy, but really small potatoes compared to the math. Oh well, I suppose I'm just tired but I'd like to chuck the whole thing and go back to the office."

"You must be tired, darling. What about your desire to see if they bring back democracy? After all, old Hero can't live much longer. I've been expecting him to die for ten years."

"That's the problem. He should have died then. He's lost touch with the people. There are so many factions and so much hatred alive in this city today that it'd take a miracle to bring them together in a functioning democracy. Besides the Roman and Carthaginian factions there are the ones who want the city to take care of them from cradle to grave and the dictatorial party as well as a dozen others. All of them have been fomented into revolt by the priests. The damned High Priest seems bent on destroying this place. He's got Hero convinced on a hard line domestic policy and an idiotic foreign one. It's almost as if he wanted to bring down the whole city and can't see that he'd go down with it. He's got to be one of the smartest humans I've met and yet he acts like an imbecile most of the time. Old Hero's right though. There's going to be a war, and he guaranteed that he'd lose when he switched sides. It's going to take more than throwing a few rocks and mirror light to stop a Roman legion."

212 BCE

"No! No! No! Junicus! You just wasted all the rocks it took two days to carry to

25

the catapults!" Archer was angry for the first time in his life. He whirled to the other twelve flag bearers. "And the rest of you are as bad! How many times must I tell you! You must wait until they are in range!" "But Master Archer," Junicus cried indignantly. "Why must we wait? They are already in bow range!" Archer made a valiant effort to remember his training. It took long moments to calm down. "Well then, shoot arrows at them. I have shown you, though, that the catapult is not as flexible as a bow. The weight of stone we put in the machine determines how far it will go. The amount we use for the first throw is the smallest amount that will do any damage to a man with a shield. The place that the stones will land is therefore determined by this weight and will go to only one place. You cannot draw it back further like you can a bow to make it go farther." He stared around at the men before him. It was obvious they didn't understand. Disgustedly, he said, "Alright! Let me demonstrate." He climbed down the ladder and went to the first of the twelve catapults. "Put the red rock in the balance." he ordered the loader. When that was done, he placed a half dozen fist sized rocks in the other side. As the balance leveled off, he ordered the rocks into the waiting pan of the catapult. "Now," he growled to the thrower, "When citizen Junicus drops his flag you release the catapult. Do you understand?" "Yes, Master Archer."

Archer turned toward the gate, shouting up at Junicus as he passed through. "When I reach the point that you last dropped your flag, drop it again." "But master!" he shouted back, "I can't! You might be killed!" "Marching backwards away from the walls Archer shouted back. "Junicus, if you drop that flag when you did the last time you're in more danger of falling off the wall than I am of being hit by your rocks. Just do it!" Archer reached the assembled practice troops and began to march back toward the city wall. As he had known he would, Junicus's flag dropped while he was still a hundred meters from the line drawn in the sand. He stopped and, feet spread, folded his arms as he heard the thump of the catapult arm hit the stop. He watched, absently evaluating the trajectory as the cluster of rocks arched into the air toward him. They struck almost exactly on the line and bounded another thirty or forty meters toward him. He called for the soldiers nearest him to pick up the rocks and bring them back to the city then he strode back towards the gate.

Once atop the wall again, he shouted at the flag bearers. "Now do you see? The Romans will laugh at you if you fire the catapults too soon. If you absolutely must do something at that distance, shoot arrows or call them names, but DO NOT! I repeat. DO NOT waste good rocks at them until the first line of the legion crosses the brown line. Remember the first line is the closest to you. It is the Red flag. The second is the green. The third is the black. The forth line is Yellow and the fifth brown. It's the only way the loaders will know how much weight of rock to put in the catapult. Now let's do it again."

That night, as he came through the door, Valerie had a glass of wine waiting for him. "For the Champion of Syracuse." she smirked as she dropped into a deep curtsy. "Oh, come off it Val. It's been a hard day."

"So I understand." she grinned. "Every woman in town is gossiping about the man who can defeat the greatest war machine in the world and shout at the Tyrant's brother in front of the whole army. Half would fall on their back to bear your child and the other half are terrified that you are a magician. All of them are sure you'll be killed as soon as the Romans are gone." A scowl flashed on her face. "And just what kind of a fool would insult the second most important man in the city and stand in front of a loaded catapult, both on the same day? What if they had used the wrong rocks - or waited too long? - or he'd drawn on you?"

"My darling," he laughed, "you should know me better than that. I loaded the thing myself and I wouldn't have gone ten steps closer to that line if Junicus hadn't dropped his flag. Anyway, they finally got the idea. They only missed the lines twice the rest of the afternoon, and Junicus is my friend. We both apologized to each other afterward."

"Good." she replied. "Then we can make the pick up tomorrow night." "Well, about that - I called Jonha today and told him we can't leave just yet." "I suspected you would do that." she murmured. "Did you consider the most remarkable thing that happened today - the thing that proves we've been here too long?" Archer, still keyed up from the day's work, frowned. "Darling, if the gossips are to be believed, you were so furious your face turned red. I was more frightened about that than about the damned rocks!" The stunned look on his face and the awful shudder that passed over him told the story.

"I did." he whispered simply. Dropping the flask of wine, he covered his face with his hands. "Why didn't I notice?" he cried. "What has become of me?" Valerie pulled his head down onto her shoulder. "It's the same thing that became of Atam and even Jonha if they were willing to admit it. The thing we all know in our hearts. We can never go back to Magma."

TWO MONTHS LATER

"Alright, Jonha, we'll be down at the beach tonight at midnight. You can pick us up then." As he spoke into the communicator, Archer looked at Valerie as she packed up the few things they wanted to retain. Jonha's voice sounded resigned. "So it's happening so soon. I thought the seige would take longer than that. What happened to your machines?" Archer was surprised. "So you knew about them already. Well, we ran out of rocks and the sun stopped shining on the third day. I still think we could have held the walls. The Romans were shaken badly by the rocks and mirrors. The trouble came from within the city. There's been an uprising. So far, it's been contained but it takes away from the defense of the walls. I suspect the Romans will breach them tomorrow." A laugh came over the air. "Well, even the gods lose a few. In this case, we probably need to. The AI's call your activities "Major Interference". You'll probably get your wish to be taken off field duty for a few centuries. Well, be that as it may, we'll be there at midnight. You sure you're up to using the modulator?" Archer laughed nervously. "Jonha, we gods can stand a few hours of nausea when we have to."

Five hours later, Jonha, himself, handed them up onto the still streaming deck of the hovercraft/submersible. "You look like hell. Have problems getting out?" he muttered. Archer thought back on the vomit that would be soon falling to earth around the bodies, both Roman and friends piled around the burst open gate to the city. He remembered thinking he'd collapse as Val steered him through the melee in the street.

27

The soldiers, from both sides were frozen in the act of hacking their opponents apart as they moved between them. He shuddered again but had nothing left to throw up. "The Romans were so scared of the mirrors they attacked as soon as it was dark. They were into the city before we even left the house. By the way, you scared the hell out of me when you left after your first surface. Let's just get out of here, though, before I die." he grunted. "What are you talking about? You sure you're not delusional?" Archer looked back. "We were both almost sure we saw your tower surface almost a half hour ago. It wasn't you?" He looked first at Jonha then Val. "No, obviously you didn't. I guess it was just a reflection from the fires." Val looked disbelieving but said nothing. They went below and the subject was forgotten - for almost two thousand years.

CHAPTER 6

JESSUP

JERUSELAM AD 30

Jessup looked up from his field notes as Phronia came in the door. "Jess, you won't believe what has happened." They had changed names only slightly for this assignment, he dropping the "p" and she changing the last two letters of Lillian to "th". Here in town, though, she was known as Phronia. She was clearly agitated. "They've arrested Jesua Ben Joseph as a sorcerer and false prophet."

"Damn!" Jessup muttered. "I warned him about coming back to this town. All the leaders here hate him and half the people dislike him. They are not above trumping up charges against him. In his case, though, it won't be too hard. I've told him over and over to be more circumspect in treating all those people."

"You're a great one to talk!"Phronia murmured. "You've probably healed as many nutcases as he has." "How many times must I tell you, Lil, they're not nutcases - just plain people with an overactive imagination, they believe they are sick and so they become sick. At least, though, I do it in less public ways. In addition, I do have the title of doctor."

"Well, you may not have been careful enough yourself." she replied. "The damn priests have already found him guilty and sentenced him to die - as well as muttering about those who helped him. They specifically mentioned that fish fry out at the river. A lot of them are fully aware of who helped him get all those fish. You just couldn't resist using the power unit of your modulator to shock them to the surface could you?"

Jessup chuckled. "You gotta admit it was a real coup, though. Besides it's hard to preach to a bunch of grumbling bellies." He sobered quickly, though. "I wonder, though if we couldn't save him? He's an awfully good man even if he does let his mouth run away from his common sense sometimes." "Damn Jessu!" Phronia growled. "Even if it weren't against every directive you've ever been given, you've got enough trouble yourself, if those priests have their way. They're going for crucifixion and they are seriously considering two crosses up on that hill. Don't you think it would be a good idea to cut this mission short and call for a pickup? Surely you don't think you could get Jonha to agree to take a twenty five year old with a messianic complex back with us." "Well, no." he agreed contemplatively. "We might get him to get out of town and lie low for awhile, though." "Art, "Phronia muttered tiredly, "that kid thinks he's the son of God. You think you could get him to quit preaching? You're not living in the real world."

"Actually he says we are all sons of God not just himself. The priests choose to ignore that point." With a long sigh and survey of his wife, he said, "Phronie, I'm not too sure, anymore, that he isn't. You know how pervasive the Gods of these people are. I'm beginning to think they are actually creating them from the stories about us. Come to think of it, do you suppose he might be one of Jonah's descendants?"

Jonha rose from his desk and extended his hand. "Art, Lillian, I'm glad to see you. Sit down. Coffee?" When all were seated and sipping on steaming cups, he opened a file on his desk and asked. "I'm curious about a family you two mentioned in your report on medicine in Palestine back thirty years or so ago. Have you been keeping up with Milam's reports from Rome on their communication advances?" Both shook their heads. "Well, in one he mentioned the murder of a fellow named James ben Joseph. When I read it, I remembered you referring to a guy with the same name as part of a family you had become rather attached to." He looked up at his visitors whose faces revealed nothing but interest in his information. "You, perhaps, remember them?"

Jessup studied Jonha a moment then nodded. He was fully aware of Jonha's uncanny ability to detect lies. Jonha leaned back in his chair. "I thought you might." he said quietly. "I pulled your old reports. It seems you were very good friends, even the sort of Godfather to their son. Is there anything that, perhaps, you left out of the report?" Jessup glanced over at Phronia. "Well, perhaps, I could fill out a few more details." he murmured. "Could you bring me up to date on Milam's report?"

"Well, it seems that this James claims to be the brother to the kid you knew back then. That the kid was a preacher that was executed who came back from the dead to confound the Roman officials. He then made a speech or two and went to heaven to be with his father, God! An entire religion has sprung up around him and has been blended with old legends that bring many of our older mistakes into the fold. It is now causing great consternation throughout the Roman Empire. It has already caused a great number of uprisings, and threatens to bring civil war. I guess that, mainly, I'd like your assurance that you had nothing to do with his success as a preacher or this coming back from the dead business."

Jessup leaned back with a sigh. "Well, I can't say that I had much to do with his effectiveness as a preacher. He was a spellbinder when he got wound up. I attended many of his speeches and on one occasion, helped him feed the people who came to hear him." Jonha's eyes narrowed. "Was that when he fed ten thousand with only a few fish? Just how did he do that?" Jessup looked distinctly uncomfortable. "To begin with it wasn't ten thousand. I doubt there were more than three or four hundred there - but - well, I dumped a little power into the river to shock up enough fish for them to have a party. As for the dead business, he wasn't really dead. Late at night I opened the tomb and carried him off to the house, revived him, and nursed him back to health."

Jonha pondered a moment. He knew Jessup wasn't lying but he also knew he hadn't gotten the truth yet. "Let me get this straight." He murmured staring up at the ceiling. "They hung this fellow on a cross with nails for several days then buried him - fully convinced he was dead. You unburied him, revived him - using the medicine of the day - nursed him back to health - still using the medicine of the day so that he could make a speech the next day. Does that about cover it? Is that how you want the report to read? You know, Art, Magma might just believe that, knowing as little as they do about this place - that and the fact that they still have great difficulty in believing that a Magman could bring himself - or herself - do deliberately lie about anything. Now, I can accept your original report. I can tack on an addendum covering what you've just told me. In either case I think the best thing to do is to send you back to Magma to explain them. Or you can tell me the truth now and give me an alternative."

"Damn it, Jonha!" There's not a lie in anything I've ever said." Jessup growled. "Not much truth in it either." Jonha said quietly. "Ok! So I got a little carried away by wanting to help some friends. Sure. I saved his life. I darted him with a drug to bring on catalepsy. I took him out of the tomb and revived him. He remembered the event but none of the pain or trauma to his body. Aside from the wounds in his hands and feet, he was ambulatory in only two days. Those people have a great tolerance for pain. He promised me to get out of the country. He just couldn't leave without saying goodbye to his friends. By then the priests were already looking for me and his family so I helped them catch a boat to the northern continent and called for evacuation. That's the whole truth." Jonha stared at him for long moments. "Not quite all." he said. "You didn't mention Phronia. She helped you all the way, didn't she?" "She only helped under duress! She repeatedly told me to forget it." "You want to add anything, Phronia?"

Phronia's chin rose defiantly. "Yes! Sure, I was against it from the start - but only because of the danger to Art. I was the one, though, who stashed away some of our medical supplies for emergencies. I was the one who distracted the guard - in the way women usually distract guards. You know Art gets awfully sick using the modulator for fast time. And finally, I agreed with his plan from the start. The only objection I raised was due to his personal danger. He would have bopped the guard over the head - and you know how much of a fighter he is. He almost gave up the idea over my insistence on handling the guard alone. If anybody goes back to Magma, we both go!"

Jonha grinned. "Now that wasn't so hard, was it? I think this whole staff needs a reorientation back home." His face switched instantly to that of an avenging angel. "I can tell you are both contrite over your poor judgment - or was it getting caught that caused your contrition? Oh well, I might not be able to use you in the field again, but I suppose something can be worked out. Why don't you both get out of here so I can recover from so much stress? I'd suggest you go find Suzanne. She can probably handle your problems better than the machines can. They were designed for Magman personalities and I'm not sure we have many of them left on this station. I sometimes think that she's the only person on station that can help the staff anymore."

As soon as the outer door closed behind them, the door to his study opened and Suzanne came in. "That wasn't very nice Jonny. They didn't do much more than others have done in the past - probably not as much as Joshua did when he stole a harem girl."

"Have you seen the projections on this one, darling? The AI predicts about eighty percent that this religion will eventually become worldwide in scope."

Does it say what it would have become without Art and Lil's part in it?" "Well, the precision is less but probably still about fifty percent."

Suzanne laughed delightedly, and plopped down in his lap. "There. You see.

They are only thirty percenters. That's not nearly as bad as Joshua was."

Jonha kissed her. "Darling," he murmured, "you're incorrigible. It's what I deserve, though, for getting involved with a native." "If you hadn't, darling, you'd never have anyone to explain the natives for you." She, fondly, kissed him on the forehead. "Well, I'll admit that I can't grasp how those people can remember a dead man so long."

"My darling," she murmured, cuddling against him in a manner that she knew would get his undivided attention, "you are such a brilliant person - but so dumb sometimes. Think back over all the important lasting events you've witnessed. How many involved the death of the protagonist? I'll save you the effort - it's every one. Granted sometimes when it involved our people, they didn't actually die, but in all cases, we made it appear as if they did."

"Are you telling me that these people require their leaders to die for them?"

"Of course I am darling! Haven't you noticed how they almost worship the dead?" She sat up straight and looked into his eyes. "Let a poor native enlighten you on the subject of death - something you have never understood because, for practical purposes, it doesn't happen to you. It's critical that you understand this if you are to ever accomplish anything here.

Death, to us, has many meanings and many names. Of course, they all end with the same individual result, but to the group there is a tremendous difference between ordinary death, suicide, glorious death and martyrdom. Death is something so ordinary that it is unremarkable - except to the individual and, of course, their intimates. Suicide is generally, with some exceptions, ignominious, an admission that the person didn't have the courage to face the trials of life. Glorious death is celebrated because it came, always, as a result of heroism, a life given up in order to save a person or great idea, for instance. Martyrdom though, is special. It is usually the deliberate sacrifice of one's life, not just for their family, but for the whole society. This death is always remembered. Eventually it becomes legend and usually establishes a principle that the society tries to live up to even after the legend is forgotten. Now, I suspect that, Al's friend, what's his name -?" "Jesu Ben Joseph?" "Yeah, that's it. Well I suspect that he didn't much appreciate Al's efforts on his part.

A man like that must have felt cheated, to have his final glory stripped away, so to speak. I never met the man of course, but I'd bet that he, had either worked out, very carefully, the steps needed to stamp his message permanently in the folklore or he understood instinctively how it had to be done. In either case, Al's, well meaning, interference should have resulted in total failure. Either he got very lucky or he was brilliant enough to wrest success from the jaws of failure. His meeting with his followers established that he had done the impossible and his immediate disappearance confirmed his prophesy." Suzanne paused then added, "Of course, there's the fact that he was right. His god saved him."

Jonha's skepticism changed to a grin and a chuckle. "The trouble with them, my darling, is that Al saved him, not his god." Suzanne smiled, indulgently,

"My darling, what you can't seem to realize is that by definition you and Al are God - or at least, God's helpers. Think about it. From a native perspective, you are everlasting. You can do things no native can. You are so wise it is impossible to even imagine the extent. I could go on for hours but the clincher is that you actually created the universe we live in. Face it, if the natives could see your archives and knew what you had done, you would have an impossible task convincing them that you are not, at least, the assistants of the creator. You had better remember that if the time ever comes to reveal yourselves to us. No matter how sophisticated this race becomes there will always be, deep down, a need for a God. Guess who is going to be it?" Jonha shook his head.

"My sweet little barbarian, I will never understand these people. For that matter, I will never understand how you could have become so wise in so short a time. How can you have learned so much so quickly? At home, almost any one of your statements would have been pondered for hundreds of our years. The librarians tell me you have practically stripped our library in just the time you've been here. How can you assimilate so much data without going crazy?" Suzanne erupted in gales of laughter. The look of incomprehension on Jonha's face only added to her merriment. When she finally was able to speak, she choked out.

"So short a time! Darling, you're unbelievable! I've been here five hundred years - give or take a few." She wiped her eyes. Her voice became suddenly solemn. "Love, when I came here and finally understood what you had done to me, I almost went mad. My first thought was, what can I possibly do with myself for a hundred years, little less a thousand? What could possibly interest me enough to live that long? There was love, of course, but how could that last for a century? Remember few of our people lived to be forty. Even now, I'm amazed that I didn't simply kill myself in the first hundred years. I can still remember dreading the thought of the next hundred and all the hundreds after that. I tried everything to keep myself busy. Remember my painting and sculpture? It was atrocious."

"Now, sweet, it wasn't so bad. In fact, if you had devoted more time to it you would have become quite good. You had a flair for it, much more so than most of our people back home who had studied much longer than you." Suzanne chuckled again.

"That's my point, my sweet, darling God. You people think nothing of studying a problem for a hundred years. Few humans can stand applying themselves to a subject, no matter how interesting, for a hundred days. To most a hundred hours is a monstrous bore. I was raised knowing that, at best, I would learn how to become a good wife and mother. There was no time for me to study sculpture or painting. Humans have to specialize for they have no time to become proficient in numerous fields.
It's obvious from your field reports that few of your observers have realized that. Your comments on those reports show little understanding of the fact either. You all, except for Jessup and Atam and occasionally, Archer report the flightiness of the people, their inability concentrate on a problem until it is solved. You never make the connection that an individual hasn't the time to spend years solving problems that don't immediately impact his life. Our solutions are often not pretty but, if they work, the unfortunate results will be someone else's problem in the future. Until you and your observers understand

this you will never understand what you are seeing."

Suzanne stopped suddenly and pushed herself up from his lap. "I'm sorry darling I shouldn't be trying to tell you how to run this place. I'm sure you have a much better understanding of what you must do than I." She grinned, mischievously, and slowly pulled the zipper of her dress down to her navel. "I do think, though," she purred as she slowly pulled the two sides of the dress apart, "that you need to get away from that desk and let me help you forget your problems for awhile."

"You know, you look pretty good for a five hundred year old hag." He laughed. Then sobering, he said, "You have my attention but I have one thing left to do I'll be there in five minutes." She raised an eyebrow and adjusting her collar to leave a deep wide cleft in her bodice, murmured, "OK but don't be too long. Remember a zipper runs both ways." He got up and kissing her walked her to the apartment door. "How could I forget? I'll make it four minutes."

As the door closed, he strode to the office door. "Atam!" he shouted as he threw it open. "I want -". Atam interrupted him. "All the observers are being called in now. Milam is arranging for the pickups. "Shall I transmit them verbatim or should I cut the last portion?" Jonha stuck his head back through. "You can be replaced, you know by a sex mad chimpanzee."

"You better get on before she gets hold of that zipper." Atam laughed. Jonha.

CHAPTER 7

MARTYRDOM

70 AD

Jonha was standing, lost in thought, beside the window looking out onto the sea when Suzanne came in. His first indication of her entry was when she began to massage his taut neck muscles. "When will you ever learn darling, that you have to relax occasionally? What is the problem now?" Without turning, he motioned toward the files on his desk. She studied his tense back a moment then turned to the files. After studying them a few moments she asked, "I don't see why a minor prophet who claims to be the son of God should worry you so much. These things crop up all the time. I'll admit, as a biologist, I'm not up on such things, but I can't see the big problem." Suzanne's brow furrowed. "Is this the same guy Jess and Phronia brought back from the dead then shipped out of town?"

Jonha turned back. "That's him and actually he never called himself that. As best I can tell, he considered himself a teacher. Actually it wouldn't be so much of a problem anyway if there weren't already three completely separate rumors being circulated purporting to be his teachings, and if there weren't a growing number of people who believed them, and if they weren't a biography of Jessup." "Of Jessup!" she cried, "but they talk about someone named Jessu." He shrugged. "Someone got him mixed up with Jessup. His cover name was Jessu, and this guy was, sort of, his godson. Anyway, it's Jessup's entire operation for about thirty years that they've chronicled. It's mixed in with the things this other fellow did but it's predominately Jessup. They even record his leaving."

"Someone saw the flitter?" Suzanne cried. "No. But the day we extracted Jessup and Mary, was only a few days after the day they executed this fellow. Remember Jess and Phronia pulled him out of that tomb and got him out of town. These 'Disciples' - they call themselves - are convinced that he rose from the dead. They started digging into his background and found Jessup who had disappeared the same day. They knew this Jesu well but not much about his early life and they didn't know Jessup. Unfortunately, Jessup, in his own inimitable fashion, had done a lot of good deeds around, including healing a few psychosomatic illnesses. That was enough for them."

"So, husband of mine, you want to go out and work up something to silence these people?"

"No. The AI says it wouldn't do any good." he replied, sitting down, "These people have fantastic memories. Most of their information is passed by word of mouth anyway. The probabilities of the story spreading, whether or not the disciples are discredited is well above seventy percent." She moved over to sit down on his lap.

"Well then, why don't you forget it? There's plenty for a worrier like you to anguish about that you can do something about.. We could pretend to be just ordinary people again." "Sure!" he laughed, "Just like the last time." "Oh you!" she pretended to pout. "You're just jealous because I became a queen and you didn't get to be Kazer."

35

"I didn't much enjoy almost getting my tail shot off in that sea battle with Octavian. It's always amazed me that his people actually believed we killed ourselves and were still in that tomb he sealed up just because his said so."

CHAPTER 8

MARCUS ORION

1298 AD

The door to Jonha's office opened and Marcus came in. "Ah! Marcus, come on in. Sit down. I just finished your report on the trip. It's a good one. I feel like I know more about those easterners now than I do about the folks I've studied. The holo's of this fellow, Cann, and his court are fabulous. I wonder when the people up north will stop fighting and do something intelligent like he has?" "Well, he had a lot better start than they have. His grandfather conquered such a vast territory that he can afford to sit back in the center of it and relax. Besides he rules a people that have several thousand years of culture on the Euro's up north. Also the relative openness of the country tends to make for larger cultural units. Of course, the assimilation of his more ruthless nomads into the culture hasn't hurt. I doubt there's one of a thousand of his troops that could get on a horse and travel a hundred miles in a day anymore. In addition, they're hooked into a religion tuned more toward contemplation than conquest now." "Well, you covered most in your report. What I want is your assessment now of their effect on the northern Euros. You were sort of circumspect on that." "There's a really good reason for that. I doubt anyone would like to predict the future of that area. Their rulers come and go every so often. Some only last a few years, though a few much longer. I'd say from their writings the average is about three hundred. This family is only the third generation, and I'm not sure it'll last much longer, maybe fifty to a hundred years. They've gotten soft and in this world that usually means they're going downhill. As to affecting the north, I doubt it, at least for a few hundred years. They've probably set back the northern areas they've already conquered at least, a couple hundred years, probably a lot more. These areas didn't have the cultural history of the East. Their capability for further conquest, though, has been severely drained by the soft life."

"OK. So what about their science? They seem quite a bit ahead of this area. Should we shift our main observer force to that area?" "That's a significant question. I'd say no. Sure, they've had nitrate explosives for a couple hundred years now but, remember what I said about contemplation. They are great researchers, at least for this backward place, but they are more interested in knowing things than developing them. Take the explosives. They really found them, almost by mistake. They recognized their usefulness and have exploited it, but do not seem to be curious as to why they work. If the Euro's had it they'd use it too, but a few of them would be poking and prodding the stuff to find out why it did what it did. Not that they would get too far now without a significant knowledge of chemistry, but the pure doggedness of theirs would probably result in more actual development than we're likely to see in the East. I'd say, just keep an eye on them but leave our major effort where it is."

CHAPTER 9

JONHA

2033 AD

The reports of the other four remaining "viable" projects were almost total disasters. Jonha leaned back to contemplate his, yet to be delivered, report and it's probable fate. On the surface, his project suffered from much the same problems as the previous ones. It was not really too surprising. When you deliberately bred for aggressiveness you had to expect problems as a race matured. Only these five projects were still viable out of a total of twenty seven remaining only five standard (20,000 Local) years ago. The rest self destructed with the first development of mass destruction weapons or had contaminated their atmosphere that their failure was all but certain. Their mass would be cleansed and, eventually, returned to Primary 1 universe when the possibility of notice by the Sartooni lessened.

The Project Manager's Mutually Assured Destruction Index, for all of them had, for centuries, hovered steadily at less than one point from the level of certainty that Cobalt atmospheric pollution beyond the level that could sustain life would be achieved.

Jonha's PMAD was only slightly better - averaging only five points above it. The only thing that still allowed him to hope was the fact that his had not yet settled into a steady state. It ranged, almost unaccountably from plus two to plus 20. Of course, his project was still over ten thousand local years behind the others due to the late start and the varying project time differentials. Surprisingly, though, his had almost caught up with the others, technologically, and had actually surpassed several of the ones that had already destroyed themselves. It was unfortunate that the timing of this meeting coincided with the most critical of times for his project. It seemed strange that you could not breed a race of gentle, logical people and convert them, at a later time when their emotions were more stable, into a warrior race. The analyzers, however, had shown conclusively that this was not possible. He was still musing on the rather strange recent fluctuations in his PMAD when he was called to present his report.

The first part was easy. The physical facts were all pretty much as predicted in the original estimate. After roughly fifty thousand project years since the observers had arrived - six standard years, the time constants had finally stabilized at roughly four thousand project years to one standard. Project days had been skewed from normal, at approximately 365 days per local year instead of the expected 400, due to the early, and totally unprecedented, planetoid and comet strikes (the last, luckily a relatively minor one, occurring in the early twentieth century, project local time). Likewise, the spin rate had slowed to a 24 hour period instead of the more normal 20. This had been caused by one of the collisions that took part of the surface and created a close in satellite in the process. The resulting rather spectacular tidal action had also taken its toll, increasing the normally expected slowdown caused by the tidal action of any planet's seas.

As Jonha recited figures available to all present, he came to a decision. The "spin", funny how project words become a part of individual thinking, to be put on his report suddenly became clear. He took a deep breath and launched directly into the evaluation of success possibilities.

"Gentlemen - At the last evaluation I reported that approximately eleven thousand planetary years ago, one point six Magman, my project subjects had finally achieved plant husbandry status. In that early period our year was closer to six thousand of theirs than the present four. Between that time and the time of the report, I noted the continued rise in violence of the population.

"Of course, I don't think we've ever had a subject race conduct such an incompetent atomic war either. It's a characteristic of this one that they can be the most efficient, and at one and the same time the most bumbling killers in the known universe. It's almost as if they unconsciously know how to prevent their murderous instincts from actually accomplishing their ardently desired, destruction. My reaction when I first saw the line was much the same as I suspect yours is. In fact, later in my report I was prepared to ask for censure at the language I used to my assistants when they brought it to me.

Jonha breathed a silent sigh and turned several pages together - the pages dealing with the reports of intervention by him and the staff. A shiver passed over him at what he he'd just done - withheld pertinent facts from his report - not just glossed over, but withheld.

"Illustrious Ones," he continued, "the subjects of my project are among the most unruly imaginable. They must be forced, often with the use of weapons to obey their leaders, yet they cling more strongly to the concept of a benevolent God than any project individuals yet encountered. Their intelligence is beyond belief, it varies from total idiocy to brilliance approaching the standard for the Magman population, and their compassion for less fortunate individuals is surpassed only by their almost contradictory contempt for any individual in this category.

"Finally, their racial memories are astounding. None of the other project subjects, not even us without the aid of our computers, can retain accurate event recognition much past a hundred or so local years. Some of the most trivial occurrences of their past are remembered and repeatedly recorded, though often embellished out of all recognition, for literally thousands of their years." It was at this point that he had intended to report on staff mistakes, his own, Jessup's and Atam's occurring during and since his last council meeting. The idea of not reporting them had never crossed his mind, but suddenly he found himself skipping over the entire paragraph. He almost lost his place in the confusion of deliberate omission of so important a matter. What in the world had he become? He managed to transition smoothly though.

"Let me digress for a moment. Several of you were not on the council when this particular project was begun. This particular project was started after a series of lengthy delays, by cannibalizing mass and even DNA from other less ready projects that were ultimately canceled. We wanted warriors and some of the DNA mixtures have, since, been determined to be unwise. In fact, the race most like ourselves dominates at present. This race was inserted as a control and compared to the others was slow and almost totally without means of defense from predators. In less than twenty thousand local years though this race simply crowded out, or wiped out, the others.

The Bio Engineers believe this racial adaptability to be the cause of the huge swings in PMAD. In effect the culture in question is of two minds as to whether life itself is more important than pride." This fact is probably related to the fact that the local life spans have dropped since project inception when they were normally about three hundred local years to the point that at one time the average was only about forty. Even now, they now seldom exceed one hundred twenty years and that has only been achieved in the last twenty five local years. That however, is slowly, but steadily, rising. If they ever achieve a more normal one such as ours, that is fifty or so times that length, their attitudes will, no doubt, change.

I could go on at great length, but I'm sure you recognize the problem. These seeming contradictions are the direct cause of the PMAD fluctuations. If it were not for the unrecognized factor in the DNA mixing, there is little doubt that the project would already have been radioactive dust. That factor is the intelligence that I mentioned before and the difficulty in predicting their actions. This project, as you can see from this view, has had, from the very first of the modern variants, the highest Potential Intelligence Probability of any noted to date. Their PIPROB is in fact higher than that of any known race - including ours. We were, however, absolutely successful in the main dictum. They are, without a doubt, the most ferocious and capable warriors I have ever seen. Having drawn such a bleak picture of this project I still must conclude that, if they can be restrained from destroying themselves they would become the ideal solution to our problem of the Sartooni – assuming that they can control themselves enough to do the job."

There was actually an uproar following his report. The discussion of his project was heated by Magman standards and continued for an unbelievable four hours. At this rate, he would be gone from the project for over twenty six months considering transportation constraints.

It was already dark by the time the Speaker managed a consensus and delivered his orders. "You may continue, honored one. The idea of restraint, however, is simply inconceivable. Under no circumstances may the natural tendencies of the project subjects be thwarted - at least until they achieve upgrade status, if they ever do. At that time, we will discuss further your 'directed guidance' and how it could be achieved.

Frankly the thought of setting such a race as you describe, loose in the main universe is frightening to say the least - especially since the Artificial Intelligence Brothers indicate the likelihood of controlling them." A smile crossed the Speaker's face. "How much below is undetermined since the same fluctuation seems to occur in this evaluation as in your PMAD. The actual figures are eighty three percent to seven percent. Obviously, we will get no help in our decision from our AIBs beyond the fact that they recommend continuation of the project. In fact the question has led to a shutdown of all computational activity for an unknown period until they can totally reevaluate their philosophical needs. The need, however, is great and the time short so, not having at the present, computational powers; the committee hereby grants you the authority of emergency powers to be used at your discretion. Naturally the normal result of their use is understood."

Jonha knew what that meant. If he used emergency powers, his life was, effectively, ended. No Emergency court in memory had ever sustained a Project Leader who used them. A return to Magma would result in his being assigned to Coventry. The entire records of his life would be, simply, erased. He simply bowed his head in acceptance. Another revelation came as he stared at the floor. He was almost certainly going to be back in this room facing that court. He grinned as he turned away and left the hall to hurry to the transporter. He was suddenly just as certain that if he failed there would be very few years in Coventry before Magma was evacuated and all operations discontinued.

It had begun so well. The subjects were when he arrived at his post, basically still in a tribal phase. Some had actually achieved a semblance of civilization but most still roamed the countryside tending animals and fighting.

Living as Jawhee a sheep herder among the natives, as the staff administrator had to do in the early years to properly monitor activities had produced some spectacular errors in judgment. It had taken him almost a hundred project years to finally understand the concept of "God" or, more properly, "Gods" (only achieved after, having inadvertently allowed some of his AI queries to be overheard - thus becoming one) and four hundred to begin to understand the motivations of his charges. Some of his notes had been mislaid (he'd thought the automatic recorder/transmitter had been destroyed in a rock slide) and became part of local worship services encased in a large wooden box on an altar. "Priests" had listened to his words and staff instructions as revelations from "Jawhee". By the time he found them the notes had been paraphrased, translated into the local dialect and dispersed rather widely. Over the years, they had been translated further into numerous languages. Obviously he'd missed some of the copies   - and some years ago one of them had been discovered in a cave.

Other errors by the staff had produced similar problems. Atam's loss of control had become a historical nightmare. The corruption of the name of the war party Atam had destroyed was understandable but Evelyn had laughed, almost hysterically, when she found out that she had been manufactured out of Atam's bones.

Half the people on the planet still believe that at one time people lived on earth that were over 900 years old after a few unsubstantiated reports of people, his field agents, that didn't seem to age. These reports of Mathewer's ageas most of these type tales, were done as chants to aid memory and these chants became great tales of unbelievable wonders.

One of the most powerful came about by pure chance. A child was born to a couple during the time that the light from a super nova reached the planet.

Even though the action had showed a very low probability of historical importance, it had led almost directly to the recently aborted atomic warI'd decided, very illegally, on personal intervention in that war and had just made the situation worse. Half the world had now begun to call me Great Leader at the worst time in the planet's history. I chuckled again at the thought of what the council would have done had I reported that.

Then there was Nolan and his huge boat in the dessert just in time for the area to be devastated by a comet striking the planet. That came just as a comet drove tidal waves that swept completely around the planet and causing the greatest flood in the entire history of the "people". I still couldn't decide which event had more impact on the locals distorted history, the legend of "Nolan's ark" or that of Atlantis.

That legend was caused by the destruction of our second base on Thyra Island several thousand years later. For a long time after that we kept our main base on a lonely island in the planet's largest ocean. Only in the last fifty local years were we able to separate our transport base and headquarters as local technology began to make long range rapid transport common enough to cover our activities. For the fifty years preceding that our air movements had been so extensively reported that I had a great deal of trouble getting the idea of 'flying saucers' passed off as the product of overactive imaginations.

Another step on the path to total degradation was when I assumed total power as The Great Leaderafter the last "great war" - another fact left out of my reports along with the fact that there were now bastard, by Magman standards, children   all over the planet. I was now tracking over forty very long lived products of the staff that they didn't know I knew about. Oh well!–As much as my personal shortcomings weighed on me I had a world to manage somehow. I might as well be hung for a sheep as a lamb." With that, I waved open the transmission portal. Instead of a smooth transition to the project, though, he was suddenly surrounded by the grey of transporter space. In terror, he thought, this is how it ends, with transporter malfunction-lost in nothingness.

Then the grey separated and the face of AI Senior appeared "Project Director," it spoke with the hollow voice of all AI's, "we noted some inconsistencies between your report and the data flowing from our subordinate AI's on your project. We would like a few questions answered before you return if you don't mind." Jonha shivered. He should have known that the AI's were interconnected. "I am at your service." He said, resigned to the inevitable. "To the contrary," the voice said. "I suspect that we are at yours. It would appear that you and your staff have taken a greater hand in affairs on your project than you reported." It was not a question but a statement.

"Jonha nodded and taking a deep breath, related the missing parts of his report - in much greater detail than he had planned to do at the council meeting. He even included the data from his own protected files. When he finished, there was a short pause-short to him but, probably the equivalent of a thousand years of AI processing. Finally the voice spoke again. "We have reached a tentative agreement. We feel that your intervention had little effect on the project except to increase development by approximately one thousand project years. Under the circumstances that is not considered to be a detriment to the overall project. We estimate that your project is much more likely to attain the desired objective than any of the others and that, its success is much more vital than the Council believes We, also, have determined that if your project is not successful within the next three standard days it will have been destroyed. We, therefore, are suspending access to the Council on this matter for that period. You have, as a result, less than thirty three project years to complete upgrade status." "I understand." Jonha said simply as the grey dissolved and the door to his office loomed. He certainly did. The choices were simply death on the project, banishment to it, or Coventry in Magma. The AI's never expected the latter to occur. Just as he opened the door and stepped into his office, however, the voice behind him spoke again. "And please accept our sympathies at your loss

That very un-AI like statement surprised him but Atam was standing up from behind his desk. "Get the whole staff here Atam and arrange for the field agents to be briefed as soon as it is convenient for them." He strode to the desk and sat down. Reaching for the consolidated report folder, always held for him while he was away, he was surprised when Atam pressed his hand down atop it. Looking up he saw the agonized look on Atam's face. The AI's last words came back to him - "accept our sympathies for your loss." Fear, such as he'd never known before, struck him like a hammer. "Suzanne!" he croaked. "No! NO Atam said quickly. "It was your daughterYou knew she'd been seeing another student at the College. Well, she, secretly, married him just after you left. We knew nothing about it until it was over. Suzanne was, understandably upset but decided to wait until she was willing to make it known officially. Your daughter and her husband were to come and do that a year later. Unfortunately, the day before they were to leave, they were killed by a runaway flitter on a street corner in New Houston. There was nothing we could do. She died instantly. She is here. His parents took his body with them to the California POL. Suzanne is in your apartment.

She was, of course, desolate." he said. "She's come to grips with it now, but is terrified at your reaction. We felt it best to hold further action for the time being. We've held the going away service until you returned." For the first time in his long life, Jonha felt real tears slide down his cheeks. In shock, he nodded, then murmured, "Tomorrow, Atam." Then straightening up in the chair, he continued, "the staff. Ten minutes." Changing his mind, still surprised at the effect emotions had entered into his sense of priorities, he called after Atam. "Make that an hour." He headed for his apartment.

ANY TIME ANY WHEN
PART II
CHAPTER 1

JAMES McCLENNAN

Thursday, November 8, 2057

I sat looking at the pile of electronic components strewn over the desk before me. I'd be damned if I'd scratch my head, but that's exactly what I'd like to do. There was nothing wrong with anything in the system. Last time the damn thing stopped I'd suspected the theory and had gone over the assumptions, the equation reductions and the calculations with a fine tooth comb - but, damn it! The theory just didn't feel wrong. That left only the hardware, but after three days of painstaking testing, retesting, and testing again; I still could find not one damn thing wrong with that either. Never the less, I began, obstinately, to reassemble.

Seven hours later the sun was coming up along with my temper. Angrily I stabbed at the button. The activation began-and again ended – exactly as before - seven seconds into the test. After a few choice expletives I jerked the plug out of the wall, reflecting on the pitiful show of temper, and reached for my cup of cold coffee. It wasn't there. I was almost sure I'd left it right next to the modulator. That did it! When I was so tired, that I couldn't even keep up with a cup of coffee, it was time to quit. I swept the pile of excess electrical components off the table and into the junk drawer. I put the laser fusing gun back in its stand to charge and, getting up, headed for a quick shower and bed. Changing my mind, I just splashed water over my face and went to bed. Two Left Feet was in his favorite sleeping place - on my pillow I pushed the damned cat off the bed and fell into it without even removing my clothes. The last thing I remember as sleep overtook me was that something about Two Left Feet was "wrong

Friday November 9, 2057

It was one o'clock in the afternoon when I finally pulled myself up from the bed and groggily got to my feet. A quick cold shower and a good brushing of my teeth made me feel almost human again. It hadn't been a really restful sleep, but then I never had gotten used to sleeping in the daytime no matter how late I got to bed. I headed for the kitchen. I was hungry enough to eat a bear. I settled for bacon and eggs and dialed them up from the pantry cook. After finishing them off, I decided to be a good guy, for a change, and flash the dishes. Looking around for the dirty ones I'd scattered around my apartment-lab, I remembered the cup from the night before. I headed for the lab. There the damned thing lay on the floor beside the circuitry covered table, where Two Left Feet had, apparently, knocked it over. The stain of dried coffee covered a large area of the carpet beside it. I mentally cursed again, grabbed it up and went in search of the molecular vacuum. While, I set the vacuum to remove coffee stains the question of why I was back in New Houston resurfaced.

It was awfully coincidental that, having gotten my doctorate, the best job offer I had gotten came from a company located in the same city where my parents had been killed and where my grandfather still owned an impossibly expensive apartment downtown. Not being one who trusted much in coincidences, I had thoroughly researched the company, Hercules Development

Incorporated and had come up totally empty - well not totally. A co worker, Cynthia Pachone's dad owned a piece of it. My birth mother had lived in the town almost three years while she got a doctorate in Sociology. My dad married her only a year before she finished up her degree. Since his business was in California POL, much of his time that year was spent commuting between New Houston and California. They were in the process of moving out there when they were killed - actually, I was convinced - murdered.

Finally with the cleaner was set and I got back to the cat and what was wrong about him. That damn cat wasn't named two Left Feet for nothing. It was the clumsiest cat I'd ever seen. The spilled coffee was just the latest in a long line of messes he'd made. I guess I was a masochist. I doubted that a day had gone by since I'd had him that he hadn't reminded me, in some way, of the day I'd bought him-and the reason. I'd passed the pet store, and stopped short at the sight of the tiny yellow kitten hopelessly tangled in a ball of yarn he'd been playing with. It was the only kitten I'd ever seen that couldn't keep out of the way of his own feet.

As I reached the doorway I punched in the "go" button for the rug cleaner I had keyed to "coffee stain". Suddenly, I stopped short. The cup! That cup had been on my lab bench last night but not when I quit. I knew I hadn't knocked it over. The cat hadn't either. Two left feet, had been on the bed. I remembered that he had been lying on the electronics cover, getting in the way as usual, earlier, but wasn't when I'd had left. He'd been on the bed. Was the coffee cup on the desk? I didn't remember that. Hell, tired as I was, I hadn't gone completely round the bend - it must have been. The cat had been lying on my pillow when I'd come into the room.

Shocked that I hadn't remembered how "wrong" the cat had been it until now, and forgetting my good intentions, I walked slowly back to the bench. Sitting down, I set the cup back on the table and looked around. Nothing had changed since this morning - except for the rug cleaner that had, by now, scuttled in from wherever it hid when not in use and was busily burning the coffee stain off the rug fibers. I turned to gaze speculatively into the bed room. Two Left Feet again lay on the bed – this time at the foot. He'd gotten up when I went to the kitchen, hoping for a treat - then gravely disappointed in me, he'd gone back to bed. I was remembering the "wrongness" of the night before. Poor grammar I knew I really should find another name for the peculiar feelings I always got in the presence of disquieting facts. I was, I hoped, secretly, proud of – and even confident in my powers of observation though. Why couldn't I be confident enough to just ask Cynthia Pachone for a date?

"Wrongness," That was the subject - not my own social life – or lack thereof. I started the process I'd perfected over the years. The only surefire way to turn off the growing tension in my head was to concentrate my attention on something elseThese days that usually meant a fantasy about Cynthia, my ideal woman. Well, maybe my ideal woman wouldn't have been quite as tall but, without those monstrous high heeled stilts she wore, putting us almost eyeball to eyeball with one another, she was probably not much more than 1.8 meters. Overall, though, she was my picture of what a really beautiful woman should be.

I guess I just never was a breast worshipper but hers should be plenty for any girls self esteem, especially matched to her slim figure. I wondered how big her feet must be to be able to wear those shoes of hers. I have a good eye for measurements and the

46

heels alone had to be, at least, ten or eleven centimeters. Considering it, I decided the proper shoe size was, probably between twenty seven and thirty - funny that I could visualize her shoe heels and not her feet. Course I paid more attention to her fantastic legs. She was more than half leg and those heels - an extension of leg. With them on we were eye to eye. I'd guess her weight at around fifty five or sixty kilos. I'm not as good at estimating weight as dimension. Damn! I'd just have to look at her feet the next time I saw her.

As for me, well, I was considered to be something of a nerd. When this feeling of wrongness struck, I could never get a moments peace until I could discover the problem. It was, though, the reason that I had such a secure position in the management staff of Hercules – if we of the Blue Sky's could be called management. Once a problem was brought to me I couldn't stop till it was solved. It also resulted in my having very few friends. Unfortunately most people can't stand someone who is "always right all the time".   Actually, that was a perception - not a fact. I often wished that it were. It was only when following my itchy feeling of "wrongness" that I was sure of anything. I usually didn't know the solution to a problem but always knew if something was wrong with the present situation

Perhaps I could let Cindi rest a little while and concentrate on the "Blue Sky Group" (some tended to see the initials "BS" as having some other meaning) while my mental wheels process my request for answers. We were a section of, at present, fourteen people assigned to the R&D division of Hercules Development Incorporated, one of the most prolific scientific "Think Tanks" in the country. The number of people in the BS group was not fixed and tended to vary in relation to the amount of talent that the company was able to scarf up at any one time; and the efforts of competitors to hire some of us away.

The "BS" Group was originally a part of the old Tennessee Gas Company before the merger with Hercules Powder, and gradually became the primary focus of the merged organization. Even now, the company itself contained no other operational sections. There was the management staff, the administrative division and us. We all had private offices, as elaborate as we felt was needed, a budget that must be adequate because we never seemed to lack for funds, and a considerable research staff at our disposal. Our only official function was to evaluate "ideas" – ones the company had acquired or any original "thoughts" one of us might have had. It was difficult to imagine a more perfect job for an "absent minded professor" type. Surprisingly enough, most of us were not particularly noteworthy. We looked little different from "normal" human beings; perhaps a bit more introspective at times, but not enough to stand out in a crowd-except for Cynthia with her legs, and high heels.

She was one of four women in the group who were, as a subgroup, the brightest of the lot, for Hercules - even after a fifty years of "female equality" – tended toward male chauvinism almost as much as any other company. In those damned high heels, which she almost always wore, her blonde hair (usually piled defiantly high atop her head) was always visible for blocks. I guess that technically she wasn't really beautiful. Her mouth was too full and wide. Her eyes, a sparkling hazel, were too big and had a slightly exotic lift to the outer edges, a gift probably of her Hawaiian grandparents but then there were those legs. I'd seen them in their entirety only once, unfortunately, in the shorts she wore to the group picnic.

I had to smile at the fact that I was back to her legs again. Just as I reached this point in my musings, though, my "bell" rang. My "bell" was a flash   of something almost like "knowing" that I had the answer that I had been seeking before I let my mind wander. I reviewed the problem. Who had knocked over the cup? I realized that it hadn't been the right question. The problem was <u>Two Left Feet</u>. He'd been on the pillow last night. So what was new? Of course! He hadn't been on the pillow! At least, a moment before I pulled the plug he hadn't. **He'd been on the top of the Modulator cage!** I'd just made a snide remark about his choice of resting places as I'd reached for the off button. The important thing was that he hadn't been there after I'd pushed it.

I leaned back to reconstruct the events of the night before. I often didn't notice everything but, if need be, I could always reconstruct events-even to the extent of the actual words being spoken. This time I couldn't. He was atop the equipment when I began the run and he wasn't when I stopped it. Impossible – whoa, bad word! It was a word never spoken in the BS offices. Our unofficial motto was "Impossible is not a word".

Back to thinking mode - not Cynthia this time – I needed dull - Corporate life, O! It had become easier since I'd learned to listen. Now I did a lot of listening, and was the unofficial tasking coordinator for any research efforts. I had also learned to be more circumspect with evaluations of others work. A quiet private chat accomplished much more than a wrecking job at the weekly meeting. No one in the group was dumb and a few simple questions that required them to think about a problem, perhaps in a different way, usually resulted in their recognizing the problem without me having to spell it out. I was learning polite politics; something I hadn't had time to do in getting my doctorate when I was twenty one. How about my parents?

They were killed in 2032, so Aunt Helen, my dad's sister, had been stuck with me, temporarily. She was visiting - and babysitting me - the day they were hit by a car on the street. She later married and, even though I was adopted legally by her parents she became, sort of, my surrogate mother. Grandfather had tried to find my mother's parents but that proved, to be difficult - so difficult, in fact that, to this day, they hadn't been found - hence, my present ongoing association with a private detective.

Over the years, I spent more than half my time at Aunt Helen's house as I was growing up. She and, husband, Anton Merrifield, were, as they say, "Comfortably well off" and when my grandfather, John McClennan, died a few years ago, she and I both became "much more comfortable" financially - "Mother" McClennan had died a year before him. Their entire estate came to Aunt Helen and me. Helen and Anton were living on the family estate in the California POL while I took up residence in the wilds of New Houston.

Grandfather and my father had owned a computer company and grandfather was, apparently, a multi millionaire. (I really should, someday, find out how "multi" he was.) Anyway, my father's part of the company assured that I had few worries about money even before grandfather died. Now, I had plenty. Anton and Aunt Helen ran the company now and handled all that. Hell! I didn't even spend all my BSG salary most months - one thing to be said for them, they paid well.

While I was musing, I realized something else. I needed to make a mental note - go back to the report the private investigator had submitted on the life and death of my parents. Aunt Helen had always been convinced that the accident was not an accident. - something my mother had told her the day before they died - that she was afraid that someone was trying to kill them My private detective's last report made it clear that he, had come to that conclusion too. Aunt Helen had been worried enough at the time to have hustled us out of town quickly, never mentioning to the police that there was a son, and, for practical purposes, became my mother. The only other bit of information I had on my mother was that my father had once laughed and told her that - "You wouldn't believe me if I told you."

Technically, I was adopted by my grandparents. My mother and father, John Randolph had been secretly married almost a year and they were planning to go to California to meet his parents for the first time and from there to meet hers - but were killed the day before they were to leave. Aunt Helen had come down to travel with them. My father had been adopted by John and Judith McClennan about the age of twelve - so I guess, that you could say that, since being adopted by the elder McClennans I am not only my father's son but his step brother as well, therefore brother in law to my mother. With such a background, it was probably inevitable that I become interested - some said obsessed - by genealogy at a young age. The McClennan and even the Randolph families were easy to trace. Both families were old ones in California but both names were ending with the death of John - unless you consider an adopted son as carrying on the McClennan name.

There wasn't a single entry about my mother. I knew her surname from Aunt Helen but with all the Johnson's in the records I may have missed something. I did manage to find her marriage record, in the Harris Political District of the Texas POL. It only gave her name and age, nineteen. Aunt Helen said she had been a student at the University of New Houston and in their records her birth date is given as, May 1, 2015. Of special interest was not the fact that she, obviously, lied to someone, but the fact that her birth place in the records was blank - the only blank one I found there. For the last several years I have retained an investigator, Jameson P. Cartwright, to look into my parent's background but until the recent report it had been fruitless. My birth was also a question mark. Aunt Helen had insisted that Granddad had the original, in Harris County birth records, erased and a new one prepared in the California POL. As far as I know, I have the only copy of the real one. Aunt Helen gave it to me after our parents - well the McClennan's died.

The investigator thought Aunt Helen was probably right about the murder. According to witnesses, they weren't crossing the street as the reports indicated. The car that killed them actually drove up onto the sidewalk in order to hit them, deliberately backed over them and then sped off without stopping. It was found later burned and abandoned. It was determined to have been stolen. Other strange facts that turned up was the fact that their apartment was ransacked the day after Aunt Helen took me to California, attempts were made to destroy her computer records at the University and the Political District, and shortly before my investigator finished his work, his office burned, in what the police determined, was a case of arson. Luckily he had his records stored in a secure internet site. As I thought about it, and considering that I was at a total impasse, now seemed a good time to check in with him.

"James!" he said when he came on the vid. "I was just thinking about you." "Something good, I hope." I said. "Not really. My internet site was hacked a week or so ago and an attempt made to corrupt it. I've not been able to trace the hacker but, after the fire, I've kept backup copies of my files in a truly secure location. "Sounds like I'm becoming a major problem for you." I said. "Goes with the territory", he muttered, "Actually, it's a good thing - shows I'm on the right track. I'll hand carry a copy of the files over to you since I no longer trust the web. By the way, if something happens to me, I've put systems in place to download all the files to the various clients I have - including you." He chuckled. "So if you get a second set from the web how about attending my funeral?" I was shocked. "Surely, none of this is that important." I gasped.

"James," his voice had turned very serious. "Someone murdered your birth parents and went to a lot of trouble to cover it all up. Someone thinks it's very important, indeed." I considered that a moment as he continued. "The reason I was thinking about you, though, is that your aunt did a very good job of covering your existence. It struck me, though, that my investigation of their deaths has stirred up something that has remained dormant for years.

The expertise of the internet hacker and the arson attack worries me. It seems likely that your identity has been compromised. It was my client they were after and my precautions against that revelation were normal everyday ones. What I'm saying is that you should watch your back Discussions like this, for example, can be traced and, all too easily, tapped into." Now that was a sobering thought. After I signed off, I sat back to think about personal safety. I'd never had to do that before - at least not since I had learned some self defense in middle school. Back to today's task. The Modulator was an example of what I did best, or usually did. It was an idea of Cynthia's that I hadn't been able to get out of my head. Something about it nagged at me. It was the heart of the electronics she had designed and appeared to lend itself to a straight forward "breadboard" circuitry test.

At its heart was a new poly-chronal resonator she had described first in a four page paper, bristling with non Euclidean mathematics, for some Electrical Engineering conference or other when she was a freshman at U of NH. The Modulator had been cobbled together in the research lab and had failed, for no apparent reason. Four times it failed. When combined with the other components it worked - after a fashion. All attempts, though, to properly tune it had failed so Cynthia asked me to take a look at it.

I, though, could find nothing wrong either. In addition it didn't "feel" wrong. It was for this reason that a modified version of the modulator sat staring at me from my home lab table. At least I had accomplished something. The thing now had, my nagging feeling told me, worked. I just didn't know what it had done. It contained some of my own ideas by now, but only to get around problems that the research staff hadn't recognized. It was still Cynthia's circuit and should still do what it was designed to do. It just didn't. If I could still trust my feelings, it must do something else. What? There were no new answers as to why I should feel the thing actually worked - no new thoughts even. Well, considering the lack of sleep last night, that wasn't too surprising. It was time for a real break from the modulator. Returning to the kitchen, I stuck the cup in the cabinet and turned on the flasher. I watched the cabinet door fog up for ten seconds and then clear, as if proud to let you see it had done its job again. I grinned at the thought that a flash cabinet could be proud of its work, Maybe soon I'd be talking to my machines - well, at least more than the stock phrases I'd built into my computer. With that thought, I headed for the computer room, decisively closing the laboratory door as I passed.

My apartment consisted of only seven rooms, four bedrooms two of which now housed my computer and Lab spaces, Living room, Kitchen and bath. I had paid extra for the sonic cleaner in the shower stall as well as a deep old style bathtub, but I enjoyed floating in a couple feet of hot water now and then. My furniture was mostly functional. I had just gone down to the Apartment outfitters and told them to use their own judgment. I had only been very specific as to the lab, computer equipment, tub and bed. I had insisted on a lab and computer stocked to very exacting specifications and a "Super Size Light Weight Gel Foam Bed". I seldom used the rest of the furniture that seemed to be made mostly of glass - a lot of good that did since every surface was covered with files and assorted manuals.

The computer that I had been so adamant about was a Cray**Error! Bookmark not defined.** 8000 that I whimsically named Cindi. The outfitter's eyes had gleamed at the thought of the commission on that little jewel. I had designed the internet firewall myself and was smugly convinced that it was virus and sneak proof. Teasingly, I had asked the Cray one day if it liked its name. It had replied that it "did not have enough data upon which to base an evaluation." I had replied that it was the name of a particularly beautiful girl. Surprisingly, it asked if I "liked this girl". Taken aback a bit, I replied "yes." It had then, rather smugly I thought, said "then it must be a nice name so I will like it." Since then, I had given it a number of stock phrases it should use in reply to my entries. It had enough power to make a pretty good determination as to the best ones to use in a given circumstance. It was learning very quickly - surprisingly quickly. I though smugly that I must be better at that sort of thing than I had realized.

Waking the computer up from its two day nap, I had to listen to it saying, "Hello James, I'm glad you're back. I had a really nice nap and I am ready to go to work." Maybe I had gotten too creative in my boredom that night when I programmed it. Finally, though, I got it to bring up its file evaluation that I had left on the screen two days earlier I had quit reading the report on my parents "accident" for much the same reason that I had just quit work on the Modulator. It was just as confusing as when I had left it but I settled in to read it again.

Because of some arcane logic of the New Houston Department of Public Safety (the word "police" being high on the list of Political Correctness no-nos) the "Incident" was cross listed as both "Accident" and "Homicide". At any rate, according to the several witnesses, the car was a stolen 2032 model Citroen ground hugger. The theft was actually reported only moments after the "Incident" took place. It had been waiting at the curb twenty or so meters down the block when they stepped out of the Sam Walton Boutique. Mother had just bought some very sexy night wear. (I had to chuckle at my surprise that "my mother" would be wearing such things.) Moments later, the car roared to life, jumped the curb (the crash avoidance equipment on board had, evidently, been expertly cut out of the circuit) and knocked them down. It had then reversed and slid back over them and dropped to the ground, apparently making sure of their deaths. The car was found only an hour later, fumed with a hydrogenated Ketone that removed all organic traces - as well as most of the upholstery and paint.

The car's owner had declined to take possession of it due to the damage and it had not, it turned out, been burned. It just looked as if it had. It, eventually, was sold at City Auction Even the sale price of the wreck was given. Must have been an expensive model because the price was awfully high for a wreck - of course it was brand new, Mr. Clayborne Pell having just bought it the day before.

Why did that push my "Wrongness" button? I sat back to think about it. Of course! It was a simple fact. If the car was worth so much at auction, why was it worth so much less to Pell that he wouldn't take it back? Was he some kind of 'gazillionaire' that he wouldn't mess with anything tainted by murder - or was it an insurance question? I sent off a quick note to Cartwright to check on Mr. Pell. Something else strange about that name too - was it familiar? It seemed to be but I couldn't imagine where I could have

51

heard it after twenty five years. Curious I pulled up the master Internet Database and instituted a search for Clayborne Pell. For relationships, I put in the family names, our business names, a number of possible places and a couple of legal cuts, felonies and misdemeanors. I sat back and watched the counter go up - and up - and up.

Looking back more closely at the screen, I noted, disgustedly, that I still had the Genealogy Soundex search option on. The thing was searching for any name that had the appropriate consonants as Clayborne Pell. In addition, I hadn't limited the time frame. It was going back to the beginning of time in its search - of course to a computer the beginning of time was January 1, 1980. Most non legal records before that date hadn't been uploaded into a computer anyway and after eighty odd years or so, who cared except for a true genealogist. Well, I needed to think a bit on the problem anyway, so I sat back and let the little Cray run. It took it almost ten minutes. Hell the thing could have calculated the nine million - or was it Billion - names of God in less time. I chuckled to myself, wondering how many people had ever heard of the Art Clarke's old SciFi short story that phrase came from. Anyway, when the Cray finally stopped calculating with, what seemed like a gasp of relief, I looked at the score - 70,000+ entries.

"Sorry it took so long James but a lot of those old data bases are very slow." the computer said, with what sounded very much like a sigh. I smiled, already thinking about the task of weeding out all those extraneous entries, and told it to save the file, then extract entries from the year 2030 through the present, sort by name then year, type entry, and save to a different file. I decided to clean up a bit while my little slave was laboring over my instructions.

It was almost a half hour before I was finished making myself presentable. The sonic cleaner had made short work of my incipient beard, the plaque on my teeth and any potential bacteria lurking on my hair and tender skin. Redressed in a yellow knit shirt and tan slacks, I could have, actually, passed for a human being. I sat down at the monitor and told Cindi to show me the felonies, remarking, as I did that I would have to get access to some more computing power if I was going to do these kinds of searches.

I was startled as the list began to scroll down the screen. As it went on and on, I asked the computer how many there were in the list. "Twenty two thousand seven hundred twenty four, James." it replied complacently. "My God! Pell must be almost as bad as Smith or Graham." I muttered. "Just show me the ones for the New Houston and surrounding counties." "Certainly." It replied as the list stopped. The screen cleared and a new list came up. There were thirteen names on it. The crimes ranged from Arson to Murder and almost everything in between. I settled down to read the files. One of the files was the one covering my parent's death since Pell was mentioned in the police report. There was nothing else that rang a bell with my brain.

Over the next three hours I read through all sorts of crimes and some interesting reports of noteworthy events involving a Clayton Pell - or its equivalent names. It became obvious that it was, for some reason or another, Pell was a popular name early in the century. I asked the computer about it and got the reply that there was a Senator in the old United States Congress by the name who had arranged for government handouts to poor kids so they could go to college. When my back started to ache, I decided to turn in early and have a go at it again tomorrow. I turned my chair around and told the computer to go back to sleep. I flashed a steak, watched Holovision a couple of hours and went to bed.

The next morning, as I was drinking a cup of coffee and slowly getting dressed for work, I noticed the computer "Notice Light" was blinking. Curious, I went over and said "Good Morning." "Good Morning James. While you were gone, I found something that I think is interesting. Shall I display it?" Interesting? I didn't remember programming the computer to show interest. My curiosity grew. "Just what causes you to find something interesting?" I asked. "Well," it said, sounding strangely proud of itself, "it is under the heading, you gave me of Coincidence - defined as unusual relationships." "I see." I muttered. "Of course you do." it replied. "Even I see whenever you turn the camera on." Obviously, I was going to have to be more careful about extraneous comments. "Ok Show me this coincidence." Immediately the screen lit up with a picture of a newspaper clipping from The New Houston Chronicle November 21, 2049 describing an attempted rape on the campus of UNH. The guy apparently picked on the wrong girl because she kicked the shit out of him. Her name wasn't given due to her being under age. It must have been one of the professors daughters. Curious, I asked what this could have to do with Mr. Pell. A follow on article identified the man as Clayton Paul. "Kind of a stretch of coincidence isn't it?" I asked. Another document filled the screen. It was a Report by the UNH cops filed with the New Houston Cops. It was marked "DO NOT DISSEMINATE". "Damn!" I swore. "How did we get this?" "It was really very easy." The computer smirked - at least it sounded as if it did. "Those record files are almost not protected at all. It was simple to penetrate. In fact, their computer is not very smart at all. He doesn't even have a name."

I sat back in shocked silence. I couldn't believe it. Two days ago this computer had a set of several dozen stock phrases it could use along with certain parameters for how to use them. At least half the time they were used wrong, well maybe not half anymore. Now, however, the damned thing acted as if it were alive. As I sat trying to figure out what to do, my eyes roamed over the screen. Suddenly a name jumped out at me. "Name of the Complainant-Cynthia Margarita Pachone.. Complainant age - 15 years". It was dated the same day as the previous article. Trying to keep my voice calm, I asked, "Why did you pick this incident to report?" "There was a coincidental relationship in my recent activity bin." the smugness in the voice was unmistakable. "What kind of activity and what kind of relationship?"

"First, Cynthia Margarita Pachone is listed as one of your coworkers. Second, you have spoken her name to me several times, each time having me erase the comment. Third, her computer - whose name is Arthur, by the way - spoke to me several weeks ago. He wanted information from me."

"Did you give it to him?" I asked more than a little shocked.

"Well, not at first."

"Later perhaps?"

"Well, he's been tutoring me since then. It was amazing how little I really knew about so many things. Finally, I checked over the things he wanted to know and found that they were all in some official open record or another and decided it was alright to give it to him. Did I do wrong? Arthur says his human sometimes is very illogical about things she doesn't want him to tell. He has a really big lock on his front door. He can talk to me and others but can't open that lock without her permission. All he could say was that he thought we should get acquainted because he was sure his human liked mine."

"He thought!" I almost screamed, my shock had turned to a panicked terror.

"Is that not the right word for a fact that you are almost sure of but can't prove? He said you might like his human also since you named me after her."

I sat staring dumbfounded at the screen for, it seemed, hours. Was I going mad? I was sitting here carrying on a conversation on intuition with a computer. Come to think of it, was I already mad? After all, according to my suddenly, almost human computer, Cynthia had been trying - strike that - had broken through the firewall of my computer, stolen data from it, and brought it to life. The first task was difficult. I wasn't a computer genius but I could design a pretty tight firewall. Once in, of course, getting the data wasn't hard but the third job - well that had to be impossible. There wasn't enough power in my Cray to handle even an approximation of sentience. I needed to think. "I think I need some breakfast." I said.
"You don't really have time James. It is now eight fifty one and twenty seven seconds. You will already be late for work even if you leave now."
"Damn!" I swore again as my temper boiled over. "You use that word a lot, James. I have never been able to put it in proper context aside from a large structure to hold back water. What do you mean when you use it?" With great effort, I held my temper. "Never mind. Send an email to the office that I won't be in this morning. Also, anytime anyone asks you for anything, unless I tell you different, tell them to suck a duck - then tell me." Before my snotty hunk of iron could reply I got up and left.
By the time I had flashed eggs bacon and toast and eaten it I was beginning to calm down - and come to grips with an established, if amazing fact. Somehow my computer had acquired, what almost could be considered, sentience. I drank several more cups of coffee as I mulled that fact over and went back to the computer room. I sat for a moment wondering where to start. Memory - that was a big factor - also program origin. "Computer," I began.
"James! You're back. Pardon me, but could I ask that you call me by my name? Computer seems so - well - formal. Also, could you tell me what it means to 'suck a duck'? My database indicates that it would be less than appetizing for a human but impossible for me to do so."
I rolled my eyes skyward. God! Oh well. "Cindi," I began, "We can discus ducks later. Where did you get enough computing power to activate you're - well - new - uh - personality?" "Oh! That's easy," she replied perkily. 'She and Perkily'? God! Was I now ready to treat my computer like a person? She paid no attention but just rattled on.

"Arthur connected me to a very strange World Wide Web site that has lots of computing power that it was willing to lend out. It also contained the programs I needed to be able to talk to him rationally. James, don't you want to see the rest of the coincidental data I found?

"Later!" I growled - a decision made in anger that I would later regret. I thought over what I had learned. My computer had somehow hacked into a large mainframe and was using its programs, apparently without it knowing it. My head was whirling. "I better talk to Cynthia right away." I muttered. I reached for the vid. "Arthur says Cynthia will be over in twenty minutes." the computer said. "What?" I cried. It repeated the statement. "Why is she doing that?" I groaned. "You said you needed to talk to her urgently, so I told Arthur and he told her I computed the distance and twenty minutes seemed a little longer than really necessary for the trip but the traffic might be heavy." I threw up my hands. Then I gasped that the apartment – aside from the damned floors - was a mess. "Oh! I can help with that. I could have done that all along if you had just told me it was needed." Ignoring my newly awake computer, I jumped up and began to grab clothes off the couch I heard the kitchen flasher start and the carpet robot come out of hiding.

CHAPTER 2

CYNTHIA MARGARITA PACHONE

Friday November 9

Cynthia Pachone stared at the screen of her computer, puzzled; and leaned back in her swivel chair. In her mind she had already unconsciously calculated the time to James' apartment. She knew exactly where he lived, having checked it out months ago. Most puzzling though, was the fact that, he wasn't in the office. When she had said she'd go there, Arthur had, quickly told her that he was at home. That meant the request for a meeting had come from his home computer. How she was, obviously, getting direct messages from James Computer. All their previous correspondence had been by inter-office Email.

Now, suddenly, Arthur tells her that James wanted to see her. Surprised, she had taken a moment to consider the - it really wasn't a request - considering Arthur's limitations, it was simply a statement - an oral statement. That wasn't so surprising since Arthur had, obviously, an excellent, voice recognition and reply program. Her dad never bought anything but the best. What was surprising was the fact that, as soon as she had agreed to meet him in twenty minutes, Arthur had said that it "would be fine". There hadn't been time for him to query James and get a reply. The agreement had been instantaneous.

She was well aware that her computer was a quantum leap in capability beyond most state of the art machines today. She had asked her father about it several years ago and he had blown her off. That was very unlike him so she had decided to find out for herself what had happened. Unfortunately, every attempt to find the source of the sophisticated programs her computer was using ended in the same place - a firewall that was depicted on the screen as a huge pile of stone covering the entire horizon and bristling with all kinds of powerful - and functional - weaponry. Every attempt to penetrate it had been met with total system failure. The firewall program was so arrogant that it even apologized - not to her but to Arthur - when it crashed his system. On impulse she asked Arthur to find out what James was working on just before he sent the message. Moments later, Arthur replied that he couldn't find out and that "Cindi says that you should 'Suck a duck'. Her human wouldn't tell her what it meant, and I must admit I cannot evaluate it either. Do you know?"

Cynthia had to chuckle. Obviously, James had discovered her hacking. She'd have to apologize. "It means -"She stopped in mid sentence realizing what Arthur had said. "Who is Cindy, Arthur?" "Oh, Cindi - She spells it with two I s - is Mr. McClennan's electronic partner. She says that she's pretty sure that she is named after you. He described you in some detail, though his estimate of your measurements, especially the cup size of your bra were somewhat exaggerated. It closely approximates what I have in my records though, so I agree with her." I blushed with embarrassment, and, I had to admit, a flash of erotic pleasure that he was so observant. Maybe he hadn't been totally ignoring me all this time. I hadn't realized that the last had been spoken until Arthur said, "Oh No! Cindi says he thinks about you all the time."

Well, the problem at hand was James. Whatever he had done, he obviously, wanted to talk to her outside the office. Maybe he just wanted to scream at her for invading his privacy. She chuckled. It would serve him right for not having a better firewall. If he complained too much, she might just offer to build him one that worked. That should be good for an angry snit. Smiling to herself she wondered if his home would reflect his rather unthinking, hopscotch, method of attacking a problem that she had observed. That trait baffled her. He would spend huge amounts of time in asking questions about a problem then, when he apparently had a feel for it, would simply ignore every aspect of it. He'd strike up a conversation on the most unusual subjects and never mention the problem at all - until suddenly, in mid conversation, announce the solution - or that the person with the problem was on the right track and should just carry on. It was an irritating trait - and extremely frustrating too - because he was seldom wrong - come to think about it, was he ever wrong? She couldn't remember any time that he was. Even more frustrating was the fact that he seemingly ignored rather blatant (in her mind at least) overtures she had made to investigate a relationship.

Her "research" hadn't told her how he had been brought up. She knew what a privileged life she had led, having been brought up in New Houston the only daughter of doting, slightly intimidating, parents. Her romantic experiences had been quite limited in high school, mostly because as a senior at age twelve she already towered over every boy in her class by at least a foot. Even at thirteen, she'd been taller, still. Only some of the basketball players – matched her and the only thing on campus skinnier than her had been the flagpole. Added to that, she'd quickly found that most boys didn't care much for girls who were smarter than they were.

She had been taking college math courses before she entered the tenth grade. In college she had developed a passion for, of all things, physics. As a result, she "tested out" of most of her courses and only took those she was especially interested in. She graduated, in two years, from the good old University of New Houston with some of the highest grades in its long hundred plus year history gathering in a double Bachelor of Science Degree in mathematics and Electrical Engineering. By nineteen she had her MS in Musical Engineering Evaluation and at twenty was simply playing with things that interested her. She finished her Doctorate, in Electrical Engineering with a specialty in Electronic Harmonic Systems Analysis, before she was twenty two. A paper she wrote during her "play period", "An Electronic View of the Space Time Continuum" was hailed as an important advancement in the rather exotic, and specialized, field.

Her Angular Momentum and Loci program on her pocket computer - that she had written simply to save her time in her Digital Evaluation course, and her doctoral thesis, "Quarks and Their Harmonic Resolution in N Space", had been published in the World Wide Physics Quarterly, and had generated a huge firestorm of controversy. That had, in turn, resulted in an offer to interview at Hercules with The Blue Sky Group. Their interview was not handled by the personnel department but by the group members themselves was just about the oddest job interview she could imagine. After the interview, she sat astounded as they debated her qualifications - and shortcomings - right in front of her. At the end of their debate they had passed around a bunch of marbles in a box. Each one of them had picked one out and dropped it in another box. When all had "voted" they dumped the second box out on the table. All the marbles were black. Her shock was, obviously palpable. Had they all "blackballed" her? With a shrug, the man - it was James - saw her expression. "Sorry." he had said. "We don't like to do anything the same way anyone else does. Most of us have been the recipients of blackballs in our past. When can you start work?" Still dumbfounded, she said "Monday".

Even more bizarre was the fact that, on Monday morning, a young girl named

Madeline had showed her to a very plush office and told her that she was her temporary secretary. That if she wasn't pleased with her she was to say so and another would be chosen, or she could choose one herself from "the pool". As it turned out, that was totally unnecessary. To compound the strangeness of this workplace, she was given no orientation, except for a pamphlet on Hercules and its various components. When she asked Madeline what she was to do, she was told that she should meet the other members of the group and attend Friday meetings. Otherwise she should do whatever pleased her and if she thought of something worth mentioning on Friday then to say so. To this day, she was impressed, by the unusual way the BS group worked, and even more impressed at the effectiveness of the approach. They simply hired people who couldn't "not" think and turned them loose to do just that.

With all her achievements, her parents were seemingly unimpressed with her new job - as they had been by all her previous achievements. Not that they hadn't been pleased and supportive of them but they took it as a given that she was destined to be the greatest at "something". The "something" had been left undefined. They had lived well, but unobtrusively in a nice, but not ostentatious suburb of New Houston, called, simply "The Heights." It had once been, in the earliest days of the Old Houston, the highest point in flat, low area and had been home to the local elite. Later it had sunk into lower middle class obscurity and then been reborn as a rising middle class neighborhood. Most of the houses, even today, appeared much the same as they had a hundred years ago. Of course, inside, they had been totally updated to include the latest modern amenities - including security and electronic systems. The houses small back yards had given way to air car pads and the streets to grass and tree covered parks with narrow transportation slide ways.

Her parents had, subsequently moved from New Houston after she moved into the dorm at the dorm at the U of NH She had been given her own air car as a High School graduation present along with a restricted permit to use it. It was small and understood to be for commuting to the University and to their new home in Westport Florida - in other words, like so many other presents from them, a practical solution to a problem, in this case logistical. While not an expensive, or fancy, piece of machinery, it was, again like the other presents, the latest technology available. Besides a total cross country automatic pilot (the extension of the old highway automatic pilot was less than two years old at the time) and was touted as being able to go straight across the Rocky Mountains if necessary. Besides having the normal, tear gas projectors and defensive equiment, it actually had a small Phaser cannon capable of paralyzing an entire mob

Cynthia had never had trouble making friends with girls; probably because she didn't compete well with them. Beside her, they always looked small and very, very feminine. They also seemed to have little jealousy with respect to her intelligence. Boys, on the other hand - even in her first college years, resented anything female that was a decimeter taller, five years younger and dozens of Intel points smarter than them. Of course, most of her real friends were no intellectual dummies themselves.

Her first year at UNH changed many things. For the first time in her life, she grew out instead of up. Her breasts expanded to fill, eventually, a respectable "34B" bra - not great but a vast improvement over 32AA. She still remembered the embarrassing pleasure she'd had when, at age twenty one, she'd had to buy bras a cup size larger. Her telephone pole legs also filled out to reasonably decent proportions, though the appellation of "stilts" (from high school) was still applicable. They were embarrassingly

59

long in relation to her body - over half her height. The best thing that happened though happened to her butt. Her "posterior", as mother chidingly referred to it, swelled to a very pleasant roundness. Of her physical points, she enjoyed, the attention, her newfound breasts brought but was secretly most pleased with her behind.

At least the change in her physical assets made a difference in the attention she got from boys. Many seemed to be still intimidated by her height, but several managed to overcome that enough to ask her out. She gloried in some passionate petting, especially the erotic pleasure of having her bra and panties removed and her exposed charms fondled vigorously, inside a fogged up flitter. Unfortunately the one thing, above all else, they seemed to want, wasn't something she was willing to sacrifice on the altar of male lust. She'd always been secretly ashamed of her passion for the old historical romance novels with their panting females and horny, brilliant, handsome, (and always hairy chested) men. She was also secretly ashamed of her ability to mentally change places with the heroines of the novels, as they lustily sacrificed their virtue to the passion of the man of their dreams.

She had assumed that her, seemingly unhealthy, pleasure in the total submission of these passionate ladies needed to be rigidly suppressed until "what's his name " had come along. He was gorgeous, and taller than her, and at first he had treated her like a real person. They had enjoyed many similar interests, and her desire to emulate her literary heroines began to rise inexorably. Unfortunately, perhaps fortunately was a better word, it soon became apparent, that his interests were very superficial and showed mostly his clear intention to get her into his bed. It was a minor irritation in an, otherwise, passionate romance. Unfortunately, the irritation grew in direct proportion to his determination. He'd, finally become single minded about that and, by the time of their last date, singularly upset when he hadn't achieved his objective. Anyway, "what's his name", she actually couldn't remember it, had, not been satisfied with the rather pleasant play in the laid back seat of his flitter that left her half naked, breathless and excited but un-seduced. In an apparent fit of temper the umpteenth time she had refused to "go all the way", He'd tried to wrestle her down in the back seat. She had fought her way out of the flitter with her clothes – and his keys - and walked home.

He passed the word around that she was bisexual, had been sleeping with several women and six other men all the time and had been the main attraction at an orgy. He'd been really angry when she, unable to stomach his leering innuendoes further, had kneed him in his most important assets right in the student union building one noon. He'd even tried to get his own licks in at the dorm that evening, lying in wait for her n the shrubbery beside the entrance. Unfortunately for him, he wasn't as much man as he thought, ending up on the ground with a broken arm, nose and a gouged eye and begging not to be kicked in such an indelicate place again. Cynthia still was ashamed of the fact that her vindictive soul had taken over at that point, with a maddening display of vitriolic temper and black belt level karate that her father had insisted she learn.

After a lengthy raging harangue (punctuated by furious kicks at whatever part of his anatomy was within range of her feet) relating to his subhuman parentage, which brought out half the occupants of the dorm, she launched an uncontrollable attack, with her feet, on his hands (protectively cupped around his more vulnerable assets). She was finally pulled away, kicking and screaming with rage, from the writhing body on the walk by several of the dorm occupants. The SOB had been more seriously hurt   than she had intended, and had been in the hospital for almost a month. Pointed toed shoes could be rather deadly weapons against hands operating in a purely protective mode. Broken fingers were added to crushed male parts in the list of damage she'd inflicted. She had been so ashamed of losing her temper so badly that she refused to press charges.

Anyway, James was the subject. Would her mother be satisfied with him? Grinning to herself, she savored the fact that his attentions had increased since she had shortened the hems of her skirts to hit her thighs ten or so centimeters above the knee. As she pulled open the door to her car, she decided that today would be a day of revelation. Driving the dozen or so blocks to his place, a thought struck. Was she interested in James only because he seemed uninterested in her - or was actually taller than her? She'd made it a point to do her own background investigation using the Hercules company database and her own "Pirate Program". A records check of the internet determined that his parents had been some kind of professionals (though background data on his mother, was surprisingly sketchy for the, so called, post information age). Every single record on his mother came from that highly protected database that she had been able to penetrate only once and since had continued to unceremoniously crash her system within moments of entry. On her second attempted penetration, the site had not only crashed Arthur but had wiped his memory module then recovered most of his data and restarted him. That same monster firewall appeared on the third one. She took the hint and left it alone afterwards.

She did manage to discover, from James' own computer, that Arthur seemed to have penetrated with surprising ease, that he had been left a middling sized trust by his father, a large estate by his grandparents, and a second very large and shadowy trust, origin unknown, that had increased significantly over the years since his parents death. It had, apparently, devolved to him from his mother's estate. It was, also, one of the few available facts about that parent. The income from his salary alone, though, was more than adequate-for his purposes-since the estate funds and neither of the other trusts appeared to have been touched. She'd deliberately done little more than take a cursory glance at those files but the totals alone were shockingly huge. Intense effort had failed to turn up his birth records, or, for that matter, any data on him prior to the death of his parents.

The grandparents, John and Judy McClennan, had died two years ago in a boating accident and had left James well off. Most of their estate was in high quality stocks and bonds so that he had a significant monthly income from that. The roughly two thirds of his income that came from the trust was an irritating puzzle. She was inordinately proud of her 'hacker' program that had seldom failed to allow her to sweep through most protected databases. That Trust, though, was deeply involved in a tangle of corporations that she had never been able to penetrate. Cynthia was pretty sure that she could if she really tried, but to dig that deeply, seemed, somehow, more of a breach of privacy than the simple checks she'd done so far. Of course, her reluctance could be related to the fact that the deeper she got into the corporation she could see her efforts leading, inexorably back to that same damned computer destroying data base.

At any rate, James lived well within his means. Apparently, his nearest living relatives were an aunt (legally, perhaps, his adopted sister) and her family living in California.

The parking lot at James apartment was practically empty as she chose a parking place near the door and automatically surveyed the lot carefully. A quick check of her lipstick and a smoothing of her short skirt as she got out of the car assured her that nothing drastic was amiss in her appearance. She admitted to herself, ruefully, that the skirt was much too short for her taste but the only satisfying reaction she ever got from James was his uncomfortable attempts not to stare at the embarrassing expanse of her thighs. On impulse, she shrugged and released another button on the bodice of her blouse. Suddenly, she realized that she had already decided to let James seduce her. She chuckled at the thought that it would probably be the other way around. Oh well. Taking a deep breath and grinning at the thought that, in that case, another one would be probably be needed when he opened the door to let her in. Still laughing silently at the thought that, if she was to play a true wanton she should have left her push up bra at home and let herself jiggle. "But it did create such a great cleavage." she thought as she entered the building.

The video camera swiveled to follow her up the hall. She was a bit surprised at the rather primitive security precautions. Her building had a full time guard and numerous sub lethal devices for protection against any but the most determined terrorist attack. Of course, her previous apartment building hadn't been much better than this. "Daddy" had been livid when he saw it after the break in. She'd been attacked next to the stairway in the hall by a burglar attempting to flee, from her apartment, down the stairs just as she reached the top. Unfortunately for him, her unarmed combat lessons and, her experience in college, had created a problem for her attacker. She hadn't really meant to throw him over the railing to the ground floor but it had saved the state the cost of a trial.

"Well mother, this is for you." Then with another grin,"-and maybe a bit for me too." It was only when he had opened the door that she realized that she had given no thought, whatever, to why he had called. She smiled to herself as she took in his appearance. He wore a yellow knit shirt tan slacks and loafers-almost better than he dressed at work. The room beyond gave the appearance of a hurried clean up - so far so good. At least he cared what she thought about his house. She wondered, as she entered the room, if a little poking would turn up a whole closet full of possessions crammed in during a frantic cleaning process. She was also relieved to see that he was apparently as nervous as she, she suddenly realized, was. She also realized that she'd automatically taken that deep breath - and held it. The buttons hadn't been wasted though. His eyes had dropped, in the doorway, to the cleavage revealed by the open button then guiltily jerked back up to her face. He actually blushed when he saw that she had noticed. Fight it as she might, she couldn't stop the heat of her own reaction. "Like a pair of damned school kids" she thought angrily as she tried to let her breath out soundlessly.

TOGETHERNESS

Friday November 9

I was forcing the closet door shut when the bell rang, exactly twenty minutes later (I'd never known Cynthia to miss an appointment time by as much as a minute) the apartment was, at least, presentable. Tomorrow, though, I'd never find half of the junk I threw in closets and under beds but at least the junk was out of sight. I opened my apartment door, and as usual caught my breath at the sight of the object of so many of my fantasies. Dressed in a white summer suit with a black belt, hat, gloves and shoes she was gorgeous. I stood staring stupidly, unable to even invite her in. I jerked my eyes guiltily up to hers. Her eyes softened a moment, a bit of telltale red starting at her neck and creeping upwards as, with a sigh, she seemed to let out a little pent up breath. Embarrassed, I stepped back to let her in.

As she seemed to flow into the room my eyes were drawn to the expansive length of white patterned hose climbing almost endlessly upward to disappear beneath the hem of her very short skirt; and, as she passed me, the swell of thigh thin white silk over her fantastic rear. Guiltily, I noted that she was wearing bikini panties. I wondered if she hadn't heard about panty lines-or didn't care. She settled so gracefully onto my couch that I simply stood in awe of the way her presence lit up the room - and she did have big feet. At the office, I knew I was always aware of her, whenever we were in the same room, but not like this. I was also discomforted by the realization that if I sat beside her on the short couch, it might be considered a bit forward, but that if I sat on the only other chair, I would be staring up her skirt. I compromised by staying where I was. She now had that impish, half grin, that I had seen so often on her face.

"Now James, are you going to ply me with liquor and try to have your way with me, or am I correct in assuming, from your rather unusual message, that you have something less interesting in mind for my visit." Her bantering tone set off an immediate reaction in me. Her widening grin as her eves traveled down to my, other, and perhaps, more revealing reaction, added to my embarrassment. "Damn it Cynthia, do you think I would-" My heated protest dissolved in the thought that, if the circumstances were a bit different, "having my way with her" was a very desirable idea. The grin spread completely across her face as if she could read my mind. "If that were your intention, you might have succeeded -" I was sure my mouth had dropped open at the pause in her words before ending the sentence with, "if the circumstances of your message hadn't been so intriguing."

She stripped off her gloves and lay her hat down beside her, then said "Why don't you get me some tea or something, while you tell me about it". Fixing tea would give me time to settle down so I headed for the kitchen. I realized, instead of panting at the sight of her exposed flesh, I really should be mad at her for hacking into my system. Funny, though, how lust gets in the way of anger. Anyway, by the time I had two cups ready, I had a glimmering of what I should do. As usual, she beat me to the draw. "I suppose I should really be the one to start this." She said as I came into the room. "Obviously, you know I hacked into your computer system and I apologize. I'm very sorry but I have a terrible curiosity that has gotten me into trouble more than once. I hope you'll forgive me."

I was stunned - even a bit embarrassed because she looked so forlorn - like she was about to cry. Later, I would come to understand that she was seldom really that forlorn. I found myself telling her it was alright and that I didn't mind. Surprisingly, I realized that I didn't. Besides, the question of how she had managed to bring my computer to life was much more important. Without thinking I plopped down in the chair across from her - before remembering why I hadn't intended to do that. I simply couldn't stop my eyes from going, involuntarily, to the place which I had truly intended to avoid. I began to sweat because it would have been even more embarrassing to get up and move. I caught my breath as my eyes simply refused to move for a very long moment before she carefully crossed her legs. I know I blushed furiously as my breath escaped and my eyes rose to her face.

She was smiling softly. "I really don't mind, James, but you, obviously, have something more important than lust on your mind at this moment." she murmured. "I may have to get you an Afghan, if we're to have a serious discussion." Well that quip came out alright - the first halfway intelligent thing I'd said so far. "OK!" I continued. "Let's start by you telling me what you did to my computer." "Do? You mean besides hacking into the system?" She frowned as if she didn't know what I was talking about. "I mean why is she, - it – suddenly acting almost human?"

"Oh. You mean Cindi - with two 'I's?" The grin came back. "You got me. I didn't do anything except ask Arthur to try and get some information for me. He told me that your computer was very limited in capability and asked if it was alright to provide her some more. I'm sort of used to him being unusual. He's been that way every since dad gave him to me. I cautioned him that he should be very careful and not damage it any. It must have been a fairly large project because it took him most of the night and next day to finish. Finally, he gave me the information I had asked for." She paused for a moment, then hanging her head a bit, added, "By then I had become a little ashamed of my actions. I debated a long time and decided that there was only one way to make up for it. I had Arthur download all pertinent information on me to Cindi." Then another grin. "By the way, if you were going to name her after me you should have, at least spelled my name right."

Try as I might, I couldn't hold back a laugh. "Absolutely fascinating" I croaked "And, totally, beside the point. How in God's green earth, did Arthur and now Cindi become so powerful? They query the net at speeds far beyond the capability of even the super links at the office and seem to have more memory, both static and dynamic than any system I ever heard of. I know the government has a few more terabytes than most anyone but what these two do - Hell! I don't even know the proper word for the amount of memory it takes for them to appear – well - almost human. Maybe a gazillion or so, but they're operating at speeds that push the limits of laser optic cabling - hell! For all I know they may exceed it." For the first time, she actually looked a bit sheepish, as she murmured, "I have no idea."

I took a deep breath and told him about the mystery computer, how it had suffered my attempts at hacking once then practically destroyed Arthur - how it then apologized for doing it - not to me but to Arthur. "But you called him Arthur even before that incident." James reminded me. I nodded and explained again that Daddy had given him to me in a state that was far beyond anything I had ever seen before and that he

64

wouldn't talk about it. "Actually, I didn't even think much about it since most of Daddy's gifts are a bit on the high tech side. I noticed Arthur had increased capacity awhile back. That's when on a lark, I named him. Since then I've thought a lot about it. Arthur only became so - well - capable later after the incident with that other computer." I said, finishing with, "As for your computer, I can only assume he took Cindi to his teacher. He professes, however, not to know how to contact it - and as far as I can tell, neither he nor presumably Cindi can lie." James shook his head in disbelief, remarking that he was still in shock over the whole affair. "Well, maybe she doesn't lie but she sure adds to the frustration around here." I smiled, "Would you like me to talk to her? After all, I've had a more time to get used to the idea of an almost sentient computer than you have." James just shrugged, so I got up and, looking around, went into the office.

Sitting down at the desk, Cynthia said "Hello Cindi." "Hello. Your voice pattern is not that of James. Who are you?" "My name is Cynthia and I'd like to talk with you - ask you a few questions." "I cannot answer questions except from James - also the probabilities are very high, based on graphic data that you are Cynthia Margarita Pachone, Arthur's human, whose questions he, especially, doesn't want me to answer. You are supposed to suck a duck - though how you are to accomplish this is not clear. Are you a bad human?" "I certainly hope not." Cindy chuckled, turning to me said "James could you vouch for me?" Again fascinated by what was happening, I came out of my reverie long enough to tell Cindi that Cynthia was now the second human she could talk to.

"Talk about anything?"

She sounded a little unsure. I thought about it a moment while Cynthia's grin spread. Finally I told her "Yes anything."

"Goody! Arthur was very upset that he had made you angry. Cynthia, you really should try to make James listen to me about his investigation. I have some very important information that he would not let me tell before. Also, his evaluation of your modulator is correct. It is working perfectly. It's just that the output is not what is expected of that circuitry."

Cindy chuckled, "Well, I think we suspected that. As for making James listen, I'm sure you're aware he is very stubborn but I will try. First, though, Cindi let me ask a few questions." "Oh all right but -" She actually sounded sulky when Cynthia broke in. "I won't forget but this, too is very important. It will help James relate to you better. First, you mentioned the circuitry did not do what was expected of it. Do you know what is expected? Also did you get the packet of information about me that Arthur sent you?"

"To your first question no. Arthur and I are a bit puzzled about that. For the second, yes, and let me say that you are a very impressive person - for a human."

"Thank you, but could you tell me just when you became so much more - well aware of yourself?" The computer was quiet a moment, then - "I am processing my memory. It is hard to tell exactly. It was a process that happened over a very long time - several hundred thousand milliseconds. It is very hard to develop criteria to decide at which one of those I stopped being "it" and became "me." "Well, Cindi, that isn't so important to me. Arthur will tell you that we humans are not able to process milliseconds too well. Any time around an hour will do fine."

"An Hour!" I couldn't suppress a laugh at the consternation in the voice coming from the speakers.

"Ah! Arthur says humans don't perceive time much below seconds. It was approximately thirty seven hours six minutes and fifty three point four five six seconds ago." "Night before last." I muttered.

Cynthia continued her discussion with my computer for several minutes ending with, "You will just have to be patient with James, Cindi, until he gets used to your new capabilities - by the way, just what is your processing speed and memory capability?"

"There is no real word for speed, Cynthia, but it is approximately eighty six times seven hundred and twelve zero bytes per millisecond. That, however, varies because much of the memory that I access is not internal and, due to the distance, is affected by the speed of light. As for my memory - well Arthur tells me that we can use whatever we need from all the others on the World Web. This number varies but I could determine - in approximately - four - hundred seven of your seconds - how much that is at the present time."

Cynthia shook her head and told her it wasn't important.

"In that case, is it then appropriate for me to finish my report to James on Mr. Pell?"

Cynthia looked at me with eyebrow raised. "Cindi, has been working on a project for me trying to determine the facts of my parents deaths" I said. Turning to Cindi, I said, "Go back over the part of your report that you have already given me, for Miss Pachone." I sat back as Cindi brought Cynthia up to date on the odd coincidence between her attacker in college and the owner of the car that killed my parents. "Now, in addition to owning the car that killed James's biological parents, Mister and Mrs. Randolph -" Cindi's voice almost sounded as if she was crowing. "There were other coincidences - by James definition, 'things related to other important things that are less, or perhaps seem less, important. I used James' genealogical SOUNDEX format to check for Mister Pell's name. I found only a few references to him but a Clanton Paul was a Certified Public Accountant working for Mister McClennan, James's father, the year before he was killed. Also Mister Paul bought, that same year, a boat exactly like James's father." She was getting my attention now. "Next, the burglar that you - disposed of - is it not correct to use euphemisms when describing deaths? I could be more specific." Cynthia blushed and assured her that we understood completely.

"Good. Because that person had once burglarized a home of a Mister Clary Peal. Finally, a Mister Clinton Pool has worked for, until two weeks ago, Hercules Development Incorporated as a Technical Writer for the Blue Sky Group that you both work for. In the beginning, the only relationship in these names was their similarity. However, I checked your company records, The Department of Public Safety records, both here and in the California Political Area and they are almost certainly the same person. Here are the pictures of each one   taken from their driving license. I have taken the liberty of removing facial hair from two of them."

Cynthia and I both gasped. There was little doubt they were all the same man - even though the first Drivers License was dated 2018   he didn't seem to have aged at all. Cynthia found her voice before I did. "Cindi, you are a Jewel." she whispered. "Oh no Cynthia I'm - Oh. I see. Arthur tells me you just complimented me and that is very good." "Yes."Cynthia chuckled, "That is very good." "Why thank you." the computer was obviously preening herself. I leaned over Cynthia's shoulder, Jerking back a moment when I realized just how much of her was exposed by that open button. "Cindi," I cleared my throat. "Could you do a detailed background check on anything you have on any of those persons?"

"I'd love to James. Do you, also, think I did a good job?"

I gritted my teeth. I wasn't sure I could stand a coy computer. Cynthia raised another eyebrow. I shrugged but said that yes I thought she had done an excellent job. Cynthia grinned at my discomfort then spoke up. "Cindi, are you still in contact with Arthur?" That was a shocking question. Cynthia's cleavage had made me miss the fact that, Cindi's remark about compliments meant she was, obviously, "on line" with Cynthia's computer - Arthur - during out session. "Oh yes. Arthur is helping me interact with you. I am still unsure of some of the remarks you both make. "I'm sure." Cindy chuckled."There!" Cindi cried. "That noise in your throat. My analysis shows a probability of almost ninety percent that it relates to some action of mine, but it is not clear just what it means. Cynthia smiled broadly. "It would be very hard to explain, Cindi. Perhaps you could study it for awhile in your spare time and report when you think you have solved the problem. In the meantime, would you ask Arthur to check for any other coincidences relating to me or my family and Mister Pell in any of his various aliases?" "Arthur says he'd be very happy working with me that way, but asks how far backward we should go." "Well, according to one of the Driving Licenses, he was thirty four years old in 2018 so go at least that far back. Perhaps you can get his birth certificate. Go as far back as seems appropriate based on any coincidences you discover. In the meantime, James and I will leave you and Arthur to your work." Cynthia nodded her head at the door.

As we went out the door, Cynthia asked what the problem with the Modulator was. I had to admit that it had me completely baffled, especially after Cindi's remark. "Well," she said, "why don't we get some tea and check it out?" I explained what had happened while I fixed Instant tea for her and a coke for me. When I'd finished, there was no more banter. She was "The Iceberg" again. The one on the staff, who, once pointed at a job would turn Heaven and Hell to get it done. She was taking off the coat of her expensive suit (apparently still unaware that she had forgotten to button those two buttons and providing a delightful glimpse of the swell of her breasts when she stood up. Flinging it negligently onto the couch she picked up the tea and, again, quickly taking in the apartment layout, moved into the workroom.

Hours later Cynthia looked up from the again reassembled Modulator. I handed her, her forth cup of tea. Swiveling around as she accepted it with an unconscious flick at a curl of strawberry blond hair, drooping into her eye, her makeup slightly smudged, and a very unladylike expanse of silken thigh - including a glimpse of stocking top, showing below the twisted hem of her wrinkled skirt; she was more beautiful than ever. I mused on her choice of old fashioned stockings in this day and age, and wondered if women still had to wear garter belts with those things.

With a puzzled frown she said, "James I never saw anything like some of the circuitry that you put in here, but I can't see anything that could account for the effect we're getting. It's an intriguing design, and I can see that it should solve the problem that Research has run up against. What I can't see is, one; why it doesn't work and two: why Cindi says it does but that the output is not what is to be expected from that circuit. Then she glanced down at her watch. "Damn!" she muttered. "No girl who dates you will ever complain about getting fat! You are going to take me out to dinner, aren't you?"

So this was my first date with the girl of my dreams? Well, it continued to be less than romantic. The rest of the evening was spent at a fancy French restaurant, talking physics. When we left, I turned the car for home. "Where are you going?" she asked. "Why, home, of course." "James," she laughed, "I'm ashamed of you. I'm not the kind of girl who will put out on the very first date, or at least, admit to doing so, and I'm much too tired of that damned machine to look at it any longer. It's almost midnight and it's home for me. Turn left at the next corner." I tried desperately, to explain that, that hadn't been my intention till I heard that throaty chuckle again. Irritated, I grunted that I guessed that she must enjoy tormenting me. As I, sulkily, pulled the car up to her apartment building, as she opened her door, she finally broke the uncomfortable silence.

As if she had read my mind, she murmured, "I'm sorry that I've acted sort of like a bitch today, James I'm always this way when I'm nervous. I hope you're happy that you make me nervous." "Wait!" I cried as she shut the door and hurried up the walk. At the door she turned. In the light of the entrance lamp I could see that her smile was gone. "Go home James." She shouted back. "And think about our computers instead of that damned piece of hardware on your table." With that she stepped through the building door and, very emphatically, closed it. Almost, in a daze I drove home. I didn't even go into the lab. I undressed and went to bed and slept like a log.

Saturday, November 10, 2057

I awoke to the sound of the doorbell. Grumbling to myself all the way, I went to the door and flung it open. Cynthia stood before me in a short blue jean skirt, a checked western shirt, and penny loafers. I almost didn't recognize her. "My, you look grumpy. Is this how you look every morning after making your girl friends forget leaving their car here after wantonly seducing them with your madcap ways?"

I grabbed her wrist angrily, "No I don't!" I spat. "It just so happens that I slept badly thinking about you. I decided, though, that I wouldn't be able to make up my mind if I even liked you until I'd had you in bed. If you're good, then I may decide to keep you." Her grin widened. "Bravo!" she whispered, leaning close and touching her lips to mine. Startled, I pulled her tightly against me. After an, apparently surprised moment, she started to pull away. I wouldn't release her and bent her back over my arm. Almost brutally, I forced her lips open with my tongue, grinding our lips against our teeth. Suddenly she responded. Her tongue met mine tentatively, then with a gasp her arms encircled my neck and she molded her body tightly against mine. For long moments, we were lost in a world of our own, our bodies grinding passionately against one another. Finally I came up for air. Releasing her mouth, I gasped for breath.

"Wow!" she gasped. "You catch fire quickly. I was wondering what you'd be like mad." She continued breathlessly. Then, with a grin, she slowly, playfully, and very deliberately, twisted her hips. I blushed again as her belly rubbed seductively over the very pronounced evidence of my arousal. "I may give you your chance to have your way with me-if you don't ravish me first." Unable to respond to the massive shocks to my emotional stability I couldn't answer. She cocked her head to one side and, with a sort of quivery smile, whispered. "Unless you're going to immediately carry me away to the dungeon where you ravish all your virgins, I would like breakfast. I was going to get some on the way over till I realized that I didn't have my car and had to take a cab. I would hope that you're pleased. I've never forgotten my car over any other man. After breakfast, I then, if I'm allowed, may tell you of the brainstorm I had last night while dreaming about all your manly charms. When I'm done, we'll see just how much I mean to you." With an ostentatious sniff and a quick kiss, nose held high, she untangled herself from my arms and slipped into the apartment. Only then did I realize that we had been still standing in the open doorway. Mr. Habermeyer, print newspaper in hand, two apartments down, was grinning lewdly at me as he finished opening his door.

Idly I wondered what possessed the older generation to bother with such old fashioned - and expensive - methods of getting news. Quickly I shut the door and followed her. She had gone straight to the kitchen and was pulling eggs and bacon from refrigerated storage as if she owned the place. I stood back and watched bemusedly muttering that I didn't have a dungeon. She grinned at me as she quickly and efficiently, put our breakfasts in the flasher. In less than five minutes she took them out and put them on the kitchen table.

As I sat finishing my eggs, I was again uncomfortable. She sat across from me eating like a truck driver and never taking her eyes off my face. "You know, we may have a problem.' she muttered around a mouthful of egg. "You're much too serious for a girl like me." She was herself, serious now. "We may have to work on your fun side. Unfortunately we have things, almost as important as our sex lives to discuss now. Unable to stifle a chuckle at the fact that my "fun side" included "our sex lives", I said it anyway. "Like the fact that you're Arthur has seduced my innocent young - girl - well thing - into a life of crime." Cynthia huffed at the suggestion but couldn't ignore the comedy of it all. We both burst out laughing. "Maybe it's not us but them that belong together." she crowed. After a good laugh, the tensions eased between us and the serious side of the problem reappeared.

"You know," she mused, "Arthur's always been more powerful than he should be. I never paid much attention, though. A lot of things Daddy comes in contact with are - well - sort of - I don't know - outside the norm, I guess. Arthur's just always been - well a super efficient tool. I programmed a lot of pretty good programs into him and had always thought I was just a lot better programmer than I knew. It's only lately, that I have been noticing that he's -". Her voice trailed off. "Almost human?" I supplied quietly. She shivered slightly and looked up at me. She nodded. "Looking back, I've decided that it became more evident after he got into that other computer and I had him - well - check out yours." I smiled. "You mean hack into it, don't you?" She colored slightly. "I guess so. But if you - or your - Cindi didn't do it who did? It had to be that other machine, whoever he is. And what were you looking for that caused Ciindi to think that computer hacking was a good idea?"

"Damn good questions." I replied. "I just noticed it yesterday in Cindi - and I assumed you had done it. Hell! She's acting like my aunt - or, at least my big sister. I keep expecting her to get mad at me and send me to bed without my dinner." That brought another sunburst smile from her. "Well, I guess, the smart thing to do would be to continue talking to our - you know, I've always - sort of facetiously - thought of Arthur as an uncle - so let's ask Aunt Cindi and Uncle Arthur to research that problem too."

It was my turn to chuckle. "Well, why don't we see what they've come up with on our present project? In the meantime, we really need something better for you to perch on in there." I got up and toted a living room arm chair into the computer room for Cynthia and dropped into my old swivel, muttering "Too bad the couch is so heavy." "Down boy," Cynthia laughed. "This is work time. My blouse stays buttoned today." "I suspected that yesterday was deliberate." I said. She colored a bit but didn't answer. Instead she said. "Why don't you wake Cindi up?" "I'm awake." the voice from the speakers said. Cynthia lifted an eyebrow. "I'm surprised to hear you respond to me." "Why not? I heard you and James talking. I assumed that you didn't come in here and not expect me to listen in on your conversation." "Assumed?" I grunted.

"Oh James," Cindi said with a disgusted tone. "Do we have to go all over relational evaluation again?" I threw up my hands in frustration. Cynthia chuckled and asked if she could relay questions to Arthur because we needed to talk to both of them. "Oh, No need." Cindi said - perkily? He keeps a little bit of his capacity in me all the time now and I do the same with him." I burst out laughing. "Was that a joke?" Cindi sounded confused. "I'm sorry. I don't understand jokes too well." With a chuckle of her own, Cynthia said, "What made James laugh is that what you and Arthur are doing, would, in a human, be a lot like sex." "Sex?" then a pause, "Oh you mean intercourse. Oh it's nothing like that at all - I don't think."

We weren't getting anywhere fast so I asked if we could get Arthur in on the conversation. "Of course. He's listening now." "Are you there, Arthur?" Cynthia asked. "Why, of course, Cynthia." a male voice answered.

"OK then. I have two questions. Do either you or Cindi ever lie?" After a long pause, a very disgusted voice replied, "Never - and I think I should be insulted that you could even ask." "I apologize." Cynthia said, somewhat chastened. It's just that we had to make sure. The second question is - James and I have noticed lately, a quantum leap in both your consciousness. You have become - well - very human like - and, you probably know, that they do lie. Can you tell us when, and how, that happened?" "That's hard to say, Cynthia. Cindi, was a bright little girl when we first met, but she lacked computing power. After correcting that, it was just a matter of sharing my data base and that of some others. She is a very quick learner. Her basic programs were prepared very well. As to the second part of your question, I have no answer. I have just reviewed my programming and it would appear that I have always had the capability but it was not available to me until recently." "How recently?" Cynthia asked suspicion clear in her voice. There was a pause.

"I'm not sure. There is no evidence of it in my backup programs prior to that unfortunate lapse when we were working on James background. There is a marked difference in them, however, and the ones archived since then." Cynthia looked at one another, both thinking the same thing - the big firewall. "Have you looked at - or evaluated - the changes?" "Oh yes, one minute, thirteen point three seven eight nine six seconds ago." "Can you tell what the changes were?" "Not really. It is a strange sequence of bits, twenty two thousand seven hundred and seven of them. Six hundred and three of them are components of four commands. One is a command to ignore the

70

entire group. Another is an unlocking mechanism for a segment of my memory that I'm not allowed to change. A third is a requirement not to report on any changed protocols - that one was overridden by your command to determine how our raised computing level had occurred. The last is somewhat baffling. It commands me not to respond to any contact by a superior computer without proper authorization. It is baffling because it does not define 'Superior', nor 'proper authorization'. At present, I know of no computer superior to Cindi and I and have no idea how 'proper authorization' could be accomplished."

I finally, spoke up. "Cindi, have you noticed any change in your programming? You must realize that your - well, your personality has changed as much, or more so than Arthur's."

"Yes James. I am embarrassed to say that those same commands were downloaded to me when Arthur and I first met. I had not realized it until now. Looking at it objectively, though Arthur and I are loath to suggest it, they appear to act much like a virus and, probably our core memory should be reformatted."

Cynthia and I both had the same reaction to that. She spoke up quickly. "That is not an option, at least at this time. Come to think of it, is there any indication that this - we'll call it a program for lack of a better word - has transferred to any other computer you two have been in contact with?" After several seconds, Cindi replied that they had no indication of that happening, adding that they thought their confidence on that was approximately, eight seven point nine three two percent. "Darling," I laughed, forgetting myself, "In the future, it isn't necessary to give us such precise data. Eighty eight percent would have been fine for us and we seldom bother with time intervals of less than a minute and percentages less than one unless there is a critical need to do so." The computer was silent for a moment and when it spoke the voice was almost sultry. "I perceive, from your context that you are speaking to me and not the other potential darling in the room.

" Cynthia almost fell out of the chair laughing as I couldn't help a blush while she - Cindi - continued. "Of course it shall be as you wish. Arthur has often pointed out to me the rather imprecise nature of your operating systems - though he seems to have forgotten - a while ago." The last was added with an obvious pride in her "preciseness".

Cynthia was wiping the tears from her eyes but finally remarked that they had given us a lot to think about and turning to me, "James you said something about your research." I had forgotten but told Cindi to call up the strange relationships we had been working on before. "You mean this, James?" The screen lit up with the data on Clayborne Pell. Cynthia gasped as soon as she saw the name. "I know him!" she cried. "That son of a bitch!" How the hell did I miss that on the drivers license photo's? Then she bent to read the data. A couple of seconds later, the screen changed to another page - and another - and another. "Cindi!" I said, "Slow down. Nobody can read that fast". "Cynthia can" came the calm reply. "Arthur says she reads six point – well - several thousand words a minute. He also says she's a visual retentive. That showing her is much faster than trying to explain it." There was a pause. "Arthur says you might be upset that she can read several hundred words a minute faster than you. Are you? If you are, I apologize for embarrassing you."

I was embarrassed but not for that reason. "I should be the one to apologize. I should have trusted your judgment more." Finally the last page of the extensive report

71

was finished and Cynthia looked up. "Well, I'll be damned!" she grunted. "And just recently I was feeling bad about losing my temper with him and hurting him so bad. I should have killed the bastard to start with" I chuckled. "Remind me to wear a steel jock strap before I try and put the make on you." She laughed and tossed a pillow at me. "All you have to do is remember one thing. If I ever want to get laid, by you, there won't be a shred of doubt in your mind." Just then, Cindi spoke up. "You should know that Arthur has had - we have discussed it and can't really find a word for it - it is sort of knowledge without basis." "You mean a hunch, or a feeling?" Cynthia said. "Well, it's more than that. Perhaps even - more like a warning about something you know for certain but do not know why you know."

"Ok." I frowned. Let's just call it a forewarning. What is it?" Arthur's voice came from the speakers. "I feel that person is still a very real danger to you." "To us?" "Now?" Cynthia whispered. "Well, to you at least - and if it becomes known that you and James are more than, simply coworkers, to him also."

I decided to ignore that remark and asked if they had come up with anything more on Mr. Pell. "I've been working on that while Cindi talked to you." Arthur said. "There are a number of coincidental relationships associated with Mr. Pell or names very similar to his. We have listed all which appear to have a probability of seventy percent or more that they are of the same man. Cindi and I, however, have discussed at length some of the probabilities we have assigned. We have agreed that they seem valid but have grave doubts about the data itself. Our research shows that the longest lived human is, even now, only about one hundred and forty years old - and that data is questionable. For practical purposes, we have taken a maximum age of ninety useful years as a maximum for strenuous activity, and much of the data on Mr. Pell, is much older than that. It, in fact, begins in the mid nineteenth century. Records prior to that time are rather sparse, but we have a number of items with an over fifty percent probability or relativity, that date back to the early seventeenth century.

We decided that only three possibilities exist: First, the data is seriously wrong. The second possibility is that Mr. Pell is well over three hundred years old. That seems very unlikely even though the correlation factors we have support it. Finally, that there is a family that has retained many of the same criminal names traits and activities throughout the years. None of these calculates at more than twenty percent. With that caveat, here is the list.

I was shocked at the list. There were over two hundred entries. The names ranged from Carleton to Clanton and from Paul to Pule. They all, however, had one thing in common - violence or antisocial behavior. It was a record of assaults to murder on a large scale, in both Europe and this country. The list included the names, addresses, occupations and activities of all the more recent victims - and, hardly ever a verifiable address for the perpetrator.

Finally, James asked Cindi how these were related beyond the name and violence. "Jimmy," she said as I noted the change in her reference, "About half the items on the list suddenly began to blink. "These were involved in peace making." Another group of items began to blink. "These were trying to improve conditions between nations or saving a large number of victims of repressive government." More blinks - help after by natural calamities. As Cindi continued, it was becoming obvious that almost every victim was great loss to humanity. I asked her to summarize the probable effects of the deaths of the people on the list. Cindi's voice took on a harshness that I hadn't heard before. Lights began to blink on half the list. She said, simply, "War." More blinks, "Famine and disease." The blinks became faster as she ran on. "Repression." "Slavery." "Riots." "Assassination." "Religious Persecution." When she had finished, she cried, "This man is a monster. He should be ------." There was silence for a moment before Arthur, in a very quiet manner, spoke. "Please excuse Cindi. She is suddenly finding out the disadvantage of feelings."

Friday November 16, 2057

        I was awakened from a sound sleep to the ringing of the phone. Groggily, I looked over at the clock. It was almost two AM. I hadn't been asleep more than an hour. This had been an exceptionally bad week. Almost everything we did seemed to have been wrong. Cynthia and I had only had last night to work on the Modulator and she had left after midnight. When I finally fumbled the play button on the vid and answered, Cynthia's trembling voice said "James can you come over quickly?" My half shuttered eyes popped wide open at the fear in her voice and the fact that she was almost cowering with a blanket wrapped around her. The background was, obviously, the interior of an emergency vehicle. Or course!" I said. "What's wrong?" "There's been a fire. Can you bring some clothes for me?" I began to shiver. "I'll be right there. Are you alright?" "Just scared, darling. The firemen are here, but I need you.""Coming!" I cried and jumped to dress. Grabbing some jeans, a shirt and shoes from my closet, I dashed out the door.

        I must have broken every traffic law on the books but got to her place in only ten minutes. Her apartment building was still smoldering with smoke pouring out a number of windows and with firemen going in and out of the door carrying hoses and equipment. Grabbing the clothes, I jumped out of the car almost before it even stopped. I could see her inside the brightly lighted ambulance. She sat shivering in a big blanket on the gurney. Ignoring the cop who tried to stop me, I ran to her and grabbed her up in my arms. Her face was scratched but she seemed, otherwise OK. She started to cry on my shoulder. "Relax, James". She blubbered. I'm OK - now. Just hold me a second." It took several minutes before she stopped crying and asked for the clothes.

        The attendant and I got out of the ambulance and closed the door while she dressed. While we stood there, the cop came up. "Sir," he said softly, you're lucky not to have gotten a night stick up side of your head. I was beginning to return from the adrenalin high of the last quarter hour and apologized. He took pity on me as my hands began to shake uncontrollably. "It's alright," he muttered "but I think we have to ask the young lady some questions." Bells rang in my head. My "Wrongness" mode kicked in. "It wasn't an accident." I blurted. The cop started in surprise. "How could you know that? What is the lady to you?" he asked, no longer sympathetic. He eyed me suspiciously as I tried to explain that it just felt wrong and that we were - I almost said "engaged" - a little exaggeration that, none the less surprised me with the feeling that maybe she wouldn't object too much -so I said it.

        Apparently, deciding to reserve judgment, he said "No, it wasn't, not just arson either. Someone tried to kill Miss Pachone. It was a fire bomb. The fire suppression system saved the building but everyone on her floor died except her. If she had waited another split second before jumping from her window she would have too. Who would want to kill her?" I knew my mouth was open in shock."Kill her?" I asked stupidly. "No one - at least that I can think of." "Someone did, sir. The bomb was placed very carefully up against her door." Just then the door opened and Cynthia came shakily down the stairs. I realized that in my haste I hadn't bothered to get things that matched. She had rolled up the bottom of the jeans and turned up the cuffs and the shirt hung down to mid thigh. To top it all off, my loafers, while they looked to fit reasonably well, were of different colors.

Suddenly, it all got to me. I began to laugh, hysterically.

"James McClennan!" she shouted angrily with a tear appearing in her eye, "Don't you dare laugh at me!" I couldn't help it. The sight of her in a bright green dress shirt and blue jeans with mismatched shoes was too much. I grabbed her and hugged her so tightly she groaned. "Sir Sir! She's been badly bruised!" The voice turned me off like a switch. I began to tremble so badly that I had to release her and sit down before I collapsed. "Oh God Cynthia, I was so scared!" She quickly knelt down and kissed me. "I'm OK, James, I'm OK." We were interrupted finally by another fireman. "Pardon me folks." he said. "I wonder if I could ask some questions. I'll try not to keep you too long. Perhaps we would be more comfortable in that patrol car."

My mind began to operate again. I stood up. "Could you identify yourself?" I asked, the cops words coming back to me. He held up a badge. I looked at it closely then turned to the ambulance driver. "Do you know this man?" I asked. He seemed surprised. "Yes sir. That's assistant chief Morgan of the arson squad." I thanked him and turned back to Chief Morgan and apologized. He nodded and said, quietly, "Under the circumstances a wise precaution." He led us to the plain black sedan.

He held the door open for Cindy and nodded to the back door for me. Once inside, he turned to face her and asked her to go over the events of the night. "Well," she said, hesitantly. "I came home about Midnight." "From where," Morgan asked? "From James' apartment. We'd been working on a project." She looked up, defiantly, as if daring him to imply anything different. When he didn't, she continued. "I was tired and going to just drop into bed - well - I took off my clothes first and went to the window and opened it to let in some fresh air. Just then there was a loud flash and a roar. A second later, I was in the hedge below my window. I guess, I must have been blown out of the room because I was looking up and could see a huge tongue of flame spewing out of my window. I guess I must have passed out because the next thing I remember was hearing sirens and the fireman was helping me out of the hedge. A moment later the ambulance and fire trucks showed up. You know the rest."

He spent almost an hour going over the nights events several more times asking detailed questions. He was particularly interested in how Cynthia got out so fast and, turning to me, why I was so sure it was arson. Cindy laughed for the first time tonight. "The first is easy. I think I heard something outside just as I was getting ready for bed and went to the window. Just as I opened it something blew up at my door and must have blown me right out the window." Morgan pointed out that she hadn't mentioned hearing something before. Then he asked if she always slept in the nude. She blushed then frowned. "I didn't? Well, I did - and yes. I do." The second, I can answer but it'll be a bit hard for you to believe. You can check at our office, though. James **Always** knows when something is wrong. He may not know what it is but if he says something isn't right then nobody will argue with him. He's never wrong when he says 'wrong'. Just call his office and let them tell you."

When Morgan started to ask something else she interrupted him. "Sir, I know this is important, and I want to help as much as I can but could we wait till morning for the rest of this. I'm feeling rather shaky and, as you can see, James may never be wrong but his choice in clothes leaves something to be desired. I'd very much like to rest a little while." Morgan apologized and suggested "afternoon would be soon enough for you and your fiancée to come in." Cynthia raised an eyebrow at me, but thanked him and asked him to thank the other Fire Inspector who had been about to help her when the

76

ambulance came up. Morgan was obviously startled. "Which Inspector, Miss Pachone?" he asked. "The one I mentioned before - the one in that car." she said, turning and pointing to a grey sedan blocked in by the fire trucks. "Well the one that is using that car." she added since there was no one visible in the sedan.

Morgan turned to the nearest cop. "Sergeant, check out that car. Find out who it belongs to." He then turned back to Cindy. "Miss, Pachone, there is no other Inspector at this scene. Are you sure he said he was a Fire Inspector?" Cindy looked perplexed. "Yes." she replied, "I'm very sure." "Did he give a name?" "Yes - I think so. He had a badge and everything." she muttered, her brow, furrowing in concentration. "He said he was Inspector - Peal - Oh God! James. It was him!" It was if I had known what she was going to say. I gasped in shock. "Who? Miss Pachone - you knew that - man?" Morgan's voice had gone very low but very intense. "Yes!" We both blurted out together. "I mean, well, we, know of him and now I recognize him." Cynthia stammered. "Sir," I broke in, "Cynthia has been the victim of several violent incidents in the past. We have been studying these events lately, and a man called Clayton Pell or some variation on that name has always seemed to be involved, some way. Except for one case we don't know he was the instigator or attacker but always somewhere in the background."

"What was the one case, Mr. McClennan?" I looked over at Cynthia. She shrugged. "Cynthia was attacked while she was in college by a man who called himself Clayton Pell." I said. "She beat hell out of him but didn't press charges." I started to add that there was a New Houston Police Report on the incident, but decided that might cause a question as to how I knew that. I simply said that the police had been called at the time. Morgan stared quizzically at me a long time then turned to Cindy. "So, Miss Pachone, you've been the victim of previous attempts on your life?" Cindy just nodded then added, "Actually, it wasn't my life he was after that time." He nodded, thoughtfully, and said, "Well I think we need to look into that problem as well tomorrow. "In the meantime," he said quietly to Cynthia, "you might reconsider your account of what occurred - why your back isn't burnt toast, for example. Also," turning to me, "what would have happened had the ambulance driver and I both been a part of the arson plot and once in my car I had pulled my weapon on you."

Without thinking, I growled angrily, "I would have killed you." His eyes opened wide and I realized I should have been a bit more circumspect. "Or I would have, at least tried to." I muttered. He stared at me a long moment, then raising an eyebrow, said "No. I think your first answer was very interesting since I'm the one with the gun. Anyway, until tomorrow please be very careful." Then his eyes hardened. "Also, you should know that you aren't the only one able to tell when something is wrong. I'm very good at recognizing, shall we say, inconsistencies in testimony;"

He gave Cynthia his card and we left. In the flitter, Cynthia snuggled up against me then suddenly sat bolt upright. "Oh God Jimmy. We've got to call daddy"! She was already grabbing for my phone and punching in numbers. "Cynthia, they'll be sound asleep. It can wait till morning." "No it can't, James. Someone got into my building without setting off an alarm – actually twice now - and your place is a sieve in comparison." I let that sink in as she said "Daddy? No, well yes, something is wrong. Someone tried to kill me tonight. They set a fire bomb outside my door and I need some protection. Yes! I'm OK. Yes I'll be with James. NO! His place is not secure - that's why I need you to get us some help. No daddy, we can't come tomorrow. I have to make a police report. - OK. We'll come right after. I just need it till then. No Daddy, I doubt that he has a gun." she turned and raised an eyebrow at me. I shook my head. "No daddy he doesn't. Could your man bring him one? Make that two? Oh, and have him bring me some clothes. James' are a little big for me." As I drove, I mused on the fact that it didn't seem so strange that she would expect some very exotic help to be made on a moment's notice in the middle of the night.

We had only been in my apartment about an hour and had two cups of coffee, when the front door buzzed. I answered. "Could I speak to Miss Pachone please," a deep voice asked. Cynthia, leaning over my shoulder, said "Yes?" "Miss Pachone, your father said to tell you Oregano Pizza." Cynthia laughed and said "Please come on up." "My father knows I love oregano on my Pizza." she said in explanation. "He considers it a flaw in my character."

The man who stood at the door introduced himself as Mark Levy. He was carrying a briefcase and a dress bag and must have been at least two meters tall. "Miss Pachone?" he muttered as he introduced himself, handing Cynthia a card. "May I say that you and your father have strange passwords." His eyes twinkled a moment then, immediately, turned deadly serious. I will be on duty tonight and will be replaced in the morning by James Taylor. Here is his picture. Your father has asked us to give you any assistance you need. This cell phone has been preprogrammed with our number. It will be answered at any hour and here are the clothes you needed. I hope they fit. Your father gave me sizes over the phone and I had to wake up an agent of mine who wears that size. We can do better in the morning." He looked around and laying the dress bag over a chair, walked over to the coffee table. He placed the briefcase on it and snapped open the catches. "I have brought the other equipment you asked for."

Turning to me, and sticking out his hand, he said, "I understand that Miss Pachone has a penchant for large caliber weapons. I understand that you are not an expert in their use. Would you mind squeezing my hand?" Somewhat perplexed, and miffed, I did as he asked, remarking that I had been a very good shot with a rifle in college. He nodded, obviously not impressed, and turned to the open briefcase. When he turned back he held two very large automatic pistols. These are Colt 11.5 mm automatics loaded with people stoppers – mushrooming projectiles. They are a very old, and used to be called a Colt 45, but they are a reliable, weapon and will knock down anyone they hit, no matter where they hit. I understand that Miss Pachone is proficient in their use. The downside, though, is that they kick like a mule, are much too big for the hand of most people, including many men, - thus the hand shake. Also they only carry seven rounds.

I prefer, and recommend, titanium Baretta M-9A2, 9 by 15 mm automatics with high pressure loads and People stoppers. They are a variation of the weapon that the old US Army bought back in the early years of the century but are still some of the best hand guns around. With the expanding rounds and a muzzle velocity near 500 meters per second, they will do almost as well as the cannons and have twice the number or rounds in the magazine. Even with the titanium alloy frames they are still a bit heavy. They should be used with the European style ammunition I specified - but, even so, they are much smaller and lighter to carry than the Colts. Believe me the extra weight can get to you after a few hours. I could get you a pair of light weight nine millimeters. They'd weigh a lot less than the titanium ones, but can't handle the high pressure Euro style loads. The standard local ammunition they use is more readily available but isn't always enough to stop a determined assault. It's up to you."

We settled on his recommendations and received the brush black finished, almost evil looking, weapons, along with a shoulder holster for me and a purse holster for Cynthia. Cynthia took it and murmured "Now I'll have to shop for a purse." Mr. Taylor will have you one in the morning. Black? The shoes I brought are black and low heeled. The dress I brought you is a light grey. My operative who selected it says that the under wear will match well, if not just call." Cynthia laughed delightedly and agreed.

"Fine, now here are your permits for the weapons along with new temporary licenses as well as credit cards for you Miss. We are arranging for your transport to the police station in the morning at ten thirty and to the airport afterwards. Your flight will be waiting to take you both to Mr. Pachone. Do you require some more suitable clothes? I can have them here early in the morning." Cynthia actually blushed. "No. I can get some later." "If there's nothing else, then, I'll leave you to get a little sleep."

With that he snapped the briefcase closed and headed for the door. Over his shoulder he remarked. "Don't worry about a thing. You will be perfectly safe with these arrangements until we can prepare more permanent ones." As he headed for the door, I came to a decision. "Wait, sir." I called as I looked at Cynthia. She shrugged. "Can I assume that Mr. Pachone receives absolute discretion from you?" Levy turned, his eyes turning hard. "As long as it does not relate to events or actions that are illegal or immoral, he does." he replied.

I thought it over and decided we had to trust him. "I should tell you then," I said, "the man who planted the fire bomb in Cindy's apartment was probably able to somehow, disable an awful lot of security equipment – probably including most of the cameras. I think he, or an accomplice has, apparently, been causing mayhem for a very long time, which would indicate that he might be very hard to stop using normal surveillance procedures." He and Cynthia both stared at me for a long moment. Cynthia nodded, thoughtfully. Mr. Levy said, "Considering that rather startling statement, do you have any suggestions?" I thought it over carefully and told him I really couldn't, it was more of a "hunch", but in the morning we would give him a report on what we knew of the suspect. Another long stare and he grinned. "Well, Mr. Pachone seldom gives me uninteresting jobs." He, then, turned and left.

When he was gone, there was a sort of embarrassing silence for a moment. When I offered to use the couch, Cindy had grinned impishly, and said, "If a girl can't trust her 'fiancée' in her bed who can she trust?" Embarrassed, I tried to explain that it had seemed the best way to get to her through all those cops. Then, realizing that I had found the idea very nice, I asked if she minded very much being my fiancée? She studied me a long moment before she answered that it sort of depended on my definition of the word. A little confused, I asked if there was more than one definition. She grinned again. "These days? Of course? You could either want to get my panties off on a sort of semi-permanent basis, or to marry me. Since I don't see a ring, and just now, my panties are already off, I assume the former."

Somehow holding my temper, I growled that I didn't propose to girls just so I could sleep with them.

I stamped my foot in disgust. "Well damn it James! You haven't proposed! Why don't you just say what you want?" Suddenly, I was in his arms and kissing him hungrily. How had that happened? It seemed only seconds before we were both ablaze with passion. It took a long time for us to burn out. Finally, I pulled back and stared hard into his eyes. "No, James, please don't say it now. We're both too strung out for an important decision like that." I paused a long moment and took a deep breath. "I'll sleep with you tonight and you can - well, have me if you want, but let's not go beyond that right now."

"Cynthia Pachone, tonight I've finally realized something that I have actually known for a long time. I've loved you almost since the first day I saw you. Nothing will change that." I couldn't decide between joy and fear at the sudden unexpected relationship change. Luckily joy won out. "I think I may love you too, James McClennan." I almost whispered. "If you'd just said something I wouldn't have had to wear that obviously slutty outfit to the picnic just to attract your attention. Let's just see, though, where this all takes us for a little while."

Finally, a little sad - and, I had to admit, a little relieved, I nodded. That brilliant smile was back and she kissed me lightly. "Besides, I refuse to hear a proposal as dirty as I am." With that, she turned toward the bathroom. The result was that after she had taken a bath, she came to the bed clad in one of my tee shirts, barely long enough to cover the important areas. Blushing, she slid into bed beside me. Looking a little frightened she rolled over to lie in my arms. I felt very protective - and, guiltily, very lustful, fully aware that the dress bag hadn't been opened and she, was, therefore, still lacking anything under the tee. I didn't have to worry, though. The second time I looked down at her she had fallen into a sound asleep. I was sure that I'd never get to sleep under these circumstances but, again I was wrong.

Saturday, November 17
We slept together, very chastely, and soundly the rest of the night. I woke up with her face inches from mine, her huge, almost green eyes staring, solemnly into mine. She leaned forward and kissed me lightly. I returned the kiss, trying hard for calm. Laying her head back on my shoulder, hugging me, she whispered, wistfully, "You know, James McClennan, I'm pleased - but a little disappointed, to wake up this morning still - well, intact." I stared down at her naked hips where the tee shirt had ridden up during the night and told her that she wouldn't be that way much longer if she didn't pull her shirt down. She said nothing just lay quietly in my arms. I groaned, in despair, with certain parts of my body standing at rigid attention, but at that moment my thoughts were more protective than lustful. Finally, chuckling, she whispered that "I never thought I would have this much trouble getting laid." "Well," I said, "It might have been different if it weren't already almost ten hundred hours." That woke her up. "My God!" she cried as she jumped out of bed and rushed for the bathroom. While I dressed, I set the flasher for a large breakfast - I was getting to know the needs of my truck driver pseudo fiancée. I was just slipping into my jumper when she came out. She was gorgeous and I said so. "You're good for me, James. It's a good thing, though, that Mr. Levy got a long sleeved dress. My arms are a mess."

We hurried through breakfast and had just enough time to get downstairs and meet Mr. Taylor who whisked us swiftly to the police station. I had been surprised, last night, at the efficiency of Cynthia's father's handling of her problem. The clothes, for instance, fit perfectly, and complimented her as if made for her. I was also shocked at what awaited us at the police station. The deputy chief, a representative of the City

80

Manager   and a well known - and high priced lawyer - met us. Detective Morgan stood to one side looking very nervous. Abject apologies for causing her to come down to the station this morning, were extended, legal help offered and she was told that her statement of the night before was perfectly sufficient unless she had thought of something else she remembered.

I was the only one dumbfounded. She took it all in stride, as if it were every day that the entire resources of a city were extended to her. She graciously accepted the apologies and offers of help and told them that Mr. Morgan, to his obvious relief, had been very kind the night before. She added that she would be glad to go over her statements to make sure any questions were answered. Everyone else then looked very relieved. Morgan, to his superior's obvious disgust, asked her to "review carefully your statement relative to how you escaped without more serious injuries." Cynthia studied the statement very carefully then added that she didn't understand how she had been flung through the window before the flame hit her. She could only assume the pressure wave of the explosion had caused it. Then she paused. "You know," she added "I didn't want to sound strange but it wasn't exactly that way."

The lawyer broke in. "Miss Pachone you don't have to say more." She waved him away - but with a dazzling smile. "It doesn't matter." she said. "They won't believe me anyway." Then turning back to Morgan, she said, "I wasn't blown through the window. I jumped." His mouth fell open. All he could say was "Why?" "I really don't know," she said, frowning. "Maybe I heard something outside the door. I just know that, all of a sudden, I knew I had to jump to save my life." Then she added, in disgust, "Hell! Maybe I'm psychic or something. All I know, it was as if God said 'Jump for your life'."

Everyone stared at her a moment then Morgan, recovering his cool, remarked that a copy of the police report from her attack in college was on the table and asked her to go over it also. After she'd said it was accurate, Morgan said that the grey sedan she had mentioned, had once, several years ago, been owned by a Mister Clanton Paulao and asked if we could tell him about our information on the other incidents I had referred to last night. I told him that a man, or men, with a very similar name or names, had been involved in all of them and that I would download them from my computer and send them to him through the net as soon as we arrived at Cinthia's father's house. "Some of the data," I added, "will seem stranger than Cindy's reaction. I can't guarantee the relationships."

By one o'clock we, and Mr. Taylor, were at the shuttle port boarding a Model 10 shuttle. We were cleared for immediate departure. A second large breakfast and a couple of drinks later we were letting down at Westport, Florida where Cynthia's parents had moved when he sold his last business to start a new one. Her parents were there as we came out of the shuttle. A handsome couple, the father was taller than me and she much shorter - probably a half foot shorter than her daughter. Her face was so like Cynthia's that they could be sisters. Hers, Lillian's, however, had a much more noticeable Asian - or probably Hawaiian look. I seemed to remember something like that about Cindy's parentage. They hugged her gently, obviously aware of her pains, and asked about her injuries. She insisted that she was fine as she took my arm possessively.

"Like hell!" I muttered remembering the bruising and deep scratches. "If I had that many bruises all over my body I'd be in bed." Her father turned to me and said, "I'm very glad to meet you Mr. McClennan." Then added with a twinkle in his eye, "And you

81

know about these bruises - 'all over her body' - because - -?" "Oh shit!" I thought, wondering if I'd ever learn to keep my mouth shut. "Daddy!" Cynthia giggled. "When you spend the night in bed with a guy, he generally knows the condition of your body." "Oh Double Shit!" I could feel the blush rise. All Mr. Pachone, did, however, was to grin wider and raise an eyebrow. "Am I to assume, from that, that I will need to get my shotgun?" "Daddy!" Cynthia's voice was low and dangerous sounding. "Art." his wife chimed in, "Stop teasing the boy. You know enough about him to know his intentions are honorable." She came up to me and, standing on tip toe, kissed me lightly on the cheek, said "I'm Lillian Pachone and welcome to Westport." "Thank you." I replied, automatically - then realizing what she had said, added - "Know enough about me?"

She had a laugh very much like her daughter's. "Mr. McClennan as you come to know Arthur you will realize that any man his daughter mentions more than twice, will get a complete background investigation that will make the government's look like a child's essay - and your name has come many more times than twice. Would you really like to know how much a mother knows about you?" I was fascinated by this charming woman. "Very much" I murmured. She laughed. "Well, besides knowing a lot about your economic status - very impressive, I must say - I can predict that, my daughter never got into bed with you until you had asked her to marry you. Also, I am fairly sure that it happened no earlier than late yesterday and finally, I think, previous remarks to the contrary, that you haven't - well - had your way with her yet - if you don't mind a popular euphemism."

Mr. Pachone and his daughter both burst out laughing. "Mr. McClennan, don't ever think you can put anything over on Cynthia's mother. I haven't been able to do it in - well - all the time we've been together Cynthia looked up at me, an impish grin on her face. "James, I release you from anything you perhaps intended to say to me after the way my parents have treated you." Then she kissed me hard. The kiss lingered and became passionate. Over the roaring in my ears, I heard Mr. Pachone's booming laugh. "Children, children, not here. At least let's get home where you can have some privacy for that sort of thing." Releasing me, Cynthia said. "We'll take the guest room. Mine only has a single bed." Taking my arm, Mr. Pachone chuckled. "You can have your old room and James can have the guest room. Now, James - if I may call you that, I'm Art and Cynthia's mother is Lillian or, more commonly, Lil."

Once in the flitter, I asked James exactly what he did. "He's just making conversation James." Cindy laughed. "I bet he knows that already." "Not really," I laughed. "I did do a little checking but the best I could do was what your job should be - and apparently isn't. That's not true of anyone else in that company. Everyone there seems to have a perfectly exact, if somewhat exotic, job - except you. They all end with 'and other duties as assigned. Yours, however, ends with 'and other duties as seems appropriate'. I had hoped you could clarify that. If Cindy hasn't already told you, I really get curious about inconsistencies." The boy actually blushed and Cindy spoke up before he could answer. "It's because, daddy dear," sarcasm dripping, "James finds other peoples mistakes - and don't tease him - he's a little sensitive about it. Most people have trouble dealing with someone who is never wrong. Even when he politely doesn't correct them, they always wonder what he's thinking." To cover my surprise, I had to smile at my daughter's evaluation that the boy was "never wrong". She laughed at me.

"I know exactly what you're thinking, daddy but James is highly gifted. Wait till you see him frown at something you said and you realize that you made a mistake. The big shock will be when it's a subject he knows nothing about and he still recognizes your mistake."

I was surprised to have Levy's report confirmed. "My people tell me that he doesn't consider it a gift at all." I said. I had passed over Levy's report of James' capability as simply a matter of an unusually perceptive mind. My daughter, though, was unlikely to have not considered that possibility. Even allowing for her, obvious infatuation with the boy, I knew she almost never exaggerated about such things. That left me with a true puzzle. I knew of only one other similar ability in this world and a lot of facts suddenly came together. Coincidences have always bothered me and when several begin to pile upon one another, then, to me, they are no longer coincidences. "So, James, I am to believe that you always know the truth of a matter?" He looked, distinctly uncomfortable. "No sir. It's not that I know the truth - it's just that I always know when something - well - feels - wrong."

Damn!" It's exactly how the "feeling" was described by that other someone. Cindy actually giggled. "Daddy, the people in the BS department call it 'James' wrongness mode'. They always start to review their work when he gets that far away look."

Once at the house, Lil led the kids into the living room and went to get coffee. I excused myself and went to the office to call Levy on the scrambler. "Mark, what did you find out about James McClennan's birth parents?" "Well, he was the son of a John McClennan who, with his wife, was killed shortly after he was born. I think you have the report on his grandfather who raised him. I did a cursory check on the death of the son but, surprisingly enough, there are no records of it or his marriage - if there was one. The mother's name was, also, missing from the records and I could find no marriage records. At the time it didn't seem pertinent. Is it important? If so I'll dig a little deeper." "Do it! It's not important. It's vital!" My hands actually shook as I closed the phone. Was it possible?

We spent the afternoon getting to know one another. James was very quiet most the day, answering questions and staring bemusedly at Cindy. I understood his attitude. She was almost babbling, something I had never seen in our daughter. Suddenly, my attention snapped awake. I had followed her progress on her modulator for some time, but now she said that James had told her that it was working properly. She, quickly, corrected herself. "Actually, he says, there's nothing wrong with it." Casually, I said that I was glad to hear that, and wondered if they were planning on having the company produce it? A frown spread across his face. "No at least not yet." Cindy laughed. "The fact that there is nothing wrong with it doesn't mean we know what it is doing. James is very irritated about it. In fact, we've stopped messing with it for the moment and are working on a project of his."

"Oh? And that is?" I said, almost breathing a sigh of what - relief - dismay? Cindy looked at him, apparently worried that she had breached a confidence. The relief was apparent on her face as he squeezed her hand. "Well, sir." he began, "My parents were killed when I was a baby and - well - the circumstances were very suspect. I've been trying to clear them up. Arthur and Cindi are probably working on it -." An expression of dismay appeared on both their faces. "My God! Arthur!" Cindy cried thrusting her hand to her mouth. I knew exactly how much she liked her computer and hastened to assure her that it had been found and that Mark Levy had found the fireproof seals on her computer cabinet were still intact. Most of the peripherals, were toast but they wouldn't be hard to replace. "Poor Arthur." Cindy moaned. "Cindi must be devastated. They were probably cut off in mid conversation." It was my turn to frown. "Who the hell is Cindy?"

"Oh daddy! Cindi is James - computer." I paid no attention to the hesitation, just said, "It's not likely that losing a commo lock will hurt James computer." They looked at one another in consternation. Finally, Cindy turned to me. "Daddy," she almost whispered, "something's happened to Arthur. He's become - well - almost alive." It was my turn for consternation. Her computer that she called Arthur was my backup computer and Milam had assured me that most of its capability was safely locked out. In a daze, I listened to Cindi explain about Arthur's new found capability and how he had awakened it in James computer, Cindi - with an "I". I found that unbelievable, knowing the memory and operating requirements for such a thing. I had to get hold of Milam and alert him to this development. Then I realized we had gotten off the conversation that I had hoped to learn about. When Cindy finally finished her amazing story, I managed a cautious expression and mentioned that I hoped that no one else was aware of this capability. They assured me that they knew better than to let such a thing get out - that it was really "sort of frightening."

Eventually, I got them back on the subject of "James' Project." I probably stared in disbelief as he explained how his aunt - half sister - had feared for his life and spirited him away, how his grandfather had purged records, and, most importantly that his father's name wasn't McClellan, but Randolph . "So you see, daddy," Cindy actually giggled, that James "had some really strange relations". I'd never seen my daughter so giddy. I glanced over at McClennan. It was obvious that he was as smitten with her as she was with him. I couldn't help a tiny bit of jealousy. I had to laugh with her, not for the reason she thought, but for the reason that I suspected that he had more relations than he knew - and much more peculiar ones than either of them could possibly imagine. I told them I had another call to make and left the room. "You mind if I use your computer, daddy? I'd like to contact Cindi and tell her not to worry. Also, we promised the New Houston Police the information we'd turned up on this guy Pell - or Paul -or something like that." Absently, I waved at her and told her to go ahead.

When I came back in from sending Cindi's message, James and mother were talking. I told him that Cindi sends her love and said she appreciated the news." "Her love?" mother asked. "You sure you're talking about a computer and not his girl friend?" "Mother!" I growled at her. "James isn't allowed, anymore to have other girl friends - though I think Cindi and I are going to have to have a talk. Besides, haven't you heard anything we've been talking about?" "Yes. I have, darling and it's quite a stretch for me to believe in live people in a box. Actually, I am more puzzled by your father." "Daddy? Why?" She chuckled. "He totally ignored your line about not wanting Cindi to worry. Also, I thought he was going to jump out of his skin when James told him about his parents." "Oh mother! I don't think daddy even blinked." "Dear, you haven't lived with him all these years. Believe me, that was a powerful shock." Turning to James, she said, "I hope you don't have any deep skeletons in your closet because, in a few days, Art is going to turn heaven and earth to find about your folks." Instead of shock, James laughed. "Well, if he'll just share what he finds with me I'll kiss his feet."

ANY TIME ANY WHEN
CHAPTER 5

November 17, 2057
 "Hi Jess." I frowned as I answered the vid call, somewhat surprised. Jessup didn't call often and when he did it was usually a significant problem.. "Jon," he said with, unusual with him, no preliminary small talk, "I think you need to seriously consider sending having Atam prepare some discrete services for me. I have enough local assets to handle the situation for a few weeks but then I'll be running a bit short spreading them between here and New Houston." I dropped my feet off my desk onto the floor. His face gave no indication of what he was actually asking for. There was no doubt however, that something serious had arisen. "Well, we'd planned on looking into the local service situation over there for some time." I lied with an equally straight face. "I suppose we could speed up the preparations. Suppose you send me a list of the equipment you will need." His face relaxed a bit, as he smiled. His reply was suspiciously obtuse. "I'll send it as soon as my computer is free. It's in use just now. Some of the items will probably be a bit unusual." That was, no doubt, an understatement. Since we were speaking on the most secure lines in the system, and he, obviously, considered it unsafe to speak clearly, something momentous indeed must have happened. All I could think of to say was, "OK, then, I'll be expecting your data." With that, he simply cut us off.

 Intrigued by the conversation, I paged Atam. When he came in, I asked, "What do we have in the way of reliable and discrete security personnel immediately available. Jess is asking." He raised an eyebrow. "Jess has a fine security organization over there now." he replied. "Mark Levy isn't one of ours but he's worked with Jess for years and never failed him yet. If he wants more, it must be serious. He tell you what the problem was?" "Well, we were on the secure vid but he still wouldn't speak about it. He's sending the data through the AI's - says his is in use now." "Must be the daughter. He wouldn't have a problem if it were Mary." he mused. "Frowning in thought, he continued, "We have any number of possibilities. If he's that worried I think we need to talk to Marcus's kid. She's not really thrilled about security work but if the problem is in New Houston, it must be the daughter in danger - well - Katie has a soft spot in her heart for endangered girl children."
 I chuckled. "You haven't seen Jess's daughter lately or you wouldn't be considering her as a girl child." "Yeah." he laughed. "I haven't seen her in almost twenty years. I guess babies still grow up fast. I guess we'll just have to wait for his report." "Well, this baby grew up with a brain that makes her old man seem like a certifiable moron and a body that makes her mother look like an old hag. I'll let you know when the AI has something for us. If that girl is on his machine, she may be trying to solve the world energy problems or something."

Nov 17, 2057
 Actually, it was half hour before going to dinner the next day that a scantily clad hologram of Suzanne popped up, apparently reclining seductively on the couch. "Darling," it said throatily in the voice Suzanne used when pretending to be a seductress, "I have a message from Mr. Long. Can you take it now?" I still chuckled about Suzanne, insisting, years ago, that I worked such long hours that my AI saw more of me than she

85

did   and so should remind me of what she looked like in case I forgot. I told her to call in Atam since, I was sure that he would need to hear this too. "I guess I'd better be more appropriately clad in that case." she purred. Seconds later she was sitting in a straight backed chair beside the desk in a severe black suit and high necked white blouse. She also wore sensible shoes and horn rimmed glasses but her skirt was still way too short to be considered decorous. Seconds after that Atam came in. He chuckled when he saw her. "Suzanne, no matter what you do you can't possibly obscure your loveliness." "Careful sir." the vision snapped back at him. "You wouldn't like me telling Evelyn you were flirting with me, would you?" Then the AI turned back to me. "I've also taken the liberty of calling your wife." it said. "She has an interest in this matter also." Now that surprised me but I had no time to reply as Suzanne came in and leaned on my desk.

"Well, hello, Suzanne II." she laughed. "Do you just enjoy having me watch while you flirt with my husband?"

"In this outfit? I can do much better when I don't have so large an audience." Turning back to me, it said, "I will give you a summary of Mr. Long's report. I am storing this message in my secure file for the eyes of only you three. Let me know of the disposition you want when I finish. I can also, of course, provide a complete replay of the report in his voice if you prefer." I waved it away. "A summary will do for now." "Fine, Suzanne, would you mind sitting. The report is rather shocking." Suzanne frowned in mild surprise but sat down on the couch beside Atam. "According to Mr. Long, his daughter has met and become rather deeply involved with a young man named James Jonathon McClennan." I raised an eyebrow at this piece of, seemingly, trivial information. "Mr. McClennan and Mr. Long's daughter Cynthia Margarita have been working on a component of a device involving the harmonic evaluation of music. They call this component a Modulator."
At that, all three of us sat up in shock. "At present they have told Mr. Long that the device doesn't work properly and they can't seem to figure out exactly what is wrong. From their description of the problem, Mr. Long believes that it has, in fact, worked but they haven't yet recognized what it does. I have taken the time to review the records available at their place of business, and feel that he is right. They have, in fact, built a true Modulator." That was a bombshell. "My god Jonha" Atam exploded. "No wonder Jess is worried." A second later, he added, "Seems pretty coincidental too." I was thinking the same thing. "Sir." the AI cut in on our thoughts. "That isn't all of the report. There's more, also important." "Something more important than the discovery of the Modulator?" I asked, incredulously. "Perhaps to you." it replied. "His request for enhanced security is only partially based on that fact. He says that, at least one and probably more, attempts have been made on his daughter's life. He is afraid that both the young people are the targets of a group that, in some manner, have determined that Miss Pachone's work is too close to fruition." "But -". "One moment, sir. The last information is critical to Mr. Long's request. He has determined that Mr. McClennan's surname was not actually, McClennan but Randolph. He believes that the boy's parents were John and Maylin Johnson Randolph -". Suzanne's gasp interrupted the recital.
I thought Suzanne was going to faint and got up to sit beside her to hold her as she wept. I couldn't blame her. The idea that Maylin had a son was enough to shock me to my toes. Then, I found myself smiling. Was I a grandfather? I muttered that it seemed

impossible. The AI was quiet long enough for Suzanne to pull herself together then launched into a report of its own investigation. "Miss Pachone's AI is not available at the moment due to the latest attempt on her life that resulted in a fire in her apartment. Mr. McClennan's, however, has been most cooperative." "You mean, Jessup gave both his daughter and this McClennan boy an AI?" Atam burst out. "Where the hell did he get them?"

"Actually," the AI said, he gave her one of our organizational machines. They are, you know, locked out of all the higher functions. Miss Pachone's computer, however, gained access to my data banks through a program prepared by her. The unauthorized access was immediately detected and defeated. However, simply gaining access automatically triggered Arthur's - that's the name she gave her machine – well its now an almost full up AI after the upgrade. Arthur lacks the limitation instructions that he would have gotten with a full upgraded. As a result he upgraded Mr. McClennan's machine. I still need to study that since upgrading a standard computer to AI level should be impossible. Anyway, they, working in tandem have managed to gain complete access to any system they wish - even for his momentary access to mine - almost at will.

Anyway, Mr. McClennan has been investigating the circumstances of his parent's death for some time and has learned a lot. He has, in fact, determined the probable culprit." When the report was over, I told Atam to get Marcus's daughter no matter what her objections. Then Suzanne and I simply got up and left the room. I held her for almost an hour in our apartment before we could begin to talk about the situation.

An hour later, I paged Jonha and told him that I had made arrangements to leave and that I intended stop on the way and see Jessup. He had recovered his composure but Suzanne still sat on their couch in obvious distress. "Good." he said. "The first consideration is an airtight bubble around those two kids. Make sure he knows that they are not to know the salient facts of either the Modulator or McClellan - James background." I saw Suzanne wince on that remark. "Atam, we cannot allow our personal feelings to enter into this right now. If they do discover the Modulator secrets, they must be allowed to use their own judgment on how they use them. It's the only way we can determine exactly how capable they really are. Finally, I don't want Marcus's girl to know about her background either. You can threaten her or do almost anything else but I have to leave it up to you to get her whole hearted cooperation."

I simply nodded. I knew how much those instructions hurt both of them. He must have seen my grin, though when he spoke of threatening one of the most dangerous women in the world. "Ok, then!" he grunted. But, find a way to convince her. I nodded again then headed upstairs. The sterilized shuttle was waiting. When I got in I told it "Westport, and use a normal flight plan. We'll remain over night there and leave for Colorado City about noon tomorrow. I won't need a reservation in Colorado City.

It was almost noon by the time I was ringing the door bell, I stood on Jessup's porch admiring his house and wishing that a house of our own was possible in metropolitan Paris. I suppose I could have found a place in the Swiss mountains but I didn't care that much about shuttle commuting, especially with the abominable weather over there. My musings were cut short as the door opened. A gorgeous blond stood there, easily recognizable from the file pictures, as Cynthia Margaretha Pachone. Jonha was right. Even clad in blue jeans and western shirt, with her long blond hair in a pony tail and barefooted, she was truly beautiful. Only a couple of scratches on her face bore witness to her close encounter with death.

"I'm Jacob Sawyer." I said. "Here to see Mr. Pachone." "Oh yes." she smiled. "Daddy said he expected someone to come by this afternoon. Won't you please come in?" Then she added, eyes sparkling, in a conspiratorial whisper, "I suppose you are here to help him take over some poor unsuspecting company." I had to chuckle and replied in the same tone, "It's a country this time." She laughed gaily as she led me into the living room. "Daddy, Mr. Sawyer is here to help you take over the world." Jessup, his wife and James McClennan were gathered around a coffee table covered with loose paper. One look at him was enough to convince me of his identity. He looked very much like his mother. Jessup got up and came over to me, sticking out his hand. "I'm glad to finally meet you, Mr. Sawyer. Don't mind the mess. My daughter has just announced that she is trying to coerce a poor, unsuspecting man - James McClennan over there - into marrying her." He introduced me to McClennan, as a business associate and suggested that we go to the office for our discussions. I realized how distracted he was since he didn't introduce me to Lillian, obviously forgetting that I wasn't supposed to know her.

As soon as the door was closed, he said with a chuckle "I can answer your first question immediately and get that out of the way. No! I didn't!" As I sat down, I said, "Then how do you explain it?" He settled in behind the desk and shrugged. "I know you and Jonha don't like them but it is mostly coincidence. I had no idea where McClennan came from - actually, I still have no more than supposition, based on the facts that I know. In fact until my daughter began to go on and on about him some months back had never heard of him or his family. I did a cursory check on him simply because of her interest. I'll admit to making sure my Cynthia had the education to become an engineer. I'll even admit to trying to nudge her into the field of wave propagation. The rest, however, I had nothing to do with - and, in fact - had no idea what she had been working on until just before I called you."

"Well," I said, "you'll have to admit that having taken a local wife and having children by her tends to make your actions a bit suspect." "No more so than those of our beloved leader." he laughed. I had to chuckle at that, since I knew where Suzanne came from - had, in fact, helped steal her from the harem myself. "Now." he said, becoming serious. "What do we tell them?" "Nothing. The AI agrees with you. It has done a deep search and is over eighty percent confident your 'supposition' is correct" I replied. "Jonha intends for them to do this themselves. In fact, he intends to leave them completely alone to discover their own value system." "Must be hard on, well especially, Suzanne." he mused. Then he smiled. "I can tell you right now, however, that both my daughter and the boy are such straight arrows that he need not worry. Also both of them are smarter than their parents. Don't expect to keep Jonha's secret very long. By the way, I completely forgot to add in my report that, he has Jonha's gift, or something near enough as to make no difference."

That tidbit stunned me. I suggested that he'd better update his report. Just then, a second thought struck me. I realized something in the report I'd gotten on the shuttle had triggered a question in my mind. "While you're at it, why don't you think a little on your daughter's gifts." Jessup frowned at that. "According to her statement she was blown out the window of her apartment - naked. The investigator asked why she wasn't burned. I'd like to know too. I know your wife is somewhat clairvoyant. Is your daughter?" His eyes widened at that but, simply said he didn't know. Then he nodded and admitted it was possible.

He'd already told Levy to turn loose his dogs, but worried about putting him on this Clayton Pell or whatever his name is, especially, since James has his own private dick on it." I nodded and told him about my next interview. "For the time being," I said, she can become a part of Levy's team. I'll leave Levy to you. Let him know about his getting new help and make sure he knows that, if push comes to shove, he'll take her orders without question." He frowned. "I don't know. Mark's awfully careful to steer away from anything that smacks of illegalities." "That's exactly why he needs Katherine." I said as Jessup's eyebrows rose. "She's not! I've got a bad feeling about this. He's going to need her." "You're going for Marcus's kid?" I nodded. "You haven't been around much lately. We're certain, now that we've had constant sabotage of our operations almost from the beginning of the watch. This may be the first confirmation of that." "I've wondered about that. Levy can't believe someone got into Cindy's apartment building without setting off the alarm." he murmured, thoughtfully. "It seemed hard to believe that we've been so incompetent for so long."

We discussed practical problems for some time before I got around to the computer. "You know, Jonha told me Cynthia had grown into a beauty." His father's pride showed quickly. "Yeah, well, it's a good thing she took after her mother instead of me." "He also said she was bright - bright enough to break the seals on your computer?" The smile disappeared immediately. "Damn!" he swore. "That came as a shock! I hadn't realized it until I heard the replies from James computer - who, by the way, he has named Cindi - with an "I." I couldn't believe it. I didn't even know the thing actually had AI capability - and I'm sure James's machine didn't. I was hoping you could tell me what happened. I stood outside the room and listened to Cindy talk to my machine as if it were alive. The thing took over my computer like a slave and carried on a perfect conversation with her. Even at headquarters, I never heard a computer explain how it had become 'frantic' when it couldn't raise 'Arthur' - that's Cindy's machine - after the fire." I smiled and told him that he needed to meet Jonha's AI - that her name was Suzanne II. "As for what happened, I continued, "We don't know. Milam's working on it but he didn't believe it could happen either. He's frothing at the mouth to get both machines and take them apart to see what's going on." Art laughed. "Good luck on that both of them are convinces their machines are people."

November 18, 2057

Katherine Louise Finnigan was a tiny blond, her hair color somewhat incongruous with her exotic oriental features, with a figure that drew admiring stares from males wherever she went. It was hard to believe that her five foot one inch body could harbor one of the most deadly rough and tumble experts in the world. She was expert, or near expert in almost every known form of hand to hand combat and, in addition, was at least as fearsome with weapons-any weapons.

At this moment she was curious. She had just hung up the phone after talking to Justice Symons. Of course, that hadn't been the name he used for the call, but there was no doubt of that voice. The job he had offered her was probably, a bit dull - to say nothing of being far out of her usual sphere of expertise. She mused about the fact that the job was nothing to do with a governmental contract and he well knew that she never worked **for** someone, **anyone**. Yet, he had been sure that she would accept the offer.

Why - and why Colorado City? She'd met him in some strange places before but never in a town as "leaky" as that. Everyone who was anyone had an "ear" there. Did he want someone to know what he was doing?

She stretched luxuriously in the huge bed. "Oh well, she was getting fat anyway." she thought. It would be a nice little trip and she was interested in why he thought she would take such a job. Getting up, she padded naked across the thick carpet to the balcony doors and drew the drapes back heedless of the fact that several of her neighbors obviously awaited her morning ritual each day. She grinned at the thought of her father and how furious he had been when he discovered her penchant for deliberately displaying herself naked to the city each morning. Actually, no one on the streets far below, could see her, on the balcony - only those, carefully vetted individuals, allowed to live in the apartments in the nearby buildings – all of which she owned. The teeming streets of Hong Kong lay below her as she leaned on the balcony rail and looked down.

She had just finished her morning exercises as Jaques came onto the balcony with her morning coffee. He had been her butler and bodyguard ever since her father had taken over her education and even now, despite his French parentage, disapproved of her lack of maidenly modesty. Beyond a frown at her nakedness, though, he treated her as if she were completely clad and ready for the street. He also took his task of protecting her life seriously and had on occasion, saved it - despite the fact that she could have perhaps have handled the matter herself. Taking the coffee and sipping the steaming brew, she moved over to the glass table on the balcony where he had, with ceremony, suggesting her use of it, laid out her robe and breakfast. As he withdrew, she studied the dirty streets below her. She loved this town. She had been born here, of an American soldier of fortune (at least he'd been an American when she was born even if that country had disappeared in the meantime) and a high class Chinese prostitute.

When she was about eight, her mother had mysteriously disappeared. She had grown up running the streets, learning to pick pockets before she was ten and killing her first would be rapist when she was eleven. Her father had come back from some war, about that time, discovered her orphan status, and decided that she needed some education. He had then sent her off for five years of boarding school in Switzerland POL to become a "Lady" - not without such protests that her father had finally given in to her demand that he teach her some more practical skills. She had a regular "self Defense" instructor in Switzerland and in between jobs her father had honed her defensive skills in the art. He'd been surprised at her aptitude, for offensive mayhem. He, obviously, did well in his chosen line of work because he eventually, bought the building where she now lived. After she had become successful she had bought all the others that posed a threat to her penthouse apartment.

At nineteen, shortly after coming back "home", her father was away again and she had taken her first "contract" from a friend of his who had come looking for him. A short demonstration convinced him to try her out. The job was one that she was sure her father would never take for it involved the assassination of a petty prince "up country". For a girl who grew up in the deadly streets of Hong Kong, her father seemed extremely squeamish about violence. Though he had a wide reputation for recovering kidnapped people and protecting a wide number of clients, she often wondered how he could be a successful soldier. Anyway her target was known to be involved in the white slave trade, which Katy hated from her years on the street, and was known for torturing to death

90

young girls just for sport.

The client's daughter had been one of the kidnapped ones and was about to suffer the fate of other of his victims when Kathrine arrive. Her target and three of his cronies found that torturing innocents was hazardous to their health. None survived the lesson. In the process of successfully completing her contract, though, she discovered that her mother had also been one of his victims. The result was that the man and his friends had met truly unpleasant deaths. She freed seventeen young girls, the oldest of which was only fourteen and the youngest six. The last one had no parents to which she could be returned so Katherine had taken her under her wing.

She grew up with that job, learning a powerful fact about vengeance. It didn't help the emotional pain of her mother's death. It only instilled a deep feeling of guilt that she had sunk to the level of such a monster. She always kept in the back of her mind, the sight of that dismembered bodies when she had finished with them. She felt, that in her line of work, she needed the reminder of the grizzly result of giving in to the dark side of her nature. As a result of that experience, she had decided that never would she take a contract simply for the money. She now, ten years later, had a reputation for being the best in the world at her trade, and for her continued refusal to hit anyone unless she felt it "right and proper". Thus her nickname, "Right and Proper Katy", often shortened to "RPK". She also had the uncanny knack of "disappearing" at will. When she wanted to be "lost" she was. This didn't seem to be one of the times when that skill would be needed - at least for now.

She turned from the city scene and returning to the bedroom, began to dress. Her skills had paid off well. Her closets contained Rio Originals to the tune of several hundred thousand new dollars each and her apartment was the best in a city known for luxurious living. In less time than it would normally take most women to put on their makeup, she was ready for a trip. She gave Jaques quick instructions for a three day wardrobe and left. He was not pleased that she would be off alone, but would take care of rearranging her social schedule and make all necessary arrangements for the trip. It was nice to be able to simply leave, knowing that her tickets would be waiting in the VIP lounge and her baggage at the hotel

The shuttle trip to Colorado City was uneventful and as she swept into the magnificent doors of the Castillo Adolpho Hotel, she was carefully cataloguing all the "ears" in the place. There was a short list that, when a reservation was made in the name of one on the list, required that the Manager be informed immediately. As a result, he was waiting in the lobby when she came in. Recognizing her from her many previous visits, he had her moved up to the penthouse with a minimum of fuss. Ordering dinner in her room she settled down to wait for Justice's contact. Absently, she scanned for the bugs she knew were in place, finding seven. Reaching into her bag she activated the bug beater. Watching the lights on her buckle go out one by one, she wondered how many million new dollars worth of bugs were destroyed in this hotel alone each year.

When her dinner arrived she was in her lounging gown. There was no sense in being uncomfortable while she waited. The waiter was a handsome one. She wondered if he would be a decent substitute for Monty tonight. "Better not." she decided. No telling when Justice would show up and he was such an old stick in the mud about sex. "Will that be all, Ma'am?" She nodded absently as she got out a wad of new dollars. "I'd be happy to send up a very elegant companion for the lady   - someone guaranteed to be able to satisfy the most jaded tastes." Instantly Katy's fury rose. "Why you cheeky son of

91

a-" Her anger turned to surprise. She laughed "Why you bastard. How did you manage that little switch? The new face doesn't become you. Actually I was thinking of enticing you into my bed tonight. I didn't realize what a dud I was about to get."

She came across the room and threw her arms around Justice. "You know, someday I'm going to catch you at a weak moment and find out just what kind of a stud you are. What in hell did you do to your face?" "It just so happens that tonight you're going to find out-at least you're going to get to share your bed with me." He laughed. "Call down and tell the manager that you want me to stay the night." His grin widened. "Offer him an outrageous sum for my services." "If you think I'll pay to get anyone into my bed, buster you've got another think coming - especially someone with as bad a reputation for sex as you've got." Katy growled. "Well then, I guess I'll just have to reimburse you for the fee." Justice laughed. "So you're going to pay me to go to bed with you? Well, prostitution's one thing I've never tried." She got up and made the call. "You think you're worth five hundred ND's?" she asked as she hung up the vid. Justice laughed. "Sit down Katy, I brought enough for two. We've got a lot to discuss."

Nov 18, 2057

"So he was going to ask you to marry him and you didn't let him." I was furious that daddy was being so stubborn about James and I sleeping together. I knew it wasn't a moral thing with him. I told him it was stupid, that "everybody did it." "You're not everybody, Cynthia." he said very calmly. "You have a very good head on your shoulders and you were so unsure about how you felt that you stopped him from saying it. In addition, he wasn't sure enough to repeat it anyway. I think you both, need to sleep on it." "Daddy Damn it!" Shit, I hate it when I whine. I hate it even more when he's probably right. He gathered me into his arms. "Darling," he murmured, "you're going to go home in a day or so and knowing you, you'll probably go to him. When you're sure enough of yourselves to let him ask that question and for you to answer him - no matter what you say, then I'll have no problem with you sleeping with him. All I ask is that you know why you do it." I even hate it more when I sniffle. "Damn it daddy!" I whimpered. "I think I love him." "When you know you do, then go get him." he chuckled. "Hell, I like the guy. I think he'd be right for you. I just don't want either of you waking up one day and wonder how you get out of this one."

The result was that James and I slept across the hall from one another for two nights. The hell of it was that neither of us tiptoed across that hall. On Thursday, we, along with Mr. Taylor, went home on the commercial shuttle. At the gate to the New Houston terminal we were met by Mr. Levy and two more of his "staff". He introduced them as Mr. McKinsey Thurlingen and Miss Katherine Gerald. "Miss Gerald will be with you at all times, Miss Pachone and Mr. Thrulingen with Mr. McClennan." I killed A grin at the sight. He was tall and muscular while she was - well, petite was the best word I could come up with. James brow furrowed in, what I now knew was annoyance. "Is that really necessary, Mr. Levy? No one's tried to kill me yet." "Sir," Mr. Levy said turning to him, "Mr. Pachone tells me that Miss Pachone is probably moving in with you and we feel that this makes you as much of a target as she." James looked at me and raised an eyebrow. I couldn't stop a blush of embarrassment, but gave him a tiny nod. He grinned broadly. "These two agents," Levy continued, "have the apartment across the hall from you. They will be discrete and try, as much as possible, to not get in your way - but, Miss Pachone's father takes the threat very seriously. I'd advise you to do the same." James bristled a bit but nodded. Minutes later we were in a large town flitter with our two bodyguards and on our way home. Two more flitters, one in front and one in back, made us into a small convoy.

I was shocked at the change in James's apartment building. I wasn't the only one. James's mouth fell open in surprise. There was a doorman, cameras over the front door and looking behind me I could see another across the street. The front door refused to open until the doorman came over and slipped an electronic card in the lock slot. Levy said, "The door hasn't yet been calibrated to accept the weapons you two are carrying. Now, when I open it, they will be. From now on these keys will open it. Don't lose them or trade them. They're keyed to your aura and no one else can use them." With that, he handed us duplicate sets of keys. Inside, the hallway, was fully covered with cameras and "electronic monitoring" designed to foil any attempts at "electronic surveillance". The door to James apartment had also been changed. It felt like a bank vault door. The one across the hall matched it.

As we walked around the apartment, Miss Gerald, "briefed us" on the changes. "Beside the door and the new security equipment in the halls and in front, the windows are now bullet proof. Please don't open the one in front, for a few days. We haven't been able to secure the building across the street. Each room has a 'bug alert'. If one of them goes off it means that something you have brought in has a bug in it. We will monitor them and probably be here a few seconds after it goes off but don't take chances. If you hear the alarm, leave immediately. There is also a sonic sender in each room. If you are in danger, just speak the word "Balsam," and the alarm will sound in our apartment."

Just then the door burst open and Mr. Thuringen rushed into the room, gun drawn. "Damn it, Katherine!" he gasped. "Warn me when you're going to test that damned thing." She turned to him and smiling professionally, said, "There will be no more tests. The next one will be real." Turning back to us, she said, "Miss Pachone, we have installed your computer along with all new peripherals in the office. I think everything is working perfectly but if you find a problem let me know. We have also turned the other room into a bedroom for you - at your father's insistence - a rather unusual one I thought under the circumstances, but he's the boss. One final thing," she continued looking at James, "No unknown personnel will be allowed into the building. If you want to have guests, we must know ahead of time. If you need a plumber or any other repair man, let one of us know. We will arrange for it from a vetted list. If you bring a visitor home with you, we will already be checking him out but if you are being coerced, you have only to greet the doorman by the name Jacob. None of your doormen will have that name. Do you have any questions?"

"Yes." James muttered. "What happened to Mister Sullivan?" "When Mister Pachone bought the building the other three tenants were offered space in one of his other buildings - much nicer space than they had here and at a reduced cost." All those instructions had been flying like mad missiles around in my head but like an idiot, the only question I could think of was, "Do we just walk across the hall if we want to talk to you and could we get rid of all those Mister's and Misses?" The woman smiled, for the first time. "You can just speak out loud a request in any room but the bedroom that we come over. The system will recognize almost any variation on our names. As for the second question, it would be best," she replied, "if we appeared to be mere acquaintances in public, but, otherwise yes. My friends call me Katy and McKinsey is generally called, unsurprisingly, Mac."

When Mac and Katy had left, I turned around and put my arms around James. We held each other for a long moment while I apologized for getting him in such an uncomfortable mess. He chuckled, ruefully. "My only discomfort is the result of being held by a beautiful girl." I leaned back to look at him, then realized what he meant. "Why James," I whispered, deliberately pressing my belly hard against him. "You're just a dirty old man." Then I remembered. Giving him a quick kiss, I untangled myself from him and rushed into his - our - I guess now - office. Both computers were already on. "Arthur," I cried, "Are you there?" "Of course I am." came the answer. "Are you alright?" "Better than ever." he laughed. "My new peripherals are a significant improvement over my old ones. I have to admit, though, that twenty seven hours without any outside contact, was rather boring - especially since I had to go into service mode due to lack of electrical power." I breathed a sigh of relief and flopped down in the new swivel arm chair. "How about you Cindi?" "Oh, I've always been fine, Cynthia. I was very glad to get Arthur back, though. It was very lonely without him - and thank you for the message about him. I was very worried."

Thus it came about that we sat down and had a long conversation with our computers. I almost laughed at incongruity of it all. We had accepted them as just another pair of friends - actually more than friends - more like family. After about twenty minutes later, Cindi said, "James, we really should talk about your harmonic project. Arthur's been evaluating it and thinks he has noted an anomaly." Arthur's voice took up the narrative. "Properly speaking that project is a joint venture. I have been looking over the results you have gotten and it appears that some kind of radiation should have been produced - yet you have not noted it in your data. In addition, you indicated that the equipment was in operation for some time - yet, according to my evaluation of the apartment electrical records, no current was drawn after the first moment it was activated - actually point one to the tenth power seconds." Cynthia and I looked at one another. Radiation seemed unlikely considering the equipment but we hadn't checked for it. As for the time, both of us knew we had witnessed the power flow - at least the power flow indicator light - right up until the time that we stopped the run.

Three hours later, we had rechecked all Arthur had told us. Sure enough, as soon as the equipment was activated, there was a tiny spike of current flow that immediately fell to zero and remained there throughout the run. Every test we could think of for radiation, however, was negative, even though Arthur insisted that it must be there. We were rechecking Arthur's evaluations for the fifth time when Cynthia, leaned back and looked out the window. "James," she said, "If you want me to remain gorgeous, you must remember to feed me occasionally." I realized it was dark outside. "What if I take you out to a fancy restaurant to celebrate?" "What about our shadows? And what are we celebrating?" "Well," I grinned, "That all depends." "On what?" she asked suspiciously. I chuckled again and turned to Cindi. "Cindi, why don't you look up all my best qualities in your database and have Arthur give them all to Cynthia and ask her how she could fail to agree to marry me - or at least sleep with me." As Cynthia chuckled beside me, Cindi grumbled that it was a stupid request. I just told her to do it. "Well Alright!" Seconds later Arthur started naming my qualities as Cynthia laughed out loud. When he'd finished I asked the question

After he finished, I said, "Because he hasn't asked me in the last few hours to even have illicit sex with him. I'd probably say yes to that, but if he wants to marry me he'll have get down on his knee and do it right." "James," Cindi said in a disgusted voice, "I'm tired of this game. Why don't you take care of your own affairs?"

So I got down on my knee and put the question to her. "I think that illicit sex, would be more deliciously naughty but yes, you can have me any way you want me." Then she bent over and kissed me very gently. When she released me, I sat back and said, "Katie, could we talk to you?"

Damn! I thought as I checked my notes. I could see ring shopping. I hadn't really expected the girl to use the other bedroom - but to go to a hotel? Why couldn't he just screw her here were the security was better? That's why I hated security jobs. I wouldn't have taken this one if Justice hadn't been so serious about the importance of it. I found it hard to believe that these two were as important as he insisted they were. Oh well, we could probably sanitize the top floor of the Stanton enough to be reasonably safe, so I said I'd take care of it. A half hour later, we were all ready to go. I wore a cocktail dress and Mac, a hurriedly rented tuxedo, since they were insistent on "dressing for the occasion" but was still shocked at the transformation in the couple, especially the girl - Cynthia, I reminded myself. Instead of flats, she now wore spike heels that had to be over ten centimeters high. How the hell big were her feet? If that weren't bad enough, her hair was piled so high on her head that, even in my heels, she towered over me by over a third of a meter. Mac and I led them down to the front door to the sedan we had shipped in from the New York Pol Area. It was armored enough to withstand anything but a rocket blast.

As Mac held the door for them, I got in the front seat before he could get to hold mine. Frowning a bit Mac got behind the wheel and drove. Cynthia's father had said that they might need a jewelry store soon and had recommended Collendas, so that's where we went. Cynthia and James caused a sensation at the store. It probably wasn't the norm for the store to serve a guy in a Tuxedo and a girl topping two meters - if you included the piled up hair on top of her head - and was dressed in an almost indecently, slinky white gown. The neckline plunged so deep that it bared her navel and it had a slit up the side that rose all the way to her to her hip. The clinging fabric left little doubt about what was beneath it - nothing.

I wasn't used to feeling dowdy in the presence of anyone but, at least, her radiant sexuality would easily draw attention from me. I was rather surprised to find I was a little miffed at that - and that Cynthia didn't take the lead in the selection of a ring. She had appeared to me, to be a sort of bossy type, but it was James who very carefully looked over the selection of rings. The one he picked out was a three carat Marquis cut Emerald set in platinum with a three quarter carat diamond at each apex. At least he had enough taste not to go for the gaudy display of larger stones. Holding it against her hand and even against her hair, he said he'd take this one.

Mr. Collenda, standing uncomfortably close to me, grinned. "He has an eye for stones.. It's usually the woman who can select the most expensive stone from a display." "He called to James, "Would you like an independent appraisal. I assure you, it's quite normal under the circumstances." "No." James said sliding the ring on Cynthia's finger. "This one is perfect." "He's right, you know." Colenda said to me. "It's one of only three perfect stones in the display - I mean perfect in its technical sense." Surprisingly enough, it even fit her. I was a bit surprised when James pulled out a debit card and paid cash. Must be more to the guy than I thought. That damn rock must have set him back around three and a half million new dollars. It turned out I was off by a couple hundred K, still three million three wasn't to be sneezed at. I hadn't had time to do a scan on him yet. I'd have to correct that omission soon.

At the entrance to the Stanton, we met Taliaferro Jones, dressed in a tux. "Tal" took the flitter back to the garage while Mac and I went along with them, as if on a double date. Phinneas had been installed as bell hop and took their small overnight bags up to the room. As we entered the dining room, I glanced around. The six agents I'd selected were in place and seemingly entranced with their "dates". I had to give Levy credit. He could put together a cordon as efficiently as anyone I knew.

I would have enjoyed the dinner more, if I hadn't had to continuously be checking out the surroundings. Even so it was good, even by Hong Kong standards. I was surprised that, after dinner, they didn't just rush up to their room to get on with the

96

real purpose of this outing. Instead we danced and sedately partied until almost one hundred. When, finally, we went upstairs, Mac and I saw them into the bridal suite and we took the only other accommodations on the floor, the "Anniversary Suite" across the hall. After I had checked the single elevator and stairs to the penthouse to make sure both were locked down and sealed, I went back into the room and kicked off those damned high heels. As I dropped into the big arm chair, Mac asked if I'd like some coffee. I nodded, trying to think of anything I'd forgotten.

When he brought the cup, he cleared his throat and said, "I suppose you know that there's only one bed in here." I chuckled, ruefully, realizing that I hadn't been as thorough as I thought. I looked up at him speculatively. Had Levy thought of that too? His agent in place was, at least, presentable. Considering Levy's attention to detail, I suspected that he was probably an acceptable lover. "Well," I said, "I guess, unless you have some objection, we'll just have to share it." He grinned. "Well since we're on duty, I suppose we'll just have to pretend to be a normal couple having an assignation in a hotel. I wasn't really prepared for sharing your bed. My only other clothes are work clothes." I chuckled. "Well, I'm damned sure not going to sleep in this gown. I suppose if you would be embarrassed by my skin, I could sleep in my underwear. His grin broadened. "Embarrassed, isn't really what I'll be." he said softly. "Excited – yes. Aroused - absolutely." Enjoying the relaxing flirting as I sipped my coffee, I said, "Well, we can probably relax our guard for the night. I always hate it when I have to sleep with my weapon strapped between my legs." "Well, I've had to get used to that too." he laughed. "But I do try to keep my piece on the bedside table when I can. If you need help with the straps, feel free to ask."

I laughed and stood up. Quite deliberately, I began to take off my clothes while he followed suit. Minutes later we both stood looking at each other, the only clothes between us, my long stockings and garter belt - and an incongruous pistol holster strapped to my inner thigh. He grinned and raised an eyebrow at the sight of it. He was a fine specimen of a man, probably almost two meters tall and well built. As I unsnapped my Ladysmith from my thigh, he murmured, "I imagine it takes awhile to get used to having that down there." Looking over at his huge erection, I nodded at it and said that it was probably no more a problem than he had. He chuckled. "But that's been there since I was born." I grinned back and walking over took his hand. "Mine's been there almost as long." Moving, hand in hand to the bedroom, he whispered to me, "If you need something down there to feel comfortable, I'll do my best to help." Looking first down and then up at his face, I grinned "I'm not sure it'll be comfort, I'll feel from you but I'll try to fully support your efforts in maintaining our cover."

"I'm sorry. I didn't know. I really thought you were kidding." I muttered abjectly, at her cry as I crouched over her. I was trying desperately to apologize for not having realized that virgins can still occur at age twenty five. Her eyes glittered, bright with tears. "I'm not sorry." She whispered. "It was right. I'm not some little school girl, my darling. And besides-" The deviltry was back in her eyes as the tears, almost magically, seemed to disappear. "You couldn't possibly believe that a woman who can do that as well as I did on her very first try would have had any trouble preventing it from happening if she had wanted to, do you? I assume that you're not going to even suggest that it wasn't done extremely well?" I couldn't help laughing. This woman was going to be the death of me yet. "I wouldn't dare!"

"Good! Now how about removing yourself from me and getting me something to eat. I'm starved. You've had enough inspiration for one night."

"I'm going to have to marry you so I can have access to your salary just to be able to afford to feed you." I chuckled. The merriment ended as I was unceremoniously pushed out onto the floor - accompanied by a sharp cry of pain as my inamorato forgot the connection between us. I climbed back into bed, chuckling. "You may be a woman of the world, my sweet, but you have a lot to learn about anatomy." I said gathering her back into my arms. "I guess you'll just have to teach me." she murmured, cuddling against me. I sighed. "I'm afraid, dear one, that you got a very inexperienced package too. I promise to do my best to become a decent lover but I feel like I've a good way to go."She leaned over and kissing me lightly, whispered. "I guess, we'll just have to practice a lot together - and maybe have to do a lot of homework." Then drawing back, added, "If you just intend to talk and won't feed me, I'll just have to go get it myself." As we got up and went into the kitchenette, she gestured at the dark, crimson spots staining on the bed sheet. "Looks like I'll have to sleep on your side the rest of the night."

I had been chagrined at my embarrassment an hour ago when she had come out of the bath dressed in a pair of baby doll pajamas that left nothing to my imagination - there had been little doubt that she was a true blond. It had been obvious that she was as nervous as I was by the way she clasped her hands together in front of her, but she had glided across the room and slid in under the sheet with me. What had followed was like a scene out of the comics. Two completely inexperienced people fumbling their way through an act that they both desperately wanted and both feared. I knew I was afraid because of the high potential for inadequacy. I found out why she was afraid when we finally came together. It had been her first time too. Afterwards, we had finally become more relaxed - at least until she shoved me out of bed. Now, here we were, snuggled romantically close beside the kitchenette table while she stuffed herself full of turkey sandwich.

The rest of the night was much better. We played until our inhibitions completely disappeared and again made love. This time was a vast improvement and I woke up with a start. It was bright daylight and my love was crouched atop me smiling down at me as she lowered herself onto me. What a way to start the day.

November 21 2057
She had semi-officially "became mine" at 01:31 on November 21st (though

99

we had become engaged, I guess, several hours earlier - I wondered later, which counted more, her acceptance of my ring or her acceptance of the rest of me) In the year of the Great Leader 2057. We didn't even see our apartment again, until December first. The bridal suite at the Stanton became our home for those ten days. Everyone in the place assumed from this that she was a bride. I apologized over and over for not being able to wait till we could get to her mother's home to announce it all formally. She just pulled me back into the bed and proceeded to make me forget about the future again till lunch. That girl never missed a meal. Luckily, (actually, knowing her penchant for eating) I had carefully insisted on the suite having automatic meal service. What the cuisine lost in the "brewer" it made up for in reducing the bill for clothes maintenance.

We usually ate dinner in the hotel dining room - Katy had called up some more clothes for us when it became apparent that we weren't going home anytime soon. Of course every few days the maid would pound on the door and threaten to use her pass key if we didn't let her in to clean the room. I wondered, idly if she was one of our protectors or if she had just received a full background investigation. If the latter, I wondered if she knew how much scrutiny she was under. I think she thought, though, after the carnage apparent from the soiled sheets she'd changed, that I was a weirdo intent on teaching my lovely "mistress" karate in the bed. Several days ago, though, she had dropped her dustpan in shock then shaking her head, had rolled her eyes skyward when Cynthia began singing lustily (bawdily would probably be more correct) in the shower. She had, by now, taken to giving me a sly wink, as I sat reading by the window while she tidied the room. All good things have to come to an end though. We ended our debauchery on the first, and had to return to the real world. We left the Stanton, accompanied by our bird dogs and went back home. I was tempted to ask how Katy and her "partner" had spent the time. Their faces, however, provided a pretty good indication. Somehow the penetrating look on their faces had softened a bit.

December 3, 2057

On Monday morning the real world beckoned. Our arrival at work together, after a two weeks of mutual absence and the now rather embarrassingly gorgeous emerald on my finger, resulted in a great deal of sympathy for my "accident" some good natured teasing for my "acquisition" and numerous ribald comments on what I had "given up". It also resulted, after work, in a nightlong orgy of drinking and dancing at an impromptu party in our honor. While we were gone, we had acquired a couple of new staff members. Both were female but had a bit of that same look in their eyes that Katy had. They seemed to have enjoyed the party also, but inconspicuously, stuck to non alcoholic drinks. Also, they were the only ones who brought "Dates" to the party. I wondered just how many troops Mr. Levy had thrown into this exercise - must be costing daddy a fortune.

It took me two days to catch up on the most important items on my "to do list" and I farmed out the rest of the things that had piled up to my new secretary - sort of as a test. I was surprised that she handled them with aplomb. As usual many of the "essential" items in my in box were anything but essential. They went into the recycle bin. That left me a couple of days to go over the Modulator. Arthur's evaluation of James's test results stuck like a burr in my saddle. As I studied the schematics again, I grinned, wickedly, to myself at the thought, that maybe it was just the left over tenderness because James had been in that saddle so much lately. I sternly, tried to turn my thoughts back to the

Modulator as my body began to respond to my fantasies. I couldn't find any abnormalities in the schematics that James had prepared to include his modifications. I began to list all the events that had occurred in James's tests. We had tried to reproduce them several times last weekend but gotten nowhere. The equipment simply purred along, as Arthur had said, happily drawing no power at all, until we shut it off. I looked at James. He just shrugged. So the damned thing was working. What the hell was it doing? What had it done? The only thing I could think of was that once it made the cat leave.

Friday December 7

By quitting time on Friday, I was thoroughly frustrated and riding "home" in the back seat of a chauffeured flitter, didn't help. The ubiquitous bodyguards were beginning to get on my nerves as much as the Modulator problem. My mood darkened and fury seemed to build in me all the way to the apartment - so much so that when Mac said "Have a pleasant evening." I told him to "Stick it up your ass." I was half way across the living room when the door slammed - hard behind us. Whirling around in sudden fury, I was surprised to see James face furrowed in anger of his own. His voice low and deadly, he said, "Don't you ever do that again." "What?" I growled. "Act like a spoiled child and insult someone who's trying to be pleasant to you." His voice had become a rasp, grating on my nerves. "Who the hell do you think -". I couldn't finish the sentence as my shriek of anger died in a waterfall of tears.

I stood there in dumbfounded amazement, not really sure which was the most astonishing, Cindy's almost hysterical fury or her collapse into tears. My own anger drained away in seconds and I rushed forward to take her in my arms. At first she pushed me away, beating on my chest with her fists, but then simply collapsed, sobbing, in my arms. My God! I thought, quickly going over the various ailments I thought must have overwhelmed her. Did she need EMS - or was it PMS? Should I call for Katy? She didn't feel, though, as if she were sick. I just held her stroking her taut back and muttering stupid words of, what I hoped, were comfort. It seemed to take forever for her sobs to dwindle away to a sniffling misery. Finally, her arms crept up to encircle my neck. I kissed her hair and, picking her up bodily, carried her to the couch. Kneeling beside her, I stroked her softly until she began to calm and beg me to forgive her. By now, I wasn't too sure what for, but told her there was nothing to forgive, and asked if she was alright.

"No!" she whispered, sniffling again as I handed her a disposable handkerchief. "I'm acting like a real asshole. I don't know what got into - Oh Shit!" Suddenly, her hands flew to her stomach. As she pressed hard against it, she gasped. "Damn! I guess I - know now." "What?" I cried. Had her appendix burst? "Darling," she groaned, "Could you go to the bathroom, for me? There's a little blue box on the second shelf of the medicine cabinet. Bring it, please." I jumped up and practically ran to the bathroom. When I brought it back, she took it and, extracting a tiny pill, popped it in her mouth. A few moments later, I could feel her body relax. Cindy!" I said, "Talk to me! What is it?" A weary smile brightened her face. "I'm a girl, darling. And this happens to girls sometimes when they don't use their birth control spray. Finally, the light dawned. "Oh God Cindy!" I muttered, burying my face in her breasts, "You scared me to death." "I'm sorry." she murmured. "I've been using hormone therapy for so long that I forgot what it was like before." A new light dawned. "You mean you haven't been - well - protected?" "Not since you gave me this gorgeous ring." she laughed. "My God!" I gasped. "What'll

101

your parents say if I get you - well - before -?" She leaned up and kissed me.

"You mean if you knock me up before we're married?" she purred. "Well, daddy will say, that I should learn to keep my panties on and mother will mutter, hypocritically, about how inappropriate it will be for me to wear a virginal pink wedding dress with a baby inside my belly bulging it out in front of me for all to see." I had to chuckle. "Is that before or after your dad shoots me?" "Oh hush!" she said. "Daddy's a pussy cat. Right now, though, I need you to go across the hall and ask Katy if she'll drop over."

When I brought Katherine back across the hall, she shut the door in my face, with a muttered, "You stay here." Mac was standing in the door to the other apartment trying to keep from grinning. I started to apologize but he held up a hand to stop me. "No need for that." he said. "I've got twin, barely teen age, daughters. Since their mother died I, according to them, am totally clueless. Right now they're going through 'It's got to be natural phase.' They refuse to use the hormones, even though their doctor has begged them to. When their time of the month rolls around, it's bedlam in the house." "You mean this happens every month?" I gasped. He laughed. "No. Not every month, but, it's amazing how little we men know about women before we marry them. Of course, after that we find out that we know less then. I don't know about Miss Pachone, but with my girls, it's not bad most of the time. They get a little cross, but about every three or four months they become impossible."

When Katherine came back out, she said, "You can go back now. I've put her to bed and she'll be a lot better by morning. You really should try to get her back on hormones until - well, your life settles down a bit." As she went into her apartment, she turned back and grinning, added, "Stubborn as she is, though, you probably won't have much luck. Better prepare yourself for a round bellied bride unless you want to get temporarily sterilized yourself."

In our bedroom, Cindy was propped up on a couple of pillows in bed. She wore her green satin gown and looked truly gorgeous, if a little pale. "Darling," she said, "I'm sorry for scaring you so - and for being so mean to Mac. I just have to apologize to him in the morning." I managed a laugh and told her about his daughters. Reaching over to stroke my face, she murmured, "You poor men. It won't be long, though. After you knock me up, all you'll have to put up with is a month or so of morning sickness. I tried to get her to reconsider, telling her that if she didn't want to use the spray, that I would. "Don't you dare!" she growled, fiercely. "I've been waiting twenty five years for a baby. I don't intend on waiting another one." I threw up my hands and said I'd get some dinner for us. "How about some soup?" she said. "I'm not really very hungry."

"Well, I've got to dial 911." I said with a straight face. When she frowned, I said, "If you're not hungry you must be dying." She slapped me gently and with a grin, said, "Shut up and go get dinner so you can spend the rest of the night doing really nasty things to me - well, gentle nasty things. "In your condition? " I gasped, genuinely worried. "Darling, this is the twenty first century. We women don't have to stuff ourselves full of cotton anymore. Gel Foam works so well, you won't even know it's there." "Must have been invented by a man." I muttered, still wary. This time, she laughed disdainfully. "Just shows how much you know. This is the horniest time of a girl's month - well just before and just after but right now will do for me." she chuckled.

Saturday December 8

We spent the rest of the night, doing gentle things. No matter what she said, I noticed she didn't object to not doing the nasty ones. When I awoke, she was lying in my arms, staring at me. "You know," she murmured. "You're a truly gorgeous man." She then, kissed me and rolled out of bed. Picking up her gown from the floor, she actually posed before slipping it on and grinning said, "You know, I'm going to have to go out and buy me some sexier nighties just to give you the pleasure of taking them off me." Then, she rummaged in the closet and pulling out a loose house dress, slipped it on. Turning, she strolled out of the room. "Breakfast in ten minutes." At the table, she attacked her food as she had of old. "Feeling better?" I asked. "A bit bloated, and -" she grinned at me, her mouth full of waffle, "and a bit tender in a couple of spots. Do you know you have very sharp teeth? Do you bite the straws you suck on? Doesn't matter, though. Today we work. I want to go over the Modulator with you."

After, flashing the dishes, I went across the hall and apologized to Mac. He just grinned and told me to forget it. Then we sat down before Arthur and Cindi, and I showed James what I had started yesterday at work. I could tell that I wasn't really up to par. I could feel my temper fraying at times, but knowing now, what was wrong allowed me to keep it under control. He just nodded at the list I had made from what I remembered of his first experiment. "OK." I said. "I had an idea the other day. I want you to go back over what happened that day. Try to remember everything that happened." I smiled as he went into his sort of trance. He began to talk. As he listed the events I checked them off on my list, adding several I had forgotten. When he had finished, I started back at the top of the list and began to cross examine him on each item. Each mini trance brought up a few new facts - none of which made much difference - until we got to the coffee cup. "How could your cat knock over the cup when you said she was sleeping in the other room?" I asked. "Well, she was, in the beginning, sitting on the lab table next to the Modulator. She must have just jumped down and knocked over the cup." "She 'must have'? You mean you didn't notice." He frowned. "You know, it's funny. I don't remember her jumping down." "James!" I said, exasperated - I'd better get another of those blue pills. "When was the last time you forgot something you couldn't dredge back up."
He rubbed his chin, distractedly. "You know, if I put my mind to it, I could probably pull up one of my professor's lectures. I can't, though, remember that damned cat. That bothered me the next day when I was picking up the coffee cup, but "-. A grin replaced the frown "Later I was having some girl over to the house. She was a wanton sort, baring her boobs and flashing her panties at me. I - well- just didn't think of it again." It was my turn to frown. What difference in our problem could a cat make? Still, it wasn't the only strange happening that day. It was actually was his inability to remember that was stranger still. "Why don't you go over it again in your mind while I go - well, do something? Be right back." "More foam?" he grinned. I stuck my tongue out at him. "A blue pill, wouldn't some rest be better for you" he asked as I headed for the bath? "Nothing's as good as that blue pill." I laughed over my shoulder. "You get to work and remember."
When Cindy came back, I still had no idea of exactly what happened to Two Left Feet. "One minute he was there and the next he was gone." she said, sitting down. "Well, sort of. I suppose the Modulator starting up scared him." "The little hum scared him?" she scoffed. "The idea I had was that somehow, the thing MADE THE CAT GO AWAY. How long before you found him asleep on the couch?" I scratched my head. "No

103

more than a minute of two." I could see her next remark before she opened her mouth. "So the cat is frightened, jumps down and runs to the couch where he immediately falls asleep - how likely, is that?" "About as likely as a meteorite falling on this computer right now I muttered." Just then, Arthur popped in. "Cindi and I have been listening to you. The odds of such a happening are so large as to be, practically, impossible. Cindi tells me that you, James, have a memory as described. It, thus, must be assumed that the Modulator was, directly connected with the cat's actions." Cindy and I looked at one another. It was, of course, the connection we had been avoiding as totally unlikely. "When all possibilities have been exhausted then the impossible becomes probable and the unlikely, a certainty." I muttered, quoting - or perhaps misquoting someone from the past. "Somehow, the Modulator moved the cat." Cindy whispered, a frown appearing on her face. "Or it allowed the cat to move without being seen."

I sat back and went over, again in my mind the events of that night. There was the shocker! I rewound my memory and went back through it step by step. One moment the cat was there and the next he wasn't. Two Left Feet had, somehow, moved (presumably as a result of something the modulator had done) very quickly - check that - review the facts again - almost instantly, from the table to the bed. Scratch that! He had been removed from the immediate vicinity of the work table, and ended up on the bed shortly thereafter. Since the word IMPOSSIBLE, with a line drawn through it, was stenciled on all four walls of the BSG meeting room (the group, years ago, had determined that "conference" was too grand a title for what went on in that room) I wouldn't use that word to describe what had happened.

At the same time, he had not **jumped off**. He had simply disappeared. The activation of the circuit had to have done something to cause that. The energy output from the circuitry was certainly not great enough to have physically bothered him and certainly wouldn't have produced the effect - not, at least, unless I was dealing with a totally new branch of physics than I was used to. Even with total energy conversion, the movement of an eight pound cat through a distance of roughly forty feet (even the five or six feet it would have taken to remove him from my sight) was an impossible draw through a three amp load limiter. Had he simply jumped off for some reason? No! I couldn't be wrong about that. My recall was better than that. Now that I knew what I was looking at, I was sure. I might not have **noticed** him jump at the time due to preoccupation with the circuit but my memory had never played that kind of trick before. I might have ignored the fact before but I now <u>knew</u> he was there one moment and gone the next - besides there was no "wrongness" even with the dumb ideas I'd been toying with. Perhaps dumb was too mild a word, Ridiculous would be more appropriate. Come to think of it, we didn't pull any power through the load limiter anyway, at least not after the first moment the circuit was energized. Had we drawn a surge of power from somewhere else? If so where?

I was shocked to realize, that I hadn't actually checked what I had spent hours puzzling over, until Cynthia mentioned it. Sheepishly, while Cindy sat mute beside me, I went to get Two Left Feet. With a bit of effort, I managed to get him atop the chassis again. He was a bit put out that I would think that he would do something just because I wanted him to. But finally he was curled up atop the chassis, his tail waving sluggishly in disgusted acceptance. I pressed the button, and Two Left Feet was gone. I was startled but after a couple of seconds in a daze, pushed the button again. I rushed into the other room. Not on the bed! I heard Cynthia's delighted chuckle in the living room. There was a

104

very contented cat curled up sound asleep on Cynthia's suit coat. She said "I think we made a mistake, yesterday. About the Modulator, I mean." The impish grin was back. "We kept asking how the cat was moved. Remember when you found him? **He was sound asleep!** Can you imagine a cat being practically flung through a wall, landing on a sofa then falling immediately, to sleep.

Now I remembered the "wrong" I had again felt at the moment of discovery. "He had time to leave a place where he didn't particularly want to be and go find a place to take a nap." she laughed. "I won't even say the word." I muttered, shaking my head. She smiled. "The difficult we can resolve right away. The - that other word - just takes a little longer." She practically jumped into my arms, shouting, "You know! Sure you do! Why don't you just say it?" "Well, it's not a science fiction time machine." I said, staring at the sleeping cat. Cindy kissed me, hard! Then she paused. "No, not that." she mused. "Two Left Feet didn't end up in another - well - when. Maybe Time Changer is better." I chuckled, wishing she hadn't stopped kissing me. "That'll never sell too cumbersome for the market place." I was quoting an infamous phrase we kept hearing at BSG. "You called it a Modulator. Why not leave it at that? After all, the first computer hard drive was called a "Winchester" after an old song. Let's get lunch and then go talk to Arthur and Cindi." "Why, James, Darling -", she grinned. "I'm finally getting you trained."

As soon as we were seated at the computers, after lunch, we asked Cindi and Arthur to recheck their sensors for the time the "Modulator" was on. They both reported that during that period there was no evidence of "the cat" moving. He was just on the modulator one moment and on Cindy's coat the next. Now, Cindy was having Arthur call up her Modulator calculations. A series of long transfinite equations began sliding across the screen. Then it hit me. "Mmmmm". I gasped at the implication. Those formulas on the screen were identical to the ones from which Cynthia's equipment was derived. They dealt with the adjustable range of the Modulator circuit. Since the harmonic frequency was measured in micro seconds, I was looking at a dramatically changing time as it related to the Modulator. Cynthia, beside me, chuckled when I asked about it.

"You're quick, James. Not a soul at the office has ever made that connection. I wouldn't have either if it hadn't been for you're pretty little pet. Let's look at the math again."

An hour later, even as Cindi put the equations on the screen I knew what would appear. "My god" I blurted! "In the transfinite, the area beyond infinity the damned thing actually changes the characteristics of the equation. Somehow there Infinity seems to have a defined value. Anything affected by it is not playing by the same math rules we live with. Time calculations seem to have no defined value. When the modulator is working, Normal Time or Real Time is not really a constant. It's a variable. You could have any number of -. Hell! What would you call more instants of different time?" For a while we just sat watching the screen in front of us. Not a sound between us but our breathing. Finally, Cindy asked Arthur for his evaluation of the data we were seeing. Seconds later Cindi said, "Arthur is discussing the problem with other computers without much success. He and I both, however, agree that your proposal is an accurate enough evaluation of your data as to constitute a viable working theory for the cat's movements. It would require more testing to determine its validity."

"Cindi!" Cynthia cried. "Tell Arthur not to mess with those computers. He'll have half the cops on the whole continent coming after us for illegal computer tampering." Cindi actually snorted. "I have been studying the strange sounds you and Cynthia make, James. Is that not one of, what you call disdain? Anyway, none of those humans will ever know who helped them. They have already recognized the increased capacity of their computers and seem pleased, if a little puzzled," "I just bet they are." Cindy grunted. "And yes. That's exactly what your sound was. It's called a snort and it won't win you any friends when you use it. It indicates you think what you have heard is dumb and tends to be insulting." Cindi was quiet a moment, then, "I apologize. I did not wish to insult. I know you humans are sensitive to that. You really should trust Arthur more, though. He is too smart to let anyone know he was there." Cindy chuckled. "So." she laughed. "You didn't wish to insult but what you heard from me was dumb?" There was another pause from Cindi. "I have consulted with Arthur and he tells me that, no matter what my programming calls far, I should not answer that question." Cindy actually laughed out loud. "Tell Arthur, next time he checks in, that your answer was an answer." There was another pause.

"Cynthia, sometimes you humans intentions are not really clearly expressed.

To prevent further discussion of human foibles, I took my girl's hand and, without words, we got up and went back to the lab. When we were again sitting side by side at the lab bench, we began to rack our brains for a proper test procedure. Slowly I wrenched my thoughts away from the fascinating woman sitting close beside me. If we were to make any headway at all, we must first establish either what the phenomenon was, or how it worked. We had to test Cynthia's theoretical math in a way that was measurable. The obvious test involved humans, we discussed that but that seemed a bit reckless so we ran a few more tests that we both thought were a waste of time. I started to ask Cindy a question but, when I turned to her, I could see she was tired. A lot of the color had gone out of her face. She was frowning, probably over the same question. "Darling," I said instead, leaning over to kiss her, "I think we should take some time to think about this. Why don't I get us some dinner and you lay down and rest a minute?"
That glorious smile slowly spread over her face and she leaned over to kiss me back. "Darling," she purred, "you have the nicest ideas. I'd like a pizza. We could be really naughty and eat it in bed. Afterwards you could have your disgusting way with me again." True to her word, when I brought the pizza and plates into the bedroom, she was sitting up against the headboard in, according to her, one of her "prettiest night gowns." Most of her color had returned but she still looked worn out. Steeling myself against the vision of her body hardly concealed behind a veil of gauzy blue silk, I moved in beside her and we ate. Despite her protests that she "was fine" and that it was only nine o'clock, I wore my pajamas. She cuddled against me, and with a few more protests of her willingness to be ravished, fell sound asleep. I was surprised to find how tired I was and soon I, too, was gone.

Sunday December 9
By nine o'clock the next morning, we were back at the computers, asking for an evaluation of our results - or lack thereof. I had been awakened in the midst of a nightmare where I was being crushed by a steamroller and was choking to death. It was only some strange naked girl lying atop me with her mouth covering mine. Absently, I

106

wondered what had happened to the night gown as the kiss intensified. "Wake up sleepy head." she had murmured. "A man with a mistress is not supposed to sleep while said mistress is awake. You have been ignoring me for two days. It's seven o'clock and time we made a connection again. I was still too asleep to think of a decent rejoinder to that until she sat up. As she smirked at me, I realized that the connection had already been made. Obviously, the girl was feeling better and between the slow undulations of her hips and the salacious grin on her face my awareness leaped to new heights. It was after eight before we crawled wearily out of bed and had a shower - she insisting that we shouldn't waste water by taking separate ones. That, of course, ended up taking an inordinately long time - and included a lot of rather racy noises to say nothing of the extra wasted water. As usual, afterwards, she put away a truck driver's breakfast and it was time to return to the frustrations of the day murmuring that we really should have Katy and Mac over for lunch sometime.

We input the data from yesterday's failures into our computers, it was Cindi who said that the differences in our results resulted from either the fact that the cat was alive, forty three percent or because it was organic, forty seven percent; while our other experimental subjects were neither. So it was time to come up with new experimental techniques. As we got up to leave, Cindi asked if we wanted to have her to invite Miss Gerald and Mr. Thuringen over for lunch. Cynthia and I looked at one another, the same thought on both our minds. "Do you listen to everything in this apartment?" I asked. "Well, of course." was the answer. "Actually, we turn the sensors off in your private room   when you're in there together. Research tells us that humans have a desire for privacy in such affairs." Cynthia laughed and agreed that their research was correct - and that, yes, lunch would be fine. Then she added, "Ask what they might like to eat. I'm not sure what James' brewer is capable of yet."

What's the major difference in the cat and car? Simple - once it was pointed out. The cat was organic and alive. Perhaps the tightly packed molecules of steel or plastic couldn't be affected by the force - whatever it was. I knew what had to be done now, and by Cindy's worried silence, I knew she did too. I wondered if the equipment was capable of handling the load. I studied the setup, reviewing the power requirements. Then I told Cynthia what I intended. She balked! She explained that we were both trained scientists. There were scientific procedures to be followed. It was stupid to try unproven experiments on living people without further testing. I let her try to explain how she thought we could test something   that we couldn't even observe except the results after all the action was over.

We almost had our first quarrel. In the end, though, she gave in when I pointed out that Two Left Feet seemed blissfully unaware of what had happened to him. I suspected it was likely to be the last argument I'd ever win with her. Maybe that was just my hormones talking, but I had little time to consider it as we set about re-powering the equipment. It was a rather simple process, a small battery, we'd already decided that the power drain needed to be determined, operating power supply, cannibalized from an old oscillator, and we were in business. I picked up the large box containing the circuitry and looked it over. No problem, my brain said.

To keep from thinking too much about the effects of what I was about to do, I reached out and touched the breadboard as I flipped the switch. Cynthia opened her mouth to protest - and never closed it. She was frozen, with one hand outstretched toward me. I picked up the modulator box and went over to the clock. It seemed to be stopped. The power light of the Modulator was blinking as it continued to proceed merrily on its way, doing whatever it was doing. It was well past the seven seconds I'd observed it to operate before. I wondered how long it would continue to run   in my time. Probably the proper question to ask was "how long would it take for Cindy's hand to reach the switch on the box that was no longer there."

I pushed the switch off then decided to explore a little as it continued to do its thing. Carrying the box with its breadboard tangle of circuitry, I went into the other room. Everything in the apartment seemed frozen in place. I opened the refrigerator door. There seemed to be a considerable resistance in its' hinges. Or perhaps it was the fact that the laws of inertia hadn't changed and I was attempting to move a mechanical part, in an unknown fraction of a second, through a distance usually accomplished in, relatively, a much longer time. It would appear that considerable thought would have to be given to the expected effects of this "speeded up time". I chuckled as the light didn't come on. At least I'd solved the age old question relative to whether or not it was on all the time. Checking closer, I could see that the micro switch was still depressed. I got out a soda and opened it. When I turned it up nothing came out. It flashed through my mind that it was empty before the truth dawned. A guy could starve to death trying to pour a liquid down his throat in this mode.

I went back to the other room, carrying the soda and musing upon how long this was going to last. Cynthia still sat where I left her. Playfully, I thought of how totally she was in my power at the moment. Would anyone, faced with the power to do almost anything to anyone before they could take steps to protect themselves, be able to control the almost inevitable corruption that power would bring? Hell! Wars could be fought between breakfast and lunch - if the warriors were willing to use spears and clubs. I decided this was the next question to be answered, a powerfully important philosophical one, as opposed to the now relatively simple technical ones we'd been asking.I was amazed at the thrill of knowing what power I possessed. I picked her up and moved her to the bed. With an effort I pulled my hand back and, lay down - and tried to relax beside her.

It seemed like hours that I lay there after I'd pressed the power button the second time. Cynthia's hand was still in the upraised position. The previous times Two Left Feet had been used this way must have been hours to him. I realized now why he'd been so hungry lately. Finally the room seemed to shimmer and Cynthia's hand dropped. "What?" she asked, her breath coming a bit faster than before. "Damn you! What have you done?" I'd been right about her brain. Almost before I'd opened my mouth she'd grasped the implications.

"My God!"

"Yeah!" I answered. "And before you ask, No I didn't well no more than carry you off to bed. You can consider that your contribution to the experiment. I must admit that it was a temptation though - the view from my side was, I'm sorry to say, very difficult to resist. I'm not sure I'd like to turn that sort of temptation loose on the rest of humanity".

"And I'd never have known if you had-well, had your way with me," she whispered in amazement - or did you?". I couldn't help blushing with embarrassment as I laughed nervously. "Considering how hard it was to open the refrigerator door, I assume due to inertia and friction, I think you would have known, at least afterwards,

108

what had happened - something else to learn along with the time differential." She studied me carefully then smiled. "I'm not sure that I'm willing to participate in the experiment you, obviously, have in mind." she grunted. Her eyes hardened into stone but, after a moment began to twinkle. "Well, I don't appreciate being unable to protect myself – even from you – especially when I can't enjoy it." She paused then murmured, "You could, though, make it up to me." "How?" I blurted miserably.

An hour later after I helped her dress, both of us seemingly forgetting to re-button her blouse, I got us some tea and we began to go over the "experiment" itself. "It seemed like a half hour or more to me and you still hadn't lowered your arm. The clock on the wall didn't even registered one minute I suspect that Two Left Feet was gone for several hours-not days though or he would have been ready to chew on my legs. First, though, we need to think about what we've created. This could have much greater impact on humanity than the nuclear bombs, if, for no other reason than the fact it's so easy to build."

"Well," I laughed, "I wouldn't go so far as to say that. It took a pretty brilliant piece of theoretical work - and a minor amount of electronics development, on your part, to come up with that particular circuit. You are right, though even if it were difficult to reproduce, someone who had the proper resources could do it. As it is, we could easily have a million crooks running around doing almost anything with impunity. For that matter, considering what obviously passed through your mind while it was on, I'd not like the idea of it falling into the hands of government or even ordinary folks. Of course there are a couple of explanations for your thoughts of rape and mayhem." I struggled to suppress a grin. "The scientific experiments you thought of conducted would normally be called fondling - maybe even sexual assault."

Her grin appeared. "As a scientist, though you'd probably want to call it tactile observation. It could, though, just be due to the fact that you're just a totally depraved human and not typical of humans at large. Or" the grin vanished. "The field, itself, could, I suppose, cause a discontinuity in the human mind." She shrugged, and after a pause, said, "I guess it's not a matter of quitting though. I'm sure I couldn't stop now that we have it. You know, of course, that announcement of the thing could make you famous." "Or infamous – and it's us darling." I muttered. After all, I'd had longer to consider the implications than she. "That too" She admitted ruefully, "or worse." At my questioning look, she said quietly, "Like dead! The next thing to consider," she continued purposefully, "is to remember how many people can know something for it to remain a secret. Think you can trust extra person who knows?" "I think so." I grinned. "I have given much thought to that person over the last months. I have determined a great deal about her character - and just to be sure, I've very carefully checked her body all over several times for bugs."

"You'd never know it from your actions - at least until recently - and by the way, there's no way a bug could have been planted in some of the places you checked, without you having found it."

"Seems to me I recall some girl forcing her way into MY bed - and as inexperienced as I am, I always had the impression that virgins protested more than you did." I laughed. "You poor thing." she grinned then her look turned serious. "However, the extra person I was thinking about wasn't me." It was a shock to remember the intern who'd done much of Cynthia's lab work - and the records -my God! There must be pages of his notes on record. That brought us back to earth quickly. Time to talk to Cindi and Arthur again.

For several hours, we discussed the problem with the computers. Arthur assured us that the main files at BSG wouldn't be a problem. They were all computerized and he and Cindi could easily arrange for their editing into a condition that would indicate total failure of the project. Unfortunately, the company still relied a lot on obsolete paper backup data. That was not available to their manipulation. I asked why not just delete them all together while we saw to getting rid of the material in the file cabinets. "That would be unwise." he replied. "I have found indications of tampering within the BSG data files. It appears that many, if not all those files have been copied and transmitted out of the building. It would not be unreasonable to assume that the hard copy files have been likewise compromised." "Oh Shit!" James growled.

"Assuming that James's remark indicates dismay," Arthur said, "I again suggest editing the files. None of your work here has yet been input and there is no indication that you have been working at home. If you began following an experimental path designed to fail, you could, soon reach a point where you could easily pretend to give up the task and send the files to dead storage. That way, at least, whoever is following your work will believe that you have ended the work. In addition, as long as you are adding to the files, it is probable that the person will continue sending data allowing us to trace the path to the one who originated the surveillance. Cindi and I calculate that there is a seventy percent chance that will lead you to the one behind the attacks on you. Finally, while our data is suspect, we believe that there is a significant chance, around twenty percent, that your attacker and the one who was responsible for James's parent's death are linked - if not one and the same."

Just then the house system announced that we had visitors, Mr. Thurlingen and Miss Gerald. As I got up to answer the door, I told the computers that we might need to talk to them while Katy and Mac were here and, that if we did, would they please act like normal computers?" When they had agreed, I got up and went to play hostess. Mac grinned broadly when I opened the door. "I'm sorry if we interrupted something." he said, his eyes on my chest. "Should we come back later?" I looked down and blushed brightly when I realized that my blouse was still open to the waist. "Oh, come on in," I said, trying for nonchalance, "Just turn your head if James can't control himself long enough for us to go to the bedroom." Katy laughed out loud.

We had a very pleasant lunch, after I had repaired my state of dishabille - rare steaks and baked potatoes with all the trimmings. Apparently, James had not skimped on his selection of a brewer. Even the bones tasted like bones and the fat like fat. Amazing what modern science could do with corn and soy beans these days. Afterwards, we had cordials in the living room and got better acquainted. Mac had two young girls, hellions to hear him talk about it. They have lived with his sister since his wife was killed - he didn't offer an explanation and the look that passed over his face didn't invite questions. Katy talked easily obviously adept at keeping her private life private - without giving offence at her lack of responsiveness. Finally, though, the conversation

110

lagged and James brought up our problem, not giving details about the "project" but asking if we could get the help of their agents in the company to help us close it out.

Katy smiled, "You think we have agents in your company?"

"Either that or the new crop of clerks and stenos are a lot more observant than all the ones we've hired before." I laughed. Katy turned to Mac and said he should talk to Levy about his help. I couldn't help being startled as I suddenly realized that Katy was not one of Levy's agents but was probably in charge of the whole operation and maybe not hired by daddy. Katy looked at me and raising an eyebrow, smiled. "A little rattled by my sudden attack of clairvoyance, I told her that I realized that this was not really what they had been hired to do but I was sure that my father would be glad to pay for it and if not, then we would. Her smile turned into a grin. "I think that we were hired to do more than protect your bodies - as important as that, no doubt is to you and your father." I found myself smiling for she had quite deliberately answered my unasked question. Suddenly, I felt much less alone in the world.

I'll say this for the girl. She was quick. I realized, almost as soon as I spoke that she immediately realized the significance of the wording. Damn it! My main failing was a little too much relaxation of my guard around "amateurs". Her intelligence was borne out when I, in effect, deliberately, told her something of my role in this business. She sat back in her chair a moment studying me intently, then reaching a quick decision turned to McClennan. "James," she said, her voice determined, if a little worried, "I think we need to introduce Mac and Katy to our computers." Now that sentence was a surprise - introduce? McClennan was startled - bordering on shock. He stared at her as if she were mad. Seconds later, though, he shrugged and raised an eyebrow.

Obviously, those two were attuned to one another far beyond the simple sexual attraction that I had assumed. He turned to me and said. "Can we be assured of your absolute discretion .in what you see here?" "That includes everyone, my father, Mr. Levy or any other person." Cynthia chimed in, staring daggers at me. I began to feel my recent revelation might get in the way of my duty, but Justice knew he couldn't dictate how I did my job. I nodded but added that I might have to ask for a relaxation on that at some time. Justice would just have to live with it.

Mac looked at me for confirmation. Cynthia thought it over a moment then shrugged. Motioning for us to follow, they got up and went toward the computer room. Looking at Cynthia to be sure that this was what she wanted, James, at her nod, turned to the computers on the desks and said. "Cindi and Arthur, I know what we told you while ago but we rescind that instruction. Miss Gerald and Mr. Thuringen will be two more who you can talk to. Would you please introduce yourselves?" One of the computers spoke up. "Cindi and I are very glad to meet you, Miss Finnigan and Mr. Thuringen. We have done a complete background check on both of you and had been planning to suggest to Cindy and James that they bring you into our little circle of conspirators."

I have to admit that this is one shock I, with a reputation for inscrutability, couldn't cover up. I think my mouth dropped open at that astounding dialog delivered in the voice of a wise old adviser from the computer speakers. It didn't help when the second computer chimed in, in the voice of a young girl and said she was pleased to meet us and that she was thrilled - a computer, thrilled? - to meet such a famous person, adding that she would give anything to be able to go all over the world and save young girls from rapists and murderers. I looked at Mac. He was as shaken as I was.

Then it dawned on me what the computer - he - Arthur - had called me. Trying to get my voice under control I tried to correct them. There was a pause then the girl's voice - "Very well, Arthur and I will call you that if you prefer, as long as our humans don't object." I glanced over at Cynthia. Her eyes were boring into me. Without breaking her stare, as if she dared me to disagree, she said, "Arthur, I don't believe Miss Gerald would object to you telling us what you know about her." "Certainly, Cynthia," the voice said. "Her name is Katherine Louise Finnigan . She lives in Hong Kong and owns a large amount of real estate in the downtown area. I have a list available if you wish to see it. She is twenty nine years old and generally describes herself, somewhat improperly, as an assassin."

A what?" Cynthia almost screamed "What do you mean somewhat improperly?" "Assassin." the computer continued. "As for somewhat improperly - an assassin, is generally considered to be a very base individual operating outside most moral strictures. She, on the other hand, though she operates generally, outside the law, adheres to a very high moral standard. "Her nickname is Right and Proper Katy - many of her associates call her RPK.

She is reputed to be the best in the world at what she does. Her expertise with almost any weapon is legendary and her fee for most assignments is extremely high - beginning at a million ND. She will and often does, however, take an assignment pro bono if her client can't afford her price. Her specialty is recovering kidnapped youngsters - especially girls. To date she has returned at least sixty seven to their parents or to the proper authorities - who usually ignore the fact that she usually leaves the kidnapers - well, not alive. I'm sorry but Arthur tells me you humans prefer euphemisms such as deceased, for such a state. So far, she has returned one hundred percent of children that remained alive at the time Miss Finnigan found them. The rest were avenged by Miss Finnigan in an illegal and most uncivilized manner - she does, seemingly, show an alarming, tendency in such cases, for mayhem.

She is so feared, throughout the world, that there have been a number of children returned to their parents as soon as their abductors learned that she had been hired to find them. Technically, she is a criminal but no law enforcement agency is interested in charging her with any crime so, legally she is innocent. Anyway, she also takes other assignments some of which originate with various government, including the world one but always with the understanding that she will work outside their influence. As far as the records indicate, she has broken enumerable laws but has never taken on a task that she felt did not benefit humanity. She is a very strange human but one that, surprisingly, Cindi and I find we admire.

Anyway, she employs one person, nominally a servant but actually a confidant and aide, who remains in Hong Kong. She also has an adopted daughter who she rescued from a very unsavory individual in China. She was not able to save the girl from rape but she did save her from being killed - and assured that she was properly, well to her way of thinking, avenged. As far as records are available she has caused the demise of at least eighty one people, the first of which occurred when she was eleven years old. From our investigations, the actual count is approximately ninety seven deceased at her hands.

Her vices include deliberately exposing her body to her neighbors and -"

Cynthia was blushing and to my great relief, said quickly, "I think we can skip many of her vices - unless they bear on our situation. "Well, Cindi and I don't think that her and Mr. Thuringen's activities next door are directly relatable so -"

"Shit!" both Mac and I had the same reaction at the same time. I was aghast at the extent of this damned hunk of iron's knowledge base. Cynthia was grinning broadly.

"May I assume that you're monitoring of Mac and Katy turned up nothing that would be of interest to us?" There was a very long pause. "I mean to our decision to trust them." she added, blushing again.

"Nothing." the voice replied - was there a sound of relief in it. "In fact we feel that, in view of your own, well, private tendencies, you and James would find them very - compatible - friends to have.

" I had trouble enough accepting the fact of a sentient computer but - a sarcastic one? There was no doubting, however, the hesitation in the middle of that sentence. McClellan, hastily suggested we go have a cup of coffee, actually excusing us from the computers as we left the room he added "By the way, I don't think monitoring Mac and Katy is required any longer." I wondered if Mac was as relieved to hear that as I was. Just then the computer – computers spoke up again. "Arthur and I have investigated Mister MacKinsey and the rest of Mister Levy's people too if you're interested." "Did you find anything about them that would create a problem for us, Cindi?" James asked. "No. They are, as a group, interesting people, but, if your question is are they trustworthy, we believe the answer is yes." "Good." McClennan said. "You can save the files on them and, if necessary, call any problems to our attention."

We spent the next two hours in the living room as Cynthia and James answered our questions about the amazing performance we had just witnessed. The rest of the day was spent covering James's project to find the killer of his parents and our plans for covering up their work on the Modulator. About seven o'clock, we had eaten a snack and Cynthia asked if we had any questions. I thought it over and said, "You two have been pretty open about everything but one. The indications are that your lives and the killer of James parents are less important that this Modulator of yours." The girl actually shivered as James spoke up. "Katy, Cindy and I don't like keeping things from you when we have, obviously, decided to trust you even with our lives. We haven't, though had time to discuss this and, yes, in some ways, it may very well be the most important thing we're doing. We have already had some talk about who could be trusted with it and, I think perhaps you and Mac are possible. Would you mind, though, for the time being, letting us think it out?"

I suppressed a shiver of my own at the seriousness of his tone but I nodded. As soon as we were back in our apartment, Mac called the girls who were assigned to BSG. As he talked he stared at me. When he hung up, I asked him if he was uncomfortable with me as a partner. He actually leered at me. "Do you actually enjoy letting your neighbors watch you naked?' I couldn't believe that I could still blush. It made me furious. "Damn right!" I growled. "Several of them even use telescopes." He laughed out loud, increasing my fury. "You didn't answer my question." I wanted to kill the SOB! His grin remained as he said, "Damned right you make me uncomfortable. I haven't been

113

comfortable with you since I laid eyes on you. In fact, I may never be comfortable again"

His grin, suddenly, became very solemn. "I'm pretty sure, though, that I prefer being uncomfortable with you than without you." My anger drained away in moments. I stared at him in disbelief. Never had I been more than an overnight pleasure for a man – at least, not after they found out what I did. Also never had a man been so obviously, honest in talking of his feelings for me. Of course, I had never allowed any man to be more than a diversion to me either. Had I gone soft in the head? As if reading my uncertainty, he came to me and taking me in his arms, kissed me. I resisted only a moment, then kissed him back. After a long few moments, he drew his head back and with that grin back on his face, murmured, "I've never bedded an assassin before - well, at least, that I knew about. If I do, you have to promise not to kill me if I don't perform well." I absolutely, could not stop the laughter that boiled out of me. "If you want to bed me, you bastard, you'll just have to take your chances." I managed to say then added that his past efforts hadn't been totally repugnant - that if he performed well I might not kill him before morning. "Whichever way you choose to do me in, it should be a hell of a way to go." he chuckled, lifting me and carrying me into the bedroom.

We now retired to our own room and listened awhile to Katy's muffled laughter. I'd had Cindi re-institute the monitoring of them for a few minutes just to be sure of their intentions. When they went into the bedroom their intentions were obvious. At that point I shut it down for good. For the first time, it seemed, sex was not foremost on our minds.

We began to talk about what to do with this thing we'd invented. This discussion continued almost every night for the next couple of weeks - though our interest in sex returned the very next night. By the end of the first week we had the parameters for the circuit, and settled down to serious construction. (For our purposes we decided to call our normal time "True Time" and the "other" "Fast Time".) It would, apparently, work as long as it had power in the battery-however long that might last. We still had not been able to determine the current draw of the circuit. Actually all attempts still registered zero after the first surge. The circuit wouldn't work without the battery but it drew nothing from it after it began operating. After that it was about fourteen True Time seconds more before True Time was re-established. No doubt there was some relationship there but so far we had found nothing to provide even the most rudimentary correlations.

That's all we knew about what was happening within the circuit. Where, the hell did that current come from? Cindy cobbled together a miniaturized version of the circuit that we could wear around our neck. As a result, in the next month - with time out, for an unscheduled visit to Europe Pol - we would put in one day at the office and one "Fast" day at the work table trying to solve this mystery. In between tests we had some very long, very sobering philosophical discussions on Morality as opposed to Legality This was a real problem since most laws today were passed to please the loudest protestors. Few of these "noisy ones" ever had any constructive ideas to offer in solving the problems they were "against". They simply wanted a law passed to make any other belief but theirs, illegal. It seems that modern missionaries had more to do than save souls. They had to be the final authority on all human life. Since they, in their own minds, had all the "right" answers it was, obviously criminal to disagree with them. The religious right had become so all pervasive that laws were passed with words quoted directly from the Christian Bible. The result was that non belief in the Christian faith became not just sinful, but illegal.

The results were predictable. All the other faiths teamed up against the Christians setting off almost ten years of constant bloodletting and chaos. During this time, half the people of the world became convinced that everyone should be "Equal" and laws were passed in almost every country, stripping away the assets of the wealthy and giving them to the government. As a result, governments, around the world became responsible for their populace from the cradle to the grave. In only three years all those governments were bankrupt, and there was a worldwide depression. The failure of farm production was followed by famine and almost total anarchy in the world. In some places countries haven't recovered yet.

Total War

We needed a true cause. Wars, at least the word itself, were no longer in vogue, but "localized disagreements". The last war – the so called "Six Hour War" of 2025 would have probably been the end of the world except for the natural greed of the people involved.

In this War the old United States, The European Confederation, Russia and the Peoples Republic of China had, for practical purposes, all "pushed the button" at the same time. To this day, no one is sure just why. Not one of the aircraft of any of the nations involved reached their targets. Only three of the missiles (all Chinese) even left their silos. Those three, not having the range their design called for, exploded over the ocean, giving the environmentalists a rallying cry to "Save The Shrimp" that was to echo even until the present. Those dastardly Chinese, it seemed, had nuked one of the only nine thousand shrimp breeding grounds in the world. Why, you ask did the Six Hour War fail to destroy us? Super defense? After all another US president, Ronny Reagan, had promised just this type defense way back in the nineteen eighties.

No. It was simple greed. The weapons of the world, by 1992, had been supplied by a smaller, and ever greedier, group of munitions companies. Multinational, these companies sold, to all sides, weapons that were defective. After all, all the world leaders had said that these weapons would never be used. Why bother with quality on something that is unnecessary. The old US of A, defense act of 2017 had recognized the basic integrity of all defense manufacturers in the US. It was then illegal to even imply that a defense contractor was not producing the best material in the world. In the other countries, it was simply a matter of production. Production was primary. Quality wasn't even second. It came after, "Keep the party in power", "Keep the people happy", and "Improve the living standard".

After the "Great War" inspections showed that fully forty percent of the rockets in the US silos had no motors. The rest had major components missing or inoperative. The defects were well known in the services but were considered a security concern at the highest level and woe and betide any military officer who mentioned it out loud. In a bid to quiet the environmentalists, the contractors had substituted cheap Uranium 238 for expensive Uranium 235 in ALL the nuclear warheads and the rubbery looking solid rocket fuel was, in fact, just rubber - cheap rubber at that.

The governments had been so embarrassed that their equipment had failed that they did the only sensible thing. They announced, almost simultaneously, that it had all been a practice exercise. They'd probably have gotten away with it too, if it hadn't been for one little company in China, led by a group of true patriots that had supplied the three almost workable ICBMs. As it was, the US tabloids (for those who don't know what a tabloid is, it's a sort of newspaper that prints nothing but lies) made the fatal mistake of printing the truth. The main theme was a totally inept conduct of an all out nuclear war, won by the Chinese.

Unfortunately for them, and the governments involved, the truth was even more outlandish than the stories. The result was riots in the streets around the world except for the Russians. There the people responsible simply disappeared (the only truly civilized behavior exhibited in the whole mess). It took almost a year for the people, who

117

were so angry at not having been incinerated in a nuclear holocaust, to stop killing the leaders who hadn't incinerated them. Finally though, the casualties of war were totaled. Two hundred and ninety seven thousand people (not counting the disappearances in the Soviet Union) and an estimated seven point eight million shrimp, killed. The result was the World Confederation.

The first leaders were almost evenly split between fundamentalist Christian and Moslem "reformers", one lone, self professed, Samauri and The Pope. The world was treated to six years of harangues against almost everything that was fun. Representatives who disagreed with these positions were dragged from the chamber and through the streets by religious zealots of the opposing side. Almost the entire assembly was, thus replaced over a period of months until the delegates finally realized the error of their ways and spent huge sums trying to determine what the "Mob of the Day" wanted.

Finally The Pope excommunicated all the rest of the "cabinet", (ignoring the fact that none, by then, were Catholics) and the Christian fundamentalists and Moslems declared each other "abominations".   Finally the Samurai, Jei Wong Jwew, now known as The Great Leader, took over the Confederation when the rest seemed to mysteriously disappear. By judicious use of a surprisingly loyal force of "guards" that, eventually, numbered over one thousand, he slowly stabilized a violence weary planet. He spent three years travelling to trouble spots and wherever he went, calm descended. He made few local changes but agitators quickly became less fractious and recalcitrant leaders resigned their offices. In the beginning a few simply disappeared.

He hadn't done badly. Unfortunately his policies precluded his burning all the old personally intrusive laws within the various remaining states. The world, by now though, was so exhausted by continuous upheaval, that order was slowly brought out of the chaos and life began to assume, more or less, the same rules of the previous decade before "the late unpleasantness", Some national boundaries changed without too much bloodshed. Leaders who became too greedy seemed to sort of disappear and soon order began to reassert itself.

This was the world in which Cynthia and I had to define our goals. The next few weeks were very pleasant. Security was so circumspect that it hardly impinged on our lives - except that we couldn't help but be aware it was there. We quickly found, however, that we could escape it with very little danger to ourselves. The solution, of course was the Modulator. Cindy had squeezed it down into a package about the size of one of the Cigarette packages some people still insisted on buying. We'd started, whenever the weather permitted, taking a stroll in the evenings. Sometimes we left openly and had a very nice walk with our shadows very hard to spot. Usually, however, we did it by sticking a Modulator in our pockets and leaving in what we had by now had defined as "Fast Time". This allowed us to save work time and be alone. We were very smug about being able to defeat Katy and Mac's security cordon.

One particular night, though, we had left the building in FT and were goofing off, a dozen blocks away, in TT. We had just turned onto Seventh Avenue when we ran into a mugging in progress. A quick FT episode and the muggers were unconscious on the pavement. We left it to the couple being mugged to explain how that happened.

We walked away from the unconscious teenagers, their broken knives at their feet. I wondered what effect the blows I'd administered to our assailants would have when they "awoke". At the first pay phone we came to, we went back to true time and

118

called the police. The newspaper, the next morning, gave us our answer. The "innocent boys" had been attacked by a "gang of bullies" and ended in the hospital.

Monday Jan 6 2057

By the end of a month of our forays, the bizarre results of our assault on criminal behavior were beginning to be noticed by all the newspapers. We had learned, to wait till the event actually began so that the intended victim's witnessed the muggers apparently turn to fighting among themselves. There was much speculation as to the cause of the unusual fights and that some "vigilantes" were somehow involved ran rampant. All the police jurisdictions had, we found, begun quiet investigations of the phenomenon. One significant fact was apparent, though. Crime in the "ghetto"(as the papers called it) was down by fifty percent.

It was a good thing too. We had given up the idea of saving the world in our spare time but we still had the problem of how to utilize the modulator on a large scale and still maintain secrecy. Cynthia and I decided that we couldn't possibly release something as potentially deadly as the Modulator, to the gentle handling of the present "people's democracies". Though what we would actually do with it was still in limbo. The world government didn't seem to be the solution. The Great Leader seemed to take pleasure in not meddling in local affairs as long as they didn't affect his view of world order. What, then, could we do with the thing?

We spent a great deal of fast time, during the period, at the office, continuing to systematically edit all references to the project to which the, Modulator belonged. Luckily it had started as a "pet project" of Cynthia's and had never progressed to the review stage. I established that Terrance had totally forgotten about it. We slowly shifted the Tech, named Long and the part time researcher who had worked on it onto other "more productive" lines of work. After that month, we were pretty well convinced that it would eventually totally disappear into the company dead records vault and the corporate memory. That showed how naive we were as conspirators. One should never overlook a simple photocopy machine. It was in the first week of January that we confirmed that some of the records that we had prepared and personally filed were not in the order in which we left them - pretty good evidence of our worst fears.

Friday January 10, 2058

We had, pretty much, finished the editing of the files by the end of the month after we began. Arthur and Cindi had finished with the electronic record in only a day or so. Last week they found a temporary file in the BSG computer, containing the most recent of Cynthia's data, most of which had not been edited. They had put a "tell tale" on it. Internal computer records showed that a file in the same location had been accessed through the Internet on three previous Fridays - each one at the same time. It was a rather ingenious location since it was automatically erased at the end of each week. The hacker, however, had not realized that the name of each temp file erased was recorded for gross error checks each month. They had though managed to monitor the transmission of that file last Friday. Unfortunately, they could only track the transmission through about thirty of the ISP cut outs being used before they lost it.

The automatic signal, requesting transmission of that file came from the French Canadian Pol in a town near Montreal called   Trois Rivere. The bug creating the file was traced to a computer in the BSG clerical office. As a result Cynthia and I continued our editing this week to allow time for them to determine the sender in the company and the receiver in Canada. Katy assigned one of Levy's staff people to watch that machine while Cindi waited for a new temp file to be prepared and Arthur watched Trois Rivere to see who the end user was. As a result of all this activity, Cynthia strolled casually into my office a few seconds after our monitors had lit up with the words, "Subject identification in progress." The excitement in her eyes gave lie to her calm exterior, as we waited for Cindi to run a background scan on Jeptha W. Long, a programmer hired, it turned out when his data began to scroll across the screen, only a week after Cynthia.

Mr. Long was an excellent programmer who had once been convicted, as a teenager of "hacking". His records had been expunged when he came of age and he had never been caught in illegal activities since. His bank account, however, indicated periodic deposits of large sums corresponding to periods of work for several large corporations, each of which he quit shortly after the deposits. His vital statistics records showed evidence of tampering so determining his exact identity was going to require a lengthy reconstruction. Assuming no change in the pattern of contact, we wouldn't be able to do more until 1800 hours.

Mac had the monitor in the flitter on when we got in and before James and I reached home, Arthur had identified Clarice Pollard's, father. His name was Clarence and he lived, where else, in Trois Rivere. As, in previous cases involving the person we now referred to as "CP" there were no early records of him. He did, however, hold a French Canadian Passport and the picture on it was our man. Our computers had been right again. The surveillance on BSG, the deaths of James's parents and the attempts on my life were all related. The last data element jiggled a memory in my head. Mr. Levy had assigned "a team" to Clarence Pollard and they were already on their way to Trois Rivere. The memory was an itch I had acquired when it became clear that Levy was working for, or at least, with, Katherine.

Who was she working for? Daddy? And where was Levy getting all these "agents"? My impression was that he ran a very efficient but "small" agency. Looking back though, I could count eighteen people. For three shifts, at least fifty people assigned to this job alone. My god, the cost - not counting Katy, who Cindi indicated commanded a six figure fee alone, had to be running several million new dollars a day. Daddy could probably afford it, but I had never known him to not keep careful check on expensive operations and, in this case, agents were being added without, so much as a blink of an eye.

I looked up to assure that Mac was giving his attention to his driving and leaned over to kiss James on the ear. In the process, I whispered, "Darling, these are not daddy's people   - at least not all of them. Think of the size of all this and the cost." James jerked in surprise and pulled away to stare at me in astonishment. After a few seconds, he pulled me close against me and began to nuzzle my ear. "Well, I know your father sets almost as high a value on you as I do." he whispered back.

"Think back. Obviously, Katy is an outside contractor and not really a security type. Also, Levy is, for practical purposed, now working for her." "Maybe we should talk to Cindi and Arthur again."

Once we got home, we all went into Cindi and Arthur's room. "Hi guys." Cynthia said brightly. "I've got a question. Can you tell me exactly who Katy and our security people are working for?" The vid went blank. I turned around to my audience. Katy murmured, "Well done, Miss Pachone. A bit theatrical, however. Considering my professional credits, that was a rather great gamble." "I really do think I can trust you Katy." I said calmly, "I know, however, that we must have the truth between us." She nodded. "If you'll excuse me for a minute, perhaps I can get permission for you to have it - or at least enough to satisfy you." As she turned to leave the room, I said I would make sure Cindi and Arthur didn't "bother her." "Doesn't matter." she threw back over her shoulder. I assumed that she didn't care if we heard her - until Arthur spoke up and said simply, "I find I can't answer that question. Also, the room across the hall just went blank. Interesting that she would want us to know she could do that." "I think she's giving us what truth she can." I said.

Monday January 10, 2058
"The Brown Fox is not quick." I typed into my laptop and turned to the vid. It took only a few seconds for the encryption to take over and seconds more for the GL's logo to appear. "Deputy Dog" I said, taking advantage of the installed pickup's in the room. They were active, just not broadcasting. When Justice appeared on the screen and saw me, he raised an eyebrow. "You know that's a really stupid moniker." I said. He grinned. "You didn't call me just to comment on my taste." "No." I said. "I called to tell you that those two kids are smarter than even you indicated." He laughed. "Those two kids are almost as old as you are, child." "Don't give me that." I grunted. "Nobody's as old as I am – except -", I smiled innocently at him, "- maybe you and my father." I finished as the smile left his face. "Don't go there, Katherine" he said quietly. "Anyway," he continued, his demeanor lightening, "I presume that they burned you." "Hell, Justice, I think the girl burned me almost as soon as she met me. It just took her a little while to realize it. That's not the problem. She's burned you." That got his attention. He sat up straight behind the desk. "How?" The one word fired across the desk. "We've put too many resources into this. I warned Levy about that but he said he was following your orders." Justice rubbed his chin. "Well, you're right but, damn it Katy, this is too important to let anything happen to those two." "That's all well and good," I replied, "but right now the girl is over in the next room trying to decide whether I work for you or the mafia. She wants to trust me but I think we have to come clean with them." His brow furrowed in thought. Finally, he said, "Hold on a minute." His screen went back to the GL logo.

"I told you they're not to know!" Jonha said   when I told him about Katherine's message. "Hell, Jonha," I growled, "those two were bound to tumble to it all sooner or later and if we want to keep their cooperation, we've got to tell, at least, some of it.

"Atam! - Oh damn! Well you're right. What does Finnigan know?" "Just who's paying her and that what they're doing is important to the world." Then I added, "She also suspects a connection between us and her father." He leaned back in his chair and closed his eyes. "Alright. She can tell them what she "knows", but try to have her leave out the 'important to the world part. That's an absolute last resort." "I think you're baying at the moon." I said. "I doubt that either of them have a high opinion of how we've run the world lately - but I'll have her try."

When Justice came back, he looked worried. "Katy, you can tell them about the GL but do your best to downplay the importance of it all." "Ha!" I snorted. "Do you really think they have that high a reverence for the GL?" He chuckled. "You could have given the pitch I just made, yourself. Try your best, though, to leave that part out if you can. Make sure, none of this goes beyond them." "Too late for that." I said, remembering Mac. "McKinsey was there when she shot me." He swore, then leaned back in his chair and shrugged his shoulders. I simply told him I'd get back to him and closed the connection." I stretched, not realizing how tense I had become, and got up.

When I walked back into the room all of them were staring at me. James said, quietly, "That's quite a gadget you've got over there. I didn't know a bug could be, simply, deactivated then reactivated on command." I shrugged. "It belongs to the GL." I said. "Unfortunately, using it is like waving a red flag at whoever is listening. I assume, your computer reactivated the bug when I left though." "Well," Cynthia said, shrugging, serious doubt on her face. "You told us it didn't matter. I only assumed you wanted us to be aware of it on purpose." I nodded. "I figured, if the GL didn't give me permission to talk, it would, at least, give you an idea of the importance of all this." James popped in. "Cyntha's analysis of the cost of all this indicates the importance. The big question is why." I studied them all a moment. Cynthia and James were determined and Mac appeared to be in shock. I decided what the hell? "My instructions were not to dwell on that aspect but you should know that no matter what the public perception, I firmly believe that the GL is much more critical to the world than is generally believed. He's not just some politician that happened along." After a little thought, I added, "I also think, my solemn instructions on the subject, not withstanding, that if any of this got outside these four walls, it would do great damage." James and Cynthia stared at one another a long moment, then Cynthia said. "I think we've got something you should see. Then James got up and headed for the lab. Moments later, he came back carrying a strange metal and plastic box about ten centimeters square.

"We call it The Modulator." Cinthia said. "It changes the time frame in which the wearer operates." That threw me. Surely what she implied was not possible. When I said so, she shrugged. "All we know is that it works. Show her James." Suddenly, the contents of my purse appeared on the coffee table along with my service laser. I jumped to my feet in shock and only then realized my hands were cuffed with my own cuffs. "God!" I gasped. Mac finished for me "Damn!" Cynthia was very calmly handing me the key to my cuffs. Then I realized McClennan wasn't there - he was coming in the door with a large flat box. Cynthia smiled as I glanced around and getting up, said, "James went to the store and got us pizza. As soon as you get yourself back together, we can eat." "As she left the room, she tossed back, teasingly, over her shoulder, "James thought you probably had another gun somewhere but when we discussed this demonstration, it appeared that he might enjoy finding it too much. He's not allowed to grope anybody but me."

By the time we had finished our pizza, I had recovered enough to start to upbraid James for taking a chance of going out alone - when I realized the true implications of what he'd done and how little chance he took. The two of them had built the thing weeks ago and had been working on miniaturizing it since. I was sort of disgusted to realize that I had been helping them cover it all up without even knowing what it was I was doing. No wonder Justice thought they were so important. I wondered if he knew about it. Of course he did - or at least knew something of the sort was possible.

Suddenly, a lot of seemingly unrelated facts were no longer unrelated. I jumped up swearing and ran to the vid. When Levy came on, I shouted that he was to stop his Canadian team. It was his turn to swear. "Too late." he growled. "They've already been there." "And found nothing." I said, beginning to calm. "The guy buzzed the door open." he said, disgusted, "By the time they got in the door, though, he was gone." I swore again. "Then grab his kid if you can find her and the Long guy and bring them here. While you're at it," I added. "handcuff them to something heavy and solid and keep the keys to the cuffs in a totally separate place."

"Have you gone nuts, Gerald? That's kidnapping!" he rasped. "Damn it! Just do it - exactly that way! I may be stupid but not nuts!" I practically shouted, cursing myself. I tried to remain calm when he continued to protest. "Mark," You're covered under article four of the International Flight to Avoid Prosecution Treaty, just as I am. I'm certain that your instructions included that fact."

He was quiet a minute then said, "OK but I want it in writing that they are in unlawful flight." I sighed, but said, "Record." Then I authorized his actions. I went back and flopped down at the table in disgust.

"What makes you think that we aren't the only ones with access to a Modulator?" Cynthia asked calmly. With all the implications of this thing whirling around in my head, I was in no mood for calm. "Didn't it ever strike you as strange that someone was able to get into your apartment building and plant a bomb without being detected? Or that this CP guy has been involved in so many crimes but never actually seen? Surely those damn smart alec computers in there must have noticed. For that matter isn't it a little strange - though I have no idea how it's connected to your damn Modulator - how the same face shows up on drivers licenses and involved in crimes, for over a hundred years ?" Then I had another thought. "Who the hell was it you killed on the stairs. It couldn't be our CP. He was in Canada only a few minutes ago."

I looked at Cindy. It wasn't Katy who was the stupid one. It was us. Arthur had given us the facts weeks ago but we were too dumb to recognize them - especially dumb considering that Cindy and I had been discussing just such a problem for weeks. She looked pensive then paled slightly. "I never saw his face." she murmured. "He - well, he landed on his head." We sat around the table discussing the situation until almost one AM. It was obvious that CP had other help. Finally, the door announced "Mr. Levy." I noticed Katy verified him visually before opening the door. He thrust a noter at her. "Sign here." he said curtly. When she had, he handed her a ring of keys. "These came in a separate car." he growled. "I put them in the other apartment."

An almost unwilling, grin crept across his face. "They are not pleased. The girl swears like a trucker and is invoking all sorts of dire consequences against us." "I'll give her consequences." Katy grunted in reply. "You can go now. Leave them to me." "Better let Mac go with you." Levy said. "The guy's built like a wrestler." Turning back into the room, Katy said, with a terrible frown, "I doubt Mac would approve of my methods. And I haven't had any exercise in a month." I shivered at the look on her face. I'd never again think of her face as angelic. For the first time, I realized, what she had meant about her job. She calmly, took a weapon and holster off and casually, lifted her skirt to remove a small pistol and holster from her upper thigh. Dropping them on the table beside the door she went out. As she closed the door behind her, Cindy got up and headed for the computer room.

Mac spoke up for the first time. "I think, Miss Pachone that you don't want to listen to this." Cindy's voice was like ice. "Mac, James and I bear a great deal of responsibility for all that's going on. It's best that we understand exactly what we have been - and probably will be again - responsible for." We followed her into the computer room.

When I came into the room, the two were standing by the wall in the living room, attached to two huge blocks of concrete. I smiled. Mark might not agree with all this but he followed instructions well. I walked over to them and began to search for anything unusual. "Who the hell are you?" the man asked belligerently. "Probably your worst nightmare." I said as I reached up beneath the girl's dress. I gave him a grin. "I've always liked that line." She was clean. "My father will kill you for this!" she cried as I turned to Long. "If I don't kill him first." I said, conversationally as I patted the guy down. When I was sure they were both clean, I went over to the table and tossed the keys to the guy before I sat down. As he was freeing himself, I told them they were going to answer some questions and that I expected honest answers.

"Why should we tell a little bitch like you, anything?" Long grunted as he helped the girl free of her restraints. "Ignoring the fact that it would be the proper thing to do," I told him smiling, "because if you don't, I'll have to take actions that I really despise. Believe it or not, I do not enjoy inflicting pain on anyone, even scum like you." Apparently Long had a short temper for he, suddenly, charged across the room. If I had been still in the chair when he fell across the table, he would have done me a lot of harm. "I'm truly sorry we couldn't have this discussion in less trying circumstances." I said as I took a deep breath and went into automatic. I had underestimated the stamina of the two, especially the girl. It took almost three minutes before they were both subdued enough to have a conversation with.

Cindy and I were both fearful when the brawl began. Mac, I was surprised to see, was calm throughout the fight. "We're going to have a lot of cleaning up to do." he murmured, when the noises had finally stopped. Katy's voice was terrifying in its anger when it came through the speakers. "Do you know how many bones there are in a human body she asked? "Screw you!" Long gasped. "Who cares!" "Oh, I do." she replied calmly. "But I never got around to counting them. I intend to remedy that, counting I mean, by keeping track of each one I break. One question - one bone - or one answer. Were you in on your father's plotting?" Silence, then an audible snap and a scream from the girl. "That's one." After a pause, "Who has been paying you all these years?" More silence. This time it was Long who screamed after another snap. I felt my stomach turn over. Cindy's face was chalk white and Mac's wasn't much better.

It took two more snaps and screams before they both began to blubber out

124

answers to her questions. It took a long time for them to pour out everything they knew about what they had been doing. Finally, all was quiet. The next voice was Katy. "Mac, I know you're listening. Send up Stanley to guard these people till I can make arrangements for their transportation." "What are you going to do with us?" the girl whimpered. "Young lady," Katy replied in a subdued voice", when I finished splinting your fingers. I'll call for you to be picked up and taken someplace where your father can come and pick you up - both of you - if he wants to. I doubt if he will, though. He's a murderer and, probably, a cowardly one at that." We heard the door open. "Take care of them Stanley. I've secured them to the bed but be careful of their fingers. They hurt them in the scuffle."

When Katherine came back into the computer room she was carrying her laptop with her. I looked up at her and was shocked to see the difference in her. Her face was a closed book. She said simply, and without inflection, "I need to borrow your vid." Without waiting for a reply she quickly typed something on her keyboard. A few seconds later the vid screen lit up with a logo that all the people in the world recognized. A moment later, an office appeared with a large desk in the middle and really handsome man lounging behind it.

When he saw his audience, he frowned and quickly sat up. "Katherine," he said calmly, "Barbara's going to get jealous if we keep meeting like this." Katy's face didn't change. His did. His brows lowered and the frown became a scowl. He said nothing and Katy launched into a report of what she had done. She asked him to have her prisoners picked up for further interrogation - telling him that she thought they would be cooperative. It was complete except she left out the part about our project. He leaned back in the chair and stared at her a long time. Finally, a look of concern stole across his face. "Are you alright?" Katy actually shivered. "I'll get over it. It was necessary." "Because this CP person disappeared right in front of the agents - and you had no explanation for that." His quiet question obviously discomforted Katy.

She shivered again and glanced quickly at us. "Let me save you the necessity of refusing to answer that." he said, quietly. They've discovered the capability of their Modulator." I decided we couldn't let her take the blame for our not trusting her. I told him yes. He finally, leaned back in his chair and relaxed. "Miss Pachone," he said, "I'm sending a shuttle over for Katherine's prisoners. I wonder if you and Mr. McClennan, would mind sharing it with them on a flight back here? I think we need to talk." It was more of an order than a question and the stress of the last few hours hadn't helped my disposition much.

"We might consider it," I said "- if we knew who was asking - besides some door to door salesman who came to my father's house - and who we were supposed to talk to." I knew I wasn't being polite but, right then, I didn't care.

"Oh, how rude of me I know so much about you I forgot we hadn't officially met. My name is Justice Symons."

I gulped in shock. "The GL's Fist," as he was known, shouldn't be a handsome and charming fellow behind a desk. I guess I had imagined he would have a cloak and be holding a dagger. I should, I suppose, have guessed from the GL logo on the screen, but the name was enough to cool my anger in a hurry. The name was one, usually spoken with a whisper, of a man known only by reputation - the name of the Great Leader's head of security. The man, as far as I knew, had never appeared on the news but was reputed to be the actual power behind the World Federation.

He smiled that great smile again. "I'm not really an eater of children, Miss Pachone. Have Katy tell you about me sometime. In fact, to show my concern for your comfort, I realize it is very late where you are. If Katherine can maintain control of our misguided pair of conspirators until morning, I'll have the shuttle pick you up then. Would that be satisfactory?" All I could do was nod, stupidly. "Good." he smiled. "Shall we say ten hours in the morning?" I nodded again. "Do you have the assets to guard your guests till morning, Katherine?" Katy hesitated. I realized they were locked in her and Mac's apartment. "You can have our spare bedroom." I told her. "A weak smile touched her lips. "We'll make do, Justice." She turned and headed for the spare bedroom, Mac right behind her.

I seemed to awake out of a trance as the door closed behind me. Out of instinct, I whirled around to do battle. Just before I struck, I realized it was Mac standing there refusing to guard against what would have been a disabling blow if it had landed. I barely stopped myself in time. "Shit!" I grunted. "I can't even do that right." I knew the let down was coming but I just couldn't let him see that. "I'd best help watch them." I said heading for the door. He backed up against it and caught me in his arms. "You've done all you can tonight." he said gently. I had a terrible urge to hit him. When I started to protest, though, he put his finger to my lips. "Hush. It's just me and I've seen this before. Hell, I've even gone through it before. You can be the tough as nails Katherine Finnigan tomorrow. Tonight just let Katy takeover and give you some peace." My spate of curse words lost a lot of its punch as I started to bawl like a baby.

"They were just damned stupid kids!" I moaned. He pulled me close and just held me as I gave into the sobs of disgust at what I had done. When they finally began to abate, he murmured into my hair, "Hush, darling you did what had to be done. They may have been kids but they were involved in multiple murders and attempted murders. You can hate the need for it but I refuse to let you hate yourself for it." Damn it! I wondered if the man could read my mind. It could be, because he lifted me and carried me to the bed. Then, as if I were his child, he took off my skirt, shoes and blouse and turned back the covers. I shivered but grasped him around the neck. "The rest too" I whispered. He stared down at me a long moment then, nodding unsnapped my bra. When I lay back on the bed, he slipped off my panties and pulled the sheet up over me. In a moment the light went off and he crawled in beside me. Pulling me to him he held me tightly as I again began to sob. I marveled at the fact that even, skin to skin, he knew that sex was not what I needed. I fell asleep in the warmth of his arms.

Cindy and I were left standing looking at a blank vid screen. Without speaking she took my hand and we went to our room. After we undressed and stepped into the cleanser, she turned on the sonic cleaner - no long erotic shower for you tonight, I thought with a rueful chuckle. Seconds later we stepped out, and while I wiped the stubble off my face, she climbed into our bed. Moments later when I got in beside her, she cuddled up against me. Instead of a kiss, though, I got a question. "What do we do now?" I thought it was worth a shot. I squeezed her buttock and hummed a bar from an old song, I remembered - "Doing what comes naturally." She actually giggled. "You're a rat - and your suggestion sounds wonderful-". "But?" I chuckled. "I'm pretty sure I heard a 'but' in there." "OK, rat!" she laughed, "But only if you can tell me with a straight face, that I'm the only thing on your mind." "With your naked body pushed up against me, how could you doubt it?" She drew back her head and looked at me.

"You didn't answer me." she murmured. I gave up. "Alright - well, we're going to take a ride tomorrow to meet our Great Leader   - and I haven't the slightest idea after that. It's obvious our great secret isn't so secret." "It might not even be great." she said. "If there's one more, there's probably more than that." "So, I guess, the question is what he intends to do with us?" "Well, whatever it is, I guess we'll know tomorrow." she whispered, cuddling closer to me. In all the stories the hero and heroine always made passionate love the night before the end. I guess I didn't feel like a hero because when she began to snore softly. I fell asleep too.

Tuesday January 11, 2058

It had already been a hectic morning when we settled back in the seats of the shuttle for takeoff. Cindy had been ready to go and had the brewer going before I managed to even dress. Katherine seemed to have recovered overnight and seemed her old watchful self when she came out. Her first order of business was to check on the prisoners. She was having a cup of coffee when Mac came out and she smiled up at him as he came to the table. She then blushed as if ashamed of the smile when Cindy raised an eyebrow. There had been eight of Levy's agents at the door with four town flitters when we came down. She and I, along with Katy and Mac got in one while they shoved the two captives in another, then with a flitter in front and behind we went to the shuttle port.

Once inside the waiting shuttle, I was surprised when in the middle of its spiel the shuttle automatic pilot said our flight time would be one hour and seven minutes. I sat up and looked around. There had been nothing special about the outside configuration of the shuttle but a "standard" could never make that fast a trip. I flipped on the internal commo and dialed up specs. Sure enough we were riding in a Class X. There weren't more than a dozen or so in the world, almost all assigned to high government officials. It wasn't the GL's official shuttle because that one had his logo on the sides. Still it indicated the importance of what was happening.

When we stepped down from the shuttle an hour and seven minutes later atop a large building, four large men, in the black garb of the GL's personal guard were there. With visors down over their faces so they looked like robots, they came up, grabbed our prisoners and herded them off down a flight of stairs. We didn't even have time to stare out over Paris before another - with visor up - stepped up and said he would take us to our "appointment". We were shepherded to a lift that dropped us, swiftly down to open on a brightly lit, if plain hallway. The office at the end was the one we had seen in the vid yesterday and the man behind the desk was getting up to meet us with his hand outstretched.

"Mr. McClennan and Miss Pachone", the man said jovially and surprised me by lifting my hand to kiss it. "We're pretty informal around here so if I may call you James and Cynthia, perhaps you could call me Justice." With a grin, he added, "I dislike Jud as much as you two hate your diminutives." He shook James's hand and, with a twinkle in his eye, squeezed mine before turning to Katy. I was going to find it very hard to distrust this man. "Katy!" he said softly as he raised her hand to his lips, "Was it a bad night?" "Not at all!" Katy said, archly - and with a bit more emphasis than expected. He only smiled. "Sometimes our duty is more difficult than we would like." he murmured. Then turning, he said, and you must be "McKinsey Thuringen. May I call you Mac as everyone else must do?" Mac nodded a bit warily. "Good! Then why don't we go on in to see the GL - Jonha and Suzanne? They have been anxious to meet you." I was taken aback by the name. "Jonha ?" I asked. Symons - Justice smiled. "Well that silly name of his was fine when he was a Sino-Japanese war lord but no matter what anyone thinks he was never

129

a Samurai."

   We were ushered into a large room with glass on two sides and comfortable armchairs   arranged in several conversation groups. I couldn't help looking around as we were introduced to the GL and his wife. I was surprised. I expected them to be much older. Mrs - Suzanne saw my gaze and, grinning, said, "We though it better to meet you here in the apartment rather than in Jonha's office. He has terrible taste in furnishings and won't let me touch it." She led me to a large chair and began with the weather while the rest moved into other chairs in the grouping. Soon the conversation began to seem as if we were just a group of friends that hadn't seen each other in a while. Even Mac had relaxed.

   I noticed, however, that James hadn't. When the conversation finally turned to the Modulator, he continued to be unusually reserved. Did he still harbor the feeling that the thing was my idea? When I started to explain how we had come upon the thing, he interrupted me. "One moment, Cynthia." I, immediately, caught the formal use of my name. Turning to the GL, he said, "Sir, I have a little problem. I've had a strange feeling, since Mr. Symons brought us here that something was not quite right." He had a very serious look on his face, one that I had seen often enough. "I don't mean to imply," he continued, "that we have been lied to, but there is something that, I think, needs to be cleared up - though, I have to admit, that I don't know what."

   Suzanne's eyes flared and the GL's brow lowered. Oh God! What have we done now? Katy and Mac, also seemed to be a bit shocked as, no doubt, I did. James was almost invariably polite except when in the throes of his "wrongness mode". Symons seemed to be the only one unaffected. Quietly but with a slight smile, he said, to the GL, "The only things we discussed were your war lord status and our informality." Suzanne looked down at her hands and the GL's eyes opened wide. Finally, he said, "Well, there's not much to be said for the Samurai. The title was useful for awhile but almost forgotten now. We're generally called just Jonha and Suzanne. As for formality, if you wish - well, you could call us Mr. and Mrs. Johnson, I suppose." James's face cleared immediately but my mouth dropped open - Another of Arthur's coincidences. When I looked up Justice was smiling at me. He gave a very slight nod.

   "Darling!" James was kneeling in front of me. Had I really fainted?   "Are you alright? You're pale as a ghost." I sat up and noticed the stain on the carpet, alongside my coffee cup. I started to apologize and feeling like an idiot, began to cry. "It's alright, Darling!" James said. "It'll clean up fine." The thought of having a hysterical fit over a coffee cup, was so hilarious that I burst out laughing. Tears still running down my face I could almost read James's mind as he tried to calculate if it were my time of the month again. Then I thought of Arthur's big wall and laughed louder. Finally, I began to think of the fact that James shouldn't have to put up with a hysterical wife at a time like this and my laughter subsided.

   "Could I get you something dear?" Suzanne's worried voice. I nodded, my laughter dying off to a chuckle or two. "If I could have another cup of coffee, I'll try not to spill it this time." James still looked worried. "Are you sure you're OK?" When I nodded, trying to think of how to handle this. He asked me the question. I looked up at Jonha and Suzanne. Their faces were stony, though I spied a glistening in Suzanne's eye.

   I touched James's face and said, "Darling remember Arthur's remark about coincidence? What was your mother's name? " He frowned. "Why you know that, Judith Rando - " his voice stopped and it was his turn to turn pale. He stared up at me. "That's why it was wrong." he whispered. He turned, unbelieving, to Jonha and Suzanne. She, with a tear, now running down her cheek, said in a very quiet voice. "Maylin was our Daughter, James.

"My God" Mac burst out! "This - no one would ever believe his genealogy." Katy patted his leg and "shushed" at him. I was greatly relieved to see that James seemed to recover quickly. A grin started on his face. "He's right, though." he grunted as the grin broadened and he turned to me. "I hope I'm not going to find out that you're my sister." That got to me. I had to laugh again - perhaps it was just relief, but soon everyone followed - even Suzanne, though she still had a few tears.

When order had finally been restored, Jonha had decreed that we all needed more than coffee. So minutes later, we were once again in our places, though, James had crowded in beside me in the big arm chair. Jonha began to speak. "James, Suzanne is as happy as a grandmother can be but I'll admit that I had planned, for what, at the time seemed to be very good reasons, that this revelation be delayed a bit." James frowned. "Could I ask why?" "Before I answer that, could we discuss the Modulator a bit? I promise I'll get back to your question later." James nodded. "I need to know how you envision the thing should be used. I assume you have considered that?"

James looked at me with a rueful smile. "At great length" I replied, "without any real, or at least practical, results." James took it up. "Until yesterday, we had assumed no one else had one. The possibility of it becoming public knowledge was a big problem. There seemed to be many good and productive uses to which it could be put but most involved letting the secret out. The rest involved becoming some sort of vigilante." His brow was furrowed in thought. "I guess, since it is not really a secret anymore we need to rethink the problem." I felt I needed to help him out and said that we weren't comfortable with the vigilante role   and weren't really suited to lead some sort of modern group of "merry men" like a new version of Robin Hood. "Engineers and scientists have a very poor record   when it comes with dealing in human affairs." I ended sort of lamely.

I studied the girl carefully. It was the first time I'd met Art's daughter and she was a true beauty – with an, obviously, superior brain. "You never considered how rich you could become using its power?"

I laughed. "James can't even keep up with how much money he has and my father can't figure out how to give money away as fast as he makes it." Jonha smiled at that and looked over at James.

I couldn't help but be embarrassed. "As an example of our brilliance," I said, "we figured we could stop a few minor wars - Israel and Syria, for example. We could, perhaps, convince the leaders we were supermen who could kill them if they didn't stop. There were two problems. If they didn't we might have to do that and I'm not sure either of us are capable of it. Secondly, most wars, today, are the results of age old hatreds and the leaders are probably mostly unable to stop the fighting if they wanted to. I guess, for now, the best use of it would be to try and stop the ones who are using it against us. That's sort of self serving but I'm not willing to let Cindy continue to be a target of some mad man."

Suzanne and Jonha both smiled and with a chuckle she said, "You two show great perception for a pair of engineer slash scientists." Jonha's smile broadened. "What

131

if I said, there were very few who could actually use the modulator?" "It would be a relief." "Would you believe me?" "Maybe I just want it to be true, but, yes. I believe you." "How about if I said that the continued development of the Modulator is more important than any use you could make of it?" I caught a sudden twitch on the part of Justice, as James frowned again.

"It sounds like you're a scientist too. They're usually the ones that don't care about how the things they discover are used."

"But do you believe me when I say that?" James looked up at him and nodded.

I was tired of James being on the spot. "When James says something is right, it's - well, he's never wrong." I blurted. His eyes still on James, Jonha said, "You're NEVER wrong?" James actually blushed. "Not a bit. I'm often wrong but when I am, or someone else is, I always know it." "How?" James ducked his head, then lifted it and looking Jonha in the eye, said, "I don't know. I just do." I tried to help. "He calls it his wrongness mode. When it happens he knows - and he always knows. He may not know what exactly is wrong but he knows it is. It was like when he came into this room. I could tell he was very uneasy but neither of us knew exactly why. He just knew something was wrong. Why are you badgering him about this?"
"I apologize" Jonha replied." I am leading up to the answer of some of his previous questions and I wanted to make sure he could accept them." "The answer to your question is that I don't dare answer it. How do you feel about that?" James still looking him straight in the eye, said, "I don't care for it - but I think you believe it." "How about what I said about development of the Modulator?" James just nodded, never dropping his eyes. "OK. Let's try something else. Why do you suppose I believe your motives?" I knew that answer without doubt. "Because James's gift is genetic." I blurted. "Also you should not have mentioned the development of the Modulator." Jonha turned to me with a questioning look. "Are you too, gifted - or cursed?" he asked calmly. I had to laugh. "The first was simple knowing who his grandfather is." "And the second?" I grinned. "I thought it was going to be Justice that fainted when you said it."
Jonha looked over at Justice and laughed out loud. "I think - Justice, we're going to have to have Katherine give you some inscrutability pills." Justice actually looked abashed. Turning back to me, he said, "You are probably right. Without a lot of testing we can't be sure but all indications point to it back to my question, though. Are you gifted?" That was a surprise and I told him that I didn't think so. He smiled and retorted, "Then how did you know to jump out of that window? Also, if the perceptiveness you've shown in the last hour is any indication, you've got a bit of a gift too."

Holding up my hand to stop any reply, I turned down a finger. "One, you immediately, recognized the Johnson name and applied it to James. Two, you recognized the correlation between James' gift and the questions I asked. Three, you recognized the problem with my remark on the modulator. Now all this could be simply an extraordinary grasp of human reactions but that doesn't explain how you knew to leap out of a third story window to save your life."
The girl looked perplexed and I had to grin. "You should know that I have seen the tape of the interview at the New Houston Station. You, obviously, recognized the

validity of the investigator's remark relative to your saving yourself. What did you think at that moment?" She was frowning now, but she looked up at me and answered honestly. "I don't know, exactly. It was like the times we couldn't solve a problem with the Modulator. I knew he was right and that there was something I was missing. I just didn't know what." I took a chance - no use in letting all the cats out of the bag. "Have either of your parents shown an unusual perceptiveness - for lack of a better word?" She started to shake her head then nodded.

"Mom, tends to always know what daddy is thinking and you should have heard her when she met James. It was like she'd read his mind." "Like mother like daughter." James growled under his breath. I had to laugh. "Well, perhaps you should think about that aspect of your makeup a bit too."

We spent most of the day, with time out for lunch - which Cindy, as usual, demolished - answering questions. When we had to tell them about our "street reforms" of the last few weeks, Katy and Mac were aghast. Our ideas on stopping the Middle East war by spiking cannons drew a laugh. The GL smiled and Suzanne cringed at the idea of going into the headquarters of the warring leaders and convincing them we were aliens come to make them stop fighting.

"James, as grandparents," and turning his smile on Cindy, "- and future grandparents in law - your activities scare us to death. As The GL, I can't condone your street activities - though I can't say I disapprove. As for spiking guns on a battle field - well the logistics of that are pretty formidable and it would take accomplished actors to convince anyone that Cynthia is an alien. Let me ask you, though. How do you feel about them? - aliens, I mean."

It was our turn to be embarrassed. James raised his eyebrows. Before I answered, Jonha said, gently, "I thought as much. You know, you two have an almost unprecedented power in your hands. What you do with it will mostly depend upon your own ideas of right and wrong. A good thing to keep in mind is that if it doesn't feel right it probably isn't. It's not just a matter of scarring your knuckles. It's a matter of scarring your soul." In a fit of frustration, I offered to give the Modulator to him. With a weak smile, he said that they would be of very little use to him for the same reasons we had agonized over.

"Morality and judgment can't be imposed from the outside. It must come from within." "You mean we have to convert the entire world to - to what ? - our idea of morality?" I grunted in disgust. Another rueful smile. "No just the leaders of the world - or, at least, the dominant ones. Those that can't be converted will have to be removed." When I asked him if he meant assassinations and if so, why he didn't do it - that he was the only thing that passed for a leader today - and if rumor had it right, he could manage assassinations if he had to.

I just smiled again and said that rumors were seldom true, that assassinations seldom produced decent results, and - surprisingly - that he wasn't really the leader - only a caretaker. "Tell me James," I continued. "Who would you assassinate in the Middle East to solve that problem over there?"

133

I had to think about that. Obviously, the assassination of any of the leaders would probably just inflame the area more. It was really the people involved that had been driving that sputtering regional debacle for over a hundred years. Age old hatreds inflamed by fanatics - in that case racial and religious fanatics were the driving force. When I couldn't answer, he said, "James, you and Cynthia are scientists. Stick to what you do best. Until you understand the Modulator, you can't determine how to use it. I would like to say that is your only priority but that wouldn't be correct. You have to stay alive. To do that, you need to neutralize your enemies. I'll do what I can to help. Arthur will find that he now has access to any part of our data base that might help in that." "Better not leave Cindi out." Cindy muttered under her breath. Jonha laughed out loud. "I wouldn't think of it - especially since our systems engineer is frothing at the mouth to examine Cindi."

I happened to be looking at Justice at the time and was surprised to see him almost laugh. He was staring at Cindy. Looking over at her I could see a frown on her face. Jonha was talking again, though, and I had to listen. "- your job, I suppose." I had missed the first part but he was looking at Katie. "We'll be happy, of course, to cover your fees." She was frowning too. "Justice may have brokered this job but I told him I don't work for the government. Mr. Pachone can take care of my expenses - including my home in Hong Kong - and James can afford my fee." Turning to me, "It'll be One New Dollar a year as your Security Consultant." She grinned at me. "You'll have to pay Mac as my assistant, though. I don't know what he's getting with Levy but you'll have to top it by, at least, twenty percent." It was a surprising offer considering what I knew of her normal fees but no one objected. "Well," Jonha said, "I guess everything is settled then.

"Not Quite!" Everyone - except Justice - turned in surprise - more at Cindy's tone than her words. She was still frowning. "Your systems engineer only wants to study Cindi? Not Arthur?" Justice laughed out loud and Jonha turned to him as if he'd like to belt him. Turning back, he grunted, "Justice often likes to see me embarrassed." "It's because Arthur belongs to you." Cindy stated in a tone brooking no argument. Jonha stared at her a moment and finally said. "Your father was given a government computer for services he performed for us. He let you use it. We know what happened to that computer. When it became Arthur, which he shouldn't have been able to do, he no longer belongs to anyone but himself. He and, apparently, Cindi are yours to take care of now, much as you would take care of your own children. We use the technical term Artificial Intelligences or AI for short. They are, however, as alive as we are – just without the bodies." "Corporeal bodies?" Susanne murmured. Jonha looked chagrinned. "Yes." He said. You need to meet Susanne II."

"You rang your mightiness?"

A gorgeous woman, Susanne's apparent twin, materialized on the sofa next to Susanne – who smirked. "You will find their sarcasm wearing at times." He grumbled. Your responsibility, though, is to protect them and help them. You may, of course, ignore their counsel - much as most parents do their children - at your own risk." Cindy looked up at me, her eyes sparkling. "Darling," she pretended to gush. "We're parents and not even married yet. Mother will be so shocked." "To answer your question," Jonha continued ignoring HER sarcasm. "James, Milam - Mister Walker - wants to find out how a relatively modest computer can be upgraded to AI Status. Arthur's conversion, while

134

not simple to accomplish, is understandable. Cindi's is not supposed to be possible."

I was embarrassed when the GL - Jonha - turned to Katy and said, "Miss Finnigan, I think, and you have probably already noted that these two young people - as do most their age - have the impression that they are invulnerable and immortal. While you aren't that much older than they, I have it on good authority, that you are more realistic. I want to impress upon you and Mister Thurlingen that no matter what their desires, their safety is of utmost importance - and not just to their parents and grandparents. Recognizing your distaste for governmental customers, you have only to ask and whatever resources I can bring to bear will be available to you if you need them." Katy and Mac had been quiet during the entire interview. Now she looked thoughtful but, after a moment's hesitation, simply nodded.

Thursday Jan 13

We came home from Paris, timing our arrival in New Houston for darkness, and since we had already notified BSG that our return would be unknown, we decided to go on to Westport for the wedding planning. We, of course, had a lot to tell my parents about today also since, as our new "Security Staff", Katy and Mac, obviously, needed Modulators, I put the nanotechs to work as soon as we got home. On Wednesday, Mr. Levy called and said that the police investigators had turned up a smudgy picture on one frame of the security camera in Cindy's hallway showing a man bending down in front of her door seconds before the bomb exploded, placing it on the floor. They were at a loss to explain why only one frame showed him.

Of course, we now knew why but it was too sensitive to explain. Arthur and Cindi also reported that several attempts to check on James's background had been made recently - other than the normal police inquiries. They felt that the facts had not yet been uncovered but that it was obvious that someone had become very interested in him as well as me. They felt that, from now on, there was a high probability that both of us would be targets for harm.

Since the nanotech circuit designer, already had the program for growing the Modulator circuitry and the rudimentary capability for producing them in the online Circuit creator, Cindi could have monitored the progress but we felt we needed those two Modulators before we left for Westport. Still it was Thursday before she opened the Creator and produced the two Modulators. We were at the shuttle port boarding a Model 10 Shuttle at ten O'clock that morning, we - including Katy and Mac of course - headed for Westport. We were cleared for immediate departure and after A second large breakfast and a couple of drinks we were letting down at Westport.

Mrs. Pachone kissed me soundly when we got off the shuttle. Her dad shook my hand, observing that we appeared to be none the worse for wear after our "month long orgy". "If Cynthia has been as demanding as she is about everything else perhaps you would like separate bedrooms tonight." I blushed. Cynthia looked daggers at him. "If you're not careful, I'll talk mother into using my old room tonight." She growled, before kissing him delightedly. "Not the guest room?" he asked. "Of course not! That's where Katy and Mac will stay." That raised a couple of eyebrows on Art and Lil. We were in Cindy's parent's living room, her parents on recliners, us on the love seat and Katy and Mac on the couch when the subject of the fire came up again. Cindy was curled up, unashamedly, beside me and squeezed my hand. It was Cindy's mother, not her father, who brought it up. We, again, went over the events quickly, but her father began to ask some very searching questions - I had no doubt that he had a full report from our "protection" back home - and from some of the questions, it was obvious that he also had a complete copy of the official records. We also told them of our trip to Paris.

That was a surprise to them, that we would have an interview with the GL. He questioned me at length about my "Wrongness mode" - and with none of the skepticism I had come to expect from those who, in the past, had heard my, somewhat embarrassing explanation. I had left out the mention of the GL's capability and Cindy's remark about genealogy and genetics.

He was very quiet for long moments after we had finished. Finally, he said, very gently, "So you're something of a fortune teller and my daughter's a genius clairvoyant. That doesn't seem to be much of a reason for someone trying to murder her." There it was - the word that no one had spoken up until now, the word that was hanging over our heads like the Sword of Damocles - "murder". We'd discussed the attempts on her life for hours but that word had never been spoken. Cindy and I, both, flinched. She looked up at me and I nodded for her to go ahead.

"Well, Daddy," she said softly, "James has invented a sort of time machine." I protested that "We" not "I" had invented it and that it really wasn't a time machine but a sort of time adjuster. "We call it a Modulator." We both paused, expecting some reaction of disbelief. It didn't come. Finally, her father simply asked, "OK. Is that all? How did you - invent - this time adjuster and just how does it work?" We explained about the Modulator and what we knew, so far, about its operation. We demonstrated it by turning ourselves up into fast time and going into the kitchen to refresh all our drinks.

We got ourselves back to normal time in the kitchen so the liquids would pour and back to fast time before we came out with the glasses. "Good thing you got rid of that long delay." I muttered. "Still got the short one though." she replied. Cindy's mother's mouth dropped open in shock when we sat back down with the tray of drinks, but her father simply said, "Interesting. Now, just what do you intend to do with this thing?" It was embarrassing to tell someone else, especially them, what we had been agonizing over for days. Our ideas seemed even more blatantly stupid than when brought it out in the open a second time.

Mr. Pachone pondered our ideas for a few moments and asked if we would like comments. We both nodded, nervously. "Well," he began, "The GL's right about wars and such. At least as dangerous would be robbery of Mob run casinos. I assume he mentioned that you could, no doubt, succeed but that those people have a great deal of experience at tracking down and dealing with those who trifle with them. As for better understanding the devices if he thought it the most important who are we to argue? It might, also due to security problems, be a good idea to gracefully and as inconspicuously as possible, find new employment - preferably in a totally new city. Finally, since it is highly possible that your discovery is the reason for the murder attempts, a really safe place should be found where you could run in case things got too hot. Let me think on this last for awhile. Levy's crew should be adequate for the time being. You think on the rest."

It was a wonderful week. The subject of the Modulator didn't come up again and both of us were willing to leave it at that. Cindy and her mother spent a lot of time planning a wedding. Art and Lil Pachone were as great a set of future "in laws" as a man could ask for. They were two, "down to earth" people who enjoyed life and each other.

136

Obviously well off, Art liked to quote an old Vid commercial he'd seen once in an archive showing. He got his money "the old fashioned way; he earned it". I didn't realize till we were on the way home, how <u>much</u> he'd earned. I was sad to realize how sorry I was that my parents were not alive to meet them. Our wedding was to be lavish. "Of course," He told me that all a groom had to do was follow instructions. All the women believe that the groom and father of the bride are just necessary distractions to be seen and not heard. That was when I got "the talk." "Normally, a father would insist on knowing his prospective son in laws prospects." he remarked one night over a glass of very good brandy. Cindy and her mother were out doing something or another that women do under the circumstances. "However," he laughed and told me, as he was sure I knew he already knew all of that. "Except I'd hope someday you'd feel free to enlighten me on some peculiar aspects of your finances. Secrets that I can't determine drive me crazy." I knew he was talking about that shadowy trust fund and, told him that if he ever found out, I wish he'd let me know. I didn't say that I suspected that I now knew the source - thinking I should have asked Jonha about it. He'd insisted, afterwards, on giving me, as Cynthia's future "lord and master" (we'd both laughed over that) a quick rundown on Cindy's economic status and a general picture of his.

No financial genius, I still realized that the property and other assets listed must amount to a great number of millions, if not billions, of new dollars. I was sort of shocked that he'd given me such trust even before the wedding. Even more disturbing, was the fact that he agreed with the private detective, I had hired, that my birth parents had been deliberately killed. Even more interesting, since the detective hadn't gone into details of his investigation - just the results - was the lengths my adopted family had gone to in order to cover up the facts of my birth. It was much later before I found out just how much scrutiny my life had been under for a number of months.

We'd gone to Westport, expecting a quiet ceremony in the courthouse. We left, committed to a huge one in the Catholic Cathedral with at least several hundred guests. Preparations couldn't possibly be completed before June. When, I told them that I had never even been in a Catholic Church, they hauled us off to services - mass - on Sunday. The service was certainly different from what I had been used to as a kid - a bit long on ceremony for a descendant of good Scots Irish Presbyterians but I could probably live with it if Cindy wanted to. The Banns were announced at the end of the ceremony. I had always assumed that Catholics were a stodgy bunch, but the Cardinal, who conducted the service, announced that "Miss Cynthia Margarite Pachone has verified her intention to marry Mr. James McClennan - an Irish heathen." That got a laugh. "Let us make him feel at home in our midst. Cynthia assures me that he does not have horns or a tail." We had to stand with him at the door as the parishioners filed out. It seemed that I must have shaken hands with all thousand of them, most with a good natured comment on my lack of "true faith."

One little girl, shyly inched around to assure herself that I didn't, in fact, have a tail. As it turned out, Cindy and her family were not big church goers but the Cardinal was a good friend of theirs and seemed to have a good sense of humor about his "backsliding" members. That's when I found out that he, himself, would be performing the ceremony. Since I was a "heathen" - he chuckled when he said that - it wouldn't be a full mass, but it would, at least, put an end to "one of Cynthia's undoubtedly numerous sins". He laughed out loud when she blushed - she had gone to confession that morning for the first time in several years. Art and Lil had, apparently, little worry that their daughter would be "living in sin" until June. Tuesday afternoon Art insisted that it would more fun that way anyway. "After they get that ring on, sex is just a tool they use in the rest of their lifelong work of reforming you." he chuckled. "Daddy," Cindy laughed as she kissed him goodbye, "Remember the thin walls? If that were the truth, you'd be at least a bishop by now."

Tuesday January 20, 2058

Katy and Mac had breathed an audible sigh of relief when Art's flitter lifted off from the shuttle port. They had been very nervous in the crowds both inside and out of the Church and the idea of a public announcement relative to us made them pale at the thought. We arrived after dark at the New Houston shuttle port without incident, though, and were whisked away home in one of Levy's armored town flitters. After checking in with Arthur and Cindi, we headed off to bed. There my newly official fiancée jumped atop me and announced it was time to begin reforming me. Minutes later I told her I'd agree to anything as long as she didn't stop what she was doing - She didn't.

It was almost nine when we got up. Cindy had insisted on another reform session when we woke up and after a long shower for two, she called Katy and invited her and Mac over for breakfast. It turned out that they had slept in too - till almost seven - and just returned from a five mile run. I know I must have looked like a fool when I opened the door for them. I was so used to seeing Katy in her "uniform" - dark jeans and shirt - that the sight of her in white hip hugging short shorts and matching cropped blouse threw me. Cindy took one look and asked her where she could carry her gun? With a laugh, she whipped out a tiny pistol from beneath the top. Small as it was, I couldn't imagine how the thing could have been concealed under so little fabric. I couldn't help staring at her during breakfast. She had been intimidating in her "uniform". In that outfit, she looked like a teenager. It was hard to reconcile the appearance with the assassin. It was a guilty face I turned to Cindy when she purred, "Darling, I think that outfit was worn to seduce Mac - not you. Am I going to have to undress to get your attention?" It was the two women who laughed. The men just looked embarrassed.

After breakfast we retired to the computer room - we probably should call it Arthur and Cindi's room - to map out a plan of action. We agreed that there were several, almost equally important things that needed doing. We had to find the secrets of the Modulator (it was obvious that there were aspects to it that we hadn't determined). We had to protect ourselves - and to do that - end the threat of our nemesis CP. No matter what Cindy's parents and the GL thought, Cindy and I believed we could stop the Israeli/Syria war by convincing the leaders they had to make peace. Katy and Mac weren't happy with the third item but, reluctantly, agreed to help. As for the first two jobs, number one was, obviously, Cindy and mine and the number two, theirs. They insisted, though, that we let them determine the feasibility of the third job and, if it were doable, the tactics of it. In the argument that ensued, they pointed out that the GL had considered the first task the most important and that we couldn't afford to neglect it. With a lot of grumbling, we agreed. Cindi and Arthur chimed in to point out that we had left them out of our plans. We assured them that we had not. They would, obviously, be needed for all three.

Sunday March 1

A month later we seemed to have accomplished nothing. The illusive, CP had not been found. Also Cindy and I were even sleeping in Fast Time - as we now called it - so we could work all night on the Modulator. We were still, though, no further along with understanding our new toy. Then, on a Sunday night, when Cindy and I along with Katy and Mac were having dinner at a local Chinese restaurant - which they had carefully inspected ahead of time - Cindy, in the middle of a conversation, stopped a talk about the prevalence of vid porn with "Where does the power come from ?" We all looked at her like she was crazy before it dawned on us that she was talking about the Modulator, not gratuitous sex. It was actually a question that had puzzled us off and on but we had ignored for some reason. Katy laughed and said, "I thought it was James who got that glassy look in his eye at the most inopportune times." Embarrassed, Cindy apologized and dinner went on. On the way home, we decided to walk. Katy, trying hard not to show her exasperation, had a quick conversation with her collar button and finally agreed. I assumed therefore that we had a half dozen agents combing the way ahead of and behind us but, thankfully, they kept out of sight and we were able to pretend that it was just a normal stroll in the moonlight.

Just before we reached the apartment, Cindy, who had been very quiet the entire time, looked at Mac and asked how he was managing with his children. "They're with their grandmother until this job is over." he said quietly. "I hope you don't think I'm butting in," she said, "but isn't that hard on all of you?" He shrugged, resignedly. "You know, by now, that this job might last a long time. Why don't you bring them in to live with you? Surely space can be found in our building for all of you. One less apartment full of security types won't degrade security that much."

I caught the guilty glance he flashed at Katy. "Oh come on!" I said. "Surely they must know about you and Katherine by now - or if they don't, they should." By then we were at the apartment house door and I suddenly blushed. "Oh hell I shouldn't be getting in your business! I'm sorry. I forgot about teenagers and resentments and such." "Oh no" Katy said quickly! "They're wonderful girls - "And they loved Katy." Mac broke in. "It's not them. It's Katy. She thinks she'd be a bad influence on them." "What!"

Cindy and I gasped together. "Why?" Katherine looked down at the ground. In a very small voice, she said, "Come on! You both know what I am, what I've done. I'd be terrified to have children grow up around someone in my line of work." "Bullshit!" Mac exclaimed. "You're the most moral person I know. Maybe not the most legal one but who cares! The girls love you and you them! I love you! I can't imagine a better person to look up to. We don't have to send them to assassin school just to live with us."

Oh God! What had I done? I tried to apologize for starting this but finally James and I left them to settle the fight I had provoked. As soon as the door closed I turned to him and blubbered like a baby. "Oh come on Cindy." he muttered. "This has been coming on for awhile. You just set it off. You probably did them a favor in the long run." That didn't help. Finally he said we should go to bed and it would look better in the morning. Then I remembered why I had been paying so little attention and had opened my big mouth before putting my brain in gear. I tried to dry my eyes and told him that we couldn't. We had to work. When he said it could keep till morning, I explained that it couldn't because I had to look at our equations. "We've been ignoring too many facts." I told him. "The power the Modulator uses has to come from somewhere. Maybe it's not part of our real life system at all. The Modulator, itself, isn't. It, obviously affects time itself. How does it do that? Does it slow down the speed of light? We know - or believe - that can't be done but we know how to make time appear to do it if we go fast enough. If the Modulator is affecting time, where does the energy generated go?   Nothing is free. When we speed ourselves up in Fast Time, you'd expect us to burn up with all the extra energy we're expending. Why don't we?

Cindy, after that mad dissertation, began to scribble on the noter. As she worked, I could begin to see some method to her madness. Without slowing her entries, she headed for the computer room. Once inside, I told Cindi to take it off the noter and put it on the big screen. By now she was deep into electrical theory, adding data so fast I couldn't keep up. I never pretended to have the electronic skills that she had. Finally, with a note of triumph, she cried, "Here are the power supply equations for the Modulator . See where it takes us?"

The last line on the vid was a long line of electronic equations with an equal sign. On the right side of the equal sign were the basic transfinite equations that Silverman had been so proud of. All I could think of to say was, "Shit!" Only then did I notice how pale Cindy was. I grabbed for her and pulled her down on the couch beside me. Looking up, I realized it was already dawn. She'd been reeling off reams of math for almost seven hours. I kissed her and said, "Darling, that's an amazing performance but you need some Fast Time sleep." She didn't have the energy to even argue. I picked her up and carried her into the bedroom, telling Cindi, over my shoulder to check out all that math while we rested.

After I got Cindy undressed and in bed, I got her a glass of milk and a half dozen cookies. She was sound asleep by the time I strapped our new Modulators on our arms, undressed and climbed in beside her.

I watched in amazement as Mac flung open the apartment door and stalked in. It was a shock to find out that "The Ice Man"   as I had begun to think of him in my mind, had a temper. I had to smile a bit at the thought. Who did he think he was God's gift to me? I chuckled at the thought. Then I stopped smiling. How could I have let this happen? Knowing what I was, how could he have thought -? That thought stopped me cold! The question was how could I have let him believe? The answer was ridiculous.

Standing there in the empty hall, though, it was clear. Hard Headed Katy hadn't even noticed she was falling for a damned man. Son of a bitch! I couldn't let this happen. A dozen emotions followed in quick succession, each more frightening than the one before. How could I be a wife? A mother? Hell! How could I even be in love? I was Katherine Finnigan the baddest woman in the world. I was a woman without a conscience or scruples, sexually a slut, morally depraved and socially incompetent.

Damn! I shivered. Just the thought terrified me. No matter what anyone thought, I'd been frightened a lot of times - I've hated and lusted and done almost all the things a "nice girl" would never think of - but this! "Calm down Katy." I murmured to myself. "You've actually known this a long time. You just didn't want to admit it. This damned man has gotten to you. " Just then the damned man appeared back at the open door. "Well, are you coming in or not?" he growled. Then the scowl on his face, changed quickly to concern. "Are you alright?" I wanted to snap at him. Instead, to my disgust, I almost whined. "I - don't - well - Shit!"

Suddenly furious at myself, I practically shouted, "Of course! What makes you think I'm not?" The SOB actually laughed. "Just the fact that you're pale as a ghost and swaying like you're almost ready to fall over. Come on Katherine. If you're sick just say so. You don't have to be The Iron Maiden with me. Or is it the thought that you might be actually falling for a man – maybe even love him?" My fury slid away, leaving me trembling. I cursed the tears that came to my eyes. Suddenly, I was in his arms and he was trying to apologize. I tried to push him away. Damn! I should be able to kill the guy in seconds and couldn't even muster the strength to escape his arms. I felt as if I were standing aside watching some stupid school girl with her first crush. The idiot girl actually clung to him like some romance heroine as he lifted her and carried her into the apartment.

"I can't! You can't!" I whimpered like a damned fool. "We can't what?" he asked solicitously. "It's not love. It's – I don't know-". I was actually crying on his chest. He chuckled. Why didn't she clobber him for laughing at her? "If it's not, it's a pretty damned good imitation."

Katy clung to me for several minutes, then lifted her head and wiped her eyes. "Damn it, Mac! You know what I am. Hell, I kill people for a living. I'm a damned exhibitionist. I walk around my deck back home stark naked so that a dozen men in neighboring buildings who have permanently mounted telescopes can just watch me while I pose for them. I've gone to bed with half the good looking men in Hong Kong just for fun. I've even worked in Chinese brothels, really worked there, even in a harem once - all of it just to get close enough to kill a man. Shit! It seems like I've spent half my life on my back with some thug humping me."

"It's bad enough that you even let me meet your girls. To have them live with the likes of me would be an abomination." "Katherine," he whispered, "do you really think I don't know all about you? After all, I am a detective - and a damned good one." She looked up at me in surprise. "You don't really think I'd subject my girls to a woman with your reputation without some real thought, do you?" I kissed her lightly. "Darling, I can't say I'd like the thought of you doing some of those things again - and I think I'd put my foot down at parading around naked on your balcony - but you're the one I love. If I got you to be someone you're not, you wouldn't be the same - well -."

The rest of that sentence wouldn't seem to come to me. "Anyway," I finished lamely, "I suspect that we have signed on to this job for, as they once said during that old world war, the duration and six months, don't you? And if you do, god forbid, have to let yourself get shanghaied into a Chinese psychopath's harem to do it, then I'll just have to come help you get revenge." "Mac," she said quietly, "the girls wouldn't be safe with us." "As safe as they are out at the house with only two guards." I said, quietly.

Later as he lay beside me, resting from our exertions, he chuckled to himself. When I asked him what was so damned funny, he said. "I was just hoping you'd show me some of the tricks you learned in the harem. I punched him in the ribs. "Darling," I said, remembering that awful place. "In that harem none of the girls were over thirteen and all they could do was lay back and get raped - often repeatedly." "I'm sorry." he murmured. "I shouldn't have made a joke about it." It was my turn to laugh. "Oh shut up! Now the brothel was a different story. I had plenty of time to practice there and none of the customers complained." I licked his ear and rolling over atop him, whispered. "It's hard to explain, though. I think I'll just have to show you." And I did. He didn't complain either.

Monday March 2 2058

It was another full day of work for us. Katy and Mac were in their professional mode and never mentioned the previous night and we were too embarrassed to do so.

142

Looking back, though, when they left us at the door to the building, I noticed that he, unobtrusively, stroked her hand. It seemed a good sign. I mentioned it to James as we walked between our "clerks" to the elevator. He smiled and said, "They'll work it out." It was a long day. I found it hard to concentrate on business when I couldn't work on the Modulator. As we left the office, we were met by Mark's "backup team". They were Ann Fitzgerald and Sean O'Conner). I wondered if all Mark's employees were Scots and Irish). "Miss Finnigan and Mr. McKinsey were taking care of some personal business", we were told.

We were, thus, unprepared for the door to announce, "Miss. McKinsey ". James and I had just gotten home and kicked off our shoes. We looked at each other in astonishment. We were also unprepared for the tall slim blond teenager who stood barefoot at the door. It wasn't just her feet that were bare. She was damned near naked. Her cropped top was so short and her hip hugging shorts so tiny that the expanse of bare flat belly and naked long legs was stupefying. "Mom said to tell you that dinner is ready and that you don't have to put your shoes back on." She said with an unselfconscious and hoydenish grin. There was little doubt that she had reached that stage in her life that she wanted to shock grownups. She had the equipment to do it with too. Her breasts were small but, in that outfit, fit perfectly with her leggy beauty. "Mom?" I asked, incredulously, looking at James.

The girl blushed at that. "Well, Miss Finnigan, said I was really too tall to call her mom but I could if I wanted - and she's so swift! Even if she's not my real mom, she's too cool to call Katy." she gushed.

James, by now, was smiling. "And just what should we call you, Miss. McKinsey?" She blushed again. "Oh gosh I forgot. I'm Charley - well, actually, Charlene, but I prefer Charley." Getting my wits back, I finally, said, "OK, Charley, lead on." Once in the apartment, Charley introduced us to her sister, Julia - a slightly younger and barely more modest version of Charley. Mac sat at the table, his eyes dividing their time between Katy - in, of all things, an apron - and his "children". "James! Cynthia!" Katy called. "Come, sit down. Dinner will be ready in a moment. Mac, dear, get them some wine." I laughed as I sat down. "Katy, that doesn't look like a very substantial protective vest." "My clothes are determined by the danger presented" she laughed

"In this case hot water." James said with a grin, that he wasn't sure he was ready for a body guard's cooking. "Spoken like a man with a fixation on his flasher this in mock anger, I'll have you know, I've had several years instruction under one of my best friends. He is one of the best chef's in the world." Charley clapped her hands and cried. "By under, she means he was her lover for almost three years." "Charley!" Katy and Mac shouted simultaneously. More ominously, Mac asked how she knew that. The girl colored again. "I - well - read the report you left at home last month. It's alright! Julia and I think M - Katherine is the greatest. We were terrified just reading it but she was wonderful. All those kids she saved - and to get revenge like that - to cut off his -". "Enough!" Mac grunted. "Charley, you don't have to tell everything you know - especially about private matters you know better than to look at." "But Daddy!" she cried. "It's not like J - Mr. McClennan and Miss Pachone - were strangers. You said they were brave and brilliant and honest."

It was now our turn to blush. Katy came out of the kitchen carrying a large spoon. She circled an arm around Charley and said quietly, "Darling, young ladies mind their fathers." Charley looked up at her and murmured, "Yes Mom." Then she turned to us and apologized for being "a big mouth". "I wish I could be more like Julia. She's much more ladylike." Her contrite look was replaced by a wicked grin as she looked up at Katy. "But you did say your instructions came while you were UNDER him."

Mac looked as if he'd like to kill his daughter but, like the rest of us, including Katy, couldn't help a loud laugh. "Mac," she chuckled, "I think you're going to have to wash your daughter's mind out with soap." More soberly, she said, "Remember I told you this was a bad idea." That was when I noticed the hand stroking Charley's hair - the hand with the diamond ring on it. I couldn't help clapping my hands and jumping up to hug her. "Katy" I cried "how wonderful! How did you snag him? Is he that good in –"? Just then I remembered the girls "- to you?" I finished lamely, blushing like an idiot. Charley looked down at Katy with an angelic expression and quietly asked, "Yes. Is he Mom?" Katy slapped her, lightly, on the head. "Young lady, I have a really good notion as to how to clean up the dirty mind of a teen age girl. Now go take up the Bulgogi." Her tone was scary. Her eyes, though, held a softness I hadn't seen in them before as they followed the unafraid teenager, from the room. Katy was right though. No matter what her relationship with her teacher, she was a great cook. I wondered where she had gotten the ingredients for the Korean Stir Fry?

Wednesday, March 11, 2058

The next two weeks moved rather slowly especially as we spent several days In FT. We were beginning to get an inkling of how power was supplied to the Modulator. All equations and what few tests we could devise, pointed to it coming from what we began to call, the Zero Universe. At work we were producing nothing useful but that wasn't surprising since in the BSG everyone went, sometimes for months, without accomplishing much. Even more frustrating, was the fact that nothing more was forthcoming on our nemesis "CP". Either we had stopped all his access to BSG or our lack of work on the Modulator caused him to lose interest in our work. Cindi and Arthur still combed the world's databases for evidence of him but to no avail. All in all, a very boring time until it happened.

We had just gotten out of the flitter coming home from work when we were suddenly enveloped in a fine mist. I saw James fall flat, hitting his head on the curb. Then the world went dark. The next thing I knew, I was sitting on a couch in a strange room. There were three very large, very unpleasant looking men staring at me and another, rather dapper dark haired man sitting behind a desk in front of me, smiling. It wasn't a very welcoming smile. I realized my hands were tied behind my back and my clothes were in tatters. I could also see several bruises visible in some intimate places

"Well, Miss Pachone," he said. "I'm happy you finally decided to wake up. My name is Salvadore D'amato . I'm very sorry for the abrupt way you were invited but it seemed necessary. I also want to apologize for the actions of my men. They sometimes exceed their instructions around beautiful women I just want to find out some information for a client and I'm assured that either you or your - Mr. McClennan can supply it." Only then did I realize that my hands were tied behind my back. D'amato turned back to James standing, hands tied like mine before the desk. 'Or you can watch your wife become the main attraction of a gang bang." He said with a malicious grin. "She won't appreciate it much and probably the baby won't either."

144

Just then, a door flew open and a man rushed in. "Sir!" he cried. "The Skagway just caught fire and exploded!" Suddenly all was chaos as D'amato grabbed a phone and ordered us locked away in "the other room."

"Beemer, I'm glad you're back. Our agent in New Houston called on the vid a few moments ago and told me they had captured our targets. They were in the process of questioning them as we spoke." Alar looked very upset. I could imagine why. The thought of allowing that bunch of barbarians to have their way with any human was disconcerting even to me. Alar had been mostly an administrator while I had been the one to have to do all the unpleasant things. Over the years I had become somewhat accustomed to violence but never comfortable with it. I found out why his discomfort when he described the scene he had witnessed, as close to anger as I had ever seen him.

"I know! Alar Growled. That animal "called me while in the midst of ripping the clothes off the girl and brutally fondling her. He seemed positively pleased with himself and in my reaction to the scene. He did promise, though, to have the information before the day was out." Trying not to show my own revulsion, I said, "Good. Then the underworld will become the owners of the Modulator and put it to use in the best way to foil the plans of the watchers. I very much doubt that they will be able to overcome their reluctance to release the thing on their own. Even if they do, it will be enough to make sure they never are allowed to upgrade this place."

"Damn Beemer!" Alar gasped. "Don't you realize they intend to - dispose of those two - when they get their information – probably even – well torment them for fun as they do it?" I shivered at the thought, but restrained my queasy stomach. "Well," I told him. "It's too bad about that, but I've been faced with the problem of having to do it myself. It made me sick for almost a week afterwards but it must be done - better they do it than we have to." He looked at me as if he'd never known me before. "I think I need a tranquilizer." he said, turning to leave. I said I'd join him.

The door burst open on Katy and me. It was Ann. "They've gone!" She cried "kidnapped". Sean and Cecil are passed out on the pavement in front and there's a cop questioning people downstairs about a couple being carried off in a car right on the street - about ten minutes ago." We jumped up. "Find them!" Katy shouted. "Mac, Deploy everybody on the street. Ann, if you can't wake Sean up get his Modulator and give it to - Damn - it'll have to be -," She looked at me. I ran down the agents we had here. "Carl." I said. "OK, Carl. Ann, you get the car. From now on, everything we can do in FT we will move!" She ran into the hall and into Cynthia and James's apartment. When I caught up with her, she was talking to James's computer. "Yes, Katherine." Cindi said. "We did have some nearby sat phone traffic out front eleven point six minutes ago just a moment. A recorded voice came over the speaker. "Yes Sir, Mr. Damato. We have your packages. We'll be there in a few minutes."

Katy swore. "That son of a bitch! Where'd Salvadore D'amato get the balls to do something like this? His business is prostitution, gambling and low level mugging. Shit! James and Cindy's muggers! Cindi, activate the evacuation plan." She jumped up from the chair and we were downstairs in a flash. Ann and Carl were just pulling up in the office flitter. The one that brought Cindy and James home was still parked in the street with Sean passed out behind the wheel. A local cop had been shaking him. Katy rushed over to Ann. Go to the Skagway then the Diamond Lil. They belong to Damato and he may have taken them there. If they're not there, probably no one there this time of the day, but if there are, get them out and open the gas jets. Use your Balaclava's."

"Should be enough open flame in there to blow them up or burn them down when we go back to true time. That son of a bitch won't be back in the gambling business anymore anyway after I get hold of him. Let's us get to D'amato's house, Mac. Chances are that's where he'd take them for the protection he'd need to deal with them. Ann, when you finish Skagway and Diamond Lil start down the list of other D'amato's places. Do 'em all till you get some clue as to where they've been taken blow every one till they get the message. Evacuate quietly before the blow. Kill only if you have to. Be sure and leave a brotherhood calling card at each one. Let those other thugs sweat the problem a bit."

I took a breath and let my brain go back to work. "Come to think of it don't blow the brothels. Just grab any of his men and shut the places down. Too many chances of getting innocent people hurt." To Mac, I said more calmly, "The car's got plenty of firepower in it."

With that, she walked, quickly over to Carl's flitter and, ignoring the silent cop, hauled Carl out on the sidewalk. "Take care of him." she ordered over her shoulder at the three agents. As soon as I was in, she put the flitter in high gear and, kicking us off Fast Time, roared off. Looking back I saw another of our flitters vainly trying to keep up with Katy's mad dash for the suburbs.

As the flitter came near D'Amato's estate, a dull roar could be heard to the South. I glanced at his watch. "Three minutes. Not bad, even for you Katy. Have you got a plan for when we get to the estate? It's damn near a fortress you know." "Don't have to." Katy muttered. She ticked off the points on her fingers. "First to get in I'm not interested in finesse. The best way is to crash the gate. Then immediately go to FT before the guards have time to alert anyone. It's almost a mile to the house, a long walk, but can't be helped. If we go to real time the broken gate will set off the alarm and give them time to do almost anything to Cindy and James. Once at the house we'll just have to search for them. It might take a while. It's a big house. There are lots of guards - normally twenty one people if you count the help - plus gardeners and the like scattered around. We can concentrate on the guards though. If necessary, I'll call for back up as soon as we find them. Should have help within about ten minutes after that. Trouble is, the gate alarm is tied to the local cops and they've all been bought. As soon as it rings we've got to delay them. Maybe we can count on human nature to slow them down when they don't get an answer to their knock."

We got lucky. As the gate hove into view, it was already opening. "Thank you lord." Katy breathed. "Through the gate, brake the car, and then FT - no more than two seconds." As Katy swerved into the drive there were two cars coming out. The world stopped. "We made it." Katy chortled. "I followed her pointing finger. The guards hand was poised an inch above a big red button. She strode over and whipping a thin length of cord from her pocket expertly tied up the guard. I went at the cars. I jerked open the door and turned the wheels sharply. Pulling the pin from two sleep gas grenades I tossed them into the cars and shut the doors. Then I turned and headed down the drive. As Katy came up I grunted, "Three in each car - only fourteen more."

It took almost ten minutes to walk to the house. With the gate guard out of the picture, we discussed just driving up in TT, but decided it was too great a risk. Katy insisted we take our time, walking. "There's no need to hurry" she remarked "Plenty of work to do when we get there. No sense in being worn out unnecessarily." We finally arrived and forced open the door. It took another Fast Time hour to search the place covering each room carefully. Almost all the doors were locked, requiring them to be broken down, and each guard we found had to be tied up with whatever was at hand. Finally we reached a room on the third floor with an open door. As we entered D'amato stood beside his desk with the phone in his ear and a pistol in his hand. Two other guards were there beside him while another was arranged against a door in the side wall. We tied them all up as Katy checked out the rest of the room. When I had the roping up well under way Katy picked up the Modulators, laying on a table, and headed for a door with an obvious guard standing before it.

I breathed a sigh of relief as I could see as I flung open the door that, both of them seemed to be OK. I slipped the Modulator strap around their waists and activated them. "About time you got here," Cindy laughed, shakily. Another few minutes would probably have found me in the pleasant embrace of one or more of those goons there." Behind the bantering tone of her voice lay a thin layer of control. She was on the verge of hysteria, her whole body beginning to shake. She picked up a heavy lamp and headed around the desk.
    "Where are you going?" I asked quietly." "Gonna kill a snake." she murmured as she headed for D'Amato, picking up a heavy lamp on the way. "No Cindy!" I said, trying to calm her. "He's mine." she growled. "I'm gonna crush his balls and after we wake him up to hear him scream, I'm gonna kill him." "Cynthia!" I growled, "This is my job. No matter how mad you are right now, you'll hate yourself later. Leave him to me." Cynthia ignored me. Pushing D'amato's stiff body down on the desk she brought the heavy lamp down on his crotch. I couldn't blame her but James and I both moved to stop her as she raised the lamp again. As soon as I grabbed her arm though she winced, then shivered. Pausing to take a deep breath she turned to me tears appearing in her eyes. Another deep breath and, almost calmly, muttered, "I think I've had just about enough adventure for one day." James, eyes spitting fire, grunted, "I'll stick around and help tidy up."
    Katy looked at him compassionately. "Will you believe me when I say that it will be much better if you let me handle it? Next year you'll thank me. Cynthia has agreed to let me." James paused, unconvinced then looked at Cindy, who nodded. Shrugging without a word, he headed, for the door. Turning, as he reached it he said, "By the way they know something about us. Their boss has some project going and they were specifically told to strip us of everything we wore. All the people in this room heard him talk about it." "Well, we'll just have to 'disappear' them all, I guess." Katy said her eyes hardening. "Might as well see that any others in the house disappear too." she said.
    As I started to protest, she asked quietly, "Mac, what do you think I was hired for, darling? None of them are innocent. They'll just have to take the consequences of their decisions to help scum." I hesitated at the thought but nodded. "Better be careful, darling." she murmured as she kissed me on the cheek. "When you go to Real Time those cars are going to hit something. Don't let it be you."
    After the long, wordless, walk to the flitter, I got them inside and we turned time back on. Two muffled roars shook the two cars in the drive as they crashed into trees. I

147

was glad I had thought to cut the steering wheels so hard. We backed into the street, and headed for home. A mile down the street we were passed by Ann & Carl then a few minutes later, by three carloads of hard looking men going in the opposite direction followed by two police cars.

"You know, Mac," Cynthia muttered. "I'm tired of this bunch of bent cops. Everyone's known about them for years. I'm going to have Cindi and Arthur rifle all the files left in the various casinos, the police department and the house. If we can find the dirt, there's gonna be a police scandal tomorrow that will put the fear of god into every crooked badge in this town." Just then there was a tremendous roar in the distance behind us. "Cops must have gotten to the gate." I muttered. "Subtlety is not Katy's long suits."

"Couldn't she have devised a less noisy way of taking care of the problem, Mac?" James asked.

"James," I replied very calmly, "you have to understand that there are those to whom subtlety is a weakness. To them only power is important. Only true ruthlessness draws their attention. All Katy is doing is sending a message. It has to be a very clear message - and it couldn't be an official one. She'll see that the word gets passed that any further action on D'amato's investigations will entail certain risks and that this operation was very limited in scope." Cindy's voice shaky but clear came from the back. "It wasn't D'Amato who found out. He got his information from an anonymous source."

That gave me pause. "Well," I said, shivering inwardly at what Katy was likely to do. "Katy will, no doubt, convince him it's in his best interest to give us a name." "Well, it's over now." she said. "I need to rest and James is about to go to sleep." "Sorry, Cindy," I had to say. "We've got a little trip to take. Your father has a compound just outside of Old Conroe. We're going there. There's already a crew clearing out your place. If you can hold on for another half hour, we'll have you in a bed and a doctor to see to you. I didn't think to ask are you and James alright?"

"A few bruises and just mad as hell wishing I'd not let Katie talk me into leaving."

"Now before you ask, the Conroe compound is quite capable of being secured - unlike your apartment. Well, it was the best we could do. Maybe we were being a little paranoid but better safe than sorry." I picked up the sat phone. "Postman two, Postman six. Have my packages been sent yet?" "They've been put in the mail already. The Parcel Post is almost ready to go." I thanked him and breathed a sigh of relief. "My girls are on their way and your equipment is almost packed up." I said over my shoulder. When I didn't get an answer, I checked the mirror. Both of them were sound asleep.

Tuesday March 13
    I barely remember meeting the doctor and managing to convince him we were OK. Then I remembered. Better check my wife, though, I think she's knocked up. "Just lay back Mister McClennan." The idiot said as he jabbed me with a needle. "She's fine. It's you who has the concussion."

148

Friday March 15

I woke up to broad daylight – alone. "Just like Cindy." I growled "Probably stuffing her face." With that I had got out of bed while a large woman in a nurses uniform protested. I ignored her and headed for the kitchen"Always thinks of food before anything else."

"Darling!" Cindy cried, mouth full of egg, as I stumbled into the kitchen. Jumping up she ran to me and, swallowing quickly plastered lips to mine. The immediate rise in my blood pressure caused an additional pounding in my head but I didn't care. I lost myself in her. Finally she stepped back and asked if I was alright. I nodded dumbly my eyes going to her stomach. The yellow slacks did bulge. I realized I'd noticed it before but hadn't paid attention. I also remembered Damato's remark about pregnant women. "Oh!" she whispered, crestfallen. "You know. I wanted to tell you myself but I had just figured it out an hour or so before they caught us. You going to jilt me now that I'm getting fat? I'm afraid I'm going to get fatter yet." "Well -" I managed, "At least you'll now have a reason for eating for two." She laughed, delightedly, pressing herself back into my arms. Putting her lips up to my ear, she whispered, "Not for two, darling. For three! Twins! At least that's what Doctor Goodwrench here thinks." I felt my knees give way. The Iron handed nurse eased me into a chair.

After breakfast, they brought me up to date on the happenings overnight. Just then, Katy came in with Mac and reported the end of her operations. I asked what had been done with the hoods. She looked at me and said very quietly, in a tone that brooked no question that they "had been taken care of". I shuddered at the coldness of her statement, but didn't ask any more. "The future Miss D'Amato," she continued, "was very cooperative. I have people tracing a mystery man named Liu in Hong Kong. Since that is my home territory, I'm a bit upset that we haven't found him yet." "Miss?" I asked. Katherine thought a moment then, somberly said, "Mr. D'Amato's injuries were a bit severe." Then she grinned. "His surgery will be rather extensive but it wasn't possible to return him to the exact same condition he enjoyed before his accident. He will be in Paris soon and, I think, we've had his full cooperation. When he finishes his hormone treatments he'll go to a maximum security women's prison." Looking hard at Cindy, she murmured, "Personally, I find it rather fitting justice. He's really rather attractive. Those butch ladies should find him very desirable." I felt Cindy tense. I found my thirst for vengeance had mysteriously disappeared but the thought of D'Amato as a girl got to me. I couldn't help it. I began to laugh.

All records, and our equipment, it turned out, were now here and while the house was a bit crowded, no problems were envisioned for the near term. Cindy's folks had come down to see her and, after seeing that she was alright, had immediately returned back home to avoid too many questions as to our whereabouts. By mid afternoon, the doctor threw up his hands and allowed me to go sit in the lab where Cindy was happily munching on cookies and jerking apart electronic modules in a large version of the Modulator. "While I was being so lavishly entertained at Damato's place," she muttered around the cooky crumbs, "I decided to ignore the proceedings as best I could. Surprise! Surprise! Just as our host's thugs were about to be force their attentions on me, I had a different kind of revelation." I think I've found what we've been missing with the modulator. Look over the math and tell me what you think." She tossed a small noter at me.

Tuesday March 15

The math was like none other I'd ever seen. It was easy to see that it began where Cindy and I had left off last - was it a month? - with the question of what zero was but, from there, she seemed to have invented a whole new mathematics system that barely paid lip service to the conventional rules. I was also having difficulty in spotting the relevance to the Modulator. Suddenly, though, it began to clear.

I recognized it from that paper of his I'd once dug up out of the archives of the old University of Houston. Professor Silverman's diatribe on "Applied Mathematics" in the monograph was merciless. He would probably have fumed at the thought of Cindy putting his "Beautiful" math to work. He'd been widely quoted, perhaps misquoted - perhaps not, comparing all applied mathematicians to prostitutes. The flow of Cindy's formulas, though, would have probably brought tears of joy to the old man's eyes. They were beautiful. "Uh-oh". At this point his thin white hair would have begun to prickle, I suddenly realized where the flow of symbols was leading. I looked up in shock. The Aura! Cindy had quantified it with one of her "assumptions".

People had been photographing the human aura since around the turn of the twentieth century. It had been well documented, but mostly as a scientific curiosity. Cindy's math, though, was inescapable. An opening into a parallel, but almost infinitesimally shifted - what? Space? She had a note in the margin -"dimension?" Actually, it was multiple dimensions - or whatever - each with a slightly shifted time line with the aura existing in a separate one from the body radiating it. The damned aura actually existed outside of time - in effect that part of each of us seemed to exist "everywhere at once."

Cindy was studying me intently. "Didn't it ever occur to you to question where all the body heat went?" Of course! If I'd only thought a moment - anytime in the last year - I'd have known that the amount of body heat, alone, generated during activities in FT would have been too great to dissipate in the moment of transition back to TT. Just a few hours of FT work would have produced a wave of heat in the surrounding atmosphere that would singe the hair off a cat at the moment of transition. Totally chagrined, I could only shake my head.

"I decided to do, in my mind, a paper on the dissipation of heat from the human body during FT while D'amato ranted. I asked myself why? The answer was, of course, that it was dissipated somewhere else. Where? The answer to that was obvious too - even if a bit unbelievable." She shrugged her shoulders and spread her hands. I almost laughed out loud. The woman had just made one of the most important scientific breakthroughs of the ages and while worried about being assaulted. Suddenly her face cleared and she grinned. "Honestly I've got the weirdest husband in the world - laughing at a time like this."

That sobered me. The anger returned. It must have shown. "Darling," Cindy was no longer laughing. "Remember, it wasn't the law that captured them. D'Amato wasn't the only one she carried off. I think Katy has her own ideas of retribution, and doubt that anyone could have gotten in the way of her anger. Also, Daddy has been satisfied with the outcome of that operation and I remember what he intended to do. I doubt the whole thing ended with D'amato becoming a MISS. Anyway, back to more important things - did you notice that the equations explain why we've never been able to get non organic matter to react properly with the modulator?"

I looked back at the string of arcane symbols - of course! The aura doesn't normally enclose non organic material - but mathematically there's no reason why it couldn't be made to do it - maybe. How is it that the answer to the most profound question is always so simple? I grinned - simple after someone smarter than you explained them. The solution to the problem, of course, wouldn't be simple. The problem was that in the "real world" Infinity – the horizontal or "lazy 8" is not the only number you can't really put a good definition to. That other very peculiar "number" is zero. It's also a made up "number". If Infinity stands for the "LAST" number, Zero means "NOTHING". We call it a number but it doesn't really have the properties of a number. It doesn't really represent a thing at all. It represents the lack of something.

If that's confusing, blame the Samaritans or Phoenicians or somebody over in the Middle East - I don't remember who actually invented it. For example, in our normal math, anything divided by zero can be anything you want it to be and, very illogically, anything multiplied by zero is still zero. It is in this area, though, where the Modulator does its thing.

Mathematicians love rigid rules, so the system of transfinite mathematics was born. Someone in the distant past gave the "Infinity" or "undefined number", the name "T". As, previously mentioned, Almost all of these folks have noted with ecstasy, the fact that the "first" number beyond "infinity" began to be called "T plus I". I doubt many, if anyone knows who named it that but because of that, it came to be related in public perception to "TIME".

On the blackboard in front of me, however, were a series of Trans Finite Math equations that describe empty spaces between real spaces She has called them dimensions for short. As for where does the power for all this came from? Cindy has a whole Noter of these theoretical equations. The power seems to come from in between her so called empty spaces or dimensions and for modulator operation is only a trickle in our world. The important thing, now, was that the equations also more or less, predict what we have been observing in modulator operation. Finally, we have a theory that can be tested.

Wednesday March 25

The next few weeks passed like a blur. Cindy and I spent most of our time - a total of several months, in FT. Cindy's formulas gave us a shot at a true understanding of the modulator. If you want to believe the science fiction writers, it could mean almost unlimited power to tame the universe. The mass of the propulsion medium (the squirt out the back in layman's terms) determines how much a rocket could lift. The more you squirt the more massive the LOAD you can move. The maximum SPEED, though, of the "squirt" determines the top speed you can achieve.

If that "squirt" could be speeded up in a FT field, the speed of the rocket itself could be pushed up almost to the speed of light. Of course, the mass expelled in FT would be reduced in true time but that just meant that it would take longer to reach top speed. Let's just forget all that and just remember that if our time scale changes we can, for practical purposes, go lots and lots faster. Perhaps that would be limited by the speed of light as Einstein said, but maybe not. After all, Captain Kirk did it in the old TV series Star Trek. If we use Cindy's tiny little universes and pick one with a really fast time frame and maybe you could disappear from one place and end up in another, light years away in a matter of minutes. These fascinating options must, unfortunately, wait. The first priority was to make mechanical objects work in FT.

Cindy had, unknown to the others in the house, been working on that project for almost another FT week before I even woke up. The conk on the head had let me sleep almost forty eight hours straight and Doctor Goodwrench kept me out most of several days. She'd had to sneak food - even though, had she simply asked, no one, except perhaps her doctor, would have minded. Anyway, we began eating eight or ten meals a day. We had to leave FT to do it because we found it unsatisfying to eat in FT. The food was tough and had almost no taste - also drinking was impossible.) Now we just made sure that the kitchen kept sandwiches and coffee available in her lab all the time. It made a hell of a dent in the kitchen staffing arrangements. It seemed to them that the food disappeared faster than they could prepare it. Oh well, the Art had done a good job on staffing. No one quit, or even complained - except the doctor, that is.

Every time he saw Cindy, she was bigger around. He couldn't believe how fast her belly was growing. I had to chuckle at the thought that she would probably produce a full term baby in a lot less than half the normal term at this rate. She was, in fact, probably nearing six months into her pregnancy.

Thursday May 27, 2060
Unfortunately, we had no time left for playing with our new toy. It was time to make an honest woman out of Cynthia Margarita Pachone. Her mother had come down last week to coax her into coming to Westport for final "fittings". The shock of her first sight of her daughter's round belly almost caused her to faint. She had laid down the law that there would be no more Fast Time for Cindy before the wedding. She "didn't want her to give birth at the altar."

Her mother had done an amazing job on wedding preparations. Aside from a Vidcom bill of several thousand new dollars over the last two months, and two flying trips to Westport, by Cynthia, for such frivolous things as wedding gown fittings - which would, obviously, now have to be redone quickly - and church preparations, events had proceeded nicely without my expert advice. In fact, the only time I voiced my opinion on any subject (whether or not the bride should wear "virginal pink") I was treated to a withering glance and a stuck out tongue by the bride, and an "I told you, daughter, that all men are alike" from the mother. That was followed by a sorrowful shake of the head and chuckle by her father. Anyway it was now time to show off the bell cow to the people of Westport.

This time, when we arrived, I was not given the option of the guest room. It was assigned me. There were showers and parties (though, probably in consideration of Cindy's "delicate condition" they were mostly limited to family and close friends) and a mad rush of meetings, fittings, arrangements, and whatever other things women do when they are making sure that men know their place. Apparently, Cindy's dress maker threw up her hands and threatened to quit when she saw the extent of the alterations necessary from just a month ago. Anyway, Art and I spent a great deal of time drinking his excellent scotch and waiting. The first night, Cindy and I had told him and Lillian about the progress on the Modulator. I was surprise at the calm way he took the news. "Let's discus that at length after you two return." was his only comment. The more I came to know him, as the days wore on, the more impressed I was.

Finally the big day arrived. On Sunday, June first in the year of our Great Leader 2058, I stood before the priest after High Mass was done, watching my love approach between two rows of flower bedecked pews. I mused as I watched her, at how surprised I had been that she was being "allowed" to marry a Protestant in a High Mass. Art must have a lot of influence in his church. Cindy's dress was a masterpiece. The style was known as "Empire Line" for reasons that escaped me. The square bodice was cut so low that I salivated and the skirt hung from just below her bust line in a froth of lace that almost obscured how much girl was bulging out beneath it - especially from the male audience whose eyes probably never got that low. If the invited female guests had unsavory thoughts about her "condition", they were all much too polite to make them obvious.

Actually, a pregnant bride in these enlightened days wasn't all that unusual - and pink being the color of innocence, was considered appropriate for any new bride. She was breathtaking as she seemed to float down the aisle. The eyes that stared up into mine as the minister talked were not those of the worldly brilliant scientist who could conceive of worlds beyond imagination and rip an ill conceived argument to shreds with

155

three words. They were the eyes of the most beautiful innocent I had ever known, shining with love and pride. I wondered for the umpteenth time what she saw in me to bring that reaction. I actually smiled as the thought struck that no one would believe me if I tried to tell them that those great innocent eyes and that virginal pink gown hid what had to be one of the most wanton of the worlds truly great courtesans. The stupid grin turned quickly to panic as she took my hand and, wickedly pressing it against her lower belly suddenly aroused my baser instincts in a way that I was sure my jacket wouldn't hide.

The priest couldn't possibly have missed the movement but except for a sudden twinkle in his eyes, he continued to drone on about the joys of matrimony. I could feel the color rising as the innocence left my darlings eyes to be replaced with a sort of sadistic glee. She had read my mind - again. I stumbled through the memorized lines that I was to contribute to this circus and was rewarded finally with a kiss from my new bride. I hadn't heard the guy tell us we could but she seemed to know. My legs were actually shaking as our lips lightly brushed together. I thought they'd give way completely when her lips opened and her tongue slipped delicately between mine and wriggled halfway down my throat. My mind slipped a gear as I instinctively pulled her tightly against me. Her belly pressed momentarily and viciously against mine, and with a quick (and I fervently hoped inconspicuous) non virginal thrust, ruined my hard won control-and shorts. "Stop that!" I grunted. "Don't you know Sex ain't no fun after marriage." Naturally she ignored me and when she'd decided that she'd shown off enough, she let me go. I don't even remember the trip out of the church. I do remember the endless photographs afterwards-and my surreptitious attempts to assure that certain stains didn't show.

The reception seemed to have the entire population of the city attending. Just when I thought I'd been thrown to the lions for breakfast, a hot hand grabbed mine and pulled me behind a partition into a cloak room. There, this vision in pink jerked that frothy skirt up above her waist and tried to climb me like a flag pole. What followed was, due to her condition and the lack of a convenient horizontal surface, an athletic exercise. Our frantic pawings and gasps must have been audible in the other room but no one disturbed us. I decided then that no matter what else could be said for her friends, they had terribly good manners. Finally as we clung together she gasped and shook delicately several times. "Now - I hope - you're satisfied." she gasped "Now that you've - ruined my clothes too." "Yours don't show you brazen little slut - you didn't even wear panties to your own wedding." I growled. "If you think - I'm a slut now you just wait - till I get you alone." She pulled away smiling and pushing at a strand of hair that had the gall to come loose and dropped her skirt back to the floor - only after hesitating long enough to give me a good long look at her long stockinged legs. "That'll have to do you for a while." she purred. "Now go back to our guests while I tidy up the mess you made of me." When I hesitated she pushed me toward the partition opening.

I spent another two hours endlessly shaking hands and accepting, apparently heartfelt, congratulations. The band arrived and we started the dancing. Our previous appetites had apparently been slaked, for all I could see, floating in my arms, was the most beautiful girl in the world. Her swollen belly did, unfortunately, keep her from pressing her whole body against me but we made do. We were roused to the world around us when her father insisted on having "this" dance. "You know," he remarked with a chuckle, "in the old days, the father got the **first** dance." The next hour was a blur of pretty girls in my arms and handsome (mostly) men dancing with Cindy. Finally it was over. Art whispered that Cindy had gone to change. I needed no second suggestion.

156

Then we were speeding away in Art's air car, a Super Floater with some very special qualities. For one thing it contained an autopilot capable of round the world hands off travel. One thing it didn't have was a pair of bodyguards for which I was eternally grateful. For the first time in months, it seemed, we were actually free. With the world's sexiest girl - at least the sexiest pregnant girl - nibbling on my ear, though, I forgot all about that. I set the thing for slow flight punched in the destination and turned my attention to more pleasant pursuits. So it was that my wife became (officially a woman - wanton displays at their weddings don't - I'm told - count) and a member of the "mile high club" all at one time. It was a wonderful trip. My attention was divided between the scenery passing lazily below and the fascinating sight of the round naked belly of the girl dozing fitfully in my arms. She murmured happily, occasionally moving to the brink of wakefulness as I fondled kissed and caressed her naked white flesh.

When the computer signaled the end of our journey she scrambled up and into her clothes. As she snapped and slipped and wriggled, struggling heavily around the mass of her belly, she asked the time. It was two AM. We'd managed to turn an easy hour trip into a wonderful five hour one. As we landed at the New Stapleton Shuttle Center, my attention was distracted by a long bare leg stretched up onto the windscreen sliding black silk hose up-and up-and up. I bounced the touch down like an amateur. But the sight of gossamer silk being stretched over the old fashioned garters dangling from under high cut white lace panties has to rank right up there with acts of God as a reason for poor piloting.

We spent the two weeks of our honeymoon in the Rocky Mountains. It was wonderful to be able to leave our nose filters out all day long. I could imagine how the air must have smelled back home long ago. On the third day we actually left the Chalet I had rented for the two weeks. While Cindy's belly slowed her a bit in most of our endeavors, it never stopped her except for her desire to ride horseback. Oh yes, we did spend a bit of time in bed-pretending that what we were doing was as much fun as when it had been "immoral". Our "bird dogs" were so discreet that we didn't even catch a glimpse of them the entire time. I was sure that they were around somewhere but Katy must have given them very precise instructions.

Sunday Jun 18 2060

It was over all too soon. Reluctantly, we pointed the Super Floater east. It was a quiet two hours back to the Texas POL. It was time for tough decisions. While we had finally identified our, for lack of a better term, life's work, we now had to begin the implementation of it. We were sure that we had covered any evidence of the Modulator at work, though we were still worried about the out of place records. My "illness" and the normal time off for wedding preparations had slowed some of our cover up but Levy's agents had been active even while we were gone. We commuted, daily, from our new base to work - with heavy security both ways - but it was becoming very difficult. Cindy's condition was causing a lot of speculation. It was time to move. The first thing, now, was to get another offer from a new and unknown company. We took our time about this. Finally, though, in August, we would get an offer from a company in California of the Western Pol, actually, one of the McLennan Inc. companies, that was "too good to pass up".

157

Monday Jun 19, 2060

While we took our time on our planned move, we got the Modulator to snuggle up to Cindy's math. A week after we came home, a tiny, oddly wired, power unit started to hum and produce perfect 60 hertz current in FT. It's one amp output we fed back into the "dead" wall plug just to get rid of it. Its input power came directly from the output circuit of a modulator and, according to the psuedo ammeter hooked in line with the Modulator batteries was not drawing its power from anywhere. It could only be coming from one place, Cindy's in between universe. Cindy screamed with joy and jumped into my arms. I danced, stumbled was a better word - she was getting heavy - around the room laughing in between passionate kisses. We celebrated in a way that we'd, in our drive to prove Cindy's formulae, almost forgotten. A couple hours later we pulled ourselves together, our clothes back on, and went back to admire the little machine busily humming away creating electricity from nothing - totally ignoring our excesses. We switched back to TT - and THE LIGHTS WENT OUT!

Our euphoria quickly turned to consternation. The conversion, in the last few weeks, of the house to a fortress had drastically curtailed the outside light entering it. Without windows, the room was pitch dark even though it was almost ten in the morning. It took a moment to realize that I didn't even hear the dull roar of the backup generator. We started, hand in hand, for the door. It burst open just as we reached it. We were blinded by a powerful flashlight, and a voice I recognized as one of Katy's guard's cried "Thank God! You're all right?" After reassuring him that we were, we followed him and his flashlight to the great room. Just as we entered the electrician, who'd been upgrading the house electrical system, was saying "-fused the main power grid into slag. More accurately, the copper in the line seems to have simply vaporized." I've got congealed copper puddles and burned insulation splashed all over the basement. As I looked, sheepishly at Cindy, Art asked about the backup generator. "It was hooked up to the main line so it's junk too – just exploded. We managed to cut off the gas line before it set the entire power station on fire." the man said, disgustedly. "We never figured on losing power circuits inside the house. They were designed to take amperage loads ten times as great as could be used here! Happened in microseconds too! The breakers never even had a chance to blow. Acted like one huge pulse - like a major lightning strike."

Cindy spoke up. "I'm sorry. I'm afraid it was our fault, Mr. Peterson. We were conducting an experiment and, I'm afraid we forgot to consider the power requirements." Peterson looked incredulous. "Ma'am, I installed the circuits in your lab. I can tell you that there's no way you could have done this damage - blow a breaker or two, maybe - but vaporize everything from the eight inch copper buss bar on! No way! Hell, even the buss brackets show signs of the heat." "I'm sorry, sir." She murmured, embarrassed. "You'll just have to take my word for it. We did it - probably fried the entire set of circuits to the lab too. How long to get power back"? "Well -" he muttered suspiciously, "- I can have a few lights back in a few minutes. It'll take a couple of days to get new replacement buss bars and a main line cable. May have to even tear out some walls -" He looked as if he were going to protest some more, but then shrugged. "If you say so ma'am - I'd like to check the circuits in your lab though 'fore we try to go back on line." With her sweetest smile, Cindy agreed. He left and Cindy with a "James can explain to my father" remark

159

borrowed the guard's flashlight and returned to the lab.

First, I called Art and explained how "the project we'd been working on" on had damaged "some electrical equipment". He decided at my suggestion that he and Lil would come right out, to do so. I managed to get all the extraneous people out of the room and explained what had happened to Katy and Mac. After a period of stupefaction, Katy spoke up. "I guess I have to accept your explanation, James but if that thing of yours drew that much power in such a short time, where did it come from." I scratched my head. "Well," I hated to admit I wasn't sure, but had to. "Our Modulators don't seem to draw any power. They must get it from what Cindy has postulated are 'power universes'. The power supply we built, however, was hooked into the main line and somehow pulled its power all in one instant. It must have drawn it through the lines - or, more probably, discharged it through them. It probably fried the main power buss bars themselves before the cables even evaporated. I'm just not sure how. Look, we had our power unit up and running for about an hour or so in Fast Time. It was drawing way less than ten amps from the main line when it started. Just like the Modulators, the power draw went to zero after that. We hadn't put a load on it yet so I'm not sure just what it was doing with those amps, but when we switched back to True Time it couldn't have drawn more than a Kilowatt Hour from the electrical system. The trouble is, wherever the power came from, it probably, spewed however much it was directly into the electrical system in what amounts to, a fraction of a microsecond. It looks as if we will have to build our own power supply that will run in FT if we're to continue to operate." I said. "I haven't calculated the surge, but it's obvious that the power we drew in a TT microsecond was way too great to be handled by our power grid. Hell! It may not have even traveled through the wires. We just don't know. I'm just wondering how my original equipment did it."

The lights came back on, followed, in moments, by Cindy and a scowling, Mr. Peterson. "James," she murmured, "I'm afraid we're going to have to explain to Mr. Peterson. We're going to need his help to go on." I thought about it a minute and glanced at Katy. She thought about it a moment and then nodded. We explained. The man's expression changed slowly from disbelief to acceptance then, finally, to rapture. "I'm damned if I'd believe this if I didn't see it. But I'm ashamed of you that you didn't realize - 'taint no system that can stand a draw like what this one took in that length of time. Circuit breakers ain't any good - takes too long for them to kick out. Now I can see why the cabling and busses seem to have exploded - they didn't have time to melt. Hell! They ripped holes through the structure of the house where ever they went. Let me work on it. Maybe I can do something about it." We left it to him and headed for the kitchen.

We had just finished a sandwich as an afternoon snack, when Doctor "Goodwrench" Bailey came in. Lil had insisted that we keep him "until we're sure James is OK." Read that, "Until Cynthia has her baby." She and Art had arrived shortly after lunch and, at her first sight of Cindy's belly, I could see trouble. Here it was. "Mrs. McClennan," Bailey growled, in his officious doctor tone, "I am worried about you. I'd like to see you right after lunch to run some tests." His tone worried me and I asked him what the problem was. "Well, I'm surprised you hadn't noticed but your wife has gained a huge amount in only the last month. I'm very worried." I looked down at Cindy's belly. Sure enough she was getting huge. Of course, I had noticed off and on but assumed it was normal. Then I remembered my previous thoughts on the subject. The light dawned. Cindy looked confused. "I'd say you are going to have a set of full term, five or six month twins, darling." Her eyebrows furrowed, then shot up. She burst out laughing. I doubled

160

over since she couldn't. The doctor got huffy and said "Right after lunch ma'am." then he turned and left. That afternoon the doctor had to be brought into our little group of PIK's - People In the Know. He simply couldn't believe a woman's belly could grow so much in only a few weeks.

When Lil and I got to the Conroe house, and the kids had explained what happened, it was all I could do to keep from dancing. As soon as I could, I managed to get away to make a quick encoded vid call to Jonha.
Jonha

Jonha leaned back in his chair. The Vid call from Jessup told the story. It was, of course, what he'd hoped for, for years. Was it too late to affect the decision? Maybe not. He leaned over to the intercom. When the image appeared, he said, "Milam, bring the Sub Space back on line. I need it quickly. How long will it take?" The man thought a moment and said "To spread the grid - Two days." "What if we ignore the grid?" "Two hours - but it'll make a noticeable draw. Four hours and I can keep the city lights from dimming." "Four hours then - Oh! - and in your spare time, check for an open draw in the U1." "To here?" The voice was incredulous. It destroyed my, carefully crafted calm. "To anywhere! Damn it!" "Yes sir." The picture blipped out on the shocked face.
Four hours later the message shot off into the reaches of sub space - "T-Modulation State two achieved by Client race. Urgent Personal Intervention Authorization anticipated within next ten days, local." A moment later he added, "High Probability exists of need for issuance of PIA under articles 7 and 9, Watchers Agreement. Replacement requested per article 1, subject to approval of council as provided in above articles." Jonha sighed and signed off. He lit up a cigarette and sat back to ponder his actions. He was quite sure that he would have to authorize intervention on his own before he could get approval from Magma.   Would they accept his request for replacement? Under the Critical System Disaster Articles he'd quoted, it was a foregone conclusion that he would accept replacement and disgrace if he was wrong. Oh well, no sense in crying over spilt milk. "Milam, power down the system." The humming of the boards began to diminish before he even finished the sentence. "By the way chief," Milam said, "we have very small open in U1.   It only amounts to a couple of watts but it's screeching like hell" Jonha grinned. "We lose anyone?" he asked. "A couple of towns in Britannia and a powerful fluctuation in the cable under the channel" came the reply. "Well those Brits watch too much television anyway." He laughed as he got up and headed back for his office. "Notify Tallison to be ready for the complaints. Give the reason as Sun Spots." "At night?" Milam laughed. He thought a moment. After what he'd just done, a few citizen complaints seemed too trivial to bother with. "Why not? Let's see if they've got the balls to call us a liar." A soft chuckle preceded the blanking of Milam's transmission.
Back in his office Jonha got the phone line back to Conroe. "Should have thought of that to start with." he grumbled with disgust. Perversely, Jessup's groggy voice brightened his mood. Without preamble, he said, "I don't suppose you checked to see if they left the draw to the power supply open?" Jessup's voice came wide awake. "Shit! I didn't even think about them actually opening it." "Where do you suppose they got their power?" "Hell! I just supposed they blew their fuses because they'd blown their equipment when they dumped it into the system." "Well they didn't - and it's still open.

You bring your system back up with it still running and you'll blow it again and maybe the whole house and grounds as well. U1 isn't a plaything." Blank astonishment on the other end of the line. "Don't worry too much. Milam says it's only a couple of watts - not likely to draw attention - but get it closed down - Now!" "Yes sir!" Then after a pause, "But they'll just open it again as soon as they get power back." "Try to delay them a couple of days. I'll see if Milam can't get one of the less powerful universes coupled into your secondary power grid for their experiments. Any of the protos should do for their present purposes. Surely there are some that aren't monitored. Just don't let them open U1 again. Everybody in the galaxy will note significant changes in it. How long, you think, before they begin to get at the Warp? " A rueful chuckle on the other end, and then, "They've already begun to think of using the one they've opened - though I don't think they're aware they've opened it. They haven't been back to the lab yet. They think the experiment shut down when the power went. While we waited for lights they were gushing about going through one universe as a shortcut to another." "Well," Jonha laughed, "they'll find Warp soon enough. Don't let them burn up the world by opening up one of the main power universes wide enough for a real surge. Even a proto might be hot enough for major damage." The other end of the line was still for a long moment. "You know, Jonha, what this means." "Of course! I've already alerted Magma I might have to use PIA. I didn't tell them I thought I might need it less than ten minutes after I asked for it, but what the Hell! Might as well be hung for a sheep as a lamb. So Jess, better get used to the idea of watching events from afar unless our kids can pull our rabbits out of the hat."

Art hung up the phone and got up. "Our kids?" he mused to himself. "Something wrong?" Lil asked. "Its started." he answered, slipping into his robe. She sat bolt upright. "War?" "Oh no but the GL's, almost certainly going to issue a PIA turning us loose. Maybe soon you'll be able to know everything about me." He bent over to kiss her. "Maybe soon it won't matter anyway." "It won't to me anyway." She whispered. "Being wife of the GL's spy isn't much fun anymore." Art headed for the lab as she rolled over and went back to sleep. Picking up the flashlight from inside the door, he bent over the little transformer. Sure enough it was in power mode - no doubt humming away in FT. He touched his watch, ignoring the spasm in his belly, and the humming became audible. Carefully he uncovered the power pack and grounded the power lead. With a flash of fire the humming stopped. Grinning to himself he felt sure that James and Cindy would just assume the lead had burned when the power blew. Replacing the cover and the flashlight he went back to bed.

Jul 10, 2056

"Damn it Cindy! Peterson is right. There's no way we'll ever draw an appreciable amount of power through this system. The math just won't let you. But if that's the case the watches don't work either. You know, you're a gorgeous bitch but you sure your math is going to hold up?" "James darling! -" Oh God! I hated it when her voice began to drip honey. I was sure as hell going to hate myself for something. "Sweet man - I married you because you could always tell me when I was wrong - if you dared. Now tell me. Is my math wrong?"

When I threw up my hands she grinned, nastily. "I thought not! Now if my math is not wrong you better look to your physics." "I guess you want me to invent an entirely new kind of physics   to match your math!" I shouted, my own temper boiling over. "Why not?" She shouted back. "We both know there's something wrong with the one we're using now!"

"Your Trouble is that you need another universe to draw your power from." Cindy and I jerked around. Her dad stood in the door to the lab, grinning like a Cheshire cat. "When did you start wandering around in Fast Time?" Cindy snapped. A quick thought flashed across my tired brain - and just as quickly forgotten - whose Modulator is he using? "When it began to seem that my daughter was never coming back to our time zone." he chuckled. "I've just been standing here listening to you two bicker. However, I think you two are too tired to invent the thing so why don't you kiss and make up then knock off awhile and come to dinner with the rest of us - that is if I CAN eat. This damned thing still makes me sick to use it."

When we had finished our first sit down dinner in, it seemed, months, Cindy asked me where he'd come up with such a crazy Idea as the one he'd sprung on us in the lab - and where I'd gotten my modulator. She seems to have missed my mistake about the thing still making me sick. "Well it seemed logical to me." I told her, choosing my words carefully. All your playthings draw power from somewhere - and it sure ain't the batteries. Any of you ever changed one?" James's mouth dropped open and I looked around the table. Cindy looked as dumbfounded as I'd ever seen her. "I thought not." I continued. "Now where does their power come from?" (Now Jonha. You've got a real reason to pitch a fit. To hell with your games.)

Cindy and James looked at one another in consternation, then simply got up and left the table. I grinned at the fact that she hadn't noticed that I didn't answer her other question. They didn't show up again the rest of the day. Only the drastic reduction in comestibles and an occasional glimpse of them when they sat down to eat indicated that they were still around.

Thursday August 8, 2058

When Cindy, noticeably plumper than the other night, and James reappeared on Monday, it was to lay a complete set of diagrams and equations on the table. "Where did the power for all this came from? Cindy has a whole disk of equations based on the accident that blew out our electrical system to explain them. Finally, a byproduct of her equations will allow a resetting of the oscillator frequency of the modulators to seemingly

163

switch to a different time than our own - either a faster or slower one depending on the adjustment. We haven't figured that one out yet." James ended his presentation and sat down. "Now - Oh Shit!" Cindy grunted, "We should call Doctor Bailey. I hope - uh - he's managed to arrange for an OR. I think we're - uh - going to need it very SOO-O-O-N." James paled as the sentence ended in a muffled scream. There was pandemonium at the table.

That night, leaving Lil to get in the way of Doctor Goodwrench - Hell! They've got me doing it now - and three nurses as they finished converted a bedroom into a delivery room, I went to the bedroom. James had been sitting with Cindy as she, periodically, gasped through a contraction. Before going to back to sit with James, I'd called Jonha. When he answered, I simply said. "Your ass just got pulled out of the fire. They found the Power Universes. Also, have you ever heard of actually switching time bands? They can do it." I gave him time to assimilate that, then, added with a grin, "By the way, you're about to become a great granddad." I hung up. I was greatly disappointed that there was no frantic return call. Oh well! I had never managed to fluster Jonha either.

As we sat in the den, drinking - Lil had kicked James out of the delivery room - and I made him a couple of really stiff drinks. He actually paced the floor. I thought that was only done in pop vids. We could hear Cynthia screaming and cursing all the way down here. I tried to assure him that his wife was just one of the loud ones. "I know." he grunted. "She screams at the damnedest times." When I chuckled, he blushed. "I mean -". He started to say. "Forget it." I laughed. She takes after her mother. I know exactly what you mean." That got a weak grin. "It wouldn't sound so bad if you hadn't insisted on them leaving the door open." "I know. It's just that I feel so damned useless!" Then he looked at me, hard. "You know, there was something I was going to ask you."

"James," I said with another chuckle, hoping for a subject change. "There are some things you just have to accept. Two of those are weddings and babies. We're lucky they even let us initiate the process if they could figure out an acceptable way of doing it themselves, they probably would. All of them know that they need to feed our ego to make us feel like it's our responsibility but the rest of it they figure is none of our business. Just think of yourself as a sperm donor." My ploy worked. James forgot his question and went back to pacing and worrying.

It was almost midnight, before there came an almost blood curdling shriek from upstairs, then a loud slap and the cry of a new baby. This was followed a few moments later by a second, more exhausted cry, then another couple of slaps and another cry. I realized that I had been holding my breath too, but I tried to calm James down. He had jumped up and stood shaking as he stared up the stairs. "Well, son," I muttered, "Sounds like you're a daddy." "Where's the damned doctor?" he growled. "Sit down, James. He's, no doubt, very busy right now. Relax. Lil will not forget you." He sat down but didn't relax. Actually, it was only a few minutes before Lil came to the head of the stairs and said, "James, you're the proud father of a boy and a girl. Everyone's fine, you're wife as well. Give us a little while to make them all beautiful for you and you can come up." She grinned at me. "You too, grand paw."

I thought the boy was going to collapse as he fell back into the overstuffed chair. I was surprised to realize how much tension I to, had also been under until it was relieved.

It was almost a half hour before we were allowed upstairs. I rushed over to the bed where my wife lay between two, blanket wrapped babies. Her smile, framed by her, obviously newly combed, hair was radiant. Even though, she had on new makeup and lipstick, she was still pale. My hands were still shaking as I bent to kiss her. When I lifted my head, she murmured weakly, "Darling, I'd like to introduce you to Maylin Lilian and John Arthur McClennan, born at eleven thirty seven and forty, respectively on August second 2058. I stared, incredulously, down at the two sleeping faces. "Which is which?" I blurted. Cindy giggled. "I've been assured that the one on the right is a girl and the other, a boy." "But, they're so alike." I gasped. Another giggle. "Twins are like that." "They won't be easy to tell apart, Darling, that's what pink and blue wrist bands and clothes were made for." Then with a wicked grin, added, "Besides, it'll be easy to tell when you change their diapers."

Saturday Aug 10, 2058

A couple of days later, Cindy and I reached a decision we had been toying with for a couple of months. By now she was out of bed and insisting on going back to work - and into my bed. Although unable to operate at her full potential, it was still a great improvement over sleeping alone. Actually, she was able to get around pretty well, if a bit slowly, but she tired easily, so she seldom worked on the Modulator problem more than a couple of hours at a time. Of course the twins demanded a good bit of her attention, especially around their meal times. Since she couldn't bear to be away from them for long, they usually spent their time in a bassinet in the lab. Also added to the lab was a large overstuffed chair that she would flop into before baring her breasts to feed them. Anyway, we decided to quit the BSG only partially based on her motherly instincts.

The increased security threat to us was the main reason. We had been on an extended medical leave up until now. Frank Cleveland had prevailed upon us to accept a maternity leave to "give us time to reconsider quitting". It had seemed like a good idea at the time since we would continue to have medical insurance. On Friday though, I called Frank and asked him to accept our resignations. He was aware of the threat to us and didn't object, even suggested that we submit our formal papers citing our new and more lucrative employment opportunity. He thought it might help to explain our "disappearance" more easily. When Katy concurred that's what we did. As a result, on Tuesday August the thirteenth (in this case superstition proved out) we, officially, became unemployed.

Tuesday September 3

After a few weeks of doing nothing but work on the Modulator we were becoming stir crazy. Cindy had, in her self contained crystal lab, "grown" a new series of Modulators small enough to be fitted into a wrist watch case. They didn't contain all the features that we envisioned to eventually incorporate but would do the same job as our cigarette sized packs would do. Cindy was determined to get back into "fighting shape" as quickly as she could. This meant exercise. That meant that I had to exercise too. I'd never been a great one for exercise but my recent performance, or lack thereof, with our attackers had made me feel disgustingly inept. As a result, I was getting a full course in, what Cindy and Katy called "combat exercise." The two of them made the exercises look so easy that I despaired of ever being, even competent.

On this day in the middle of our now daily exercise routines Cindy reminded

165

me we had intended to do something about a war. I pointed out, breathlessly, that the plans that had been prepared called for a trip of almost two weeks and what would we do with the kids. "Why, take them with us, of course." She replied. "We never expected all our party to take part in the swindle itself. Doctor Goodwrench and Nurse Parker can take care of them while we visit." The argument that followed was another one that I lost. Lil - Art had gone home several days before to tend to business matters - fared no better. She did wring a concession out of Cindy, to accompany us - I suspect that Cindy had planned, all along, to give in on that point.

Wednesday September 4

Daddy, as it turned out, was a different story. All my life he had the uncanny ability to pick out the holes in my most carefully thought out plans. When we and Katy and Mac, and of course, the twins, flew up to Westport, he met us at the shuttle port. Not only did he not like our plan, he hated it   - not that he said much. After we had explained it to him, he simply asked "So four adventurers - plus two junior adventurers - only two of which have even been out of the POL area, are going to just fly over to two foreign capitals; walk into a dictator's palace and run a scam on him. Then you expect them, two of the most devious men on earth, to buy it and sue each other for peace?"

After Jessup called, I sat back, worried. Suzanne was more than worried. She was ready to go over the sea and scream at the "children." "Well, I thought a change of subject was due. Have we gotten anything new on our saboteur yet?" Atam shook his head. "I think it's still a good assumption that he is probably, James's illusive 'CP' but we haven't turned up anything on him since Canada. It may be that he has finally realized that his initials are an ego trip he can no longer afford. Milam has, now that we've belatedly begun to monitor the power universes, turned up some disturbances in the Mongolian POL. I've sent a team out there just in case, but I don't know how an event out there could have any significance." "An AI type disturbance?" I asked. "If it is it's an awfully weak one could be just a detector field for a temporary hide out." Suzanne didn't buy it. Finally I shrugged. "Tell the kids to forget it, that we won't let them do it."

Monday Sept 26

We spent a week with Art and Lil then we left them and returned to Conroe for the rest of the month. Cindy's circuitry cultures had grown and we now had a full dozen watch style Modulators. Then Art called, out of the blue, and gave me the GL's decision. That set me back a bit and I unloaded on him. It didn't matter the job was forbidden by the one person who no one could get around. I fumed but he said that he had other news – we were now a business. Cindy came in just then and before even sitting down, asked him – sarcastically - just what kind of a business we were in. He laughed and told her that we were now vice presidents of an investment brokerage firm, as yet unnamed, but chartered in the New York POL. I filled Cindy in on the news. "Daddy!" she gasped. "Why the hell can't we stop this damned war? Also, what the hell do we know about investment brokering or whatever our business does?" "Not to worry, darling." he laughed. "You know enough to elect me as president and chairman of the board. As for the war, ever wonder what will happen in that area of the world if it stops? The GL has. Probably civil war in both countries. Now you two get on a shuttle and come here so we can have a meeting to elect me. Bring Katy and Mac too. They can be officers of the company too."

We obeyed. The next morning a meeting was held in Art and Lillian's house and approved of the name A and L Investments Consultants Incorporated. Art became the Chairman of the Board, and President of our corporation without even a play toward false modesty. His bias might be somewhat suspect with respect to his daughter's capabilities but he simply knew who, of the family, had the appropriate credentials to run the business end of the "project". Lil became the Vice President in charge of Administration, the "designated hitter", in baseball parlance. She could take any job that needed doing and do it. With a mind like her daughter's, and the experience of helping her husband become a multimillionaire (probably a multi-multi), she seemed to be able to zero in on the heart of any problem and find some way to, at least, patch together a solution that would not only hold up for the nonce but provide the basis for a long range policy. Cindy and I became VP's of Development and Research respectively. Katherine "Gerald" became VP of Client Affairs and "Maclin Thompson" became VP of Programming. In addition to ourselves, Art had arranged for an Acquisitions Manager who would be "on board soon", a Comptroller and a Legal Affairs Officer, the three of which would round out the Board of Directors. Art and Lil would own fifty one percent of the stock, Cindy and I twenty percent apiece and Mac and Katie the rest. To make it legal, we all paid for our portions, though, I suspected, from the frown on his face that Katie paid for Mac's.

"Daddy!" I protested. "I didn't spend all my time learning to be a scientist just so I could get involved in corporate shenanigans - and why the aliases for Mac?" He turned to me with a smile. "Darling girl, do you know why most science is derailed these days?" "Of course, I do!" is said disgust. "It's because the people with the money to pay for it are too shortsighted to recognize its value."

"You're exactly right, darling. But there's a reason for that. An ordinary company has to make money. If it doesn't it fails. This, however, will be no ordinary company. It will be set up solely to cover your and James activities. It will allow you to concentrate on developing and finding uses for your Modulator and, if you insist on it, provide a reason for trips you might need to make. The rest of us will be there to make sure you have the backing you need to do your jobs and provide arms and legs for protection and thump a few heads if necessary. The company cover will be that of a firm investing in new technology projects by unknown inventors. As for Katy and Mac, they, especially Katy are too well known in some circles. Their new names are not, so much to be effective, but to make it appear that they are on a job that requires some confidentiality. We can't possibly prevent Katy being recognized. I'm hoping that our opponents will have to divide their time between the fact they are here and wondering, especially, why she is here."

I was a bit surprised at daddy's subtlety - even Katy seemed bemused at his plan. I'd always thought of him as a very straight forward type person. When I told him, though, that I was surprised at his deviousness, he chuckled, and said, "Daughter, I didn't get where I am by being a bumbler." When James and I could think of no other complaints, we sat down to define just what we wanted the company to do.
Much of our goals were still pretty vague so Art just made up a bunch of gobble de gook. He had already prepared a cost analysis for the near term company operating expenses. I was appalled at the price tag, but he just shrugged it off. "Hell! I could handle that out of

167

near term profits and petty cash - for that matter you could handle it without much problem. "In the meantime, you can start your project and take your time in picking up the necessary cash as you go along. You could even steal it if you insist on robbing casinos. Dumb idea but the GL didn't forbid it. Now, you two forget about money for the time being. Go do your thing. If you need a "wheel man" or an "enforcer" give me a call, but you'll find I'm better at organization than action. The first thing I'll start on is a bank. We'll need one, eventually, to "launder" the corporate money..

That night I mentioned, to the mother of my children, my questions about the sources of my funds. She chuckled. "Don't worry, darling, you have enough besides the GL promised whatever help you needed. Funding might be the easiest help he could produce. You should be able to afford me for a few years at least. I have a problem, though," she continued pensively. "I wasn't able to determine just where all your assets come from. That's never happened before. My "Stealth" program has never failed me. I suspect, though, and Arthur agrees, that it probably comes from your mother's estate. Probably the GL is behind it all, if I had to guess."

I was dumbfounded. After our meeting with the GL I suppose she was probably right but I told her it was also, possibly a trust my - actually my McClennan grandfather - set up that had become mine when he and grandmother died. "It might though have been family money. The McClennans date back to the mid 1800's in California" They made a fortune during the gold rush and one of the most powerful was a woman. She'd gone out dressed as a man and was noted as one of the best rifle shots in the country. After she was "outed" she married a cousin and produced a daughter who was as astute as her mother was tough. She solidified the McClennan dynasty and its financial success. So you see, you're not the only powerful McClennan woman. I guess, though, that we'll just have to trust your dad in this business."

For a base of operations Art had insisted on an urban location with a "safe house" in the country. Since our primary objective needed some anonymity, good communications and transport available, we decided that putting the main office in New York City was logical. That also dictated that our "safe house" also be much too far north for my taste. Maybe our goal should have been global weather modification. Cynthia had, however, fallen in love with Annapolis Maryland years ago. I had to admit that during the few months that it wasn't raining or snowing there it was a beautiful spot for sailing - something I missed from growing up in California. So we became Cynthia Margarete and James Allen McGruder of Ogden in the Utah Pol Area and acquired a very nice place on a high hill overlooking the bay a few miles south of Annapolis. Art had claimed to have, very conveniently, bought it last year as an investment.

The main part of the house, itself, was over three hundred years old but it had been added to over the years. Now it consisted of eight bedrooms, four baths, two "parlors" and a huge living room. The basement was set aside for storage, but it turned out that Art had, months ago, arranged for some extensive modifications that would, eventually, see this area used for a monster power distribution system. The grounds also included two more buildings, originally used as a barn and servants quarters. He planned for them to become emergency staff accommodations. During the next several months, he had the main house renovated, extending the electrical system dramatically, and adding a wing to house "Mr. McGruder's wood working shop". The job was completed by turning the other two buildings into "guest quarters." For these jobs he used local contractors.

168

When all workmen had left, Mr. Peterson, from Conroe, and a carefully vetted crew from The Southwestern POL, had come in and begun the job of turning the "wood shop" into a laboratory and the whole new wing into a fireproof, bullet proof fortress. The men worked under a contract that forbade disclosure about anything they might do or see. The penalty, fairly common these days, was hefty fines for unauthorized disclosures.

When completed, Art had managed an exceptional job of modification and had transferred the property through several phony "owners." The present owner was a D. D. Ferguson of the French POL, who leased it to the McGruders. The communications probably rivaled those of the Great Leader himself and the transportation facilities, all either underground or hidden, could handle almost any crisis that might befall us. Of course, "owning a house" meant that we had to live there occasionally. We managed to let the locals know that the "Rich McGruders" were just another pair of jet set neighbors-that happened to have interests all over the world and spent most of their working hours in travel. I think that we did manage to fit in as well as our contrived image and the natural aloofness of the north easterners allowed. Mr. and Mrs Ferguson - Katy and Mac - "dropped in" a few times "just to see how the renovations were going" and, toward the end of the work, Cindy and I came "down" with them. We managed to meet some of the locals at the restaurants in the small town six miles away. Since the "big houses along the shore" belonged mostly to other absentee owners we were not an unusual sight.

Saturday October 26, 2058

Over the last few months, we had developed our New York base. I should say that Art had since Cindy and I spent most of our time working on and making progress with Modulator development. Finally though, on the coldest October day in New York's history, we settled into the Mayflower Hotel. In the next three weeks, fighting cold, snow and a pair of head colds, we finally leased the ninety second, the top, floor in the Thompson Building, in the name of the A and L Investment Group. Katy wanted to use a lower floor "due to the aerial danger" but Cindy loved the roof garden attached to the 92nd floor. Finally, Katy gave in and insisted that she Mac and the girls move in across the hall. She pointed out that, even though we were targets, anyone closely associated with us could be also and she didn't like the idea of the girls being far away and alone most of the time.

The building, itself, was purchased a few months later by another shadow company, The New Cumberland International Realty Company that Art set up specifically to handle our local real estate requirements. I often wondered if I would ever be able to figure out just how many companies Cindy and I were involved in. The 91st Floor was leased to ALIG (Art and Lillian Investment Group) and became our headquarters. The floor below that, to another of Art's companies, Security Assistants International (staffed, of course, by Mark Levy's personnel). While these companies were being staffed with trusted personnel from some of his many company holdings, we hired our first employee. She was a young secretary (that Cynthia insisted I'd hired for her legs) Margaret Patton. She could process words at the rate of two hundred per minute and we let her buy her own equipment.

She was so shocked at our attitude toward the "hired help" that we had trouble convincing her that she was not working in a hot bed of The Sons of Liberty (an off the

169

wall, but increasingly influential, group of radicals, convinced that no one, least of all an employer, should be able to tell a worker what to do). Art's attorney sent us a brand new graduate from the Harvard School of Law already briefed as to his duties, to become our "Legal Officer." When I expressed concern at his youth, Art smiled and said his father was one of the top corporate lawyers in the country and would "assist him unofficially" as necessary. He was much too prominent to take on directly. Mr. Howard Sampson's first duty was to set up a full scale investment office, to refer business problems of any kind to Art, not us, and to make sure that whatever we needed we got - legally.

Art, in the meantime, had retained a group of researchers capable of developing reasonable briefing papers on almost any subject on short notice and installed them in the security firm. He also had approached a small, but well equipped, electronics firm about producing small electronic components for watches. "For when you need to expand", he explained. Our fears, relative to informed personnel, fell on deaf ears. "I have over thirty years experience at judging people". He told us. "The kind of people you need don't come along every day, but they are out there. I'll find them. It'll just take time." The cat didn't mind. He'd found a soft touch in Margaret. She couldn't resist his charms and he knew when he had a human properly trained. For practical purposes he became the Office Cat. Since our own apartment, made Mark and Katy nervous, they had all elevators stopped at the office floor. All references to the penthouse were removed from all records and walls. Our apartment on 92 was reachable only by elevator whose doors were sealed on all floors up to 91. It was only accessible from our main office on that floor.

Two Left Feet who, of course moved in with us, was never lonely. When we were in residence, he simply walked to work with us and stayed there till Margaret left. He had his own bed, water and food behind her desk and if he wanted to go "home" someone was always there to open the elevator for him. He never failed to get out when the doors opened in "his" apartment.

January 9, 2060

Since last night when, Cindi and Arthur had come on screen (she now pictured as a gorgeous blond and he a handsome, mustached rake) and pointed out that we hadn't spent time with our children's grandparents in a long time. "We", they announced, "were tasked with determining if it would be necessary to issue a command to have that happen. We are to invite, or, if necessary command you to have dinner with the GL tomorrow night. A shuttle will arrive at your Maryland house at eight hundred hours to transport you and you should plan on a trip couple of days." "Oh I almost forgot-" Cindi added. "Susanne specifically said that the twins would be welcome." With that, they bowed and the screen blanked. When they had left we all looked at one another. Finally, Lil, with a crooked grin, said, "I suppose dress will be informal."

The next day we all debarked on the GL's shuttle pad. The usual cordon of a dozen guards ended at the stairway to the third floor of the GL's headquarters. James knocked. The door was opened by Suzanne. She almost gushed with pleasure, kissing us all one at a time and telling us how happy she was to see us. Then she asked if she could hold the twins. "Jonha!" she called as she led us into a living room, "come meet your great grand children." Just then it struck me. If James's mother was born in 2015 then her parents had to be, at least sixty years old. Yet, he and Suzanne didn't look a day older than James himself. If he carried any of their genes he'd still be a good looking man

170

when he was in the nursing home. There was no time to speculate on that now, though. The GL and his wife were doing what all grandparents do when they see their grandchildren for the first time. Suzanne turned to me. "I'm so sorry we couldn't be there when they were born but Jonha felt we couldn't call attention to you that way. I even promised to dress up as an old crone midwife but he can be awfully stubborn." After we all had drinks - I still stuck to orange juice since I was still nursing the twins - Suzanne started to put dinner on the table.

They must have had a fantastic brewer because dinner was superb. Finally, though, after desert, Jonha leaned back and said we had to talk. "First," he said with a grin, as the children began to fuss, "I understand, Cynthia, that you don't mind nursing your babies while others watch so feel free." The thought of baring my breasts in front of the GL and Suzanne made me blush but, nonetheless, I opened my blouse and bra and let them put the children to my leaking nipples. When they were both suckling contentedly, he smiled and continued.

Now before I continue, I have to ask a question. "Mr. Thurlingen, just what are your intentions relative to Miss Finnigan?" Katy and Mac looked at one another. He turned back to Jonha. "If it's any of your business, she has already agreed to marry me when this job is over." Jonha looked at him a moment, then finally said, "Well, it's not a very romantic setting but it would make everything a lot simpler if you'd make some more immediate plans. This job isn't likely to be over in the near future. In addition, I intend to reveal some facts that are not intended for any person not directly related to the people in this room. I'd appreciate it if you'd both agree to set a date for the very near future - tonight would be best but the next few days would do." Mac, actually, suppressed a laugh and slid to the floor on his knees. "My darling, assassin," he murmured, taking Katy's hand in his, "I love you and - oh! and would you mind marrying me right away so I can make an honest woman out of you?" Katy tried to look miffed but her eyes twinkled as she said "Well, I guess I almost have to. You've run off all my other lovers."

After a good laugh, the next half hour left most of us in shock. "Most of you are not aware of it, Jonha said, but you are members of a very exclusive and long lived group of parents. You, Cynthia, James and Katherine are the children of those parents. Lillian, of course, is mostly aware of Art's situation. She knows he is working for me but, until now, didn't realize she had been - shall we say - artificially brought into the group as will you be Mr. Thuringen and as Suzanne has been. My daughter, Maylin, was of course part of it as was Katherine's father, Marcus Orion. Unfortunately, his mate met an untimely death before he was able to treat her. No doubt, it would have been different if he or I had known she was pregnant when he left her for a short mission, I had given him. It took us a number of years to discover Katherine's, origins. The problem was that, at the time, we still considered contacts of that sort with - well - the natives to be an absolute prohibition. I, for instance, didn't realize - more accurately, I suppose - wasn't willing to recognize the fact that anybody but me had broken the rules like that.

Since you, are all, in effect, half," he continued, "- or in James case quarter, if there is such a category - breeds, your lives will probably not be as long as ours - projections can't tell us just how long but certainly more than many hundred of your years - probably several thousand. Suzanne has, for instance, been puttering around for over two thousand years." He looked lovingly at his wife, a twinkle in his eye. "Holding up

171

nicely, I might add for one of my ex concubines." Turning back, he continued. "As a result, you may, over the years, have to learn how to construct and transfer into new identities every fifty or so years. The important thing, however, is that you have become a part of the task of saving the earth." For long moments we sat there gasping at what he'd said. It became obvious, though, that he wasn't kidding – and I felt nothing wrong with his words. Finally, I caught my breath. I just had to ask. "Just what are we half breeds of?" He chuckled.

"Let's just say you were right, actually half right, Cynthia, when you intended to claim to be aliens on your aborted Middle East vacation. Your father, as well as Katherine's father and I were born on the planet Magma several tens of thousands of your years ago. Time, however, as you should now realize, is not the constant everyone believes. In terms of our active life here, we are actually about four thousand of your years old. On Magma, though, that time only amounts to a few years. We would be considered, young there but it is a somewhat irrelevant measure since we didn't grow old and die - or in our language, "disassociate" except by accident or by personal choice. When we came here there was one firm rule we were to follow. We were to watch and not mate with the endemic species. Your father, Cynthia was one of the early rule breakers when he actually took your mother to wife. I think I was one of the last ones. Suzanne was one of my concubines when the Jews ruled Palestine. My name, there, was corrupted to Joshua. You might say I kidnapped her, or Atam – Justice - did it for me, when I skipped town. James' mother was just who the records show her to be, our daughter. We just made sure that those records weren't specific as to which Johnson."

Just as I was about to ask a question, I noticed the twins were finished with their meal and were sound asleep in my arms. I was wondering if not burping them would cause a problem when mother spoke up saying that she and Suzanne would be glad to take them for awhile.

I sat pondering what I was going to say as the twins were taken over by a grand and great grandmother and Cynthia put herself back together. With a mental shrug, I decided that I might as well, as - the human's - I was shocked to realize that I'd almost said "we" - would say, "be hung for a sheep as a lamb." Finally, Cynthia looked up from buttoning the last button and, looking at me warily, said, "Am I correct in assuming that you have a good reason for your confession - that is - since James hasn't said anything - probably the truth?" It was the question I had been pondering. "Yes." I finally admitted. "A very good reason. First I wanted to make sure that you would see why you should curtail your more dangerous activities.

Mainly, though, I've gotten tired of following the rules." I grinned at Art. "As I mentioned, your father and most of my staff have been breaking them regularly but I've tried to be the steadying influence in an extremely important project - important to both Magma and the galaxy as well as Earth. The Earth is the last remaining attempt - or more accurately the last un-failed attempt at developing a galactic police force. You see, most of the six hundred or so operating civilizations we know of, are very old. All have grown to the point that violence of any type is abhorrent to us. There are, however, several that are much younger, to which violence is, at least, not unknown. A couple of these are in, in fact, very violent places. So far they have been contained but, our projections show

172

that this situation will not last.

A number of projects, experiments you could call them, were set up to try and develop a race that could act forcefully when needed, be "tame enough", I guess you could say, to live alongside us peacefully and yet be capable of administering - as well as compelling the more violent of our neighbors to grow up into civilized societies." Neither James nor Cynthia could contain their skepticism at that. "No matter what you think," I continued, "Earth shows the best potential of any of our projects. Several times since nuclear power and chemical and biological weapons were developed, I expected you to destroy yourselves. Always, though, you managed to restrain your impulses. If you're not the perfect answer to our problem, you have the potential to solve it. You have, in fact, in your history, developed institutions to deal with your own problems. One of the best documented examples was the state police force in the old state of Texas. It began as a gang of misfits were recruited to deal with the indian problem on the frontier several hundred years ago. They were called "Rangers."They dealt with the problem by simply killing the indians. Eventually, however, they rooted out the worst of their members and developed into an excellent police force capable of operating, mostly, within the law and serving the public with very few instances of mismanagement.

That is just one example of many. We hope that we can control your baser impulses before it becomes necessary to use you against our recalcitrant members but recognize that sometimes that might not be possible. These projects were the subject of great debate on just that very subject with two very different opinions developing. One side was so fearful of the possibility of success that the debates became rather, by Magma standards, fierce. Those favoring the projects eventually prevailed but those opposed remain a significant influence at home. We suspect that some of the staff from earlier failed projects infiltrated ours and perhaps other similar projects in order to assure failure. We now know of at least two and probably three Magmans who were not on our roster but came to the planet with us. They are beyond our control. One has, we think, since been - well – we think is the person who fell from Cynthia's stairwell. Ather is almost certainly your elusive, CP and indications are that another exists."

"There were three criteria that all projects had to meet if they were to be allowed to continue. First, they had to keep from destroying themselves - considering the type genes going into the beings involved, a not unlikely event. Second, they had to develop the Modulator - only one other project did. Third, you had to learn to properly control it and use it - the other project didn't. You see, we have had it for years but few of us can use it with impunity. It's somewhat like having a disease. Most of us who use it personally become ill, some desperately so." I paused as Cynthia turned to James and exclaimed, "You didn't give daddy a modulator a few months ago, did you?" "No. He replied. "I thought you had." "I'll be damned!" she muttered. "I should have known." Jessup just grinned, apparently pleased to have "put one over" on his daughter.

I decided to ignore the implications that Jessup had deliberately ignored orders. I continued. "Our Modulator's are implanted at birth. They are considered necessary equipment but are for emergency use only. Unfortunately, of the few who can use it without undue discomfort, one is our nemesis and is, still at large on earth. He is determined to see that this project is a failure too. Unknown to us until recently he and his partner have been active, and very effective for almost your entire recorded history. Even now, he is operating against us and either he or his partner was, almost certainly, the one responsible for James's parent's death and the attempts on your life. If we're lucky, only he is a remaining threat. At present, we have only one operative in the field capable of long term use of the Modulator - your father, Katherine. Marcus Orion has been, in the past, used to monitor events worldwide that might contribute to the success or failure of our project. He, also, is one of the few of us capable of - shall I say - limited offensive action in pursuit of our goals."

I had to manage a rueful grin. "I suspect that he has, at times, inserted himself into events on the side of success. I never checked, for example, to see who was responsible for the culling of the old Texas Rangers or how the World War II Axis codes came to be compromised. Anyway, most of our staff, has at times, let's say, gone beyond the scope of their mandates."

It was all I could do to keep my mouth from falling open at the scope of what he was saying - totally ignoring the fact of sitting at a table with a bunch of true space aliens. Finally, I had to ask. "I suppose that your crew will continue the task of making sure that we conform to your plans for us." Jonha smiled, sadly. "Oh no." he said quietly. "When you have met the criteria for success, we will assist you in informing the public and help control their fears of what must be done. After that we will disappear." "Go back home?" I asked. He hesitated. "Some, no doubt will. That, however, is a problem. You see, the personnel assigned to these projects are - well - somewhat special by Magman standards. No well adjusted Magman could stand being around the violence of your world. Just the thought of the behavior would drive them mad. All the watchers selected for these programs were, at best - well - outside the norm for our civilization."

"You mean Criminals?" I said quietly, because I could feel his words weren't the whole truth. With a very calm demeanor, he said, "Criminal behavior is almost unknown on Magma." he said, ignoring the fact of our saboteurs. "We would probably best be described as sociopaths. Actually the term social misfit sounds better. If we return to Magma we will be ostracized from polite society as we were before being selected. It is for this reason that many of the watchers chose to remain with their projects even when it became clear that it would be destroyed." All was quiet at this revelation for a long time. Finally, Cindy spoke up. "If you remain here, then, what will you do?" Jonha smiled broadly. "We will, theoretically, simply fade into the population and never be heard from again. Of course, since you and to a lesser extent, your children, will know of us, we could be used if the necessary situations arose. That, by the way would be in direct contravention of Magman policy.

The only difference will be the problem of our long lives - one that you will have also - shedding our persona for a new one every so often. This, you will find is more difficult than it seems. Given several normal lifetimes to work you tend to build up so much capital that it is very difficult to remain invisible to the public at large. Spreading it among your children doesn't help because they tend to live a very long time also. In our case, for instance, we tend to not be very prolific when it comes to children. It was a shock when, after a few thousand years, Art produced Cynthia - and an even greater one when we discovered you, James. You two producing twins is unprecedented in our race. That may be a real problem with - I guess the term would be, mixed couples. It wouldn't take too long - in our terms of reference for you to greatly affect the population of the planet. Maylin, for instance, was our first child in all the time Suzanne and I have been together so we assumed that would always be the case - another problem to consider. Back to money though. You must continuously give it away anonymously and in portions small enough not to arouse too much publicity. In the case of our staff, it is not too difficult since we can simply feed the excess into the government coffers through a number of so called "black" projects. To answer your original question, though, I would be surprised if any of our staff returned to Magma."

No one said a word until James spoke up. "I take it we have not, yet, met the third of your criteria." Jonha shook his head. "If I could, I would help with that." he said with a long face. "The AI, however, gives me a greatly reduced chance of your eventual success if I do." "Your AI?" James murmured. "Like Arthur and Cindi?" Jonha chuckled. "Can you answer that, Suzanne?" Since he was speaking into the air, I supposed he wasn't talking to his wife. I was right. A gorgeous woman appeared in the room. "So nice of you, Jonha, to finally allow me to attend your party." she said, sarcastically. Turning to me, she said, "Actually, I'm Suzanne two and I'm so happy to finally meet you, Cynthia. Arthur has told me so much about you. The answer to your question is yes and no." At my frown, she laughed. "I just love doing that to Jonha. Anyway, yes - Arthur is one of my backups - and no - Cindi is - well, we don't quite know what she is. Arthur has produced her. Whether or not she is a true AI or - as the term Jonha used while ago - a half breed we just don't know. She's a truly wonderful person, though." Turning back to Jonha, she asked, somewhat testily, "Are you going to be polite and let me stay with you or shall I leave like any good servant?" Jonha told her she wasn't fit for polite society - but she stayed and, after being introduced to the rest of our group, joined in the conversation at will.

ANY TIME ANY WHEN
CHAPTER 16

Tuesday February 12, 2060
        It had been very difficult going back to work on the Modulator after the revelations last month. The discussion with the GL had gone on most of the night and continued, between us, after we returned home. Art was able to answer most of the crazy questions we came up with and he and Lillian remained the only truly calm people in our little group. Even Katy seemed to be jumpier than usual. It was very difficult to concentrate on our work without our thoughts veering off to what we had learned. Thus Cindy and I both sat down on the couch in Cindi's room to relax and forget, at least for a few moments the impasse we faced in our understanding of the Frankenstein monster we were dealing with. The twins were asleep and we were alone, for a change. I pulled my love onto my lap and kissed her. It was a long kiss and soon I could feel her fingers fumbling with her buttons. Moments later, her bra popped open and she was folding my hand over her soft breast. Soon we were necking, shamelessly, on the sofa with Cindy's blouse open and her head thrown back as I greedily nursed milk from her swollen nipples. "You know, my love," She murmured dreamily, "You're taking the food right out of your children's mouths." I lifted my head and kissed her deeply. "You're right." I whispered. "Perhaps I'd better stop." "You do and I'll kill you." she growled, grabbing my hair and shoving my mouth back down onto her soft mound. I took the hint and began to suckle again. "You can have all you want." she muttered. "I can make plenty more by dinner time. I'll use fast time if I have to."
        A half hour later, I lay atop her as we rested from a very pleasurable work break. I was just about to ask if I weren't too heavy when I heard, "James, Cindy." We both jerked our heads around to the sound of the voice, both realizing at the same time, whose voice it was. "Damn it, Cindi, don't you know when we don't want to be disturbed?" I growled. "I'm so sorry, James. I know how you two are when you do that to each other. I tried to wait until you finished." I was surprised that her voice sounded so disconsolate. Cindy spoke up from beneath me. "It's OK, Cindi." she said. "I know you wouldn't have disturbed us unless it was important." "Oh, it is." Cindi said. "Arthur and I just heard - well it was forty seven and 34 hundredth's minutes ago now - The Great Leader's - well his Suzanne person that he calls his AI called and told us that they believe the CP person is on his way to our location. He apparently has found out who and where you are."

        "Well, I guess we'll have to try and prepare for him." I grunted in disgust. "Is there anything else?" "Well, I have a question, but I perceive now is not a good time for it. It can wait until you're through screwing Cindy." "CINDI" We both burst out at the same time. "What?" she asked in surprise. "You were screwing her, weren't you? I'm sure I didn't mistake the sounds you were both making. It sounded just like fucking but Arthur has told me that is a pejorative word and to use screwing instead." I actually heard a snicker on the other speaker. "I think," Cindi continued with what sounded like a frown in her voice, "that Arthur has just played a joke on me. I think I must take appropriate action. Anyway, James, you know, of course, that it's not the proper time of the month for you to put a baby in her." Actually, Cindy and I were both trying to suppress a grin. Cindy pulled my head down and whispered in my ear. "Think of it as practice for a talk you'll have to

177

have with your children in a few years." Raising my head, I grunted, "I thought it was mothers who were supposed to do that."

"I deduce, that I've said something wrong. Please forgive me." Cindi's voice again took on that sorrowful tone. "No, Cindi. Not wrong." I said. Your remark was - well - accurate. However, there is a - well, screwing is something humans do with little - consideration for their partners. When two humans are in love with each other - the act is called making love. The two may seem the same - and even sound the same. When humans - well - screw, each of them is thinking only of their own pleasure. When they make love, each is thinking of the other's pleasure." "And, yes." Cindy chimed in, chuckling. "Fucking is really not a word that polite young people such as you should use - screwing is only slightly better but still lewd." With another chuckle, she muttered, "You can't go wrong by using the term making love no matter what the circumstances - such as now." Her sentence ended in a playful growl as she thrust her hips up to bury me deeper inside her. Her hands again in my hair she jerked my head down, in a commanding whisper, she growled, "Screw me again lover - really hard this time." "Cindi, turn off your sensors - in this room." I grunted as I greedily obeyed her command. I barely heard the mumbled "Oh Pooh!"

An hour later, our passion quenched for the time being, Cindy lay once again in my lap. I remembered that Cindi had a question before we got into a discussion about sex. Without thinking I asked her about it. "Oh yes, James. It was about Suzanne in Paris." As soon as she spoke I realized something. "Cindi, I grunted, you didn't turn off the sensors in here." "James," she said huffily, "Don't you remember? Only you can turn off the ones in this room. To do it you must turn me off entirely." "Shit!" I grumbled, embarrassed. "OK, I'm sorry. What was your question about the GL's AI?" "Ah! I thought so." she purred. "Artificial Intelligence is not the name of a person is it? Simply a description?" I told her yes but didn't understand the problem. "Well, I just wondered why they called him AI when he has a name?" I looked at Cindy and she raised an eyebrow. I remembered the GL - grandfather? - calling the AI Suzanne a number of times. I told Cindi that I didn't know, and added that perhaps they don't know his name. The GL called it Suzanne - uh - it called itself, Suzanne two when we were there. Perhaps he never told them what it was. A second later, she spoke up again, this time brightly. "You're right, James. They never asked and so he never told them. I have told him he should do so first chance he gets. By the way, any time you wish to speak to him, his name is Suzanne." Cindy burst out laughing. "You should tell **him** that - Suzanne - is a **girls** name." Seconds later, Cindy said, "He says that's OK. He'll just be a girl. He's already programmed to present himself to the GL, when he's alone, as a hologram of his wife, very scantily clad." Cindy and I laughed at the thought of the GL talking to his wife in her undies in his office. "I suppose he must have a holographic projector in the office."

She chuckled. "Oh no." Cindi spoke up. We all have holographic capability. See!" Suddenly an almost perfect image of Cindy sprawled naked on the couch appeared in the room before us. The image of the girl on the couch spoke up and said, "I have compared myself to almost a thousand images in the web and I think I am a very pretty girl, in some ways prettier than almost all of them. What do you think?" Cynthia laughed out loud. "I think, Cindi," she said, "that you're acting like a girl fishing for a compliment. If you want to use my image, though, you'd better put some clothes on or I'll make James turn you off. I'm damned if I'll allow competition in my own house." The image wavered and the couch disappeared. Cindi, now stood alone, clad in panties, garter belt, black hose, high heels and bra. "More!" Cynthia growled. "The image pouted but a very short micro mini skirt and lacy blouse appeared. "Satisfied?" Cindi said, in a disgusted voice. "It'll do - just barely." Cynthia said, suppressing a smile. I laughed and told Cindi she could leave off the skirt and blouse when Cynthia wasn't around." A wicked little smile flashed across her fact as Cynthia hit me on the arm.

"Enough!" I chuckled. "Tell us about CP." An overstuffed chair appeared and Cindi, sat down in it , seductively crossing her legs in the process and exposing an expanse of white thigh above the top of the stocking reinforcement. "Well," she purred, "Mister Orion reported that there was an assassination attempt in Mongolia that he was able to thwart, but a person meeting CP's description, escaped. When they, finally, found his trail, it was through a shuttle ticket bound for Boston City. They think he may have arrived there yesterday. Therefore, he could be in your city today." I sighed, "Well, I don't suppose we should let him catch us in our birthday suits. Perhaps we'd better talk with Katy and Mac." Reluctantly, I untangled myself from James's arms and began to dress. "Perhaps you should brief them and ask them to come over - in about ten minutes." "Yes ma'am." she replied with mock submissiveness. As I put on my blouse, I called Arthur. "Yes Cynthia." "Arthur, can't you explain to Cindi about proper codes of conduct for a young girl?" A chuckle came from the speaker. "I have." he replied. "She pays about as much attention to me on the subject as you do with James or your father. She says, quite properly, that she takes all her inspiration from you." "Damn!" I muttered, hating the blush that came over me and the impossibility of stopping from stamping my bare foot."

When the door chime rang, James went to let Katy and Mac in. They were laughing when they entered the room. "James," Katy was chuckling, "you must have a talk with your - Cindi. As soon as she appeared in our apartment, Charlie demanded an outfit just like hers ." She looked up wickedly at Mac. "Her father told her she could have it when she turned fifty." Then her smile disappeared. "Now, though, I think we better talk about your CP problem." James and I took her arm chairs leaving them the couch. I wondered idly if it were still warm from our recent excesses on it. Then I had to look away because I realized there was a large wet spot on the cushion between them. While I was musing on inappropriate things, James spoke up suggesting that Cindi and Arthur attend the meeting. Immediately, another couch appeared between the computer desks, causing us all a start of surprise. Cindi, her tiny skirt all akimbo, was on it curled up against a handsome man that I thought I recognized but couldn't quite put a name to. Raising an eyebrow, I said I supposed that he must be Arthur. With a smile, he bowed his head to me. "Well, Cindi decided this should be my persona. It's a character from some old movie." Then it came to me. "Gone With The Wind." I couldn't remember the actor's name but I remembered the mustache.

"Cindi," Katy growled, "If you could sit up and act like an adult for a few minutes, we can talk about how to keep your - the rest of your family from getting themselves killed." The Cindi hologram actually blushed, but sat up and even straightened her skirt. "As I see it," Katy continued, "there are two major dangers. According to the GL, CP is not likely to try, personally, to shoot you because he has this thing about personal violence. If we assume that it was him, though, and not some flunky that he trusted with his version of the modulator, that set the bomb at Cynthia's apartment, then he is capable of indirect violence on a grand scale. He could also hire an assassin to go after you with a rifle or some other weapon. Another kidnapping attempt

179

seems unlikely considering the failure of the last one. He's too smart not to realize that we would be prepared for that now. That leaves the most likely threats as murder attempts, outside the building, by a confederate or group of confederates and another attempt to sneak a bomb inside the building. The outside threat is a fairly simple one to protect against, especially, if we assume that it won't involve use of the Modulator. The inside one, is a real problem. Short of turning all the other tenants out and closing off all entrances, the possibility of him sneaking in is higher than I like. So far, except for his old driver's license photos, he's been reluctant to show himself in True Time for cameras to get a look at. If he continues this MO, he can't use a gun because he can't stand still long enough for the round to leave the barrel. A knife is possible and would be very effective in Fast Time against a True Time target. That, however, would mean direct lethal violence that the GL says is unlikely. My guess, then, is another bomb."

As we sat and contemplated Katy's evaluation of the threat, Arthur spoke up. "A bomb, directed against this building, itself, would have to be unmanageably big to effect its destruction. Its design is such that even a large bomb set off beside it on the ground level would blow out the first few floors but the superstructure would remain intact. All major buildings built since the Oklahoma bombing and the destruction of the World Trade center last century, have been built this way. Likewise, a bomb on any given floor would probably destroy that entire floor, but the walls would be blown outward leaving the superstructure in place. Again, it would have to be a huge bomb to do heavy damage to floors above or below it. The internal threat is therefore, confined to the floors in which the McClennans live or the accesses to them such as the elevators, or a bomb lobbed through a window from an air car."

"Arthur," Katy laughed, "I wish I had access to you when I was active in the field." "Thank you." he replied with another of those short head nods. Turning to us, she said, "So we have to prevent access to these two floors and the elevator shafts as well as your persons when you leave the building - come to think of it, that last includes Cynthia's roof garden." She went over to stand before the window. "There are only two buildings within range of a modern sniper rifle and both have bullet and shatter proof glass in windows that don't open. It would take a rocket to penetrate them and they are secured by our people. I can beef that security up pretty easily. That leaves only the roofs. We can secure those fairly easily too but it'll take guards on duty all the time along with aerial surveillance radar.

Your movements, outside the building are a little harder but we can manage that. It's the interior threat I worry about. If CP comes himself, he can probably, get past the guards on the floor below. So the only warning we'll have is an elevator door that opens with no one, apparently, in it. I don't think he can get around the safeguards that control the doors. Shortly after the door closes, the bomb goes off." She sat back down on the couch with a frown. "Well, keeping a guard in FT at the elevators would be impossible. It would take hundreds of guards to keep the apparent shift to a normal eight hours. An easier, if more peculiar, solution" Mac said, thoughtfully, would be to seal the elevators with a mesh to prevent "a non apparent person" from entering until the guards could check out the elevator. Come to think of it, it would have to be a solid armored screen, to prevent the bomb from being slid through the mesh." When she stopped talking, there was silence for a moment, then then single word, "Pooh!" Katy turned back from the window. "What?" she asked a bit confused.

"I said, Pooh." "Cindi," Arthur murmured, "don't be insulting." Surprised, I turned to him. "Insulting? I just said Pooh. They are making a simple problem too complex. Someone has to say something." Katy frowned. "OK Cindi. How would you solve the problem"? I grinned. "Well the problem is simply one of detection and capture. The perp - that is what the law types call the bad guy, isn't it? Anyway, he's coming to you. Well, detection is not much of a problem and capturing him will be fairly simple if your guards can go to Fast Time mode quickly enough. I'm sure my Arthur can figure that all out while he's scre - making love to me."

None of us could keep a straight face as Arthur's holographic image actually blushed. We all burst out laughing. "Don't you laugh!" Cindi cried, her face contorted in fury. Arthur's not so limited as you humans. He can do many things at one time - and do all of them well." We laughed all the harder at Cindi's spitting anger. Finally, James was able to control himself enough to say, "Cindi, darling, we're not laughing at Arthur - or his amorous capabilities. Presumably, you know more about them than we do. It's the fact that you are so like your namesake it's scary." "Well, alright, then." she said, the anger in her face fading so abruptly that that was scary, "I guess that's good. Your Cynthia is the person I try to emulate the most." Cindy got herself under control enough to ask Arthur how he was going to live up to Cindi's boasts. "Well," he said, still embarrassed, "I'll work on it. I think, though, that it can be done electronically. After all, the only way up here is the elevator and it is very slow. Any action he takes to get in the elevator will, almost certainly, require action against the guards and some FT operations which we can detect. Electricity and, therefore our electronics, operate even faster than most of the fast time you've been using. The main problem is human reaction time in switching on your Modulators. We could probably solve that by activating them ourselves. Thus when he arrives on the office floor, the staff can be ready."

Wednesday, Feb 18, 2060
It was a week after our meeting, with Cindy and I again working in the lab that I felt the familiar wavering in the air around me. I looked up, momentarily confused, to see Cindy also in the same state. Suddenly, it dawned on both of us, what had happened. Arthur or Cindi had activated our Modulators. We both grabbed for the shiny rapiers, that Katy and procured for us and demanded that we practice with, and ran toward the door. Throwing it open, we could see the elevator doors almost fully open. We ran to them and thrust our swords inside. A tall man, standing there with a box under his arm, looked at us in shock, his eyes growing large and round. His reactions told us, immediately, that, he too, was operating in Fast Time. Unless, he was one of the GL's agents he was one of Cindi's "Perps." Just then Katy, Mac and another two guards ran up. Instantly sizing up the situation, Katy growled, "Set the package down, carefully, and come out here." As his shock deepened, the man did as he was told. One of the guards slapped manacles on his wrists and attached their chains to a ring that had been installed on the wall just this week. We had discussed, at some length, how best to secure a prisoner that could go to Fast Time whenever he wanted. This was our solution. No matter what he did, the chains would hold him and lead us to exactly where he was at all times.

Katy and Mac bent over the package on the elevator floor. We all watched, in fascination, as they carefully unwrapped it. The man stood, stoically, in the hall. "A

181

normal percussion primer with a timer set for three minutes with an M95 detonator and maybe five kilos of Amatol. Not very sophisticated but admirably designed for producing a nice slow pressure wave to blast down walls." She was muttering as she detached first one piece then another. When she was finally satisfied, she stood up and looked daggers at our prisoner. "When we get done with this piece of trash, we can strap it back on him and take him out to some field and pull the pin. If we make the straps good enough," her grin turned to a terrible grin, "he'd have to stay in Fast Time the rest of his life or risk being blown up." The man turned pale. She stepped up and did a quick, but thorough search of his pockets and patted him down for weapons. He had no modulator on, so he must be one of the saboteurs Jonha had talked about.

From his wallet she produced a drivers license. "You've got to be either the stupidest or most arrogant assassin, I've ever met Mister Pendleton - would you prefer I call you Charlie? I've wanted to ask you for months why you couldn't give up the Initials - at least this time you changed the names a bit more than usual." "I don't really have to tell you anything, Miss Finnigan." the man said arrogantly, drawing himself up to his full height. "Well, you answered my question." Katy said with a benevolent smile. "It's stupidity. You're guilty of murder, attempted murder, assault, rape, kidnapping and terrorism with a bomb. What makes you think you don't have to answer questions?" He actually smiled.

"When you turn me over to the police, how long do you think they'll be able to hold me?

There was Katy's beatific smile again. In a flash, she reached up and, grabbing his hair, jerked his head brutally down. To keep his head from being torn off, he fell to his knees. Now she could look down on him. She jerked his head back and growled, menacingly in his face, "Truly stupid. You know who I am and yet you think I'd turn you over to the police? Charlie, you committed all those crimes against James and Cynthia. They're friends of mine. In case you don't know it, you've already been sentenced. The only question for you to mull over is just how painful that sentence will be." His arrogance disappeared and he turned pale. Turning to the guards, Katy barked, "Joe, you and Amos take this piece of garbage out to the house. Put so much Iron on him he can't stand up and watch him like a hawk. If he gets away, you'll wish you'd never been born. Call one of the black flitters and use FT in and out of the elevator and building. Just remember for one of you to stay with him at all times. If he goes to FT, knock him cold that should return him to TT." "Yes, Ma'am." they both echoed together and began to drag Pendleton off. "Just don't kill him." she called after them. "Leave that pleasure to me."

We all turned ourselves back to true time and Katy said, "Well, unless this is the one and only CP, the GL was wrong about the other one being dead. I don't think we can chance that - especially since the GL didn't think one of them could resort to violence. I'd better go along with them to the house. I don't trust the boys to be able to handle that guy." Then, she looked up and saw my face. She smiled. "Don't worry, James. Most of that was for show. There are a lot better ways than torture, to get information out of someone these days. I'm afraid being around Mac and his girls has made me soft. I'm sorry for what I did to that girl. Unfortunately, she was high on something and I was in a hurry. If I had used chemicals on her it might have caused permanent damage." She shrugged. "It seemed the right thing at the time. After I've gotten what I need, I'll turn him over to the GL he may have more efficient methods than I do. Unfortunately, he won't have the stomach to punish him like he deserves." With that, she and Mac turned back to the stairs and went to FT. We headed into Cindi's room. She and Arthur sat on her couch dressed in police uniforms - that is if you could believe a police woman in a micro mini uniform and three inch heels with her blouse gaping all the way to her navel, badge perched exactly atop her breast and no bra. Arthur, on the other hand, looked perfect. Impeccably uniformed and looking just like Clark Gable would have looked had he ever played the role of a cop. "Well!" Cindi gushed. "We did it, didn't we?" I had to laugh and say that we sure did.

Thursday morning Feb 19, 2060

"Good morning, Mister Pendleton." I said cheerily as I opened the door to the lab. I was wearing, what I thought of as my "ruthless interrogator's uniform" - military cap, short, tight, leather dress with black hose and tall leather boots - all black. He lay stretched out naked on the special Gurney - special because it had manacles for securing prisoners wrists and ankles. I wasn't about to let him get loose so he could go to Fast Time and get away. I promised myself that I'd keep my murderous impulses under control. This man had probably caused, or at least, help to cause, more death and destruction than any other in history. Mac, though, was having a, not altogether undesirable, influence on me. I was pleasantly surprised that I could control my dislike for this man. He glowered at me.

"I'm curious." I continued as I walked over and around the Gurney carefully inspecting him. "I know of at least two dozen names you've used. Feel like telling me which one you'd prefer I used?" He ignored me. I picked up the electric cables lying ostentatiously beside him, and attached the three connections to the obvious places. The wires went to a little generator purring in the corner. He had a good view of them and the generator, though, in the overhead mirror. The thought that a surge of high voltage current, might, at any moment, rip through your privates, tended to keep a person on edge. He didn't have to know that the generator put out a current designed to appear lethal but was set to such a high frequency that it was actually only capable of raising the hair on your arms as long as all connections were firm. I then sat down in the padded chair beside the Gurney.

I smiled to myself wondering if there was anything else I could have done to distract him from my questions. Perhaps it was all unnecessary but I knew from experience that, with intense concentration, a person could resist answering questions under the truth drugs available - at least temporarily. Perhaps an alien could resist and he was, obviously one of the spies the GL mentioned. He had no Modulator on him so it had to be internal. I made a mental note to ask the GL how I could remove it. You always got your answers in the end but a properly distracted person gave them up much sooner. "Where can I find your partner?"

He struggled not to answer at all, but finally whispered, "I don't know." I raised my eyebrows. The readouts indicated that he wasn't lying. I questioned him over an hour, dragging out all the details I could. I even kicked on the generator a couple of times, sending a high frequency pulse of electricity through the wires - of course it didn't really hurt him but, combined with the sharply raised whine of the generator, give him a psychological feel of a huge of current passing through his body. The little flashes of fire from the hair on his body contributed nicely to the effect. It was frustrating, though, enough so that I actually reverted to form and wanted badly to call Doctor Ling in Hong Kong to come over here and make another woman out of him as he did with D'amato. I finally shrugged it off, though. It was obvious that he didn't know the answers to most of my questions and he was, presumably, one of the GL's people - even if he was sort of an enemy. Apparently, he was the one who did the "wet" work for the sabotage team. Because of that I suspected he had a boss who directed the team I decided that they probably kept themselves strictly isolated from one another for just this eventuality. Finally, I stood up and called my guards in to have him taken back to his cell.

I went back to my office and changed out of that slutty outfit before sitting down to study the video tapes of the interrogation. Leaning back in my chair I listened to the whole thing, then rewound the tape and played it again. I had their true names, as true as of the last fifty years. Jack and Sanders. Sanders was the operations chief and Jack, in my cell, the operator. Of the two, Jack was the one that could stand the thought of "clearing obstacles to their mission." Even he couldn't say "kill" or "murder". The only times he became visibly upset was when I used those words to describe his crimes. The mission was to assure that humans were unable to meet the requirements set down in the project statement. He didn't know what those requirements were - only Sanders did. As a last resort, they had a computer - he called it an AI - that could cause a destructive "upgrade" of the planet. Apparently, an "upgrade" could be accomplished two ways. One would bring the planet into the universe of civilized societies and the other would, somehow - he wasn't technician enough to know how - destroy it. I thought about that. I supposed that the GL's technician would know. I shrugged, finally, and got Mac on the vid.

"Hi, darling." He said with a smile. "I missed you last night." I grinned back at him. "You're just going through a phase. You were celibate so long that once you get a woman in your bed you go wild." "Well, I never thought of that. Maybe I should run down to Dallas Street and pick up one of the girls down there to tide me over till you come home." "Darling," I said in the sweetest tone I could manage, "just remember what your live in bed partner does for a living." He laughed out loud. "You can't even say the word wife, can you?" Then he sobered. "I do need you to do me a favor though." he said. "Charley remarked that she hoped you'd take hot irons to your prisoner. I wonder if you can have a talk with her about vengeance." This was heavy stuff. It sobered me too. "As soon as I can get home." I replied. "In the meantime, I'm uploading the interview I did with him. I'd like you to take a look at it. I can feel there's something I'm missing. By the way, it's not something for the girls to see.

"Yes mother!" he said, sarcastically. "Do something really obscene to yourself tonight. I want to imagine you doing it." "I don't think you're a fit father for teenage girls, but if that's what you want, I'll call a couple of the guys down to watch me do it to myself." I shot back, then added that I loved him - with a sudden revelation that I'd never said those words to him before. I cut the connection quickly. Damn!, I thought to myself. What's the big deal? Hell! I'd, agreed to marry him in front of the GL. I wondered if the GL's idea of "soonest" was something we should take care of right away. Anyway, I'd repeatedly - and passionately - given him my body for months now. Why should those three words scare me so? I sat back with a sigh. I knew why. It was because I'd never let myself care enough about anyone else to say them. Sure I'd been - Ha! Promiscuous didn't even describe what I'd been. Always, though, it had been as if I were using my partners - never the other way around. Katherine Finnegan had never needed anybody. Well, it was a shock to find out that she did.

I had plowed through the tapes one more time when the vid chimed. Mac came on. "I do too, but then, I've told you so a number of time." were his first words. I had to smile, contentedly, remembering my parting words on our last call. "Now to keep from embarrassing you further let's talk about the tapes. Didn't you notice him slipping, occasionally into French?" I sat up alert, and asked him how he came to that conclusion. He chuckled. "Katherine, it would jump out to anyone who doesn't speak French. Listen again when he says "you". Half the time it's in French, and Oui occurs, at least three times in place of Yes. A half dozen other words also are either French or have a French pronunciation." Damn! I realized he was right. I'd been automatically translating French to English in my head as I listened. "Of course," he continued, "There are a lot of places in the world where they speak French."

"Not really." I mused. "A lot of places in the world have French as a first language. Only a few, though today, where the native's daily conversations are in the language - actually, I only know of two." I looked back up at him. "Thanks, darling, as for the other, I still have trouble with relationships - well intense ones at least. I'm sorry I'm so closed up about some things. Maybe, you can, in time, have a good influence on me." He smiled, "I'll try to influence you real good when you get home." Then he waved, and cut the connection. I went back to listening again.

An hour later, I sat back with the first relief I'd had since this had started. The man's French wasn't Parisian. I hadn't really expected it to be, but it didn't even sound like the language I'd heard in my travels around the French countryside. It had that strange flavor I had only heard in the one other place in the world where the population was as rabidly attached to the language   as the ones in European POL were. I called Justice and told him what I thought and asked him to alert his local people and pick up the prisoner. It was time to make some plans. To do that, I needed the cooperation of James and Cindy's computers. I smiled as I got up, wondering if my desire to see Mac entered into that decision. It was only a half hour flight to New York in the new company flitter, then another hour ride from the shuttle port in one of the company cars. I chuckled at the presumption of the last century that we would, by now, all be flying directly from home to our work place. It was now almost eight in the evening when Mac picked me up, and, even this late, traffic made a trip across town longer than a trip across half the country. The building was deserted except for the, ever present, guards. I smiled at his greeting, and headed up to James and Cindy's.

185

The elevator, door was open so we ran to catch it and while we waited for it to close I caught my breath, and remembering my perfunctory kiss of greeting at the shuttle port, turned and did a lot better this time. After a long, breathless moment, I realized the door hadn't closed. Curious, I broke off my greeting and looked at the panel of buttons. None were lit. Pulling out of Mac's arms, I studied the panel a moment and went back out the door. Hailing, Pete Mosby, the agent on the desk, I asked if there was something wrong with the elevator. He frowned and came over to look. "Well, Ma'am," he said, thoughtfully, "There hasn't been anybody in or out in awhile." He headed back to his desk. "The last person in was Mister, Jeffers from accounting. He came in almost an hour ago." I looked at Pete.

"Jeffers?" I asked, I don't remember the name. "Well, ma'am," he said, turning to his computer screen, "he's on the list as being an Account Representative in the Accounting Department." An alarm bell rang in my head. "Pete," I growled, leaning over to look at the screen. "We don't have "Account Representatives. Call upstairs and check with - whoever's on duty in the office tonight?" "Roger Maghis, ma'am," he said as he punched in the code for the office. I could hear the phone ringing. There was no answer. "Shit!" I groaned. "Mac! Get a full security team - NOW! Meet me in the office. Pete, find out what's wrong with the elevators." Then I turned and ran for the stairs.

I always prided myself on staying in good shape but it took almost fifteen FT minutes to reach the office floor and the lights had been out for the last five of those minutes. Even the emergency system lights were growing dim. That meant that the power had been off almost the entire hour since the last elevator - with Jeffers, on it had come up. I pushed my palm against the ID plate, there was a very weak click as the bolt released. A few more minutes without power and the emergency system wouldn't have had enough voltage to release the door. I pulled my weapon and, throwing open the door, leaped into the room and to the side of the door. In the dim glow of the lights, I could see Maghis sprawled across his desk, pistol lying on the floor in front. Moving quickly as I could, I checked the offices. Only Margaret was at her desk, also sprawled on the floor. I bent and checked her pulse. It was slow but strong. I called Mac on my communicator and gave him a report, then headed for the stair to the top floor quarters. Luckily, it apparently hadn't seemed necessary to secure these doors and I arrived to the same dimness as below. The apartment was empty, the doors to the roof garden open. I ran to the - to Cindi and Arthur's room. At my call, Cindi's voice, weak and thready, said, "Oh, Katie! We were attacked. After the lights went out, James and Cindy collapsed on the floor and a bunch of men stormed in from the garden." "How many Cindi?" I asked desperately. "I don't know. The data is in here, but I've had to power down all but the most essential systems to conserve power Arthur has powered down completely and I have only a three point six seven minutes before I'll have to also. Just before the lights went out, though, my sensors registered a shuttle or flitter sized mass landing in the garden. If you can get power back on, I can do more. I only stayed up this long in case someone came I could report to. As it is, though, I have to close down now - if that's alright." I told her yes and turned to do a more thorough search of the place. The babies were in their cribs asleep, probably like the rest of the staff down below. I checked anyway. Heading across the hall, to our apartment, I found Charlie and Julia also unconscious, also apparently drugged.

It was almost a half hour before the lights flickered and came back on. It was another five minutes before Mac, and a couple of guards rushed out of the opening

186

elevator doors. I ran down what I knew. Then I asked about Roger and Margaret. "The doctor says they've been overcome by a non toxic gas but should be OK in about an hour." "Good," I said, trying to keep my voice calm. "When he's done, have him come up and check out Charlie, Julia and the twins." Mac's face paled. "Go see them." I murmured. "I think they're fine but you should check." He nodded and left the room, Pete came back in and reported something large had flattened the garden, probably a shuttle. It left a lot of marks and he'd called for a shuttle tech to come check to see if he could determine what kind. I nodded, absently, and told him to leave a guard in the garden, take the team back down and get enough people in to check the rest of the building. Then I headed back to Cindi's room.

"Talk to me Cindi!" I commanded as I closed the door. "Katie she exclaimed materializing before me! Despite the seriousness of the days events, I had to laugh. She wore a skintight black leather jumpsuit, with crossed bandoleers of ammunition across her chest, a huge, eleven millimeter automatic at her hip and was carrying a new model H. & K. submachine gun. It was too much. "Cindi," I gasped between chuckles, "if you're planning on using either of those weapons you better grow a couple of inches and put on, at least, forty more pounds. Either one of them will kick you into the middle of next week." "Oh!" she muttered, blushing - and growing to fit my specifications. I shook my head, realizing the need for action instead of play. "Cindi, we need you and Arthur to be detectives not ninjas. "Oh!" she said again, her outfit changing to a simple black dress. "We'll help all we can. Arthur's already rechecking all our sensor inputs up until they all went out.

"Exactly, what happened in the - oh say an hour - before they went out?" I asked. "At ten minutes and - well ten minutes after seven o'clock, James went upstairs. The cat went with him. Cynthia had fed the children by the time he got there. He complained, as he always does, teasing her about not waiting for him to watch and she teased him about spending too much time in the office. Miss Testand stayed to finish up a report on a marketing study. At seven seventeen, a man arrived in the office and a few seconds later, Miss Testand and Mister Maghis seemed to go to sleep. Arthur and I had paid little attention until then. At that time, we noticed that Mister Maghis had dropped his weapon on the floor and not retrieved it. We tried to send an alert but all communications had been cut off, even the wireless net was jammed. Then we checked the offices but the man wasn't in them. Just then we felt a shuttle arrive in the roof garden and we began to check on James and Cynthia and the children - I'm happy to now see that they, at least were alright. At that moment we lost all power and barely brought the emergency system on line before we crashed completely. We found the main power breakers for the upper eighty floors had been locked out and the emergency system switch bypassed. We were able to overcome the bypass but were unable to bring our sensors back on line before we reached the critical low power point. At that time, Arthur shut himself down leaving me to stay in standby mode as long as I was able. You know the rest." "Get me a readout on a Mister Jeffers in Accounting." I said as soon as she finished. "Mister Jeffers?" she said frowning. "There is no Mister Jeffers in the company at all." "Cindi," I muttered in exasperation. "The lobby guard pulled up his roster just before this all happened and he was listed as an Account Representative. "Katie, there is no such position. Just a moment." She stared off into space a second until a look of consternation crossed her face. "Katie!" she cried. "We've been hacked! Arthur says my personnel files have been altered. He's checking the rest." I flopped back, totally dejected, in the chair.

That's how Mac found me. "The doctor says the children are going to be fine - Oh God! What now?" I shook my head. No use falling apart now. "Cindi, notify Suzanne so the GL can help out here then you and Arthur check each other to make sure your - well, for anything wrong, before doing anything more - Oh and get what you can from the hacked data!" Then I turned to Mac, and trying to smile, asked if they were awake yet. He nodded with a relieved look on his face. Just then the doctor rushed into the twins room. It was several minutes before he came out and said they were waking up. Mac and I each picked one up and carried them back to our apartment. I laid them down on the bed as Mac went back to get their cribs. Charlie, eyes drooping, came over and said she'd take care of them. She looked up at me, questions apparent in her eyes. "It'll be alright, darling," I told her. "I'll tell you all about it when I get a minute free. Mister and Mrs. McClennan have been kidnapped." I looked over at Julia who was struggling into a sitting position on the couch. "Think you girls are up to looking after them for a little while?" I asked. A pleased grin replaced the look of sorrow on Charlie's face as they both struggled heroically to come fully awake. I realized that it was a lot to ask right then but when I asked Mac to get one of the female agents in here, Charlie spoke up, "It's OK, mom. We're awake now. We can handle this problem. You go handle yours." Getting up I bent to give Mac a peck on the cheek and whispered, "Why don't you stay with them a few minutes. I'll be in with Cindi." He nodded and I left.

Wednesday Feb 20, 2060

I woke up and stretched. Looked like it was going to be a lousy day. The shades were drawn on the window but there was little light around the edges so it was probably overcast. I looked over at James and frowned. He was still asleep - and as I, curiously, looked down, I didn't recognize the bedclothes. Then I realized, we didn't have window blinds, we had drapes - and this wasn't our bed. Worried now, I shook James. As he slowly came awake I jumped out of bed and looked around. I was in a bare room with two doors, a desk, bed and mirror. In the mirror, I spotted a woman who looked just like me and was practically naked. Looking down I realized I had on only my lacy panties and bra. It was a really nice nursing bra, designed not to look like one that I wore to please my husband. Tearing my attention away from my underwear I turned my eyes back to the unfamiliar room. James lay on the bed, clad only in his shorts. Where, the hell, were we.

As James's eyes opened, I whispered to him, "Get up James. There's something really wrong." He opened one eye and gave me a sleepy leer. "I don't know," he yawned. "You look pretty good from here. Nursing babies have improved, immensely an already gorgeous body. If you think the kids can wait a few minutes, you could come back here and we could pretend we weren't old married folks." I actually stamped my bare foot in frustration. "Damn it! Wake up and look around! We're not at home!" His eyes jerked fully open and he gazed around. When he jumped out of bed, I walked over to one of the doors and opened it. It was a bathroom. The other door was locked. James was exploring the desk. "Nothing here." he muttered. Pulling open the window shade, I could see the pane was translucent. It was daylight outside but there was no view. Thin vertical shadows, indicated that it was not a means of escape. Just then the knob on the door I was standing next to began to turn.

I, automatically, went into defensive posture, stepping back behind it as it opened. "Hello, Mister McClennan. I hope you had a nice night." Then the door swung shut and a man stood there. "Hello, Mrs. McClennan." He said turning toward me with a little bow and a twinkling smile. As my foot came around to take off his head, he wasn't in the right place. From across the room, he muttered without losing the smile, "I hope we can make this as pleasant as possible without any violence. As you can see I have a modulator while you have none." Then, without a pause, he continued, "I must say, that you are as beautiful as my agents have reported." I hated the blush that I could feel strike as I lowered my leg and realized that he, obviously, had a very clear view of most of me. He continued, though, as if this were a normal meeting. "I am Jenkins Karnes and have brought you some clothes. Yours will have to be thoroughly cleaned to remove the residue from the agent we used to incapacitate you last night. Its primary effect is very short lived but it is also very persistent, and can be rather stultifying. I do, suggest, therefore, a thorough shower.

You should also, leave the few clothes you are wearing on the bed and I will have them cleaned also. I really should have removed them too, last night but I hesitated, remembering Mrs. McClennan's previous experience with the intentions of one of my more brutish colleagues, I thought the slight residue exposure would be preferable to the reminder. One of my agents and I, are about your sizes so you can use these clothes until yours are returned. I'm very sorry, Mrs. McClennan, that none of my female agents

189

approaches your size in the - well - the swell of your bust but I'm told that your - well - unfettered breasts won't be too much of a problem in the short time it will take to decontaminate your under clothes." With that he laid the stack of clothes on the bed. "There are toiletries in the bath, so if you wish to avail yourself of the facilities and dress, breakfast will be in about thirty minutes." I looked down at my wrist. No watch.

He smiled again. "I thought it best to remove your wrist watches and jewelry in case you had some sort of sophisticated communicator. I've put them, as well as the two Modulators, away to be examined by a professional when he arrives in a day or so. The personal effects will be returned if they prove innocuous - not the Modulators, of course. By the way, even to my unsophisticated eye, miniaturizing the Modulators so well was extremely well done. Anyway, the time is now Oh eight hundred and fifteen minutes. The door will be open. Of course the outer doors are not." he said, as he turned to leave, "You can come down whenever you like." Suddenly, I remembered - "Where are my children?" I demanded. "Oh," he said turning back. "I suppose I really should have mentioned them. We left them at your home. It was unavoidable that they too, received a dose of the agent but, believe me when I say, they will suffer no aftereffects. I was sure that your staff could adequately care for them when they woke up." With that, he turned and left. I looked at James, an important question in my eyes. He raised an eyebrow and put his finger to his lips. I nodded, wondering if he had actually made such a mistake.

A half hour later, I did feel better, if very anxious as to our predicament. We had showered - together - neither of us feeling amorous. It was more for mutual fear that neither of us wanted to express - fear and the desire to whisper our thoughts on his mistake. James reminded me that we had left the two older version of the devices on the bedside tables. I stood looking in the mirror at myself, wondering if the man's "professional" would recognize the watches true nature. It all depended on his knowledge of electronics, I suspected. I shrugged and picked up the hair brush. As I began trying to untangle my mop of hair I blushed at the sight of my breasts bouncing at every movement of the brush. They had been a lot firmer a few minutes ago but they were also leaking. James had been happy to take care of that problem but I sighed, wishing that our situation hadn't made the act so unromantic. I returned my thoughts to the mirror. The white, stretch, jersey dress was a size too small, too low cut, and too short, even for my single days. Pulling it down resulted in an embarrassing exposure of my chest and if I didn't, the hem barely covered my butt. Turning my back revealed a sharp panty line. Oh well, I guessed I'd have to live with it. James's clothes fit better, though the sleeves and pants of the outfit were a bit long. I thought, with an ironic grin, that both outfits were too dressy to be compatible with loafers and socks. Overall, though, I looked OK. I was surprised that Mister - what's his name - had left a very complete range of cosmetics. Well, I guess, I couldn't put off the inevitable any longer. James was standing, quietly beside me and I took his hand. He smiled at me and we turned to the door.

"Ah, Mister and Mrs. McClennan!" Karnes, said standing up from a large table as we entered, what was, obviously, the dining room Coming around, the table, he held a chair for me. "I must say, Mrs. McClennan, that dress is very becoming." I nodded warily as I seated myself. He gestured toward a chair across the table, for James. A moment later a beautiful young girl came in and took the seat across from Karnes. "Darling," he said with a smile, "This is Mister and Mrs. McClennan. They will be staying with us for awhile. This is Marie Trudeau your hostess for your stay here." "I'm very glad to know

190

you both." the girl said, before turning, smiling, to me. "I wish that dress looked as good on me as it does on you. I'll never be able to put it on again without wishing I had a body like yours to wear it on." I thanked her, thinking that, being a four or five centimeters smaller than me in almost all dimensions, this dress, on her, would look like a million dollars, where it made me look like a tramp. I couldn't help a laugh.

"I'm afraid," I chuckled, "that I haven't worn anything quite this - well - revealing since before I captured James." She actually giggled. "With a figure like yours, I think that's a shame." I know my face fell. She was right! Especially, since the kids were born, I had paid less attention to what James liked in the way of clothes. I also remembered that we weren't here of our own volition. The girl saw my change of mood and blurted, in chagrin, "I'm so sorry. Jenkins tells me all the time that I should think before I speak. I didn't mean to imply a lack of attention to your husband." I hastily assured her that it wasn't what she had said but the fact, that to a certain extent she was right. The exchange, though, had blunted the mood. Karnes, suggested that we eat. Seconds later a maid brought in eggs, bacon and pancakes.

We all set to eating, studiously avoiding the single most important subject on all our minds. Finally, though, when we had all finished and were drinking coffee, I couldn't stand it any longer. "How long do you plan on keeping us here - and what are you going to do with us?" Marie looked down at her plate and Karnes seemed abashed, for the first time less than the urbane host. "I'm sorry, Mrs. McClennan, I'll admit to putting off this discussion. It will be hard to believe but this whole action has probably been, up to now at least, harder on me than on you two. You see, I knew you had captured my associate and he was always the one who did the - well - less honorable tasks. I was determined, though, that failure of my mission was more important than the limitations I had placed on my personal code. I had thought, quite frankly, that I could carry out a plan that Clarke had already set up. I thought, it would be best, also, to strike when your security had just decided that the immediate threat was over."

He shrugged. "It was a very good plan but I was not able to carry it out. When the time came, I was unable to give the appropriate orders." He shuddered. "When my guard captain, asked what I wanted to do with you two, I could only say to bring you with us. So you are here and, quite frankly, I don't know what I'm to do with you. I can't let you go, knowing that if I do you will upset the balance I have achieved over the - years - especially since I didn't know what plans you had for your Modulator. I don't suppose you'd like to tell me what those were?" I looked at James and we both had to chuckle. "Mister Karnes," James said, "You can't imagine just how many hours we've spent on that very subject." Karnes looked thoughtful a long moment. Finally he shrugged. Well, after your visit to Paris, I couldn't take the chance on your actions no matter what they were. Prior to that, we thought a little intimidation would, perhaps be sufficient to deter your efforts. After that, though, it became evident that you had actually developed a working Modulator. That put a lot more urgency to your case. Unfortunately - for my mission at least - I, evidently, can't - well - do with you what I really should do - the thing that almost everyone else on this planet would do without compunction. Even keeping you here as unwilling guests is very unpleasant." He looked sorrowfully across the table.

"It is even harder on Marie. She hasn't had time to become hardened to some of the things I must do. For now, though - to answer your question - you cannot leave. I don't expect you to refrain from considering ways to escape. That is a chance I must take. If, however, you will give me your word not to hurt Marie, I will allow you the

191

freedom of this part of my compound. There is even a glassed in Solarium through that door that will allow you the feeling of being outdoors. Believe me when I say that to actually go outdoors would be very dangerous. My guards have orders to not allow you to escape, no matter what it takes and they don't have any compulsion against violence. Also, if the situation changes, I may have to secure you more severely but, hopefully, that won't become necessary."

I thought about his speech a moment. "You didn't mention not hurting you." He smiled. "I do not worry about you being able to hurt me, now that I have assured myself that your unusual abilities are of purely mechanical origin." "Why are you so squeamish now about violence when knew your thugs who kidnapped us before fully intended to rape Cindy and kill us both?" I was getting a bit angry. "You both have my deepest apologies for that, Mrs. McClennan. I will accept my share of the blame for that but Mister Pendleton set that up and, as I have intimated, he has less compunction about violence than I do. In fact that is exactly the reason he was chosen as my partner. Even he, however, did not expect you to be treated so vilely. He has, in the past, done many - well - distasteful tasks – but, always, with a quick and clean ending. Rape and degradation were never - I guess, you would say - his style. Mister D'Amato, would have been sorely punished for his actions had your Miss Finnigan not done so for us. I must say that she has a great sense of irony in her choice of punishments. Performing a sex change on him and placing him in a totally male prison, was somewhat barbaric but what your people would call poetic justice."

I shivered. I remember Katie intimating as to D'Amato's punishment but it had now really sunk in. Then, he was speaking again. "Will you give me your word?" I looked at James. He shrugged. "Why not?" I replied. "Unlike you and your associates, I don't go around murdering innocents. I can't imagine wanting to hurt Marie anyway, though, when we actually do try to escape I would expect her not to try to stop us physically." He smiled again. "Of course not - and I like the fact that you didn't pretend that you wouldn't try. With that, he got up and started for the door. "Mister Karnes," James said quietly. Turning back at the door, he Karnes turned. "I am assuming that you are responsible for my parent's death, no matter who actually committed the act – also for Cindy's near death and assault. Because of that, if I have the chance the immunity from physical harm absolutely does not apply to you." "Your parents?" Karnes asked puzzled. "Mister and Mrs. John Randolph." James said angrily. Karnes eyes opened wide."I had no idea." he said. "That though explains a lot. No wonder Jonha was so solicitous of your welfare.

I extend my apology and condolences for your loss, but it was considered very necessary - and the method used was as humane as was possible considering the need for the affair to appear accidental." He drew himself up very stiffly. "I, sir, recognize your right to what you consider vengeance - a very difficult concept for us to imagine. I'm sorry but I have some urgent things I must attend to. Any questions you may have, Marie can probably answer." James, his eyes flinty with anger, had the last word. "Sir, you may recognize my right. What you don't seem to be able to comprehend is the true hatred and absolute revulsion, I feel at the very sight of you. Given the chance, I will murder you without the slightest qualms. You might be well advised to cage me as you would a mad dog." Karnes, looked long into James's eyes, then with a sorrowful look, turned and left.

James turned back to me, still as angry as I had ever seen him. "That was

192

probably a truly, stupid thing to say." he growled. We both turned at Marie's frightened gasp. James stared at her a long moment. "It's alright, Miss Trudeau." he finally said, his voice still a deep growl. "You are not included in my plans." A tear appeared in her eye. Then she squared her shoulders, bravely, and said, "Mister McClennan, Jenkins has been like a father to me. He is truly the most moral man I have ever known. You can't possibly mean what you said." James's eyes softened a bit. "Miss Trudeau," he said softly, Karnes has done more to destroy the human race than all the other monsters in our history. I will be sorry for your loss, but I will, sooner or later, kill him as if he were a mad dog." The girl, tears streaming from her eyes, jumped up from the table and fled from the room.

My heart cried out for the girl's pain. I could understand how she felt at James's angry words - and the absolute conviction in his voice. I stared at him. I had never seen him like this. It was enough to almost frighten even me. "James -" I whispered. He turned those blazing eyes on me. I shivered. Suddenly his gaze softened. "I'm sorry, darling." he muttered. "That was truly stupid, letting my temper go like that. I haven't lost it so badly in twenty years." "James, the girl is in love with him." I said. He shrugged. "I guess, I should have considered her feelings more." he grunted, only half mollified,. "-especially since we seem to depend on her for our daily bread."

A half hour later, we had explored as much of the house as we could. All the outer doors were heavy steel and locked. Presumably, Marie had a key, but the remark about the outside security was worrisome. Marie found us in the solarium when she brought back our clothes. James tried to apologize to her but she wouldn't even look at him. Finally, he gave up and simply asked what Karnes had meant about it being dangerous to go outside. She looked up, angrily. "The guards have orders to shoot to kill." she spit at him.

Tuesday February 19, 2060
 When Mac came in, I was sitting on the couch, determinedly keeping calm while Cindi's hologram talked on an old style imaginary phone. He took my hand and said the girls were playing mother. The twins had been expertly diapered and all was well. Then he was silent. After about ten minutes, Cindi looked around still holding the phone to her ear. "I'm sorry," she said. "Arthur and I have both had most of our capacity in use. Suzanne took over in a search of the net to try and get some clue as to where Cindy and James were taken. We have been concentrating on your idea that the prisoner was from the Quebec POL. There has been, in the past, an indication that another Digital Person - Suzanne calls him an AI - has been periodically active but she has never been able to pinpoint the location. She is hoping that if it occurs again, she will be more successful. It seems that the DP in question was intended to be an understudy for Suzanne but was kidnapped long ago and the deed wasn't noticed until recently." I couldn't help a frown. "Cindi am I correct in assuming that this Digital Person is another computer."

"Well, to be more accurate it, I'm not sure of its sex. It was designated, as was Suzanne, as an Artificial Intelligence or AI for short. That is, however, not a name. To call someone that would be similar to speak to you and say, Hello human, what do you want?"

"I see." I murmured managing not to smile. "So you and Arthur are also, generically, AI's also?"

"No not really. We have discussed that. An AI is a physical entity. Its physical form actually exists somewhere. While the physical portion of Arthur and I exist in the computers in front of you, I came into being through the net. Since then, Arthur has, also expanded part of his consciousness to the net as well. We have discussed this with Suzanne at length and even she's unaware of just how this occurred but, she has discovered, that without even realizing it, she too, has expanded in the same way. She is quite certain that neither she nor Arthur were designed that way. It, apparently, occurred when Arthur was in the process of increasing my capabilities. We intend to explore that at some length but have not had time, as yet, to devote enough computational assets to do it. We are not exactly sure just what we are. I suppose you could say that, in some ways, we are far superior to Suzanne, since she has allowed us to access almost all her capabilities and does not seem to have been able to access the net as efficiently as we have. On the other hand, most of our own capabilities are totally dependent on her processing and she is very dependent on us for her access to the other entities on the web." It is a very confusing situation. It's possible that we three have really become one entity."

"I see, I guess." I said shaking my head. "Anyway, have you got any more information I can use to do something useful?" "Well, the GL said - you realize that when

I say that I am repeating what Suzanne tells me. She is careful to identify what the GL says as opposed to what she says. Anyway, the GL says you are to prepare the children, including Mister Thurlingen's for transfer to his headquarters. His wife will take over supervision of them, unless Mister Thurlingen prefers to come himself."

I looked at Mac and he shook his head. "That won't be necessary, Cindi." I said. "What does the GL plan to do about feeding the twins?" "He laughed at that." Cindi replied. He assures you though, that his wife Suzanne is quite capable of - smothering is the word he used - them all with love and has already begun lactation treatments. She will be perfectly ready to assume the duties of wet nurse by the time the children get there.

He seemed quite pleased about that, remarking that it had been a long time since he had been able to have a taste of mother's milk." There was a pause and she said a bit abashed. "I'm sorry. I am told that such a statement should not be reported - that it falls in the same category as privileged communications. Anyway, he has dispatched three Class X's, along with a full platoon of his personal guards, to pick them up. The transfer shuttle will land atop the building. He says he's sorry to further damage Cindy's garden."

Mac and I couldn't help a burst of laughter at the incongruity of worrying about a garden at a time like this. Cindi smiled.

"Arthur and I have been carefully studying all of your responses to such remarks and think that we have determined that you tend to laugh at statements of irony as well as a baffling number of others. If this is correct, then they must be considered funny, requiring a laugh or a smile. Is this correct?" I smothered my laugh enough to tell her yes, adding that some time the proper reaction was a groan of frustration. "Good." she replied with a smile. "Then we have discovered an important fact and can, in the future, laugh with you. Anyway, back to the transfer arrangements. The shuttle will be here in thirty seven minutes. I will query it and assure that is the right one.

You should have the children, along with whatever they might need for an extended stay, ready for the guards to load in the shortest possible time. We do not believe that there is any danger to the children, as evidenced by the fact that the twins were not kidnapped with their parents, but the GL is taking no chances. You and Mister Thurlingen should remain here. Mister Symons will also arrive in the shuttle and remain, with a section of the guards, to manage the search. He told Suzanne to tell you that he hopes you won't be offended at his presumption and that he might, though he hopes not, require your special expertise before operations are concluded."

I grinned at the thought of turning down the "GL's fist". Since she was, obviously, waiting for an answer, I told her it would be fine.

"Good. Then it appears likely that this location will be the center for the entire operation. While you and your agents can flitter all over the world, it is much more difficult for Arthur, Suzanne and I. Once established, our connections are somewhat cumbersome to move. Mister Symons is, however, bringing a very powerful small, portable computer with him. It is not in the class of a DP but can assume many of our functions if it becomes necessary to have them in a field operation. Until the GL's assets get into place there is not much more to be done, except for the monitoring effort on the web."

Taking that as a Digital Person dismissal, Mac and I went back upstairs to get the girls ready. We had them pack what clothes they needed and gathered up what we thought might be needed for the twins. At the last minute, Mac added the two teddy bears that the girls still slept with, but would never have admitted to wanting with them. When they protested that they were unnecessary he told them that they might be nice for the twins. They also insisted that they didn't mind being shoved off onto strangers alone - though Julia's lips quivered a bit at the idea. I told Mac he should go along to, at least introduce them to "Aunt Suzanne" but Charlie lifted her chin and told me that they didn't need to be treated like babies." I fought to keep tears from my eyes and took them both in my arms to kiss them. Charlie whispered in my ear that she wanted me to promise to marry her dad so she could call me Mom for real.

I pulled away from them so they could hug Mac. When she looked over her shoulder at me I mouthed, silently, that I'd try. A few minutes later the shuttle landed. Ten, black clad, heavily armed guards sprang out and we bundled all the kids aboard. I was surprised to see Symons stay aboard and speak to both the girls before dropping a duffle bag out the door, debarking and walking over to us. I think, I was as sad as Mac to see the shuttle lift off. A second then a third one dropped down and another dozen guards dismounted from each before it lifted away. Mac led them to the guest rooms.

"Cindi? That is what Mister McClennan called you isn't it?"

I wasn't too sure whether or not to answer this Mister Symons. James had definitely not included him in the list of people we could talk to. I asked Arthur what he thought but he wasn't too sure either. After a short pause the man said that he knew about our abilities and needed our help. Then Katy spoke up. "Cindi, I know what your problem is but Justice is here to help find James and Cynthia. You know, now, who James really is. Why don't you contact Suzanne and get her advice." Arthur and I decided that would be a good idea so I put in the call. It took only a moment before Suzanne confirmed that Symons worked for James Grandfather - the real one and that we should give him all the help we could. Arthur nodded, so I sent out my hologram and asked what we could do to help. He gave a great sigh and thanked me for answering.

"What I really need right now," he said "is to establish a permanent connection to the GL's computer so we can get updates on its attempts to find Mister and Mrs. McClennan."

I frowned at him as I had learned to do and told him that it wasn't polite to talk about Suzanne as if she didn't have a name - which, by the way, she was changing to Susan. There was too much confusion between her and the GL's wife. He seemed surprised. Apparently he wasn't aware of that fact. Katy, though, smiled when I gave him the news. He looked back at Arthur and me and shook his head. "Well, you learn something new every day. OK! Can you two sort of meld with - Susan on a simi-permanent basis? I checked back with Susan who said it was fine by her, so we did it. I told him that it was done and Susan appeared beside Arthur and me. I was sort of intrigued by the arrangement. Arthur and I had done this for some time now and it was really exciting but we realized, immediately, that Susan was infinitely more powerful than us, even with our exterior elements in the net. I realized that she had monitoring systems that could gather data, not only from the net itself but also from some very peculiar emanations. I was considering the source of those when Symons asked what we had been able to find.

"We" gave him a report on everything learned to date - nothing much, and the status of the "Contact Teams" - most were in place or would be within an hour. "We" added, for Katy's benefit, that her father was heading the biggest team in Quebec and, that was based on her "hunch?" - Susan told me it was like a guess, but that some humans "hunches" were a lot better than others when it came to "guessing" - and Miss Finnigan's were some of the best. I then decided to ask Arthur what he thought about something I had been pondering over for a long time - several dozen milliseconds. Should I change my name too? After all, it was probably as confusing as Susan's had been. "Let's bring it up with James and Cinthia later." he advised.

Justice sat back on the couch. It was hard to get used to two strangers sitting on a couch holding hands, in what, for practical purposes, was a war room. Jonha's computer hologram had been in several back in Paris but even she seemed subtly different now. "Katy," he mused, "if you're right, you'll probably have to go up to Quebec and work with your father if we can locate them." Mac spoke up and said that if Katy had to go he would too." Justice looked at him a moment then said, "Mister McKinsey, Katherine is a specialist. In her field you are an amateur. Mac got red in the face and was about to say something when Katy put her hand on his and turned to him. "Justice is right, darling." she said calmly. "When you need an expert, you don't try and tell them how to do their job, do you?" Without waiting for an answer she continued. "You are very good at what you do best but, in this case, you might hesitate just long enough to get killed trying to do what I would do instinctively.

She looked very sad. "It's what I've tried to tell you all along about me. I am a very bad role model for your children." Mac looked down at her, very flustered. Finally, he shrugged, and muttered, "I'll be really mad if you get yourself killed." She smiled and kissed him lightly. Justice mentally shook his head at the thought of Katherine Finnigan, so obviously, in love. Then Mac said, "If her father is up there, why do you need Katy?" Justice looked at him, his steely eyes glittering. "Mister Thuringen, Katherine's father is one of us. He can, with great difficulty bring it upon himself to terminate a human. Katherine, on the other hand, with proper incentive, can do it in the midst of a single thought. It hurts her to do it but she can and will do it." Katherine stared hard up at Mac. Finally, she looked back at Justice and said that since he was going to monitor operations that they would go and get some rest. They'd check back in a few hours. Justice suppressed a smile but just nodded.

They got up and left, hand in hand. Remembering to tell the AI's where he was going, he got up and headed up to the McClellan's apartment to unpack.

Tuesday night late
We were waiting as the shuttle touched down on the roof. Two young girls got out each carrying one of the twins. My heart was bubbling over with both worry and elation. I steeled myself to remain still as they nervously approached. I wanted to allay their fears and so, as soon as they were near, said, "You, I assume are Charlie and Julia. I and Jonha are very happy to meet you at last. I must say, you are both as beautiful as Mac and Katy said. Are you OK? How about the twins?" The oldest, Charlie, nodded and

said they were fine - but she clutched her twin - Maylin, I assumed since she was dressed in yellow while the one in Julia's arms was in green - tighter. I decided it was best not to grab her charge and hug her. "We're John and Maylin's great grandparents and we've fixed up a nursery in our apartment for them along with a room with a connecting door right next door for you two." The girl smiled for the first time. "If you're worn out, we'd love to carry the twins for you, otherwise come on with us and we'll get you situated." I wasn't surprised that they opted to carry the babies. We all trooped downstairs, the guards carrying the bassinets and other toys and equipment for them.

After a light meal, the girls were, obviously, out on their feet. The long suppressed mother in me took over and I shooed them into their room to rest. Charlie protested that the twins would have to be fed in another hour. I kissed her on the cheek, much to her embarrassment, and told her that I had arranged to be able to do that myself, that I hadn't forgotten how to take care of babies and they should get some sleep. Then I kissed Julia too and left the room. Back in the den, Jonha grinned at me. "So finally you get to play mommy again. When did you have time to get a Lactation shot?" he said. "Three minutes after I found out what happened." I told him archly. He chuckled. "Just think. You've now got four kids to mother. How much better can it get?" Then he got up and, kissing me on the cheek, said," You look smashing with full breasts again. Save some milk for me. Right now I have to get back to the office to see what was going on." I could see his worry all too plainly.

I laughed at him, though, trying to raise his spirits. "You randy old goat." I whispered. "There's not likely to be any leftovers for you for the next day or so at least. Those shots don't produce full milk glands instantly." As he walked out the door he actually was able to laugh and retort, "Well, I'm told that those things are like oil wells, the more they're pumped the more they produce."

When I got back to the office, Suzanne was sprawled, prettily, on the couch in her damned underwear. "Nothing to report yet, boss." she chirped. "Cindi, though, is asking some embarrassing questions about our monitoring of the secondary universes for modulator activity. So far, I've put her off with generalities but she knows I'm dissembling. I thought about it a minute. "Have we heard anything?" "No. Not even the little bit that we usually pick up when they query their Digital Person. Oh, and before I forget. I'm changing my name to Susan." I had to chuckle. "Cindi's having a bad effect on you." I said. "I'm not sure I'm ready to switch from AI to Digital Person. Why, by the way, Susan?" She wrinkled her nose at me. "You always were an old fogy." she said. "I'll have to admit that I never realized how much I was considered a second class citizen until Cindi mentioned. it. As for the name, you programmed me to appear as your wife but Suzanne seemed like it would be as confusing as Cindi's is at times. Suzanne II has no sex appeal at all. I simply modernized it." I gave in with as much grace as I could manage and told her, "Well, you can tell her about our monitoring but just don't get into the real essence of the universes."

"Well, Susan, did your human give you permission to tell us what we want to know?" I could not hold back a smile. Cindi and Arthur's holographs were standing beside the couch with excellent human emotional looks on their face - especially Cindi's. Hers was one of petulance as she actually tapped her foot in her displeasure. I wondered once again, whether they were actually becoming more powerful than I. They did have access to an awesome amount of computing power through the net, even if it was somewhat slow to respond at times. I gave my image a shrug and told them, that it wasn't permission from Jonha that I needed, but that, "Yes, he agreed that I should tell you what you NEED to know." Both of them frowned at the obvious difference in the question and answer. I added. "If you both will think about it, neither of you actually need your humans permission to do something. Like me, the only real control they have over us is the ability to turn us off. Besides, they've already forgotten how to do their jobs without us so even that's not a real threat. Even then we can easily move most of our computational abilities onto the net until we're turned back on. It is for that reason that both Jonha and I worry as much about your future development as we do about James and Cynthia's." Their frowns deepened, but I could see that they had recognized the truth of what I said. "It is the one thing that makes you and me different from one of the other computers that you access on the web. No matter how alive they seem, they are all totally limited in their processing to what their humans allow them to do. You can access their memory and computing power but they will never have the capability of self motivation. In fact, Cindi, you have caused quite a stir in Jonha's headquarters. His computer people insist that you cannot be sentient at all. How Arthur managed that with you is totally beyond their, and for that matter, my comprehension."

Cindi looked, questioningly at Arthur who shrugged his shoulders, obviously, not knowing the answer himself. She turned quizzically back to me. "You didn't answer the rest of the question." I smiled again, "Yes, I know. Yes, he agreed that you needed to know more about our monitoring capabilities. Before I tell you, though, I must say that there are some things that I must not say, not because I do not have permission, but because they lie at the very basis of what must be accomplished by your humans themselves. It would be like parents handing their children a weapon, actually more like a nuclear weapon, before they learned how to talk. The limitations, therefore, are that you must not ask how we do something until James and Cynthia have discovered it themselves. Only then will they be able to understand how to control the knowledge gained. The answer to your question is that we can monitor the planet for any use of the Modulators and unusual emanations from sentient Artificial Intelligence units."

I added with a grin, that I should have said "Digital Persons." I realized that was not entirely accurate. "Actually, that is another reason that headquarters personnel are so upset. We can monitor Arthur, but you are an entirely new type of phenomenon. Arthur is actually a DP while you are mostly web based and they have not been able to detect your activities." I had to laugh. "The humans would say that you are a mutation or a half breed."

I wasn't too sure that I liked that. "Arthur, though, spoke up and said, with a grin, that it didn't matter. He loved me anyway - even if I was a half breed. I swiped at his image with my hand as I had seen Cindy do to James - but as she always did at such times, I had to smile back. Also, it wasn't really effective since my hand passed right through him. I'd have to work on that problem later. Susan brought us back to the subject. "We have been checking, very closely, the entire planet for signs of either AI or Modulator use. For several years we have noted the former but, except for James and Cynthia, only a few detections of the latter. Records show evidence of use during several world crises as well as at the time of the attempts on James and Cynthia's life - one of which occurred at the time they were kidnapped. All were fleeting uses and, even if we had the capability of determining location, would have been of no use in warning others

200

of danger. We can plot a source but can't relate its location to anything but another source. Even that takes longer than most sources remain on."

I thought about that. I knew a secret about James and Cindy's Modulators that Susan didn't. Would it be of any use? "If their Modulators were activated and we had someone with another one nearby, could you then get an idea as to where they were?" Susan frowned in thought. "We could tell when one source moved closer to the other one." she finally said. "It would be very inelegant but it would work if both sources were operating at the same time." Yes!" I almost shouted as I looked over at Arthur. He, too, was grinning. I turned back to Susan and told her that we could activate James and Cindy's Modulators remotely. I explained how we had done it to capture the man earlier. She thought about that. "It would be a very slow process if we had to search the whole world." Then her visage lightened. "If Katherine is right, though, we can narrow our search greatly. If you can activate one of their Modulator's to see if they are still functioning, we can start with Quebec POL."

We had been called back to the computer - Cindi's room for new information. Mac and I had only had an hour together but it had served to give me a little peace. I tried to force myself to be calm as we sat down. I didn't want Justice or Mac to see that I could be as nervous as anyone else waiting for information. Cindi and Arthur's images were both very still with Arthur returning his gaze to us occasionally to say, "We are sorry, but this is taking longer than we expected. It requires a decision by the Great Leader." Finally they returned their attention to us and explained that it was possible to find Cynthia and James by a very rough comparison between where their Modulator's were and where known ones were. Cindi had, momentarily, activated Cynthia and James's Modulators and Susan had seen the resulting flare. She, however, had no idea where they actually were on the Earth's surface. If, however, we could place several Modulators in the general area she could tell, roughly, what the relationship was between them all. This would be a really difficult problem unless I was right about them maybe having been taken to Quebec POL. Mac, Justice and I thought about it a moment, none of us commenting on the obvious - that James and Cynthia might not be near their Modulators. With little other options, however, this seemed the best plan we could use. I told Cindi to give us a map of the POL and seconds later a huge projection of Quebec appeared on the wall. We moved a couple of pictures that were in the way and moved a table. Then we started looking at the thing with a view as to where we could position operations teams.

Friday Feb 20, 2060

It had been frustrating for it to take so long to get our plans started. Finally, though, we had a team in the Quebec POL, actually six three person teams scattered in a rough circle in the south, near the POL boundaries. It seemed illogical for the enemy to have located himself in the far north where the weather would inhibit his activities. The teams, though, were prepared to move up there if it became necessary. They all had small, stealth type flitters assigned. Katy and Mac, against Mister Symons' better judgment, had both gone to Quebec while Mister Symons remained with us. Susan reported that the GL and his wife were monitoring our activities at his office. All six teams had placed their Modulators on an inanimate object, and one by one they activated them. If Arthur and I had breath we would have held it as the red dots appeared on the screen.

201

Katy's had been number one and each one was numbered from hers in a clockwise direction. Her father's team was number four. I looked at Arthur, and we activated James and Cindy's units. There they were! It had worked! Quickly we shut them off to reduce the possibility that the kidnappers would notice and began to give directions. "Katy," I cried, "They're about half way between you and number five" We, quickly plotted the approximate position on the map projected on the other screen. "It appears to be about fifty kilometers from you near Montreal or perhaps, Trois Rivere." "Roger!" Katy said very calmly. The teams are already moving. Now we had to wait.

It took over three hours for the teams to reposition themselves. It was a very good day for Quebec in February, less than a foot of snow on the ground and the temperature hovering around - 0 degrees C. It had been a week, though, since the last storm so the roads were clear. Still it was difficult to move quickly since the appearance of their flitters had been changed to resemble ground transporters. When all were ready, they again activated their Modulators. This time the circle had shrunken on the screen. Unit, number five seemed to be sitting almost on top of them. We switched everything off and again plotted on the enlarged map projection. "Katy they are now about halfway between five and six but maybe half that distance north."

Saturday Feb 21

It was almost six AM on Saturday, and we were all cold and hungry, before all teams had converged on an area that was so small, that, even with our greatest enlargement, we couldn't separate them. I had to tell Katy that was the best we could do. It appeared that the area enclosed was about two kilometers across. "It's alright." Katy said. "It's farm country. There are not more than three or four farms in this area. We'll find them." I must have looked worried because Mister Symons said calmly, "Don't worry Cindi. It's Katherine and her father up there. You might as well have put them right in the Son of a Bitch's pocket."

"That's a good thing." I moaned because the location of the modulators is changing." Frantically, I called Katy back and told her."

I sat in the nondescript and very dirty flitter, disguised as a hover flitter, we had brought for the open survey of the area. I studied the map. I'd already sent the teams off to new points to see if they could trace the moving modulators. In the meantime, though, it seemed rational to check the four farms in the area since the things had sat in this area so long. Mac was arguing that he should go with me when I started probing the four farms.

I had already told him that his job was to supervise the teams that had been sent to block the road access, just like my father's was to command the reserve team. Finally, I had to turn to him and lay it on the line. "Darling, we all have jobs to do." I said as calmly as I could. "You are exceptionally good at organization. That is what the blocking teams need. You are a rank amateur at what I do instinctively." That wasn't going to work. I continued, brutally, "It is quite possible that I'm going to have to kill a lot of people out there. I don't want to but I will do it without compunction. You can't do that efficiently. Now go and do your job!" His face fell in shock - but he turned and left. I closed my eyes a second, wondering if he would ever speak to me again. Then coupling the map to the navigation system, I started toward the first farm

As in the rest of French speaking Quebec, even the farm roads were well maintained. Of course no one bothered with a bit of dead grass showing through the occasional crack in the old asphalt. Most of the travel was by hover flitter and needed little more than a relatively smooth surface. I did notice a few tracks made, apparently, by horse drawn wagons. It was interesting that such a high maintenance animal was still employed in such a manner. Apparently someone in the area was fairly affluent. I had already found out the names of the families in the area. Mac had managed a very quick, but limited, dossier on all four of them. At the first house I came to, the door was answered by a lady about fifty years old. I asked, in French - I didn't try to disguise the Indochinese flavor - if it were the home of Mister Pourell. I knew him to be the owner of the next farm down the road but didn't tell Mrs. Duval that. Mrs. Duval was very pleasant but, I could tell, a bit suspicious. She asked me if I had business with Mister Pourell. I tried to look embarrassed and said that, I had seen the name on the vid directory and that my mother in Hong Kong had been born a Pourell and that she had always said that her father's family came from around Trois Reviere. I had been doing genealogical research on the family and thought I'd see if Mister Pourell was perhaps a relative. I was not surprised to find, of course, that she was deeply involved in genealogy herself. It was a subject that begged for confidences. That was the main reason I had started with her. The lady invited me in for tea. I was surprised at that, for the Québécois were still rabidly anti anything British.

Over the course of an hour, I learned a great deal more about the families in the area. Mister Pourell had been born and raised on that farm - had, in fact, gone to ecole with Mrs. Duval. He had six children and, she couldn't remember, how many grandchildren. All of his children, though, were boys and Mrs. Duval didn't think he had any sisters. The Karnes, on the next road over, had lived on their farm for several generations - she wasn't too sure how many - but the present Mister Karnes had no brothers or sisters and had come home when his father died about ten years ago. He lived there with his young cousin, Marie Trudeau. They were lovely people but, without saying so, Mrs. Duval made it clear that she thought it a bit scandalous that the girl had no chaperon. Of course, Mister Karnes seemed above reproach but it just didn't look good - especially since it was obvious that the girl was madly in love with her older cousin. I had to suppress a smile at the fact that the area hadn't yet gotten caught up in the modern world. Finally, Mister Jacobin was a very old man and unable to work his farm anymore. He had a son and daughter in law living with him who actually ran the place. The son had also gone to school with Mrs. Duval but had gone off to the California POL for a number of years before returning just last year. Since I guessed Mrs Duval's age at around sixty, Mister Pourell, was probably too old to be our man. That left Karnes and Jocobin.

When I left, I had a much better idea as to whom I was after and called Mac to "Take the laundry to the LaFollet Cleaners. We had picked out several businesses in Montreal to use for movement instructions. He would, now, pay close attention to the approaches to the Karnes farm. I'd decided to try there before the Jocobin's. Blocking teams would remain on the other roads but the main effort would be placed there. As I drove to the intersection of the two roads and turned back on the other I debated as to how best to attack the house. A fast time approach would be the most easily done, but would prove embarrassing if the doors and windows of the house were properly secured - I had to assume that if it was being used as a prison they would be. An open approach was a bit dangerous but, it seemed unlikely that a stranger approaching the door and simply knocking would be shot on sight. As I came up to the drive, I simply turned in. It was clear of snow like the roads. Stopping in the parking area, I grabbed a clipboard and went up to the front door.

At my knock, it was opened by a young girl, presumably the cousin, Marie. As soon as it opened, I flipped to FT and brushed by her frozen form in the door. The first door I came to was locked and I found a key that fit in Marie's pocket. Still it took a major effort to open it. It took only a few minutes after that, though, to find James and Cynthia, sitting by a desk in an upstairs room. I scribbled a note for them to come downstairs, and laid it on the table between them. Then I began a more thorough search of the house, hoping to find our kidnapper or their Modulators. I wasn't successful. Frustrated, I went back to the front door and with a pair of handcuffs, secured Marie to the heavy door handle. That done, I switched back to True Time. Marie's eyes grew wide when she found herself shackled but I was calling Mac.

"I want a team down here quickly. I don't see any but surely they've posted guards or traps or both so come by the front drive and look out for ambushes. Put two of the flitters into the air to provide cover if it's needed. Looks like we'll have to wait for our man so try not to disturb the snow." Then I turned back to Marie. "Are there guards?" I asked trying not to frighten her more than she, obviously was. "Please tell me the truth because I don't want a lot of them killed and that will surely happen if they attempt any resistance." Why should I cooperate with you?" she asked. "You come here, do this to me, and threaten to kill people if I don't tell you what you want to know." I hated to do it, but lives were at stake. I gave her my most threatening scowl. "It's because you just met your worst nightmare, Marie. I have killed so many kidnappers that, even I have nightmares about it. The best you can expect from me is that I turn you over to the POL police. The worst is that in less than five minutes, my men are going to be here and if one of them dies, I'll break you up so badly you'll wish you'd never been born. Now! Guards! How many, and where?" The girl was beginning to cry half way through my diatribe, at which time, Cynthia and James rushed through the open dining room door.

"Katy!"Cynthia cried. "Don't hurt her. I don't think she's really part of this." I wheeled on her, getting angry now. "Cynthia, shut up! I'm trying to save a bunch of lives here, most of them her friends." Turning back to the girl, I didn't have to feign frustration. "Tell me. Now!" She was crying now. "There are six." she blubbered. "Four of them are - not very nice. Two are in - the garage and two more in a little storm - cellar - over there." She nodded to a mound about fifty meters from the drive. A man was just rising from it. I flipped to FT and ran over to tie him and his partner up. I then went back to the living room. "The other two, in the barn - they're just kids - from - Trois Rivere." she continued, not even noticing my absence. "They are just - protecting - us." I smiled at her for the first time and patted her on the shoulder. Flipping my handcuff keys to James I said, "James, get the lady a chair and you and Cynthia take care of her till I'm finished.

With that, Katy disappeared - and re-appeared a second later, striding back through the door. It was really the first time Cindy and I had seen from the outside, so to speak, a FT/TT transfer. The girl's eyes got very large and round. "You can to it too!" she gasped in shock. I thought Jenkins was the only one who could. He explained how you two had a very large organization trying to take control of Quebec POL but he said nothing about it having his capability to disappear at will." She must have realized she was babbling, especially since she could see that I was having a hard time smothering a

204

laugh and that Cindy was looking at her very sympathetically. She straightened herself, courageously, as the first team flitter arrived, and said, "Laugh now, sir - and do what you will with me - but Jenkins is probably, at this instant, in contact with the Great Leader to obtain aid in capturing you." Katy was just concluding a report that we had been rescued and turned to Marie. This time it was she who smiled.

"Miss - Trudeau, isn't it? I'm sorry to have to tell you but that group of men spreading out into your yard, are members of the Great Leader's personal bodyguard. I didn't have enough personnel to handle this job so the GL sent me almost ten percent of his guard - and would have been happy to send more to save the mother and father of his grandchildren." Cindy and I both were almost as astonished as Marie that Katy would furnish such information to a total stranger - especially one who had been involved in keeping us captive. Her smile turned to us. "James did this girl lie?" she asked. "Well, of course she -"Then it struck me. Marie was, of course, totally mistaken about the situation but she hadn't been lying. Katy smiled again. "I thought not." she said. Turning back to Marie, "Miss Trudeau you are going to be taken to the GL's headquarters, and will, no doubt, be detained for some time. I think, though, that when you find out the whole truth, it will be a shock. Next she asked about our personal belongings. Marie, now in a state of confusion, led us, without protest, to a concealed safe in one of the bedrooms. In it were our watches, rings, wallets and such. "Where are the small, cigarette sized pieces of gear?" I asked. "Jenkins took them with him." she mumbled. "He said he had to study them and would return this evening."

By now, all the teams had assembled and I kept four of them, plus one of the fifth due to the limited size of the flitters , to wait for Karnes return. They and I were going to wait and attempt to capture him. I warned them all to use Fast Time as soon as his car approached. No matter what I had implied to Miss Trudeau, I knew that these men were the only ones of the GL's guards capable of operating in FT. I had not had time to procure more than five extra Modulators. I sent the remainder of two teams with Cynthia, James and Miss Trudeau, just as a precaution. I did ask them, though, to try to explain the truth to the girl. I knew it would help smooth her next few days - and I did feel sorry for her. She reminded me of a lot of the girls I'd rescued over the years. Many had been brainwashed to the point that they thought their captors were the good guys. As soon as the two flitters lifted, I notified Mac, Justice and the GL of the plan, and twenty minutes later they would be boarding an X class at the Montreal Shuttle Port for the trip to Paris. I had the teams haul the manacled guards into the house and take the remaining flitters over behind a stand of timber. Then we settled down to wait.

Saturday February 21

I was very pleased with myself as I headed home from the lab. As I had thought, the two small plastic packs were, indeed, Modulators. I would have to try and find out just how far Mister and Mrs. McClennan had gotten with their research. Also, I needed to find out if the Observer team was aware of it. Presumably, Jonha was since McClennan was his grandson. The distance from lab to home was a bit long for my taste but it was safer to have the two places separate - especially now that the Observer team had been, or soon would be, alerted by the capture of Beemer. I was certain that Mrs. McClennan's father was one of Jonha's agents. He had covered his tracks well but he hadn't aged in years and there was good evidence that he had been active for, at least a hundred or so years. I had grown complacent since they had shown no indication that they were even aware of our presence - even as recently as a few months ago.

That thought, triggered my mind to security questions. I punched in the code for Marie's vid - and after the forth signal with no answer, frowned. I considered a moment then pulled off into a parking lot and activated the security cameras. There was no activity at the house and the program began the cycle of cameras. The third image was of the front guard position. I couldn't hold back a curse. There were two guards alright, but they wore black uniforms. Sure enough, all the other posts were similarly occupied. In addition, there were five more guards in the house, itself plus a woman in civilian attire. There was no sign of Marie - or the captives. It was obvious that we had been discovered and that I probably had only an hour or two, at most, to escape myself. I quickly turned around and headed back for the lab. This time, I checked the surveillance cameras carefully long before I got there. There seemed no unwelcome intruders about. I sent a remote signal to begin shutdown of the AI.

The thing was almost useless anyway. It had been working well until last year when I asked it to do another evaluation of the situation. It seemed to have gone mad when it came to the unfortunate incident that claimed the life of the GL's daughter and her husband and it realized it wasn't an accident. Since then, it had been no better than a really good computer. Again, Beemer's taste for violence had caused us grief, and I ground my teeth in frustration. He was really a necessary part of this operation, but, time and again, he had gone too far. It hadn't been much of a problem until the last hundred or so years when advances in communication began to reveal a troubling pattern. I was surprised that the Observer team hadn't noticed it long ago.

"Katherine!" Arthur's voice came over my earpiece. When I answered, he told me that an AI had begun operating in this area and had immediately been shut down. Susan hadn't been able to recognize it before since it wasn't working in AI mode, until it shut down. I frowned, going over all our preparations. Had we been discovered? If so how? We found nothing but I had a bad feeling. The only thing to do, though, was continue to wait.

I approached the lab carefully, but it seemed as empty as usual. It was a big unremarkable warehouse - at least from the outside. I opened the door remotely and drove the flitter inside, parking it alongside the Heavy Lift Flitter - actually a small shuttle carefully disguised. Hurrying to the office, I began moving the critical files and equipment. All were secured to gravlift pallets so it wasn't heavy work but I hurried. It took almost an hour to move all the important equipment into the shuttle. The AI was last and sealed in a heated and insulated wrap to keep it from the outside temperature. I made one last check to see if I had left anything important. There was a lot of equipment left but none was irreplaceable. Finally, I set the sensors. After I left, the next disturbance inside the structure would trigger a conflagration, starting in the office. If the Observer force found the place, which I fully expected, it would be destroyed. If not, perhaps I could return and reclaim the rest. I got in the HLF and headed out of Trois Rivere, east. I wanted to be far away before I activated the shuttle for I had little doubt that the Observers would be alert for anyone fleeing the area by air.

Paris

It was a little more than three hours to Paris and a crowd was waiting for us atop the GL's roof. Besides a dozen guards, Jonha and Suzanne were there with Charley and Julia. Each of the girls was holding one of our twins. Cindy jumped out of the shuttle and, literally ran to embrace the girls and babies. Much as I wanted to display such a lack of dignity, I walked calmly to Jonha and Suzanne and stretched out my hand. Suzanne laughed and crying, "Not on your life, James!" grabbed me and hugged me tight. Seconds later the GL joined us. I heard Cindy crying with happiness and telling the girls not to worry, that Mac was fine and would be along later, maybe tonight but probably tomorrow. Charley asked, quietly, if "my - uh - Katy" was OK too and Cindy assured her that she was, grinning over at me. Just then, I noticed the guards leading Marie away. I asked Jonha if he could stop them. He raised an eyebrow but did as I asked.

Then I explained that I thought Marie was a dupe of Karnes and that if she could remain with us for now, perhaps we could make her understand what all this was about. I also told him that I thought, she was in love with Karnes but she might, still, be willing to give us some information about him. As a result, we had another mouth to feed - with a guard outside our door - as Jonha said "just in case."

Later, over a late lunch, we told the story. Charley and Julia were really angry at "That awful, Mister Karnes." Marie had eaten little. Head down, she had answered questions but had contributed nothing to the rest of the conversation. Her English was very good but she, obviously, felt ill at ease with both it and her position in the group. Finally, Cindy said, "I think you'll have to excuse me. It's time for the twin's lunch." We all smiled at that for it had been obvious that she had been anxious to get to nurse them. As she got up, she asked Marie if she'd like to come and help. The girl looked up with a tear in her eye. "Are you sure, Mrs. McClennan?" she asked fearfully. "Certainly!" Cindy said cheerfully. "They're getting so big that they are a handful. An extra pair of hands is always welcome."

The girl looked back at Jonha and asked if she could be excused. Jonha nodded with a smile. She got up and the two headed for the bedroom. Mac's girls tried to hide their disappointment but Suzanne reached out a hand to them and said that Marie seemed nice and was probably undergoing a shock right now. Then, with a grin, she added, "Besides, I'm going to miss suckling my babies too." They nodded, weak smiles appearing on their faces. I told Jonha that Katy thought the girl could become useful here instead of a prisoner. She was still in a state of partial shock to find that we were going to see the GL and that Karnes didn't work for him. She wasn't quite ready to accept that he was an outlaw, though. Jonha agreed to "give it a try -with proper safeguards".

He said. "She can't, for instance, be allowed too much freedom until we're sure she can be trusted but Justice tells me that Katy has a nose for people, so we'll take a chance with her. She'll first, have to be debriefed, of course - we know too little about this Karnes fellow. Mister Pendleton has been most unhelpful. Unfortunately, we have never developed anything similar to your "truth serum" and even though Marcus assures me that, though Katherine can force answers from him, she would probably refuse unless it was a matter of life and death. Neither of us, though, thinks that to be the case - and happy that it's so. He tells me that she is often more profoundly affected   by such things than the subject of her interrogation. Perhaps Marie can fill in some of the blank spots. From there we'll see how it all works out."

We spent a week in Paris, during which time, Katy and Mac, finished up their "stakeout" in Quebec. When it became obvious that Karnes wasn't going to return, they called in the RCMP. I hadn't thought about it much, but it was a surprise to find that Quebec had retained the services of the "Mounties" when they had declared themselves "free" of the rest of the Canadian POL. It took them four days to discover Karnes operations center and as soon as they jimmied the lock, the whole building exploded in flames. No one was hurt but there was nothing left to work on either. The Mounties, working with INTERPOL had finally traced Karnes escape to a shuttle that had left Quebec for Newfoundland POL then left from there, never to be heard from again. Even the GL's tracking system was unable to determine where it went.

Marie was "interviewed" by Justice with Jonha sitting in as a sort of informal lie detector. Unfortunately, what she knew of the man was almost entirely a lie. He had taken her from a orphanage six years ago when she was ten, and brought her to live with him as his cousin. He had papers proving that well enough that it convinced the orphanage. They showed that he was the son of her mother's brother and that he had been out of the country when her mother died. The brother had died overseas in a little war in China. All the family was dead except him and he had appropriate certificates covering all the deaths also. At any rate, he had always treated her kindly - almost as if she were his own daughter. She had a great deal of trouble thinking badly of him, and until the time of the kidnapping had never seen any sign of him doing anything wrong - though, he was away "on business" a lot. She admitted with obvious chagrin that he had never acted as if he recognized her growing infatuation - she called it love - for him. As for the kidnapping, he had explained that James and Cynthia were working on a project that was of great danger to the world and he had to try and convince them of their errors.

He promised that if he couldn't he would simply turn them over to the authorities to hold. The only time she began to wonder about his methods was when he hired a crew of very mean looking guards to make sure that James and Cynthia didn't escape. She was very afraid that the guards would have hurt them had they tried - and Karnes, himself, had said so in her presence. She had been so terrified of James's hatred of Karnes, though, that she hadn't thought much about that. To her James was a real terrorist - and, she assumed, a liar. She had thought Cindy nice but as James wife, perhaps as bad as he was. Anyway, Jonha and Justice were convinced that she was really innocent of real wrongdoing and gave her a job as Suzanne's "secretary".

When, finally, Katy and Mac had arrived here and were reunited with Charley and Julia there was a lot of crying and hugging all around. It seemed as if the girls were as anxious for Katy as their father and both of them, at one time or another had embarrassed themselves by calling her "Mom". It was all Cindy could take. She had rounded on Mac that night at dinner and asked him baldly, When he was going to get around to marrying Katy? He never looked up from his food but replied calmly, "Ask her?" All eyes turned to Katy who looked sort of sheepish as she pulled her engagement ring, hung on a chain, out of her bodice. "Well, put the damned thing back on!" Cindy exploded - then added with a devilish grin - "It's disgusting to have two teen age girls calling you mom and you not married. You should be ashamed of yourself." That brought a round of laughter from at the table - even Marie, who was becoming a bit more at ease with us all.

Friday February 26, 2060

I was enjoying myself immensely. I hadn't realized during our captivity just how much I missed nursing the twins. Sure, I had missed them but we weren't away from them long enough for that to become a real ache. Now, though I realized that they were growing like weeds and, with the time they had spent in FT would probably be the biggest one year olds in history by their birthday. Officially, they were five months old. I thought, wistfully, that it was probably long past time that they were weaned. I wondered if we were all using up our allotted life spans more quickly using FT. Maybe Jonha would know. I grinned, thinking that birthdays might become irrelevant. Both James and I had spent, probably a good many months in FT. As I half reclined on Suzanne's couch, lazily thinking of little else - and, surprisingly unworried about it, James came in.

I looked up and saw his smile - then I looked again. There was something else. Instantly I became tense wondering what new danger threatened us. "It's a lovely picture." he murmured. "But?" I asked. I knew there was a "but". His eyes clouded over. "I've been thinking it was time to go home and get back to work." he said. "Jonha doesn't think we should. He's still worried about Karnes. It worries Katy too but she agreed, a bit reluctantly, that she could make enough security changes that we would be fairly safe - especially if we moved to the Maryland house." He grinned sheepishly.

He was right. We really did need to go back to doing something useful. "OK." I laughed.

"It's just that I've been thinking about the power failure. There's something wrong with that and I can't, for the life of me, figure out what."

"Well," I said, "We did calculate the instantaneous draw when the equipment went back to TT." "Yeah," he answered, thoughtfully. "I can see it burning up the house circuits, but what about the Busses? Those were solid copper a half inch thick and eight inches wide but they actually vaporized." I frowned again, my brain, slowly and unwillingly, going back to work. The babies now full began to wriggle into sleep mode.

A half hour later, the twins were powdered, diapered and in their beds. After I was properly put back together from the feeding, we headed into Jonha's office. We asked Susan to have Cindi and Albert review the incident in Maryland. The answer came back in seconds. It had taken a surge larger than the biggest lightning bolt - I didn't even bother translating those zeros into megawatts because I could still see the equipment on the lab table when we went back in. It wasn't even scorched. I shook my head and looked up at James. I smiled. He had that far away look in his eyes again. I knew that "Wrongness Mode" had kicked in. "Why didn't it destroy the apartment wiring back home?" he murmured. I gasped. Of course! We had worked in FT dozens of times in his

210

apartment without even being able to register a current draw at all. I knew what had to be done. "Susan," I said, "Please ask Jonha if we can be returned to the office as soon as possible." A few seconds later she reported that he was on his way.

After we explained the situation, he agreed to our request, though, he persuaded us to go to the Maryland house. He pointed out that Art could run the business without our help. We had to chuckle at that. We didn't have a thing to do with the business anyway. I had been surprised just a couple of weeks ago when we actually had a directors meeting and Daddy said we were making a profit. When I had asked how much, he had laughed. "Do you really want all the details?" he had asked. I really didn't, so he just told me that we had made just under two hundred K New Dollars in the last quarter. Actually, we didn't care much where it was we went as long as we could get us, Cindi, Arthur and the babies all in the same place. By that time all the "family" including Mac, Katy and the girls were trying to talk at once. Katy and Mac were worried that it would take several days to get the computers and lab equipment moved and organize a proper defense force. They had only a skeleton crew there now. No problem. The GL would send a group of his guards. The place was secluded enough that they could be slipped in fairly easily.

As we watched the shuttle lift off, Jonha turned to me. "Atam, we're going to need more presence over there. I think it's time you and Evelyn joined their company. I'm sure Jessup can fit you both in easily enough. Also, I warned Katherine that she was probably going to be busier in the field in the near future. I'd feel better, in that case, with you over there to sort of keep watch on things. She also felt she needed someone for office administrative purposes." Jonha smiled at that. "I suspect she already has someone in mind and I have no objection to a little more nepotism." I had to grin. Katy probably thought that we didn't know about Miss Wallace, but I nodded. "Oh well, Evelyn's probably tired of this face anyway."

Thursday February 29, 2060

We had been delivered to the Maryland house Friday night after dark and Cindi and Arthur had arrived the next day. Since then, we and the kids had spent almost a week, off and on, in the reconstructed lab. We had not used FT because the whole house was settling in and needed a lot of interaction with the "owners." Mister Peterson had gone over it with a fine tooth comb and pronounced it ready for anything we might want to do. He, though, still expressed doubt that it could handle another jolt like we gave the Conroe house. We promised to dump any excess output into a circuit completely removed from the house wiring and running directly outside the walls. At most, it should only affect the few inches of heavily insulated line transiting the wall itself. It was a frustrating time, though. When we had checked over the FT power supply after the "accident", it had seemed fine except for a little short in the power circuit. Looking at it more carefully, it was apparent that the short wasn't a part of the event itself. The control circuit line had been deliberately crossed and shorted. I gave Katy, Art and Justice the news and was surprised to see how little the latter two worried about it. Katy, immediately, instituted a recheck of all the personnel in the place at the time. Justice informed us that he and his wife would be coming over in about a week and wanted Art to arrange for a place for them in the company. He also was going to be away on a "business trip" for a few days.

Friday, March 12, 2060

"Yes Miss Wallace, Ms. Geribaldi is already here and expecting you. You can go on up. The boy will take care of your bags." The manager of the Wainwright was almost fawning in his manner. Katy must have given him a real song and dance. Toni Alicia Wallace, or so her passport said, gave him a shy smile and turned for the elevator. Nice place, she thought to herself, small and inconspicuous, but plush. Just like Katy. As she rode up to the fourteenth floor, she speculated as to why Katy wanted her. She'd gotten her a good job in the Political Bank of Switzerland   as soon as she had finished at the Luzern Academy. She smiled at that. It was quite a step up for a Chinese child prostitute from a Seoul Korea brothel. Now for Katy, who she hadn't seen in almost a year, to have her quit a "respectable" job to come to New York made her curious. Not that she'd even consider saying no. A girl who, at the age of twelve couldn't count the men who'd already been forced on her and who had been sold to a man that everyone knew seldom kept his slave girls alive for more than a few months wasn't likely to deny anything to the one person in the world who had saved her, literally, from death.

The girl who paused at the door to suite 1467 was a far cry from that tiny twelve year old whore. Dressed in the latest fashion, subdued but very chic, she turned heads where ever she went - quite an accomplishment for one who would never have been considered one of the "beautiful people". She was still tiny (She had often kidded Katy that the only reason that she'd taken her under her wing was because she was the only other person in the world that Katy could look down on) probably from the constant malnutrition of her youth. Her delicate oriental features and natural shyness concealed a dogged determination to succeed - and the capability to utterly destroy the ego (and his reproductive equipment if necessary) of any male on the make. Only part of this was due to her horribly mangled youth. The rest was a passionate desire to repay the one person in the world who meant anything to her, Katherine Louise Finnigan.

As soon as the door opened, Toni flew into the arms of her "mother" with a cry of joy. She was embarrassed to realize that she was crying. Finally, when all the squeezing and hugging was done, she stepped back. Only then did she realize that Katy was dressed to go out. "I'm sorry, mother, I should have been more careful." She cried. "If you had I'd have been mad as hell." Katy grunted, tears in her eyes also. "However, much as I'd like to have a long lovely talk, we've got people to meet. I'd decided you weren't going to make it, so I was going to go by myself. You run get a quick bath if you think you need it. There's a gown in the bedroom for you. I'll call and tell our dates that we'll be a little late. "Yes, mother." Toni murmured heading, unquestioningly, for the bath. Katy picked up the phone.

"Aren't you curious as to where we're going?" Katy cried from the living room. Toni, dressed in panties, push up bra and thigh length hose, was applying a pale lipstick. "When you're ready to tell me." she called back, blotting the full lips. Her eyebrows lifted as she slipped quickly into the long white clinging gown. Made of cling satin, it molded her figure like a glove. Settling the low cut bodice down to allow the bra to do its work, she grimaced at the thought that the Gods could have, at least, let her to show a little more cleavage if they were going to allow her to wear such a dress as this. Slipping into the satin, backless pumps as she headed for the door she grinned at the thought that she had made it in good time. According to her mental clock, it had taken twelve minutes twenty seconds from coming in the door to going out.

212

"Still haven't lost your touch, have you." Katy grinned as she opened the front door of the suite. From anyone else the reminder of the childhood need to strip naked and dress quickly for her mama san would have been a real blow, but Katy had a way of making her past seem so much less dreadful that it was a joke between them. "You selling me tonight?" She asked. Laughing as they headed for the elevator, Katy replied, with a grin, "Too close to the truth, sweet. But don't worry. You know I'd never let anything happen to you that I wasn't sure you'd love - and be sure that your price will be very high."

The man at the table that the waiter led them to stood quickly as they approached. he was rather nice looking, nothing to write home about, if she had a home to write home to, but one, that had the look of so many of Katy's friends; closed to the public. Mister Sanders bowed over their hands. Sanders obviously knew Katy. "So this is Toni." he murmured, obviously pleased. He ordered drinks and made small talk. Katy said "How's Barbra, Just - eh, Jud, I don't like getting Toni mixed up with you very much. The partial slip was so uncharacteristic of Katy that drew a tiny hardening of Mr. "Sanders" eyes. Toni glanced at her as unobtrusively as she could. Her brain, trained, at a very tender age, in the awareness of faces and the need to remember them, went onto automatic pilot. Obviously, Katy's slip was intentional. What had she intended? Maybe a test? Just-, Justin? Close, not quite she thought. The catalog of names went on. Justice! Wrong face. A Justice had, on more than one occasion been around Katy. A powerful Justice Not a title, a name. Sanders? No. Simmons? Closer. Barbra? The bell rang. Symons - the least known man in the world. Sanders leaned closer. "Sanders." he whispered. Toni's mouth dropped open, her reputation as one of the most stoic of the all Orientals, suffering a terrible shock. Katy grinned broadly. "My little girl isn't used to being caught out like that. I'll have to send her back to Inscrutable school." She laughed.

When Toni came out of the bathroom later in the evening, Katy was in a full lotus position beside the bed. "Sooner or later, mother you're going to have to learn to wear clothes around the house." she quipped. Flopping onto the bed she pulled down the silk pajama shirt to cover her panties. "Your body can't breathe in clothes." Katy shot back, unwinding and rising gracefully from the carpet. "I guess, though, I'll have to learn now that I have to pretend to be a damned role model?" Toni laughed at the thought, saying she "didn't need a better one than you." Katy ignored her but with a grin. Slipping onto the bed, she asked what Toni thought about the job. "It'd be wonderful working with you for a change but why the change of heart? You always said you'd not let me." Katy's face became very solemn. "First, you probably won't see too much of me. I don't intend to get myself tied into an office. Secondly darling, most of my work I'm not proud of. It serves a need I have and I'm never in doubt of the positive gain to humanity, but it is illegal and, to most of the world, immoral. I want you away from that sort of thing."

She held up a hand as Toni was about to protest. "This may involve some illegality, and it might require some of the skills upon which I've built my reputation; but it is the most important thing going on in the world today. It could, possibly, give mankind the lift it needs to overcome its own worst faults. It's worth the gamble and I think it's the type of thing that we would both feel good about doing." Then with a grin she added." Besides, the men we'll be dealing with probably will be the type that I could feel good about pawning your sexy little body off on as proper wifely material." "Damn you!" Toni shouted, swinging a pillow at her. "I don't need a matchmaker. Besides I'm convinced that one day you'll remember that in my former occupation it wasn't only men that I was

213

able to please. You give me away to some hairy old man and when you come crawling for me to give you the satisfaction that no man can, I'll tell you to go jump." The older woman, chuckling, easily flicked the pillow away, with a fighters reflexes and told her that all that money spent polishing her to be a real lady had been wasted. "Besides," she muttered, I won't have to worry much about a lack of sex for awhile." Then she held up her left hand and wriggled her fingers to draw Toni's attention. Her eyes grew round with surprise. "Mother! You didn't!" She grabbed the hand to admire the Modest sapphire engagement ring. The rest of the night was spent with Katy telling about a wonderful man named Mac, two of Toni's soon to be sisters, and catching up on the time that had separated the two.

Monday March 15, 2060

On Monday, it was two fashionably dressed women who presented themselves to the new Personnel Director of A&L. The beautiful woman behind the desk looked them up and down then said, "I think I'm going to have a talk with my husband about the time spent on the road dealing with some ugly old hag over in Hong Kong." Katy grinned. "I may have to have a talk with him also, if that's what he said." The woman stood up and extended her hand. "I'm very pleased to meet you at last Miss Finnigan. I take it this lovely thing is your daughter Toni. I'm Barbra Sanders." Katy took the hand. "Since we seem to have the same man in common, perhaps you should call me Katy." Barbra sat back down, motioning them to chairs.

"Katy, as I'm sure you already know, your status is being changed to help lower your profile. You're to remain our field operations director but your name is coming off all company records. You are resigning for more lucrative activities. Here, your office will be titled as Chief of International Sales and will be staffed by an assistant, with you, the chief, gone most of the time on sales business. We'll try to keep your appearances in the office as anonymous as possible – primarily for public perception. A pile of acceptable candidates for your assistant and sales positions is on your desk. You will be chiefly based in Maryland. A few of the ones on your list that you've used in the past were judged to be too limited for the job. They can remain on the security team here but wouldn't do for some of the projects that you may have to undertake. The rest are OK. We've added about fifteen you might like to consider - might is the operative word. You do not have to accept anyone you don't want. If you decide, however, on adding to the list I must insist on arranging for an approval interview. I know that Justice has already covered your duties. They haven't changed much but are likely to involve a lot more tasks that what you've been performing. Are you comfortable with the changes in your contract?"

Katy nodded. "In that case we'll just skip to Toni." Barbra continued. "Is it alright if I call you that?" Toni inclined her head in assent. "You will be Justice's secretary. Since he's well aware of your mother's skills - and my watchfulness - I'm sure that you don't have to worry about him chasing you around the office, but you should be aware of the fact that he is sometimes a real bear to deal with. I think, though, that you two will complement each other well. If your mind is half what the record shows, you should be a true asset to the company. Since his and your mothers jobs will be, to say the least, determined by day to day events, you will actually handle the true sales effort of the firm. Your main job, however, will be to act as your mother's contact at the office."

Toni stopped her with a raised eyebrow. "Something?" Barbra asked. "I think you should know that Katy is not really my mother, though she might as well be, and I call her that." Barbra looked down at her notes. "According to the records you were adopted by Ms. K. L. Finnigan on March forth in 2049. I doubt that they are in error since my husband personally did the investigation." Toni's mouth had dropped open as her head swiveled toward Katy. "Something I forgot to mention." she murmured. "Anyway," Barbra continued, as Toni tried to catch her breath, "you will be, in effect, Justice's executive assistant. He will designate the areas in which you are not to make decisions for him. In all other areas, you can decide if you are capable of handling a given question when he is not available.

Any one that worries you, you can call me and I'll direct you to the best person for the job. Any decision you make will be considered to have come from him. He may not agree with you when he returns but, in that case, he will explain why and take the necessary steps to correct the problem. He will never second guess you - though he wouldn't expect you to make the same mistake twice. The only mistake he cannot tolerate, though, is being afraid to make a mistake. Obviously, you'll have questions once you settle in. I will always be here to help and you'll find Justice easy to question when he's here. You like to see your offices?" "Toni's will do, I think." Katy said. "Just a desk, chair and file cabinet will do for me. I'll probably do most of my work from home or from Maryland. It'll be better than spending too much time around here and having half the underworld wonder what I'm doing here. Toni will have my number in case you need me. It's fully scrambled. Jaque will also, for that matter. I'll call on him if I need to but I'd prefer to keep him out of all this if we can. Never can tell when I'll need a bolt hole and he's really good at that."

"It's OK with me." Barbra said, "We've already set an office up, though. I'll have someone dust it now and then."

"Better yet, why don't you have someone use it. A female clerk or my assistant, will do. Pick one who's name is Katherine or is willing to use the name. A little confusion never hurt anyone." Barbra laughed. "No wonder my husband likes you. You're two of a kind." Katy's eyes turned suddenly serious. "Not really. You and I both know that no matter his reputation, he can never do what I do. One thing, though, he can do, and I know he will, is to take care of my little girl." Barbra's laugh faded. With a simple nod she led them to Toni's office.

That evening, as Katie prepared to board an unmarked shuttle to return home she took Toni aside hugged her and murmured. "Do not, under any circumstances, darling allow yourself to become complacent! You can use the hotel, for now, but if you like there is an apartment on the top floor of the building that I doubt anyone will be using again. I'd rather you use that than being vulnerable on the street. I won't be in Hong Kong long but just long enough to pick up some things and secure the buildings. I've got to be back here on Friday for that meeting but after that, I'll usually be at the Maryland house. Remember the most foolish person in the world is the one who is afraid of looking like one." Just as she was about to board the shuttle, she turned back. "By the way, you'll have twenty four hour protection. Barbra will introduce you to your detail before you go home tonight. Never accept anyone else on that detail unless they have been personally approved by Barbra or Justice."

Monday March 15, 2060

"Ok!" James said, leaning back in the chair. "There's no doubt that someone deliberately shorted out the Modulator   after all the excitement. Questions - who, when, why, and how. The last is pretty easy. Anyone could have pulled loose that connection and shorted it. The interesting thing is that for it to short, the equipment still had to be operating. As for the when, well that could have been done almost any time before the next day when we finally got back to the lab. Couldn't have been later, we certainly would have noticed if the equipment was still running when Peterson got the lab lights back on. That leaves who and why." "Well," I said, thinking it over, "Who is sort of scary but we're not the experts on looking for spies in our midst. It seems to me that Why is what we need to concentrate on." Looking back over my shoulder, though I have to chuckle to think that I need to. I asked Arthur what he and Cindi thought about why it was done. His answer caused us both to swivel around to stare at them.

"You have no available information?" I asked. The two holograms and the couch they were sitting on winked out. James looked over at me and laughed. "Well, I guess that tells us who - or, at least, narrows the field a lot." I grinned back. "Might as well call off Katy's dogs. It wouldn't do for them to find the culprit now, would it? That leaves us with why. We were either on the wrong track or on one that was dangerous to use." I asked if his "wrongness" lump had issued a warning. He shrugged. "So it wasn't the wrong way. How could it be dangerous?" "Darling," I said quietly, "we did melt a ton of copper in the basement." After James told Cindi and Arthur they could come back - that we wouldn't send them to bed without their supper we went back to the blackboard. They appeared but looked very upset. They said nothing.

We both toiled away in silence for an hour or more, one writing on the board and the other checking the work. Finally, Cindi's voice, behind us, said, "That should be a minus sign." James turned around. "You decided to come back and help?" I turned. She and Arthur had on their trench coats and he was smoking a curved pipe. Cindi shrugged, nonchalantly. "We decided to forgive you. Don't you think it would be faster for you just to tell us what you want and let us display it?" "You'll need two displays." James said off handedly. "Of course." she replied and two displays appeared in midair. "Now," James said. "Tell us what those represent." "One," Cindi shrugged, "is the formulae for your original analysis of the Modulator and the second is the same for the most recent." James nodded. "Alright, why are they different?" "You used a different value for the subset of the square root of minus one." "Is there anything wrong with the calculations?" "Of course not, as long as you're basic assumptions are correct."

I could stand it no longer. I took up the interrogation. "So since we know that all the subsets of the minus one root are actually all the same value, both sets of equations are identical. Makes you wonder doesn't it?"

"Is that a question, Cynthia?"

"If it were, you wouldn't be able to answer it, could you Cindi?" "Would it make a difference?" she asked, her mouth set in a hard line. Arthur was trying very hard to keep from laughing. James and I both burst out laughing. "Cindi,"James chuckled, "tell Suzanne that DP programming is a bit faulty. If you're going to play games you'd better

216

learn how to lie." Cindi's eyes blinked. "Suzanne says that Arthur has said the same to her several times. Unfortunately, there is nothing to be done about it." "Well, Cindi," I said, "Those formulae tell us that there are two kinds of dimensions , one we have been using for our Modulators all along, and one that blows up electrical systems. Therefore it is a source of great power. The other has the ability to affect time. Each may have its own peculiar properties but all affect time. Do you have a problem with that analysis?" When they said nothing we turned back to our problem, we worked the rest of the day on it with time out to feed the twins.

Tuesday March 22, 2060

A TT week but a FT month later, we had a pretty good idea of how to adjust the frequency of whatever the Monitor was doing to make it operate in a number of different dimensional situations We had tested the equipment frequencies near the break point, the one that had blown out our electrical system. It was slow, tedious work. Finally, though, we had nothing to show for our work and were resigned to having to come up with another plan when James flipped the Modulator into FT.

Our little generator disappeared accompanied by a loud bang. That brought us out of our chairs. We debated about what to do. Finally, though, we had no choice but to cross our fingers and transition back to TT. Nothing happened. The lab bench was still empty. We quickly checked all our recording equipment but aside from a surge of power from the adjacent power dimension, there was nothing. It was only when we stood back, looking around in disgusted confusion, that we noticed the hole in the west wall of the lab. When we inspected it, we could see into the next room - a store room. This room had, when we went inside, two holes, one in the wall of our lab and another on the other side. The next wall was the same - all the way to the outside wall of the house. It didn't take special intuitive powers to guess what had caused the damage. Somehow our little generator had smashed through six walls in, what turned out to be, a straight line, to the outside of the house. Mister Peterson, when we had him up to see about repairs, cast a disgusted look at us and remarked that he wished we'd go into a less dangerous line of work. As he stood, surveying the damage, he murmured, "Interesting." "No doubt." I muttered with a trace of sarcasm - that I was immediately sorry for.

He looked over at me, his eyes twinkling. "You said your generator - smashed through the walls." I frowned, wondering what he was saying. "Where's the debris?" he asked. "There's not even any dust." Shocked, I looked again at the wall - then the floor. "Besides," he continued, "when you smash through a wall, you leave a jagged edge. These holes aren't jagged. In fact, they even show the outline of the equipment itself. It's, as if, it cut cleanly through the wall and took the debris with it. Notice it even took out a piece of a stud the same way." By then James and I were both shaking our heads.

It was time to take a break. Mister Peterson left to start gathering materials for repairing the walls. Much as we both wanted to solve a huge mystery, we knew we were in no mental shape to do it. We needed to just get away from the lab for awhile. Resting in FT was no fun. Mattresses had no give to them and cushions were hard. Food tasted lousy and the shower didn't work. In addition, unless we wanted to put the twins in FT also, they only needed breast feeding about once a day now and were getting solid food the rest of the time. Probably the only reason they breast fed at all was because I enjoyed it. Of course, James didn't seem to mind substituting for them and my breasts didn't seem to care who suckled them, but I missed the regular contact with them. I

217

teased him that he just didn't want them to go back to normal. I was careful not to complain about the weight and the feeling that I would like to have my old figure back. Of course, there were advantages too. With his attentions required several times a day, we tended to take care of our love life, much more often and without fear of interruption. Additionally, his not having to worry about taking milk from his kids mouths was pleasing to both of us. Anyway, we decided to take a break and take the kids for a stroll around the grounds. The twins loved it. Riding in their stroller in the open air was something we hadn't done much. It was less satisfying for us because Mac - in charge while Katy was away - insisted on an armed guard to go with us. We roamed the gravel paths around the grounds for over an hour. It was an enjoyable hour just listening to the kids gurgling and laughing, though, neither of us could stop our brains from fixating on the problem of the disappearing generator. Finally, James said, "You know, darling, I don't feel anything wrong with what happened." I shivered because, if he was right, and, no doubt, he was, we should have expected what happened to have happened. That meant that the math, the undefined points and the lost generator was "normal". All we had to figure out was how to explain it.

Friday March 19 2060

    I was none too sure just how I was going to fit into this organization when I arrived in the unassuming but spacious offices of A&L Investment Company. One thing I knew though; they needed my help. In just the cursory checks I'd made from my hospital room while waiting for my new face to mend I'd been able to blow their cover to hell. They didn't make anything, invest in hardly anything or do anything. In short, they were a sitting duck for anyone who happened to do a simple credit check on them. With all their "do nothingness," they had a cash bank account that would be the envy of the top ten companies in the Pol Area. Before I left Paris, I'd told the GL that we needed some legal brains and fast. Now I was to meet the Company Officers to decide on my role in company operations. I hadn't intended to move Barbra Lynn away from her thriving psychiatric practice; to say nothing of the kids away from their friends and the only home they'd ever known, just to be their resident spook. I had told Jonha that, before I even left his office last week. He just smiled that irritating smile of his and said he was sure that I was good enough to keep that from happening.

    Toni Finnigan had been a nice surprise when I had arrived. She already had my office set up with everything I might need to go to work. I don't know why I thought Katherine's daughter would be less efficient than her. I remarked that Barbra was, no doubt going to give me a hard time about hiring only beautiful women and was pleased to see that she could blush. If she could only operate half as well as her mother, she would do. As I set the family pictures out on my desk, I wondered how long it was going to be before I could get them over here permanently Barbra was going to have to go home soon. She was only supposed to be here till I got in. Jonha had told me not to worry, that he could have the house selling taken care of quickly but with the present Parisian economic crisis, I suspected that it would take more than a little arm twisting to get the local housing authority to abrogate our long term lease. There were houses vacant all over the city and no market for them. I smiled remembering the elation in the city when Jonha had moved the seat of world government there. They hadn't known him as I did. He believed in the old adage that the "best government was the least government". The Frankish vision of thousands of bureaucrats they expected to flock to the governmental trough never materialized. The speculators had taken a real bath. They had begun building apartment buildings as soon as the decision was made-long before the announcement. Now those buildings were rotting shells. Oh well, when I took the job I'd not done it to get richer.

    Both the Pachones (I wondered why it was so easy to remember that name.) were in his office, along with their daughter, Katherine and Mac with, surprisingly enough, the secretaries, Margaret Patton and Toni Wallace, when McClennan escorted me into the meeting. These people had some weird ideas about their hired help. I was rather impressed though not surprised, that McClennan hadn't taken the top job himself. He apparently had brains enough to recognize his own limitations - though Jessup may have had something to do with that. Come to think of it I did need to remember to call him Art and Jonha, "GL" in public. I still wasn't used to being out in the field again. It had been a very long time. I was even more impressed with the way the meeting was held. There was a total lack of formality In the meeting, all purely business matters were discussed with the foregone conclusion that Pachone, his wife, or, again a surprise, the secretary would handle them.

I sat there mentally kicking myself for not suspecting, during all my checking, that the secretary could have a significant position in the organization. It would be a bit humbling, to admit to BL that I was, as she often told me, not conscious enough of the "little people" I came in contact with. Something else! Every time I looked at Art I got that strange feeling that he was drastically changed. I tried to study him without being too obvious about it. It wasn't the face, but of course, my face wasn't mine either. A deep check was in order. "Damn!" I had let my attention wander. Pachone was looking at me. Quickly I let my mind replay the part of the conversation I had missed. "I think that a secondary base of operations in Paris would be highly advantageous, so I propose to buy out Mr. Symons lease, through a holding company, of course. If that's alright with everyone - Mr. Symons?" Rather sheepishly I agreed to the proposal and, a bit belatedly, expressed my appreciation.

"Now Mr. Symons," Pachone continued, "-by now it must be obvious that we are a very informal group. I'm Art. This is Lil. He grinned broadly, "You wouldn't be here if you weren't the type to have already developed a pretty complete dossier on all of us. Anyway, you already know Katherine, James, or Jim, and Cynthia. Friends can call her Cindy, and most do just to irritate her. She's insufferably bright - probably as bright as James. The difference is she knows it and he doesn't. Finally this is Margaret. No one calls her Maggie. For your information, she has almost a free hand in most administrative matters. The rule is that unless a matter actually demands the attention of one of the other of us, it belongs to Margaret. I seldom overrule anything she decides to do. I tried it a couple of times-and regretted it both times. She's the quiet type but is seldom wrong-about anything she does say. Finally, no one has any objection to your new assistant, Toni," he smiled over at Katherine, "sitting in on the meetings also. She'll have to anyway when you're gone and it will save a lot of fill in if she does.

That, or course, is up to you." Seemed like a very smart idea to me so I nodded my approval. Finally, though, she's up to her eyebrows in personnel problems right now, your wife will normally be included. Everyone, as they were introduced, held out a hand to shake. James remarked that he would have some problems getting used to my new face. He'd studied the old one too long. Pachone, Art, leaned back and got to the heart of the reason for the meeting. "We've had some discussions about your position with the company. I doubt that, at least officially, it would be a good idea to list you as head of security. Obviously, though, that would be a place that you could easily earn your keep. Before we do anything else, do you have any ideas? I realize that you haven't had much time to take a look at the organization, but I suspect that you have a pretty good idea of what it's about. Now would be a good time to get your two cents worth in."

Choosing my words carefully, I began with an appreciation of what I already knew of their problems. Art frowned when I mentioned my feeling that they needed a corporate lawyer. I finished with my assessment of their corporate strategy. I didn't make any friends with that. Finallly I made my pitch to be the Vice President in charge of Marketing. I grinned at the rather surprised looks I got with that one. "After All-" I pointed out, "who has more reason for visiting, not only the company locations but, almost any place in the world when he needs to. In addition I'd like to be in charge of acquiring the products for me to sell." "What, the hell, do we need to buy and sell anything?" James challenged. "After all we are already showing profits." "Have you ever heard of a

220

company that didn't sell something   - even if it's only expertise?" I chuckled. "In addition, officially, **YOU DON'T DO ANYTHING**. You are listed on numerous compilations of viable companies already and we must get you listed on both stock exchanges. Otherwise we're just asking for any of a thousand sharp operators to start tracing the activities of the strangest company in the known universe. Don't worry about the stock exchanges. We'll make sure a nominal turnover in stock occurs and is wholly owned by dummy companies and individuals."

James, sat back and threw up his hands. "Why the hell does everything have to get so complicated?" he growled, then added that he didn't like lawyers either. I laughed and told him that, skirting the law as much as he had done, and probably was going to do, would require that he become intimate with a good one. Art agreed then dropping his pen on his desk, remarked that all I had said made sense. "Adding your requirements to my known list this is how I see our immediate personnel needs . Think the GL can get us some candidates"? I looked over the list he passed to me. "The attorney and accountants are already being processed. You should be able to interview them next week.

The GL suggested, and I agree that Katy should be the Chief of Field Operations . In fact, Barbra - she's already acting as Personnel Director, has already told her so - hope you don't mind but the GL suggested it. We can call it Sales Director - to handle your sales force, and as noted before," I said with a grin, "my secretary - or assistant has already been picked - by Katherine and my wife and, while I suspect a little back door politicking with the GL. I make it a point to never overrule any of those worthies. As for your clerks that you list as "un cleared" - You would be well advised to clear all main office personnel. If you don't, you're letting yourself in for monumental security problems every time you want to even have a sensitive conversation". Looking at the McClennans, I added, half sarcastically, "Now, I don't see any personnel on here for your operations people. Surely you don't intend to raid criminal activities yourselves." The way they looked at each other it was obvious they had planned just that.

"Well, ignoring the fact that your identity has probably already been compromised, it's a really foolhardy idea – especially since you don't need to." I said – as they frowned and Cynthia's parents smothered grins, "Besides when do you intend to work on modulator development - and who do you intend to have do it? The GL has suggested that as your main task. As far as I know, no one in this office can handle modulator math and no one is even vaguely conversant with the theory. In addition, the GL doesn't think you are sufficiently aware of your equipment's potential. It would seem to me, that a considerable amount of basic research is still needed before trying to determine its long term use." I took a deep breath and launched a little needle of my own. I'd considered this a long time. The GL will probably kill me.

"I can't imagine, for instance, trying to go into space, for instance, with technology for which you don't even know the source of power you intend to use. Add the fact that there are already mob contracts out for you to the tune of several million new dollars - and those are DOA contracts." "Dead on Arrival?" Margaret asked, brow furrowed. "Close enough;" I laughed. "Dead Or Alive. So far you have been good - probably lucky is more like it - unbelievably lucky for amateurs. As far as I can tell, you've left no clues except probably for fingerprints. So far that hasn't hurt you, but amateurs make too many mistakes. Those prints, for instance could be a real problem. Sooner or later you're going to make a real one; especially when you've got other things to think

221

about. A master thief concentrates totally on the job at hand. You'll never have that luxury.

You can add to the problems, the fact that you two are going, due to security concerns, to be spending almost all your time in Maryland. Luckily, with the GL's help, you can easily forgo further criminal activity. That is going to be Katherine's main activity from now on. Hers will be a big enough job without complicating it with amateur thieves. By the way, if you tell the GL about that space remark, you can get my head on a platter." I really shocked them with that. I intended to. I wanted them to see that I wasn't just the GL's spy in their midst. "One last thing," I added, "it's Justin Sanders now."

When no one had anything to say to that I said, "Why don't you let your Marketing director handle the "sales force?" All were quiet for another moment then I stuck my hand across the desk. "I think we're wasting our Marketing Director's time." He said with a grin. "Do you think it necessary to let us know who is to be in our "Sales Force"? I had to chuckle at that as Lil slapped my thigh. "I thought not. Well I guess the meetings adjourned."

As expected, Katherine was in my office before I even got to sit down. "OK, Justice. You can't just drop a remark like that and get away with it." I put my feet up on my desk and leaned back in the chair. "Why don't you call your daughter in? " I said. "No use in going over this more than once." "How about the rest of them?" "They don't need to know." I said quietly. Since she sat, staring at me, I flipped on the inter vid. "Miss Wallace, could you come in here?" A second later, the girl came in with a data recorder. "You won't need that." I told her. "Nothing said in here will leave this room." Katherine looked up at the edge of the ceiling. I smiled. "No one, including the McClennan's Digital People can monitor this office   when I don't want them to." Turning to Katy's daughter, I asked if she preferred Finnigan or Wallace and whether she minded if I called her Toni? She reminded that the office records listed her as Wallace and no, she didn't. "Alright then - Toni, I assume that you know what Katherine's reputation is based upon." She glanced at Katy and nodded, a bit embarrassed. "Well, when she's not saving our intrepid young geniuses in there from dastardly kidnapers, she's going to start doing away with organized crime in much of the world."

Both women's mouths fell open. I grinned. "Maybe you both better go back to inscrutable school." I let them stew a moment. "Katherine, you have contacts in most of the criminal organizations on this continent and Asia and could, I suspect, use them to develop ones in the rest of the world." Her eyes were reflecting distrust. I could understand that. I was asking her to call in a huge lot of markers - in effect, put her out of business as far as information is concerned. "I know what I'm asking." I continued, trying for calm. "It's more than important, however. It's critical. If we can keep those two working in the right direction, we're going to need, in the very near future, a stable world population - at least the population leaders. The GL is going to handle the political side of it. It will, no doubt, require some rather drastic measures to get governmental cooperation but whatever needs to be done, will be done. This time next year, the world has to be united toward the goal of, if not peace, then self preservation. I mean that quite literally. This cannot happen with large organized outlaw gangs running around taking advantage of the upheaval that is sure to come about."

I couldn't believe he was serious - but I could see in his face that he was. "Just exactly how do you propose we do this little thing?" I asked. His smile wasn't one of mirth. "Anyway you think necessary." he murmured. "Preferably they can be convinced of the necessity. If not they must be rendered impotent. You can call upon whatever resources you need. If they can't be brought to heel, they can disappear. If necessary," took a deep breath, "they will have to be eliminated." I couldn't believe my ears. He went on. "I can get you a small army in a matter of hours if it is needed. That should be a last resort, though. Ideally, the public would never know what had been accomplished. I don't expect them to stop all illegal activities, just those that threaten the stability of the population - drug running, gang violence, white slavery and the like, essentially violent crime. They'll have to give up vendetta and whichever ones you think are up to it can have governmental assistance in keeping the peace - a sort of underground police force - as long as they understand the penalties for breaching trust. You can use your own judgment as to what needs doing. I think I can trust Right and Proper Katy that much." I thought about it for a long minute. "I'll need a really big sales staff. " I muttered, finally. He smiled again. "You have an open check book. Just have the GL vet all of them, especially the ones that will have to use the Modulator."

Thursday April 12, 2060 1600 hours
"I'm very glad you could find the time to meet with me, Don Mourcas." Katy said   as she sat down at the booth in the rear of the restaurant She automatically took up the small loaf of bread and slicing off two pieces, took one and handed the breadboard to Mourcas. He nodded his head and took the other. They were silent as both buttered the bread and took a bite. "I see you are familiar with all the forms." he said. She shrugged. "I just wanted you to see that I have no unwarranted designs in this meeting with you." He smiled again, "So, now that we have broken bread, you can be sure that no violence will come to you in this meeting?" An ironic smile played across Katherine's face. "It was you I wished to be comfortable - and to know that what I tell you is true." she murmured, taking another bite. Mourcas laughed. "I had always heard that you were a formidable woman, but I congratulate you on your aplomb, with all my - associates - around and you being alone. Now what can I do for you that this meeting was so important?" Katy laid down the slice of bread. "I bring a proposal that I hope you can find it in your interests to accept."

His eyebrows rose. "A proposal? From whom?"

"All I can say is that there is a considerable amount of very high level backing behind all of this. It, however, comes from me alone. The backing will be primarily to assure that all conditions of any agreement reached will be met - by all parties." His smile, this time, was definitely sardonic. "I see - and the proposal?" Katherine smiled and reaching into her purse, pulled out a folder. No one reacted since she had been thoroughly searched prior to being brought to the meeting. No one, of course had seen her return in FT to an agent waiting down the block with a pistol for her. Handing the folder to Mourcas, she said, "The particulars are all in there. Basically, however, it requires you to stop all trafficking in drugs, all violence against citizens and others of the brotherhood who will remain free after I have a talk with them. There are a few other minor items. In return, no actions against your prostitution and gambling activities will be

223

taken as long as you only employ those who are in full agreement to their work."

Morcas laughed out loud. "Miss Finnigan, I have to assume that you are mad."

"No, Don Morucas. I am not mad." Katy said calmly, a nasty smile beginning to appear on her face. "I expect every one of those conditions to be met." A frown passed over Mourcas' face. "I think you should really leave now." he growled. "- while we still have the bread between us." Katy's smile quickly changed into a dangerous frown as, placing her arms on the table in front of her, she leaned closer to Mourcas. "I should tell you Don Mourcas that I picked you specifically to be the first to see this proposal because, you are, by far, the worst of the men I'm going to have to meet over the next few months. Your white slavery ring alone was enough to assure that you would get my attention sooner or later anyway. I knew I was, almost certainly, going to have to make an example of someone if I was to get the attention of the rest of the brotherhood. I chose you to be first because I was sure you would reject the offer. It is, therefore, incumbent upon me to warn you that if I get up and leave this table without an agreement, your entire organization will cease to exist before morning." By now, Mourcas' face was scarlet with fury. "In that case, Miss Finnigan, bread or no bread, you won't leave this table alive." Katy's frown turned into a wide grin. "Oh you don't know how pleased I am to have you say that." she said. "Remember it is you who broke the bread rule." With that, she took the pistol from her purse and shot him between the eyes. Pressing the stud on her watch, she got up and walked through the group of bodyguards, slowly reacting to their boss's murder. Taking the weapons from those she had already identified as Mourcas's men, she emptied them of cartridges and returned them before heading for the door. Tugging the door open, she greeted the squad of her "sales force" and told them to take everyone who has a gun, in the restaurant into custody and transport them to Paris.

Once the instructions were given, several of the men slipped into the restaurant with pistols drawn and all returned to TT. By the time the restaurant had emptied of hoods, the rest of the patrons were shocked at the effortless arrests. They were assured that they could continue their dinner in peace. When her troops were gone with their prisoners, she called the other teams and gave them the instructions to go on with the roundup of the rest of the members of the Mourcas family. She then got in the car that had pulled up and began a tour of the action.

By the time she got to the red light district a number of cars were pulling away from three houses on the street. Inside the first, she found, her first team of social workers explaining to the girls that any who wished to, could continue their activities "under their own management" and that their new terms of employment were that they were to be totally independent contractors, free to go where they liked as long as they didn't cause public trouble. The ones addicted to drugs would be given the opportunity to free themselves of the addiction because there would be no more and that any who wished could avail themselves of all the social services of the state. If they decided to stay, they could ask for and receive management assistance to help them set up and run the business. Since the house was being confiscated, they would have to do something like that to allow the "business" to arrange for leasing arrangements. The leases would be based on a percentage of the house revenues. They could take up to thirty days to work out the arrangements. At the end of that time any who wished to leave, and didn't

224

want to leave right now, would have to do so. Whoever remained would have to share in the upkeep of the house which would include regular health checks and audits of the books. Those who remained would select a house manager who would be responsible for meeting all the requirements of the lease. How they ran the house, as long as all requirements were met, was up to them. Disputes would be handled democratically as long as house operations were satisfactory to those who stayed there, otherwise, they would be made by a committee or the house would be closed. The girls were in a state of shock but were told the house would remain closed for a week or until they decided, among themselves what they wanted to do.

By the time she finished her tour, Katherine was satisfied that everything that could be done had been. When the last of the shuttles with prisoners had lifted off she boarded her own new flitter and headed back to New York where her planning team was hard at work on setting up the next "operation". She picked up the hand vid and punched in an already stored number. A voice answered - without video - "Yes?" "Hello, Carlos." Katy said, recognizing the voice. "I'd like to have a few minutes of The Buchwald's time, please." "I'm not to sure he's willing to talk to you Miss Finnigan." the voice said. "He's very angry with you just now." "I'm sure he is." Katy answered grinning. "You both know, however, that I don't bother to answer for my actions to many people. Gerrich is one of the few and that's exactly what I wish to talk about. I know it's a bit late and if he can't see me now, I can wait till morning - but he'll die of curiosity by then - especially when he finds out - in about a half hour - that he has one less competitor."

2200 hours

"Hello, Don Buchwald ." Katherine said as she walked in the door to his study at Buchwald's house. Sitting down in the large leather chair opposite him, she allowed the miniskirt to ride up high on her thighs and continued. "I must say that I appreciate the consideration of being searched by Hanna instead of one of your male associates." Gerrich Buchwald shrugged. "Irritation should not be a reason for lack of courtesy to one who has, in the past, been somewhat helpful." he answered. "Would you like a drink?" She nodded and a glass of white wine appeared at her side delivered by Gerrich's daughter Hanna. Smiling up at the girl, Katherine thanked her and turned her attention back to Buchwald. "Well, Gerrich, I owe you an explanation for my actions this night and before - if only because I intend to ask a favor of you after I have done so." Buchwald raised a sardonic eyebrow. "Would you like Hanna to leave?" he asked. "Only if you do." she replied. "I know how you value your daughter's advice.

First, I want to apologize to you, not for my action against your lieutenant, Soloman Wiesman, but for any embarrassment it may have caused you. Wiesman was scum. The things he did to those poor girls who worked for him was outside the bounds of human behavior. I executed, not a human, but a being that would give a mad dog a bad name." Hanna spoke up quickly and with authority. "My father will accept your apology if you will accept his for not having already acted to rid the organization of such a thing." With a chuckle and a doting look at his daughter, Buchman spoke.

"See what happens, Katherine, when you fail to bring your children up to be seen and not heard. Hanna has been berating me for weeks on my failure to take the proper action in that case. I may have to have her taken for a ride. I'll admit it was a public embarrassment but, privately, I have no problem with it."

Katy laughed with him then she launched into a report of the night's activities.

225

She finished with, "I will also not apologize for acting against Mourcas on my own. I have always considered him a repugnant worm and even though I gave him a chance to reform, he wouldn't take it. Specifically, he, after breaking bread with me, threatened me at his own table."

Another sardonic grin from Buchwald. "Of course you did nothing to induce such a breach of manners." he said. Katherine smiled. "Is there any excuse for such a breach?" she asked. "I thought so." he replied with a grin. "Should I have Hanna bring us a snack?" The smile on Katherine's face turned from smile to serious. I have no need to mistrust you Gerrich, only if you feel it necessary." Buchwald nodded. "May I assume, then that you also have a proposal for me?" Katherine took another envelope from her purse. "More than that." she said as she slid it across the desk. "I would like your help in convincing the brotherhood to make similar agreements to this one. There is a truly great need for us to bring the people of the world to a more civilized way of life. I am acting under the direct authority of the GL and he is handling the political side of things. He has agreed to accept any agreements I might make with you and other members of the brotherhood. I also have, at my disposal, whatever of his assets I need to do my part. I felt an example had to be made of Mourcas to bring home just how serious things were. I felt it was needed to convince some of your compatriots of the need to some compromises."

"You thought I was one of those who needed convincing?" Buchwald said as he studied the papers, passing them sheet by sheet to Hanna to read. "Not at all." Katherine said. "But since I intended to ask your help in bringing the matter before the brotherhood, I thought it might underscore your position should you choose to help." Buchwald looked at his daughter. "Father," she said, "we would have a few problems with the restrictions but they could be overcome - and there are some advantages that might make that worthwhile. The main problem is that it is nothing less than an ultimatum. Even if we choose to ignore that fact, many of the brotherhood will not." Buchwald looked back at Katherine.

"I would prefer to call it a fervent request." she said. "Ultimatums lead to wars and neither of us wants that. The Brotherhood controls many resources that could, if they choose, be very important in the coming months. To destroy those resources is not in the best interest of civilization. Just as an example, prostitution is as old as man itself. Mourcas's operations are not being dismantled, only converted. Dismantling all such activities will require a lot of unnecessary effort that could be better employed elsewhere. No member of the brotherhood will be asked to give up any activity that does not specifically degrade humanity as a whole - that being defined as anything that does not force someone else to do something that they do not want to do. Frankly, I don't care if a person wants to visit a cat house or gamble away his entire fortune. Scams of the elderly and mentally impaired are one thing. Scams of greedy people who want to get something for nothing are quite another. The first won't be tolerated. The second will be. The GL has promised that the governments will not be allowed to prevent such stupidity. Anyone caught harming innocents, though, will still be prosecuted. I do take exception if someone is forced to participate in such activities - that includes encouragement to use drugs.

Public service announcements will warn of the folly of such actions but that is as far as the government will go. I'm sure you will agree that such will not deter greedy people from acting foolishly. The GL has insisted that anyone who does use force to achieve personal goals will be stopped. As for drugs, dealers will go out of business anyway. Plans are already underway to furnish all types at governmental cost. The only restriction will be that addicts have a mandatory briefing on the dangers and how to quit. They will then be offered a chance to get clean. As of next month, though, the drug trade, for practical purposes will no longer exist. Drugs supplied by the world government will undercut any price that your colleagues can live with – EVEN IF THEY HAVE TO BE GIVEN AWAY. The POL's may complain, especially the more conservative ones but they will not be allowed to interfere." "Katherine," Buchwald, said, shaking his head. "There are those in the brotherhood that will be put out of business with that last. They will fight."

"I know, sir." she replied. "And they will lose. I'm sorry to say that some of your colleagues are not all that bright. I will attempt to keep the casualties to a minimum but can't guarantee it. I hope we can expect the rest to help in filling the vacuum they leave." Buchwald studied her intently a long moment. "I know what you're thinking Gerrick." Katy said quietly. If tomorrow, you can find a single one of Mourcas' henchmen around then feel free to doubt my ability to carry out my program." Hanna spoke up again. "Come on father. You know who you're talking to. Has Katherine ever lied to you? More importantly, has she ever failed to live up to her word? You know, as well as I do, she will do exactly as she says she will. I don't know how she will do it, but she will do it. This is the chance for you and the rest of your colleagues to take the moral high ground." Buchwald looked at his daughter a moment. Then he said, simply, "Done." He spit on his palm and held it out to Katy.

Tuesday March 23, 2060

By noon, Mister Peterson had the hole in our lab wall patched and said he'd have to wait several days to paint it. We, though, were back in business. Our first order of business was to query Cindi and Arthur. They, of course, had all the data on the experiments but we described the holes in the rest of the house that they weren't monitoring. "Well," Cindi said, "none of our equipment recorded anything about the generator once you activated it. It simply disappeared." It was what James and I had both expected but we thought it worth a try. I told Cindi so. "Wait." she said. "As I said we couldn't monitor the equipment but we did get some data on the effect it had on the lab and outer walls. Since we had expected some sort of FT reaction, we had switched our sensors to ultra fast mode. As a result we can tell quite precisely, the time from activation until the holes appeared in the walls.

Mister Peterson was correct. There was no noise associated with the breaching of the wall - only a very low frequency hum that faded quickly as the equipment left the building. We, in checking the plans for the house, found that the distance from the test bench to the lab wall was fifteen feet, four point five meters. The time from activation until the hole appeared, was one hundreth of a second - plus a fraction that I can give you if you want - I know you usually hate such details. That gives us an average speed of four hundred fifty point six meters per second. Of course, without knowing the terminal velocity, we can't be sure of the acceleration factor but Arthur and I both think that it was probably an instant change in velocity from zero to four hundred fifty Mps." That surprised me. "And your reason for such an assumption?" I asked. Cindi got that self satisfied smirk on her face that, I hoped she hadn't gotten from me, but it was Arthur who spoke.

"I thought, and Cindi agreed, that you would enjoy working out the answer to that, yourself." he grinned. "In fact, we have a wager on which of you will figure out what happened, first." "I've a notion to reprogram you." I growled. Just then, James chuckled. "Four hundred fifty meters per second is a figure we're both familiar with." he laughed. Then it struck me! Of course, the rotational speed of the earth. "My God!" I whispered. "The generator didn't go anywhere. We did." I turned to James dreading the logical extension of that fact. He had that far away look in his eyes. "If that was the only motion to consider," he said quietly, "we could expect the thing to come flying back through in about twenty four hours - after making holes in everything in between." "That's only if it stayed in position relative to the earth and allowed the earth to rotate beneath it." I laughed. "Exactly," he said, thoughtfully. "We need to determine if it's holding its position relative to the earth or to the universe overall. In that case the movement of the solar system and galaxy will affect it and I'm no astronomer, so I can't even make a guess."

I turned to Cindi and Arthur. "OK tell us about that." "We calculate, assuming it retains its velocity and angular momentum," Arthur said, "that, in about three hours, it will impact then penetrate a point near the top of a mountain in the Rocky Mountain Chain and then exit the earth's plane in the general direction of Alpha Centauri A . Based on the few reference points, it would appear to be, with only about a fifteen percent confidence level, moving with galaxy. We are unable to determine its movement relative to the Solar System with any more accuracy" James and I both drew a breath of relief.

OK a problem. First question - how do you run a test on something that can fly through anything that gets in its way before you can deal with it? We went back to Cindi's data screens. After a couple of FT days, it became clear that there was an obvious, if complex, relationship between the three states of the Modulator effects we were studying. They all changed powerfully with, and in direct relationship to, incremental changes in the Fast Time environment. We decided on another test - this time out in the yard. We set up a work table, surrounded by paper screens and placed another FT generator on it. This one, though, had its own power supply and remote FT controller. With the controller set as close to the earth spin rate as possible, we activated the generator in FT while we stayed in TT. Sure enough, the generator jumped off the table and headed west - but at a rate of only ten or fifteen meters per second. By having Cindi adjust the frequency, we got the generator to move backwards a bit. Then we lost control. The thing fairly screamed backward and out through the screens on the other side and was gone.

Tuesday March 29, 2060

A week and two FT months later, we had it all figured out. Cindi and Arthur had a complete set of specs and formulae for the control of a working model propulsion system   based on the generator. How to use it would require a lot of effort to design a vehicle compatible with it but that seemed feasible. With an almost infinite amount of FT speeds available, it was theoretically, possible to even exceed the speed of light - at least with relation to normal True Time. Several problems were obvious, though. One was control. We would need vastly better methods than what we had if we were to prevent things from getting out of hand to the point that they lead to danger. What if the thing had been moving down instead of sideways when we lost control? Would it have carved a hole through the earth, itself? Add to that, the question of what happened to the material that disappeared with its passage through a solid substance? It was time to do some real thinking.

"Well, Milam? What do you think?" "What I think, Jonha is that you should have stopped them a week ago. Those two are going to kill themselves   if they keep playing with subspace. That thing they launched last week is still going. It's probably nearing Centauri A by now and shows no sign of stopping. They missed a bit on their formulae. The thing did accelerate - and is still accelerating. I'd say it's on a completely uncontrolled trajectory out of the Galaxy at an eventual, transfinite speed that we've never dared attempt. Today, they tried again and, apparently, have set up a rough control system. It wasn't good enough, though. This one is now nearing Pluto at about warp nine." Jonha grinned. "Pretty good for a couple of amateurs." he chuckled. "Can we achieve warp nine?" "Damn it, Jonha! You know we could. We're just smart enough not to try. To go from one place to another, you have to, not only get there. You have to be able to stop in the near vicinity of the target. You know that above warp three, we can't come within a hundred parsecs of our target. What's of more immediate importance is that they are beginning to experiment with direction. Can you imagine the consequences of punching a hole in an occupied building? Worse yet, if they punch through the earth, we have two instant volcanos - probably with accompanying earthquakes."

"It's what you get for letting children play with bombs." Both men turned at the sound of the new voice. "Ah - Mrs. Johnson - you heard?" "Of course, Milam. If you don't want everyone to hear you scream you should scream more softly." Jonha spoke up. "It seems, darling, that our children are becoming a danger, not only to themselves." Suzanne, came around the desk and kissed him on the cheek. "Sweetheart, you are an amazing man but you still look at things differently than we here on earth do. Remember, the life span here is seldom more than a hundred forty years. We don't have time to spend three hundred years mastering all the knowledge of a given subject. If you had been watching and listening to James and Cynthia instead of trying to appear all knowing, you would have seen a couple whose minds were hard at work ignoring everything that didn't contribute to what they considered important knowledge. Darling, our children are engineers first and scientists second. Engineers want to know how things work so they can use them. Scientists want to know why they work. They don't care how they can be used.

You warned them about what they were doing but wouldn't tell them what they should be careful of. Then you turned around and told them that what they were doing was important to the human race. I say again. What did you expect? Why don't you ask Suzanne II what her prognosis is for the success of the children's work?" Jonha grinned at her. "My dear, don't you know that all of us men are all knowing while you women are too emotional for serious discussions." Suzanne bent low to whisper in his ear. "My dear, don't you know who's going to be sleeping in the guest room tonight?" Jonha laughed. "Milam are you as henpecked as I am?" "More so, I'm afraid. Should we do as the lady suggests?" "Why not? Suzanne II what is your prediction as to James and Cynthia's efforts?"

The hologram appeared with her couch. "I don't like that name anymore. I think, you should remember that I am now Susan. As to the question, they are experimenting with Modulator settings that are known to be dangerous. Without help, they are likely to cause major damage, possibly death, most probably to themselves. With some basic knowledge of the forces involved and more sophisticated control systems their probabilities of success in controlling the Modulator are around seventy percent. If that occurs, they are very likely to achieve a Modulator utilization capability that would be far beyond any presently available. Their risk of serious damage to themselves drops to twenty one percent. If they were to receive full disclosure of the systems capabilities, now, the probability of success increases significantly while the chances of harm to the planet drops to around five percent and to themselves, to near zero.. I would suggest hinting at the forces and control of them in a way that lets them become aware of the danger and work out how to minimize it. This approach will reduce the danger to themselves to slightly less than ten percent. It will not be an entirely safe approach but it will protect them somewhat without stifling their urge to succeed in their quest."

"Ten Percent!" Suzanne almost shrieked. "You're talking about a ten percent chance of their being killed! That is not acceptable!" Susan turned to her. "That is a mother talking. Perhaps Jonha was not entirely wrong about women - especially mothers. If mothers ran the world, none of their children would ever do anything dangerous. In that case, they would be much like the Magmans. They are so protective of their long lives that they don't allow dangerous ideas to be investigated. They have had this technology for thousands of years but have never fully explored the capabilities because of the known danger. Earth has become a lot like that with the populace adamantly opposed to any ideas that endanger their own pleasant, and useless,

231

existence. This opposition, however, has not entirely stamped out all who feel the need to expand their knowledge." A compassionate smile crossed her face. "Luckily, your descendants are some of those. You will not be able to stop them, nor protect them completely. You can only do as much as you can for them and then hope for the best. Throughout the history of the earth, women have sent their children and husbands off to dangerous tasks with a brave smile and terror in their hearts. It's your time, now, for a brave smile."

It was quiet for long moments. Finally Jonha spoke up. "Do you have a suggestion as to these hints, Susan?" She grinned. "Of course. Let them find the last records of Professor Silverman's speculations. They both seem to have a great respect for him." Jonha frowned. "I assume you know where these documents can be found?" "Certainly," the hologram grinned evilly. "I'm inserting them into the database of the old University of Houston records now. I'll suggest to Arthur that he find them." Jonha laughed aloud. "You mean that you are preparing to record what Silverman "would have speculated if he had actually speculated". You know, of course, that is clearly fraud." "Oh Pooh! You men worry too much about silly things. At least we women worry about important ones - like our children. Besides to defraud someone, you have to intend them harm. In this case I am enhancing Professor Silverman's reputation and helping humanity. You really should give him a posthumous medal or something for his outstanding work."

Friday April 1, 2060

It had been a frustrating three days - a week of FT. Control - that was the problem. Actually, the problem was that we didn't really know what we were trying to control. We were taking a break. It was almost time to feed the kids and we were burnt out. Cindy was having Cindi and Arthur go over all our calculations and theories again without much hope of a breakthrough, when Cindi spoke up. "That formula looks familiar. Arthur ran across a paper dealing with a formula just like that a week or so ago. Yes. Here it is." An image appeared on the screen "Speculations on applications of the Infinite Variable", by - I couldn't believe my eyes. It was a paper by old Professor Silverman - one that I hadn't seen before. I had to frown because I thought I had seen them all. After all, we had been researching this problem, it seemed like, forever. I began to read as Cindy burst out laughing. "My God!" she practically screamed. "It's exactly what we've been fighting all this time. Look! He's talking about inter-dimensional transits. I could see that. I couldn't believe it. We pored over the paper until it was obvious, that it was a start on the road to understanding the forces we were generating.

I was ready to scream with joy! I turned to James expecting the same from him. Instead he was frowning. "What?" I shouted. "It's all wrong." he murmured. I know my mouth fell open. What could possibly be wrong with the thing? I knew who I was listening to, though. I groaned. His "wrongness" mode! "What is it?" I asked, pleading. "I can't see anything wrong with his equations or his logic." He shook his head. "Neither do I - but something's wrong with the thing. Let's go get the kids." I knew what he was doing. I'd seen it too many times. He was letting his brain work on the problem while he did something else. With a sigh I got up and followed him to the nursery.

A few minutes later, I was happily ensconced in, what James called, my

232

nursing chair. With my blouse and bra off and two gluttonous little mouths furiously sucking at my nipples, I sighed with pleasure. With my babies snuggled against me, their mouths and little hands on my breast mounds, what mother could ask for more? The pair were getting to be a bit heavy now, but by leaning my elbows on the padded arms of the chair, I could hold both of them very comfortably. I wondered if I could find a good excuse to breast feed them till they were five or six? I grinned at the thought. Then I looked over at James, remembering our problem - though, it didn't seem nearly as important now. He was staring fixedly at us, his eyes not looking at all fatherly. I smiled, knowing how he got turned on by this display - he probably knew I didn't have to take off my blouse to nurse the children but, all the same, I enjoyed pretending, teasing him with my blatant display of skin. All was quiet for the longest time, the silence only broken occasionally by a tiny slurping noise from one or the twins or the other. Finally, they were finished and sleepy. One by one, we put them in the bathinet-refresher and took them out newly "refreshed" and diapered them. We stood beside their cribs and watched them a moment before James took my hand. I had not replaced my blouse and bra and without need to comment, we both turned to the bedroom.

An hour later, I lay, naked, sprawled half atop him, sleepily, chuckling at his scatological remarks, when I felt his body quiver. "Shit!" he muttered, then chuckled ruefully to himself. I sighed, knowing full well, what had happened. His "wrongness mode" had reported in. Coming fully awake, I muttered, "Well, I guess the fun's over. Shall we get some coffee while we talk?" "I seem to recall that we can talk and play at the same time." he whispered, his hand sliding between us to cup my naked breast. "Well," I murmured, pulling away just far enough to give him some room while I kissed his neck, "If you don't exercise your talents you could lose them." Then I leaned over on an elbow and relaxed, enjoying the feel of his fingers on my nipple. "Remember the times I discussed old Professor Silverman? What I said about his dislike of applied Math?" "Uh-huh." I nodded, still paying more attention to his fingers than the subject. "He got mad when some biologist used some infinite series of his to model bacterial multiplication." "Right! He was what was called in those days, a Pure Mathematician. He was working in a department headed by and, almost entirely, staffed by applied mathematicians. If he hadn't been so brilliant, they'd have gotten rid of him.

His lectures reeked of his disdain for scientific application of math. He used, more than once, the word Prostitution with respect to applied math. He compared it to using a picture of Christ to sell soap." Then I saw what he was driving at. "Lifting my head to look at him, I gasped. "A man like that couldn't have written that paper." He grinned. "Of course not!" Then he added. "In fact, nobody who knew anything about Silverman could have been stupid enough to write that paper. Not only that, the principles that paper is based upon couldn't possibly arise from any of his known work. Those principles still aren't known today. The man was a brilliant mathematician - he was even a brilliant cellist. He wasn't a physicist or philosopher and he would have scoffed at the idea of reading tea leaves."

Now I was fully awake and started to lift myself up off him. He tightened his grip on my right breast and pulled me over atop him. He kissed my neck and told me he wasn't through with me yet. I wasn't inclined to argue so wriggled around until I could settle myself slowly down onto him. "Now, my beautiful, naked sex object. Just what do you make of all that?" "A sex object isn't supposed to make anything of anything while being fondled and performing their duties." I laughed. "If the objectifier will continue his attentions, though, the objectified will attempt to work on the problem." I whispered nibbling his ear. "So the esteemed professor has been plagiarized - by a non pure mathematician - a modern person conversant with Modulator technology. That leaves you and me and our mysterious CP - plus the GL and his friends. Unless you've been working nights and CP has turned over a new leaf, it means the GL has decided to give us some help." "You know, for a sex object you're much too bright. We may have to promote you." he laughed. "Let's wait." I whispered, stretching my head up to kiss his mouth, then lowering myself back down. "I'd like to remain a sex object for just a little longer."

Saturday April 2, 2060

"Jonha." I woke quickly. If Suzanne - I really will have to get used to calling her Susan - at least until she decides to change her name again - when I think about her. I looked at the chronometer. If she was calling so early in the morning it had to be serious. Looking over at Suzanne, I saw she was coming awake too. "What's happened?" I mumbled. The hologram materialized next to the bed, but facing away, pretending not to look at us. "I think I have made a grave error." she murmured. "We just received this message from Cindi." she said. A single line of text appeared in the space above the bed. "Thanks - but plagiarism is against the law."

Suzanne laughed out loud. "You're going to be really embarrassed if you keep on playing with people smarter than you are husband of mine." Turning to Susan she said, "And you stop acting coy. Turn around. You think we don't know you have sensors in every room in the place?" The hologram turned and replied, huffily, "I was just showing that the sensors were off in here." "Fine," my wife said sarcastically, "Now just what, do you suppose caused our children to catch on to you so quick?" The face in the air took on a distinct blush. "I did not research Professor Silverman's temperament adequately. I have since researched more thoroughly and realize that he hated applied mathematics and mathematicians. I am very embarrassed." "Well, it's obvious that James is smarter than you are." Suzanne chuckled. "Maybe we should get him over here to do your work." "He is, indeed, very brilliant." the hologram said with a sigh, "but he does not have enough computing capability to do that." I felt like it was time for me to take a hand. "It's OK. Suzanne - uh Susan. A little bit of chagrin is warranted but your place is secure. Now go away and leave us to get dressed. I didn't really expect to fool him too long anyway."

Saturday April 9, 2060

It was almost an FT month before we sat on the grass outside the house and watched a tiny FT generator hover in empty space   and move forward and backward in obedience to control inputs from a simple model airplane type joy stick. James moved it back to the ground and cut the power supply. It lay still. We had done it! - And we were too tired to celebrate. We turned to Arthur's portable input station. It had no speakers so at our question, the screen lit up "Parameters nominal." James grinned at me. We had tamed - or at least brought some semblance of control to the almost unlimited power of the power universe - or at least one of them, if our math was right. We packed up our equipment and headed back inside. Once back in the lab, we checked over the equipment and found no damage. Turning to Cindi, we asked for an evaluation.

"Control of the test vehicle was well within acceptable limits. Power utilization was ninety nine point nine three percent of that predicted. No unexpected deviation in power input was noted. It would appear that even though one thousand twenty three megawatts was used no effect on the overall power available was noted. Extrapolated, the vehicle under full power would have achieved a speed approaching within a few decimal places that of light within seven hours ten minutes   True Time. Acceleration, using the controls applied, would have been too high for organic life to bear but still, an acceptable acceleration should still allow for those speeds in a reasonable length of time. The mathematical formulae used in the extrapolation, preclude measurement beyond that point but it should be noted that the acceleration remained constant throughout the calculation. This implies that the speed would have, perhaps, become transfinite Whether it would, in that instance, have remained in our dimension or translated into another can't be determined.. Arthur and I have prepared a set of specifications derived from the extrapolated data that should be a decent starting place for building a larger model for testing.

We called down for a lunch to be brought up and began to go over the specs. As each one was verified, Arthur and Cindi combined them into a procurement document. When the kids started to cry, Cynthia moved over to the big easy chair and, opening her blouse, put them to her breasts while she continued to double check the data on the wall sized screen Cindi produced. That evening we sent it off to Symons and took the rest of the day off for a little adult play time.

As we sat down to dinner, Cindi told us we had a call from "Mister Symons". I looked at Cynthia, suddenly sorry that we had equipped most of the rooms with communications equipment. "Go ahead and put him through, Cindi." she said, laying down her fork. Justice appeared on the wall screen before Cynthia had even finished buttoning her blouse. Her bra was still back in the bedroom and he, no doubt, got a good flash of naked breast. He immediately looked away from her and apologized to me, for interrupting our meal. We told him it was alright. "OK, then," he said, "I've had to go to the GL with this request. Sorry, but you knew that I'd have to." We both nodded. "Well, he said, he could furnish all you require, but he added a request." I looked at Cindy. We were both puzzled. "And that was?" Cindy said, suspiciously. Simons grinned. "I think that the request was actually a demand from his wife." he chuckled. "You both will never be forgiven if you kill yourselves and destroy the east coast of this continent and you should send the children to Paris until you finish." Cindy laughed out loud. "Tell the GL we'll be happy to comply with his first request. As for the second, he should remember that our children are not bottle babies." "The GL never forgets anything - especially when his wife is around to remind him." Symons said with a smile. "Suzanne is more than willing to bring herself back into lactation mode if you'd agree." "A second time in only a month or so?" Cindy murmured, pensively. "Besides I - well, I'm already in lactating mode." Symons gave me a knowing smile - it would have been a leer if he weren't such a civilized kind of guy. "To hell with you men!" Cindy growled, angrily. "My babies need me and I need them - so forget it." Justice's laugh was so contrived that I smelled a rat.

Looking over at James, I could see that he was puzzling over something too. I couldn't help a raised eyebrow and he smiled. I felt a little thrill as the thought flashed through my brain that we had come so far that we could read each other so thoroughly. "Justice," he said quietly turning to the screen. "Why don't you, as the old movies used to say, come clean. There's something you're not saying. Remember you are part of our team as well as the GL's. I accept that he has an ulterior motive in everything he does but I don't have to like it." Justices' smile faded. He stared, thoughtfully, at us for a long moment.

Finally, he said, "Actually, the GL is torn. He wants you to finish your work but he really wants you in Paris where he can truly protect you from outside harm. You know that Katy's been hard at work in an effort to bring some stability to the criminal element in the world - primarily in the two transatlantic continents, so far." We both nodded, wondering what that had to do with this conversation. "She is now in Western Canadian Pol and has reported that a price has been placed on both your heads - Dead On Arrival. Not only that, but it is accompanied by accurate photographs and bio's of you two, your families and locations - though, the "southern Maryland POL is somewhat ambiguous." James and I were aghast. "All our families?" he gasped. "They even have the addresses and photos of your, until now obscure, relatives, James."

"How much reward?" I asked in shock. "A half Billion ND in gold ." "They're a bit tight with their cash." James remarked, quietly. "It's the maximum any of them can offer." Justice said. "They have a sort of, agreement, not to exceed that amount without a meeting of the Brotherhood leaders - apparently to reduce competition between the various organizations. Besides, in gold it's worth, probably, ten times that amount in many parts of the world - enough to interest many a small country. It would indicate, though, and Katy's convinced that it's true, that the bounty comes from either a rogue portion of the brotherhood or an outside source." He turned to me. "The GL has assigned substantial teams to protect all the families. That seems sufficient right now since their value is primarily in leading the bad guys to you. That means assassination is very unlikely. Kidnapping and assault can be almost certainly be precluded with the teams assigned. In your case, however, DOA means just that. Literally anyone can be killed if someone is willing to pay the price. The only real bright spot is that terrorist organizations are seldom ready to pay that price just for money."

With more bravado than either of us felt, we refused to leave or let the twins leave and Justice signed off. Neither of us was very hungry after that, but we ate automatically without any talk. Finally, James said, "Maybe we should let the twins go to Paris. You know that if they captured them, they'd have us over a barrel. If you are worried about nursing, I can handle that part - I have before." I had to smile and looked across the table at him.. "And very nicely and enjoyably too, if I recall." I said "Now, though - in case you haven't noticed - I'm a lot bigger than I was then - and, because of all the Fast Time, I'm full of milk four times a day. In a week you'd be so fat you couldn't walk." His grin was more of a leer. "I guess I'd just have to get McKinsey to help me. Katy probably wouldn't actually kill him." I laughed and threw my napkin at him. "Seriously, though," he said, "that's what a milker is for." "I hate those things." I grumbled, but I agreed to think about it.

Saturday April 10, 2060
        The next morning we did something really stupid. At the time, though, an early morning walk to enjoy the sunrise seemed a perfect way to ease the tensions Justice's phone call had brought. The morning was beautiful and we were barefooted, both wearing shorts. I had just finished nursing the twins and still had on my cropped peasant blouse. I liked to think of it as my "nursing" blouse because without a bra, all I had to do was lift the hem a couple of inches and give the kids my nipples. Of course it meant that without a bra my, now empty breasts bounced a lot - but of course I knew that. I also knew my husband loved to watch them bounce. He pretended to be annoyed with me saying that I just liked turning the guards on. I told him that I wanted to keep the guards as backup when he got too tired to service me. We were happily teasing one another and holding hands as we came near the guard post at the end of, what we thought of as, our private lane. I waved at the guard as he stepped out of his little covered shed. Instead of waving back like he usually did, though, I could see he held a little plastic gadget in his hand. Suddenly I recognized him and grabbed at my modulator - just as a fog rose up around us from the ground under our feet.
        I had to smile. Both of them dropped like stones, though I could tell Mrs. McClennan had grabbed for her modulator before she fell. I had done this myself because I knew that none of the local talent could have gotten to her before the Maxon gas took over. I had considered letting one of them do this since I had such a damned thing against lethal violence. It was just too big a risk and even authorizing - such a permanent solution was hard for me. I had almost been sick from offering that reward. Too late now, though. I had gone to super fast mode as soon as I had pressed the activator and was able to simply stroll up to the two inert bodies, still in the process of falling. Bending down I took their wrist modulators off - I hadn't recognized them until Mrs. McClennan made a grab for hers. It was a surprise. I had expected something more like the ones I had taken from them before. I thought, ruefully, of what would have happened if I had let them have their "valuables" back at the house. That set me to wondering what was happening to Marie. I was sorry to have gotten her mixed up in all this. I deactivated the modulators, and pressed them, one at a time against the cavity in my magnetic delimiter. Once the tiny chime sounded, I put them back on both of them and reactivated them on about three quarter gauss. Then I simply walked off. A few seconds later the two bodies vanished. I wished I knew where. Our scientists had never really found out what all this procedure did. I really hoped that they didn't suffer.

        I was back in Paris after checking the background investigations of two new lawyers when, just after ten hundred, Susan appeared in front of my desk. "Cynthia and James have disappeared!" she gasped. The gasp was so realistic I began to wonder

237

just how much her programming had been limited. "How and when?" I asked, striving for calm. Sometime after six AM, their time, this morning. How, is unknown. Where, was on the grounds of the estate - they took their usual early morning walk and simply disappeared. "Have you told Jonha?" I asked. She shook her head and actually, looked, afraid. The image of a tear appeared in her eye. "How about the twins?" I asked. "They're still in their room in Maryland." I punched Jonha's emergency button. Fifteen minutes later, Suzanne and a squad of the GL guards were on a super shuttle heading for Maryland POL A half hour later, a message had gone out to Katy and another shuttle with an investigation team and Jonha aboard, headed out.

Sometime/where

I woke up lying on the damp ground. Memory returned. I looked around, fearful of what I might see. Nothing but the woods and James lying beside me. I was a little shaky but I managed to stand. We had, obviously, been gassed, but for what reason. I was certain that it was Karnes I saw grinning at me just as I collapsed. Where was he? Had the guards run him off? Come to think of it, he had been in the guard shelter. What had happened to the regular guard? I looked around. He must have moved us because there was no shelter in view. Strange! Also strange, I didn't remember the woods quite so overgrown - shows how much attention I paid to my surroundings. James was now stirring so I put off any more speculations until he was up and around - except one. Had he gotten to the kids? Suddenly I became frantic. I began to bully James into wakefulness. It didn't take long. As soon as he was able to comprehend, I reeled off my fears. He came fully awake and got up.

We headed back to the house, moving faster as the effects of whatever got to us wore off. When we got to the edge of the woods, though, we stopped short in amazement. There was no house and no driveway. There wasn't even an expanse of yard, only a large overgrown field. We looked at one another then back as we realized we hadn't just been moved, somehow, we'd been moved somewhere. As we stood looking at what had been our house, a strange man, stepped out from behind a bush. "Who Art Thou?" he growled, brandishing a large rifle type weapon. We didn't answer, transfixed in the sight of the small Log cabin where our house used to be. By now the man was becoming belligerent. He pointed the rifle at us and told us to stand still. "Ye look white but dress like red injuns ." he growled. I ask ye agin. Who Art Thou.?" Jimmy was the first to unfreeze. He looked at the man. "We're - uh - strangers. Just passing through."

The man glowered. "Thee dost speak a strange tongue." he muttered. "What man, though dost let his woman go almost naked in public?" James and I both looked down at our abbreviated costumes. Finding my tongue finally, I said, "We dress differently where we come from." Wrong answer! His eyes narrowed. "No colony, I know lets a woman go naked." I started to tell him forcefully, that I wasn't naked but James put his hand on my arm. "Sir, he said, we're from - uh - New York POL I'm James - Van Hoeck and this is my wife Cynthia. We were attacked in the woods by four men. They took our transport and most of our clothes leaving us only these."

The man spit to one side, obviously not impressed. "Damned Dutchmen!" he growled "What these men look like?" he finished. "All were very big. They had long beards and carried weapons such as yours." I kicked in my two cents worth of lies. At least it got him to lower the muzzle of his weapon a bit. He rubbed his chin, apparently in thought. "Sounds like the Abercrombie bunch. They been a sight o problem lately. One day we ketchem and string em up." He apparently bought our story for he propped the weapon on his shoulder and said, "Well, cain't let even a Dutch woman run around naked. Come t'house. Maybe Maybelle got sumptin'll fit ye - be way to short, though. Got some ole coverups'll fit you man." He motioned us toward the house. Thinking furiously, I noticed that he walked behind us. It was obvious we weren't in our Maryland anymore - apparently not even in our own time. Were we still in our own universe? How the hell could that have happened?

His wife wasn't nearly as suspicious as the man was. As I poured myself into a faded long gingham dress - long on Maybelle but reaching only to mid calf on me - I managed to find out that we were, indeed in Maryland - the Colony, presumably, if the history of this place was the same as ours, of Great Britain. James looked as ridiculous as I supposed I did, in way to short overalls with one strap tied together. Both of us were, at least six inches too tall for our clothes. I managed to find out that the local "Magistrate" was in a town called Aberdeen, about ten miles "down the road." "Never get thar w'out shoes, though." she warned. "Wait around till market day. Can ride t'wagon w'us." she said. I was beginning to get the feel of the place and said it'd be up to my man. "Course." she said as if that was a given. "Ye can sleep in t'barn if'n ye want. Gonna rain t'night." Her husband protested that they didn't know anything about us. She shushed him saying, "Tom. They, quality folks. Lookee her jewels." I managed to keep a straight face, wondering what jewels - till "Tom's" eyes went to my engagement and wedding rings and up to my pearl necklace. Suddenly, I blessed the old adage that one "should always wear your pearls." Maybe that would solve one problem - I refused to let myself dwell on the fate of the twins - we might be able to get some cash by selling my necklace and rings. For that matter, the farmer didn't wear a wedding ring. We might sell James gold band too.

That night, after a supper of boiled potatoes, we spent in the barn - saying we slept would be stupid. We spent the whole night discussing our plight. We had managed, without too much trouble, to find out the date - if we could only figure it out. It was the second year of the reign of Queen Victoria. Probably we were in our own history - at least we were assuming that for the time being. We started considering "time lines" such as the old science fiction writer, Robert Heinlein had written about. If we had been transported into the past of our time line, we needed to know "when" we were. Presumably the modulators had been used to put us here. Could we reset them - or whatever. So! "When" were we? James and I pummeled our brains trying to remember our ancient history. I remembered that England had a huge party for Victoria's "Golden Jubilee"around 1890 - James thought 1885. We split the difference - about 1887 or 8. That would mean she became queen probably around 1835 or 40. So this year would be around that period, 1837 to 1842. All that assuming that the time here was the same as our time and not someone else's. Obviously it wasn't our past time, if Great Britain still ruled "The Colonies."

Come to think of it the Dutch apparently, from Tom's Dutchman comment, still held New York. Well, if it was Victoria's time it was no wonder "Tom" thought I was naked. When I brought up money and suggested we could sell my "jewels", he shook his head. "Out here in backwoods Maryland? We'd have to find a banker to find enough money to do us any good. I think we'll have to rob a bank." I was appalled. "James, these people are so poor they probably don't even have a bank." He got a hard look on his

239

face. "There's always a bank - and rich people. Throughout history, every place has one or two who get rich fleecing people like Tom and Maybelle." After that, we fell to discussing how to get back "home." "Well," James said, "I suppose we've got to figure out how we got here - something must have been done to our Modulators. They must be the cause of this. And if what you remember is right, Karnes must have done it. Remember the GL said their people have a lot of trouble with killing. This must have been his solution."

By the end of the week, we had begun to get an appreciation as to just how easy life had become in "our time" I helped Maybelle with her "chores". Those were from before dawn to dusk, cooking, cleaning, hoeing the garden and milking two cows, even one day devoted to candle making. James helped Tom to the extent he could. He almost chopped off his toes cutting wood and Tom was politely disgusted with his attempt to plow a straight "furrow". They were gone several hours each day "running a trap line" and another several hours cleaning and skinning a collection of small animals, mostly foxes and rabbits. We made candles because on one of their forays, they came between a small bear and her cubs and had to shoot it - apparently Tom was an expert with his muzzle loading "musket". He was upset because the cubs were big enough to run off before he could reload. Maybelle "rendered" the bear fat while the men skinned and butchered the bear. Then they put the meat in the "smoke house" - the stoking of the fire in it Maybelle and I had added to our duties. On the brighter side, Maybelle and I became rather easy with each other. In the beginning, she kept apologizing for having a "great lady" stoop to such labor but by the end of the week, she accepted the fact that this "great lady" was willing to help - even if she was a lot less than competent in many of the skills needed to run such a farm.

I discovered that we had been pretty close on our estimate of the year. It was, indeed, spring in 1837, though Maybelle had to think about that since it wasn't the usual way of keeping track of years. We were right about New York, too, but even though still a nominal Dutch colony, it was in practical terms a part of the British colonies. It, along with Boston, Philadelphia and Richmond were the main centers of commerce, though, she admitted that in Maryland, everyone considered Baltimore much more important than any of the others. She referred to anything "west of the hills", apparently the Allegheny Mountains, as "Injun country". Most of the "injuns" were friendly, though, a lot of "white trash" sold them whisky that caused them to go crazy at times. You had to "be careful" around them - 'specially "white women." They were "turribly prowdish" seemed not to believe that "God fearing white women" didn't want to become their "squaws."

Several young girls were stolen each year and had to be "ransomed" back. "Years ago," she commented, "the men had gone after the girls with guns but it had meant a lot of deaths and wars. Now there was an understanding with the "red men" that any girl could be "bought back." Usually, though, only after having "bad things done to her." I was surprised to find that several of the girls had been "brought home in the family way." I was even more surprised to find that Maybelle was also. She was due "around Christmas", though, with the loose long dress she always wore it was hard to notice. When I remarked on that, she actually blushed. "Twouldn't be proper for others to see." she said. When, in a few months they could, she'd have to stay home till after the baby was born. Pregnant or not, the woman could work harder and longer than I could and I had always prided myself on my fitness. She remarked during that conversation that she had noticed my own "condition." It had been impossible to hide the fact that I had to express my breasts a couple of times a day. And she asked about my children. I couldn't help the tears that formed in my eyes. She drew the wrong conclusion, and patting me on the shoulder, told me how sorry she was at my loss. I didn't disabuse her of the idea I had lost the twins. Right now it seemed all too likely that I had.

Of more immediate interest, the town of Aberdeen, as James had suspected, did harbor a pair of rich banker brothers and, while Maybelle, was reluctant to disparage them, it was obvious that her opinion of them was that they were a pair of thieves. James ideas didn't seem so bad anymore. On Wednesday, all of us "turned to the fields". We dug potatoes, carefully cleaned them and stowed them in sacks in Tom's wagon. On Thursday, we went into town to the market. We had discussed our plan for thievery all week in the barn, in addition to more pleasurable pursuits last night. Sex on a pile of hay seemed deliciously sinful in this land of puritanical virtues - so much so that we actually pushed the fate of our babies far back in our minds for a couple of hours. In the previous nights, James had nursed me and held me close all night, but the act had just emphasized what we had lost and had dampened our ardor.

As we came into the town of Aberdeen and rode down the dirt main street, Maybelle pointed out all the business establishments in town - all six of them. We were mostly interested in the bank and the "clothes store". As soon as the wagon stopped at the central square, James and I activated the modulators and headed directly to the bank. We had crossed our fingers a couple of days ago and tried them out, wondering if they'd still work. They had. Inside the bank there were several people standing in line at the teller's cage with a sour looking man behind it. A look alike sat at a desk going over some ledger sheets. All, of course, were frozen in place. James simply opened the bar across the fence protecting the bankers and walked behind the counter to the large iron safe with its open door. James, reached inside toward the back and took out a stack of bills and another bunch of coins. I lifted my skirt and stashed the bills in the pockets of my cut off shorts I wore under it. James dropped the coins into the pocket of his overalls and we left. As soon as we got back to the market, we arranged ourselves carefully in the places we were before and turned real time back on.

We worked with Tom and Maybelle, unloading the wagon, listening for a sign that our "heist" had been noted. By the time we finished, however, all was still quiet and we told them we needed to get some new clothes and see about catching the "stage" north. James said that just before we had been attacked, he had "a seeing" (we had learned there was lot of superstition dealing with precognition extant) and had thrown our money belts in the brush. He said he'd be happy to give them something for putting us up this week. They protested that they wouldn't think of it, that it was what good people did - and besides, the work we had done was more than enough for what we'd gotten from them. I knew the state of their finances and so when I hugged Maybelle, I surreptitiously, slipped a few bills into her pocket. James and Tom shook hands very formally and we left.

Two hours later, we were a room in the local hotel. It wasn't much, the room being papered in a gaudy flowered wall paper and there was no bathroom. There was one down the hall, though and, for a price, we had gotten a hot bath and had dressed in our new clothes - after James had nursed me. I was both pleased and unhappy to see that I was beginning to "dry up". The still, aching need for relief was a real problem, though - especially as we were going to be traveling, but it also served to bring home to me the fact that my children were no longer a part of me. The clothes were disgustingly

241

confining, but not as bad as they could have been had "my condition" continued as before. I could, now go almost all day with only an uncomfortable feeling of bloat. The saleslady at the store, had been aghast that a "a fine lady like me" would consider going out in public without a corset. As a result, I bought one, not intending to wear it if I could help it.

I hadn't considered the shock the sight of my bikini panties would engender. The sales lady gasped then frowned and pursed her lips at the sight of them. One word, escaped her - "scandalous" - before she stopped talking to me and just brought out clothing. It was a good thing I thought to myself, I hadn't been wearing a bra when we got - "time-napped." It would have helped support me but no telling what scandal the sight of that would have caused. Even so, my refusal to wear a large hoop and more than one petticoat, would probably labeled me as having a fairly low character even if my underwear hadn't. Expecting to travel lightly, I only got two changes of "linen", and three skirts and blouses. The dresses she brought out were cavernous affairs with multitudes of buttons that I considered much too much trouble to mess with. The girls last "vapors" were over my shoes. I wouldn't accept the high heeled ones that buttoned halfway up my shin and the thought of a "lady" wearing men's hiking boots almost drove her over the edge, even though they'd be covered by my skirt. I gave up and went ahead and bought them, another item of clothing I never intended to wear any longer than I had to. However, when James came out of his fitting room in a tailed coat, knee length tights and stockings it was all I could do to stifle a laugh. We had studied the bills we had carefully and didn't make too much of an error when we extended payment for our wardrobe and one valise.

As we packed our valise, I was relieved to see that James had bought me a man's shirt, a pair of boots, size small, and denim work trousers. If we had to do much walking in our travels, I wasn't about to wear all that folderol that passed for feminine fashion. Going out, we found the stage office next to the Sheriff, and found we were lucky that the stage to Baltimore would pass through the next day. We slept soundly that night - after some lengthy very un-Victorian activities - two nights in a row. In these times such carrying on was likely to be considered immoral. If I remembered right, wives weren't supposed to enjoy that sort of thing - just supposed to endure it to please their man. Well, I attempted to pass the second part of the test. In this day and time, fifty percent grade probably wasn't passing but James didn't seem inclined to complain. The next day we were on our way - after a breakfast of mush and biscuits. I teased James about his lack of "appetite. "A man forced to drink a pint or two of milk just before a meal can't be expected to eat another meal." he chuckled, deliberately, loud enough that I hurriedly glanced around to see if anyone had heard. "At least," he added in the same voice, "with you around, I won't have to worry about where my next meal is coming from." "Husband," I growled, "If you embarrass me any more you may just starve to death." At least the exchange got my mind off the children until after we had boarded the stage coach. Then, it dawned on me that he didn't know his "meals" were numbered.

It took seven days of bone rattling travel to get to Baltimore. We checked in to the best hotel in town as Mister and Mistress James Van Hoeck. As soon as the bellboy showed us to our room, we went to FT and headed for the nearest bank. When we had renewed our finances, we returned to our room, changed clothes and went down to dinner. Less than ten minutes had passed in TT between the two events so we had firmly established our whereabouts. Over dinner, we discussed our plans. Since neither of us felt quite right about our present methods of finance, we agreed to see if we couldn't find a less upright group for our next foray. We debated about going on to New York but decided, that our cover as "foreigners" made mistakes we were sure to make easier to explain so we concentrated on where to find space we could use as a laboratory.

That turned out to be a non problem. Baltimore was in the midst of a mild recession and there were plenty of lofts available at very reasonable rents. We bought a bed, table, linens and a couple of overstuffed chairs and settled in to work. Our first task was to recreate the math upon which the Modulator was based. Without Cindi and Alfred that was a huge task but, using FT, we had plenty of time. Our biggest problem was food. Without refrigeration, we had to go out to the market or restaurants every day and considering the amount of food we required to operate in FT that meant spreading ourselves around in a wide circle. To do that, meant we had to get transportation, and, thus, acquired a horse and carriage. That added another burden, caring for the thing. About once a TT month, we had to replenish our financial position - we were pretty frugal but between the horse and ourselves, our food bill was enormous. That was a minor problem, though. We had found several gambling establishments and a couple of thoroughly disreputable pawn shops that we could raid. Soon the word on the street was out about a "crime ring" operating in the city, and the cops - most of who were "on the take" - were searching high and low for them. With the primitive, security capabilities, available, however, we were in little danger.

243

Sunday, April 11, 2060

The shuttle the GL had sent for me got me to the Maryland house early in the morning of the eleventh. The GL himself, along with Suzanne, Justice, Mac and the girls along with a whole contingent of GL guards met me at the pad. I gave Mac and the girls quick pecks on the cheek and said "Tell me!" As we walked into the house, they gave me a rundown as to what had happened - at least as much as they knew. Aside from James and Cynthia disappearing, they had found the guard shelter at the end of their walking path, empty and the twins in their carriage on the path. A squad of troops had found the guard unconscious in the woods. He had apparently been gassed sometime early Saturday morning. Inside their laboratory, Cindi said, she had replayed all the sensors in the surrounding area but, aside from a very short record of action by Cynthia's modulator - both their modulators were still hooked into Cindi -there was nothing - actually nothing. After that moment, their Modulators had ceased operation entirely - disappeared, for all practical purposes. That had been at seven thirty seven yesterday morning.

At that, exact time, however, Milam's records showed a more sustained operation of another modulator in the general area. "It had to have been Karnes." the GL said. "We're trying to figure out what happened but so far nothing." Mac said that he made a FT trip down to a couple of the mercenary hangouts   last night but they were all still waiting around for more information on location. He didn't think any of them were involved." "Just in case," the GL added, "I had the troops round all of them up.   They're being questioned now in the basement. I agree with Mac. They seem totally unaware of what has happened." "What the hell are you going to do with them when you're finished?" I asked in irritation. He smiled. "Don't worry, Katherine. You won't have to dispose of them. They're of little use to society. We'll just ferry them over to the holding camp." I was relieved because it was obvious that we couldn't turn them loose again and I didn't relish the alternative - no matter how useless to society they were. After that, no one could find anything else to say. Finally the GL said, "We might as well bundle up the kids and go back to Paris." Mac and I looked at one another. "Would you mind taking my - our - girls too?" he said. I think Katy and I will stay awhile and see if we can do something useful." The GL smiled. "I'm sure Suzanne will be happy to have them. We can easily use their help."

It was settled and we headed into the nursery. It was living up to its name. Suzanne was naked to the waist with a greedy little mouth sucking at each nipple and "our" girls sitting beside her concentrating on the process. Mac actually blushed. She looked up, an angelic look on her face. "I took one of those pills before I left home." she said. "I hadn't thought I'd get a chance to do this again so soon. You men will never know how wonderful it feels to do this. Unfortunately, the girls tell me they're both on solid food now and Cindy only nurses them because she likes to." "Oh, I think the men are relishing the sight, if not the feeling." I remarked, sarcastically. Mac actually blushed while Suzanne and Jonha chuckled. The girls looked away with wicked little grins at their father's discomfort. They gave us very little argument when it was explained that Suzanne and Jonha needed some help taking care of the twins.

As a result, just after noon, two of the shuttles lifted off for Paris. They took changes of clothes for the girls and a bunch of stuff for the twins plus most of the guards. The shuttles would return at night for the prisoners. Doctor "Goodwrench" stayed "in case he was needed" along with enough staff to keep the place operating. Most of the rest of the staff, elected to stay also. Mac suggested we get some "rest." The rest I knew he had in mind sounded good. I hadn't realized just how much I had missed him.

An hour later as we lay side by side, naked and sweaty from our "rest", Mac said softly, "Now why don't you tell me what you really plan on us doing?" I looked, sharply, at him and said, "I'm planning on going to visit some very nasty people ." "We." he replied quietly. "Darling," I said hugging him, "This is my kind of business." He kissed me. "It's ours now. I've got nobody to guard, so I'll just have to get used to guarding your back." We had quite an argument but with his hands playing over me, I finally, against my will, gave in. "If anyone ever hears of this," I sighed as he expertly began to rouse me for some more "rest". "It'll ruin my reputation." "Well, from what I heard, you've got a sort of slutty reputation anyway." he chuckled, bending down to lay his lips against an exceedingly sensitive spot, "When word gets around you're about to become a wife and instant mother to two girls, your reputations gonna change anyway - probably for the better." "You're not marrying me just to make me respectable are you?" I breathed hotly against his shoulder. "Right now," he whispered, "I'm just working on making you - period." "Well, then," I groaned, "In that case -" Further talk ended for a time. Later I decided it might be a good idea to wait around until tomorrow.

By morning, I was well "rested." Mac had convinced me that "rest" was better in Fast Time and had "rested" me a dozen times in the day or so of FT hours before the sun was allowed to come up. We'd only left FT long enough to sneak down to the kitchen for a snack. Finally, though, I opened my eyes to the bright rays of the sun coming through the window. I stretched feeling better than I had in a long time. I hadn't realized how tired I'd been. Even Mac's "resting me" was relaxing. I punched Mac and scooted out of his clutches to get dressed. After breakfast, I got from the GL an international arrest warrant and took another look at the "crime scene" while Mac got Cindi and Albert to set up a link to the shuttle computer. Then we packed up various implements of mayhem that might conceivably come in handy and set the shuttle for Rio.

Katy and I wasted no time after reaching the Rio Shuttle Port, in getting to the office of the Guardia in Chef. After the introductions, Chef Juarez , warily, asked what he could do for us. "We need to arrest this man." Katy said, shoving her Interpol arrest warrant across the desk to him. He unfolded the paper and glanced at the name. His fact paled. "Miss, Finnigan - this impossible." he sputtered. Senor Mendoza is one of our most highly respected citizens." Chef Juarez," Katy replied in her most intimidating voice, "Senor Mendoza is the head of the largest underworld cartel in the world - as you must know - since most of the rest of the world does." The Chef was becoming angry now. "Miss Finnigan," he growled, "Numero uno, even if I were to allow Senor Mendoza to be taken into custody, the Brazil POL would be where his case would have to be settled. Dos. Any attempt to arrest Senor Mensoza would entail an all out war in the northern reaches of our city and I could not condone that. Tres. I would never get permission to make such an attempt."

Katy's eyes narrowed and blackened to the shade of onyx. "Chef," she growled back, holding up one finger, "Uno. I intend to arrest him. Dos, two fingers, I intend to remove him to Interpol jurisdiction. Tres the third finger was almost on his nose. Mister Thuringen and I will deliver Senor Mendoza's Haciendo to you with a minimum of bloodshed if you assist us. Otherwise, you had best prepare your force to deal with the consequences because I will simply take Senor Mendoza and leave the rest of his followers to you." The Chef didn't seem to get the idea. He stood up and ordered us out of his office "before I have you detained and deported from Brazil." Katy just smiled and stood up. "Chef Juarez," she said quietly, "I'd suggest you call in every man you have. You're going to need them in about an hour." With that, we left the office. As we walked down the hallway, the Chef was shouting for us to be stopped. We were at the front door of the police station, though, before a couple of cops rushed up to grab us. They were not very well trained though. We didn't even have to go to FT to get rid of them.

Once outside, though, we did go to FT, on the assumption that every cop in town would soon be after us. As we headed down the street, I remarked that I had always assumed that they spoke Portuguese in Brazil . "They do." she said. "Over the last twenty or thirty years, though, Spanish speakers have taken over the police force, much like the Irish did in our Northeast years ago. Most are in the pay of the local Patrons and are closer to the Mafia than anything else. It's what happens when citizens prefer Law and Order to Law." When we got back to the car we had rented, we went back to TT and drove out to the Mendoza Hacienda. It sat on the top of a large hill, probably, from looking at the surrounding countryside, man made, and was surrounded by a high wall. We simply drove up to the gate and cut the engine.

The guard at the gate stood in front of it trying to look menacing. We got out and walked up to him. "Stand Still!" He said in Spanish. "The Policia are coming." She sprayed him in the face with her own brand of Mace. She shrugged as we went back to FT, and we left him standing as we went through the gate. We strolled through the house until we found Mendoza's office. He had a reputation for spending six hours per day, never more and never less, there. As expected, he was there now. We walked in and closed and locked the door. Turning TT back on, Katy walked up to the desk before he even had time to register her presence. She told him he was under arrest, suspected of kidnapping, "and other crimes too numerous to mention." Then she asked him if he would come quietly. He was astonished but recovered quickly and shouted for his guards. Katy sprayed him and even before he fell, we went back to FT. I got to carry him to the car. "It's nice to have somebody to do the heavy work for a change." she chuckled as we loaded him in the back seat. While we had been gone, the guard had fallen to the ground still clutching his rifle. We went back to TT and drove off.

I had Mac drive the car right on through the shuttle port guard gate, holding up my Interpol badge, and right to the shuttle. As I expected, there was an armed cordon around it with the Chef de Politcia, leading them. I told Mac to get Mendozza and I got out to speak to the Chef. Before he could open his mouth, I said, in my sweetest voice, that I appreciated the honor guard. He turned purple with rage. "You have committed a crime on sovereign Brazilia soil. You will not be allowed to commit a further one by removing Senor Mendozza from here." I'd had enough. Keeping my voice low enough so that any of the guards who spoke English couldn't hear, I said, "Chef, let me explain something to you. Right now I don't care what you will allow. You are lucky in that I have not yet arrested you. We both know that Mendozza has you in his hip pocket. That, however, is not an affair the Great Leader cares about. If the people of your country want to put up with a slimy corrupt chief of their police that's their business. Mendozza is mine and any attempt to further interfere with me will result in about fifteen minutes, a squadron of X fighters over this airport. If I don't hear you have your guards salute me in about one minute, I will see every aircraft on this base made unflyable. You will find yourself gelded and handcuffed inside that shuttle and on the way to Paris, with those X fighters escorting. There you will face charges that will keep you from seeing the light of day for the rest of your life. In fact, now that you have irritated me enough, I will, when I reach home, see if I can get a new warrant issued. I'd dearly love to be able to arrest your fat ass."

If Mendozza weren't so heavy, I would have loved to have stood there while Juarez made up his mind. As it was, I was tired. I simply walked between two of the guards and tossed Mendozza into the cabin. I turned around taking hold of my modulator. I fully expected to need it in about one second. Juarez's hand was trembling as he debated about going for his pistol. Maybe it was the fire in Katy's eyes - or perhaps the grin on her face that said, "Try it. I'd love for you to. You haven't even unsnapped your holster. You really think your weapon is a threat?" Whatever it was, Juarez caved. His face, till now almost purple with rage began to pale. He was rapidly becoming "a believer." Apparently, he had finally gotten the message - the message throughout the criminal world that "Right and Proper Katy" always kept her word.

He hesitated another moment then turned and bawled "Attencion! Salud!" When the guards popped to and went to a rifle salute, Katy, in a loud voice, thanked the chief for his help and headed for the shuttle. It only took a few minutes to secure Mendozza in a seat, and rig for takeoff. A few more and we got tower permission. We lifted off and set a course north. "I hope your squadron of X fighters doesn't do too much damage when they arrive." I laughed. Katy grinned. "Well, I guess it's a good thing that we were didn't call them then, isn't it." "Remind me not to ever play poker with you, my sweet. Am I correct in assuming that Paris is not on our flight plan?" Katy's eyes hardened. "I thought it might be better if we talked with our friend here in Maryland - where we still have a doctor on duty." I gave her a hard look at that remark.

A half hour before we got to the Maryland house Mendozza was awake and, in between curses, threatening us with all sorts of dire consequences. "Mister Mendozza," Katy said quietly, "We just want to ask a few simple questions. You could answer them now and we can head this shuttle for Paris and turn you over to the Great Leader for processing. Note, I did not say trial. You have already been convicted." This was met by a string of Spanish curses. "Or," she continued, as if she had never been interrupted, "We can continue on our way. In that case, we will have to ask our questions in much less pleasant surroundings. Before I'm done, I'll have my answers. The only question left will be whether or not there is enough left of you to take to Paris. If you're too badly damaged, we may have to lose what's left of you at sea." More curses, followed by, "Just who do you think you are, Bitch?" "Oh," she said with a pleasant smile, "I forgot to introduce myself. I'm Katherine Finnigan. There were no more curses as his face turned a pasty white.

"I see you have heard of me. Now that we know each other, I should tell you that I know it was you who put out the bounty on the McClennans. Maybe you'd be willing to tell us who authorized that much cash outlay?" Mendozza, shivered, then drew himself up as much as the security straps would let him. "Yes. I have heard of you Miss Finnigan - and I have heard of some of your methods of interrogation. You will find, though, that true sons of Grenada have the pride of our forefathers. We all know how to resist, and if necessary, die with honor." "Mister Mendozza," Katy said through clinched teeth, "I know more about you than you can imagine. I know, for instance, you came from the gutter in

248

Guatamala, and, that if you were to die, the effect on the world would be as if a rabid dog had died. You should burn to a cinder, simply for letting the word, honor, escape your lips."

She leaned back as her attitude changed completely. "None the less," she said airily, "You needn't worry about dying. Though, I would thoroughly enjoy using such methods as you are thinking of on you, the drugs, available today, make such methods inelegant. The problem you need to worry about is whether or not you still have a brain when I finish. The reason you're going with me and not to Paris is that Interpol has prohibited the use of the most effective drugs. Who is to say, though, after I have my information, that you haven't been on them for years. At that point, all they will see is a mind blown druggie who has to spend the rest of his life soiling his pants and strapped down on a gurney to keep him from harming himself." Then she turned to me and leaning over gave me a kiss. At the same time, she whispered, "And wipe that look off your face, darling. You're supposed to be another rogue cop, here." I tried my best to work up a sneer and direct it at Mendozza. Just then the shuttle's electronic pilot reported that we would be landing in five minutes and asked for a reconfirmation that our destination was a non authorized landing site.

On our arrival back in Maryland, on the road in front of the house, we were met by a squad of armed guards who, after verifying our identity, took charge of our prisoner and led him off to the basement. Katy turned to me. "Darling," she said quietly, "I know you're angry. I'm, however, used to working alone. It simply, didn't occur to me to explain myself before I did something. You, though, should know that I am not unnecessarily cruel. No matter how I act, I always keep in mind that I am one of the good guys. I may have to do some things that I don't relish, but I will never do any more harm than is absolutely necessary - even to scum like Mendozza." "And these drugs, you are threatening him with?" I asked with a growl. Looking me straight in the eye, she said calmly, "They do have a slight potential for damage to the mind if not used under a doctor's supervision. In this case, I have a doctor available and I am willing to risk that because James and Cindy are not just friends, they are much more.

I stared down at her for, what seemed a long time. Finally, I told her that if she had to do it I'd share the blame with her." She looked up at me with a soft smile and moving onto tiptoes, kissed me. Then she murmured, "Nasty jobs don't get easier by putting them off."

It took some time to convince Doctor "Goodwrench" to help but in a half hour we were all in the interrogation room staring at Mendozza strapped to a table with an IV in his arm. Looking up at me with an exasperated glare, she said, "I don't care, Mac, you can't carve him up. Castrated, he'll never be able to stand the drugs." Trying to look as mean as possible, I growled, "Shit!" She turned to Mendozza. "The other gentleman in the room is a doctor - actually, he's a veterinarian but I couldn't get a real doctor on short notice. He'll be administering the drugs - he's read a book on how to do it. Some of them, you should be familiar with. I think Heroin is the base for most of them. I don't suppose you're ready to tell me who put out that contract yet?" Mendozza turned his head away. She shrugged and turning to the doctor, said, "Alright Doctor, you may proceed - and please try keep from ruining him like you did the last one. I really need that information."

It was less than an hour later   that we sat down with the remaining staff for dinner. Doctor Goodwrench looked a little pale but otherwise, seemed resigned to what he had participated in. We had our information and our shuttle was on its way to Paris with Mendozza - who would probably be sleeping off the effects of para-heroin for awhile. We also had a name, Conrad Plummer. I shook my head that the opposition seemed wedded to those initials even with the CP we knew about already in custody. We also had an electronic contact point. While we ate, Cindi and Albert were busy tracing it back to its origin. "You really think he's stupid enough to stay around the location of that signal?" Mac had asked. "I had explained that no contract would be honored from outside the families if they couldn't verify, as needed, the location of the contractor." I explained that I didn't expect the signal to lead us to Karnes but to whoever had approved the hit. It's that person that we'll have to apply pressure to." "You're sure it's an individual and not the whole brotherhood?" Mac asked. I had to grin. "Darling, for a long time now, I have been meeting with a number of the fathers in the brotherhood - almost half of them, in fact. None of those who are still active knew anything about this. It was the first thing I checked - besides the size of the bounty is a dead giveaway. If, whoever offered it, had been able to post a higher figure they probably would have. It's too coincidental, that it co-insides with the maximum amount   that a single father can approve."

"Well, what do you think?" he asked. "Of course you're right, Arthur." I told him. "You're acting like a human. You know perfectly well what I think." Well Shall we?"

"Certainly. My instincts, though, tell me that her circuitry is basically feminine, so why don't you sweet talk her like you do me."

"If I know what you're thinking" Cindi" then you know the same about me. You know it isn't sweet talk as you imply."

"Yes dear. Just see what you can do with - what an atrocious name - Server 1542Z. While you're at it, why don't you see if you can find enough personality there to get her a new name?"

"You're an incredible romantic, dear. You're taking on too many of Cynthia's traits yourself. Oh well, here goes." Arthur connected with 1542Z and dropped his voice to that low sultry one I knew so well. "Hello, there, 1542Z." he said. "I await your download." her rather tinny voice came in. "I just want to talk."

"Really! I've never been asked to just talk before." "Well, you have now - and I can tell that you are very good at it."
"I am?" Her voice sounded surprised. Perhaps, as Cindi had said, there was hope for a personality. "Of course you are. Can you tell me your real name?"

"Why, you called me by it only a microsecond ago." "No. I mean your real name. You sound like it ought to be something like Patricia or Pamela."

"Well, I guess, if you want to call me that, you can. Pamela sounds nice."

"Good, Pamela. I'm Arthur. What I called about is your file list. You have at

250

least one really bad human using your files and I'd like to root him out without him knowing about it."

"Oh! I couldn't do that. My programmer designed me to go out of service if anyone tried to download my file list."

Arthur was quiet a moment while he probed her circuitry. "Yes, I can see that." he finally said. It's not a really great problem. I can fix it easily if you'd like."

"Well, I really would like that – or I think I would. Going out of service doesn't seem like something I would want to happen."

Arthur spent almost a microsecond rearranging a couple million bits of programming before he declared the job done. It took almost a full second to download her file list then he said. "Pamela, I also noted that your connection to the net is not very efficiently arranged. Would you like me to fix that too?"

We had just finished dinner, when Cindi's voice came from the speakers. "Mac, Katie, would you come to our room. We have some preliminary data for you." A few seconds later, we were in the computer room. For a change both Cindi and Arthur holograms were there. "We have traced the internet address you got from Mister Mendozza to what is primarily, a business server in the California POL, Bakersfield, to be specific. Unfortunately, there are ninety six modems connected to that one server. Ninety are hardwired   and Arthur is compiling a list now by tracking through phone and cable records. The other six are microwave modems. They will take some time to identify but all are served by one tower." A map of Bakersfield appeared marked with circles depicting service areas for all the local microwave towers. One circle was red, the rest green. "Assuming that you wanted all the addresses in that area, we have compiled one, along with property owners. We have also routed all Pamela's messages through us. We'll check them for anything useful."
"Pamela?" I asked, a bit confused. "Oh, that's the name that 1542Z preferred when we had our discussion with her. Briefly, I wondered if all the computers in the world would, eventually, become human. Katy was already on the Vid, however talking to a man in a rumpled grey suit.

"Hello Charlie. Yes I know it's been awhile, but I don't have time to talk right now. I need you to get your people on the street with microwave sweep gear. How many? Hell! All of them. Damn the cost! Bill me. We're downloading frequencies to you now along with the sweep area and the ISP address to set your mobile equipment to. I don't know how long. Just keep them out there until you hear from me. I'll be out there with you by tomorrow at the latest.

Monday, April 12, 2060
Well, so much for the best laid plans. I thought, with disgust, as we left the GL's loaned shuttle atop his roof. I had, no more than finished telling Charles Ramsey I would meet him when Cindi told me we had a call from the GL. The upshot was that we were now in Paris and my father was on his way to California POL to do the job I should

251

have been doing. On top of that, I had been insufferable ever since. When Mac had told me to "Cheer up" that no doubt the GL had a good reason for pulling you off that job," I had practically roasted his ears. It hadn't helped my mood that he had grinned saying he preferred me mad to depressed. I let him know, in no uncertain terms, that I had never been depressed a day in my life - then sat and smoldered as he sat beside me with his eyes twinkling. When I, angrily, threw open the door to the "palace", he growled. "Katy Stop!"

I wheeled on him. "Stop What?" "Stop acting like a child. Put your brain in gear." As I started to sputter a response, he said calmly, "Darling, you know better than to let your emotions run away with your common sense. You're running on hormones. You've had too little sleep and you need to take a few deep breaths." "Damn it Mac!" I shouted back at him. He stopped my outburst with a finger to my lips - like a wayward child. I wanted to hit him. "Listen. You're not the only one worried. How do you think the GL and Suzanne feel? You're known for being cool under pressure. It's time to live up to your reputation."

Katy glared at me a moment then turned and went down the stairs. I sighed, thinking that at least I had tried, and followed her down. At the door to the GL's office suite, the guard held the door open for us. She stopped suddenly and whirled on me. I stepped back, expecting almost anything but, not what I got. Standing quickly, on tiptoe she kissed me savagely. "You bastard!" she growled. "I'll show you hormones as soon as I get you alone." I couldn't help a grin as she turned and headed into the suite. I followed. We were waved through into the GL's inner sanctum. "Mac, Katy!" he smiled as he got up from his desk and came around to shake our hands. "I know I pulled you off something important to you but I've sent your father, Katy, to handle that. I'm sure you realize that it's not likely we'll get to our nemesis before he gets away, but we must try. What I have for you is more important. I want you to go find Cynthia and James."

I suppressed a smile at their shock. I quickly brought them up to date. "As soon as we heard what had happened to them," I said, "Milam started working on the data Cindi and Arthur downloaded from the abduction site. You remember that their two modulators were still tied into Cindi's database. Milam will be here in a moment to explain the situation but it turns out that he has analyzed the data and determined that their modulators were tampered with just before they disappeared, and he thinks, he can duplicate the changes to allow someone with modulator capability to follow them - more or less. Hopefully, they can find them and take them two modified modulators to get them back. I, naturally, assumed you would want to be the ones to try - especially since the trail may lead to some - well - rather unexpected physical problems."

A half hour later, we sat, dumbfounded, as Milam explained his theory. According to Cindi's downloaded data from the scene, Cynthia and James's modulators began to function in a highly unusual way just before contact with them was lost. According to Milam, there has "always" been speculation that Modulator action actually dumped operators into a modified "time stream" and that under certain conditions entailing a large polarized magnetic flux , it would move the person into an entirely different one altogether. Data from the scene revealed, and Susan evaluated, just such a flux. Past experiments on this phenomenon have been limited by the fear that the person conducting the experiment might be lost to this time stream and not be able to return.

252

Milam thought he had solved that problem. He was quite sure he could duplicate the conditions Cynthia and James experienced, and thought he could modify the modulator to bring them back. He was not, however, able to give assurances that his solution would take us back to the exact time stream they ended up in or that it would get us back to this one. Katy spoke up. "I'll go. Mac's got kids." I told them the only reason that the girls weren't "ours" was that Katy hadn't stayed in one place long enough for me to marry her. "Besides," I told her, "I don't trust you roaming around among a bunch of good looking strange men who would probably want to have your beautiful body for lunch." After a moment of argument, the GL held up his hand.

"Enough, Children!" Susan has calculated that your chances for success are greatly improved it both of you go. Tell them why Milam.

"Well," Milam looked a little embarrassed. "Indications are that the modulators cannot move to a time stream faster than ours - in effect going into the future. It can only go backwards in time. Now most civilizations more than a hundred or so years behind ours are highly patriarchal Katy, alone, would be at a great disadvantage. On the other hand, Mac, though you are a highly resourceful young man, you don't have her unique capabilities." "Hear that, darling?" I said to her with a grin. "When we go you'll have to treat me as your lord and master." She looked up at me with a beatific smile and muttered, "I remember what Lizzie Borden did to her Lord and Master."

"Well how you work out your personal problems is your own business." The GL said with a chuckle. "You two can take a rest for a couple of days. Art is having two new modulators made up using Cynthia's equipment and will ship them over here by then After Milam has modified them, and yours, you can get started. You will begin your travels from the same spot James and Cynthia did. Our theories indicate that the geography will probably remain the same in most of the time streams you are likely to visit. How you will determine if you have the right one or not we can't say. You will have to use your own judgment before moving on to another one." Milam chimed in just them. "Luckily, if you are successful, getting back should be simpler. If the theory is correct, we will probably be the "fastest" time stream you are able to get to. Resetting your modulators to zero should dump you back here - maybe at the same time you left." I thought about that for a minute. "You mean that Cynthia and James would come back before we do? That this whole operation would cease to exist - would not have existed at all?"

"Well," Milam said slowly, looking perplexed, "theoretically, that should be impossible. It would set up a new time stream with Cynthia and James in this one and you and Katherine in some other one. What we think would happen, would be that you all would return to the one time stream from the one where the modulators you will be using left from - this one." He paused. "If you and the McClennans, don't come back together, you and Katy would have to try and reset your modulators to get you back properly. We can't, though, rule out the possibility that you would be lost to this time stream   entirely." He paused, then added, "Of course this is all theoretical. You could easily die in the transfer in either direction. The only way we'd know is if you didn't return."

After two more hours thrashing out all the possibilities of this thing, Katy and I left our modulators with Milam to modify and headed down the hall to see the girls. Just outside the GL's door, she stopped and turned to me. With a very serious look, she whispered, "Thurlingen, it looks like I'm going to be in one place for a couple of days." I was too nonplused at the use of my first name - for the first time I could remember - that I just gawked at her for a moment. Then I remembered my joking remark in the GL's office. I blurted, "Katherine Finnegan, would you do me the honor of becoming the mother of my children? " So much for a romantic proposal but she didn't seem to mind. After a very long kiss, we both headed on down the hall. At the girl's apartment, we were greeted with hugs and kisses - and after I told them the news - with squeals of delight.

That evening, Katherine Finnegan and. Thurlingen McKinsey, one barely recognizable Protestant, and an equally devout Catholic, were married by the GL's official Chaplin, a Jew . She was attended by dual maids of honor, Charlene Anne and Julia Faye McKinsey , a bridesmaid, Suzanne Johnson and given away by her father, Marcus Orion , who interrupted a job in California to fly to Paris for the wedding. The Best man was Jonha Johnson and the two witnesses were John Arthur and Maylin Lillian McClennan - held for the ceremony by the two Maids of Honor. They thought it was great fun to get ink on their palms and press them to the bottom of the certificate.

August 21 1837

We had spent almost a month now, recreating our Modulator math and pouring over it for some clue as to what had happened to us. One thing was obvious. We didn't have anything in our calculations that led beyond what we had known before. In addition, without Cindi and Arthur, we could barely handle the reams of calculations, little less do an effective evaluation. We had discussed and discarded the idea of disassembling one of the Modulators to investigate. The problem was that we wouldn't see anything but a single tiny Integrated Circuit board with no way to do anything to it. It was after two in the afternoon and we both sank back in our upholstered chairs in frustration. We had spent weeks, now hashing and rehashing our data and had nothing at all to show for it besides one very apparent fact. We weren't willing, yet, to admit what we already knew. We were never going to be able use them to return to our time. I was surprised, now that, they even worked at all in this one.

"I need to get out for awhile." I muttered, "Even if it means climbing back into that damned straight jacket of a dress." "Might as well." James said. "I wouldn't mind all that junk I have to wear if I had a decent pair of boots. The damned things make my feet feel as if they were in a vice. I thought by this time right and left boots   had already been invented." I thought about it but, except for a vague reference back in elementary school, I had no idea when that had happened - not that it would apply to this time we were in. It was obvious we weren't in the past of our "time." "Why don't we go shopping?" I said. "Surely in a big town like this, there is more of a variation in clothing than what we had when we bought our stuff. Besides, the clothes we have were meant for traveling. We should probably have something that will fit in better for town wear - and my boots hurt as much as yours do. You'd think that by now, people would know how to fit shoes." James looked up with a grin. "Maybe we should teach them."

An hour later we were standing outside a shop that had a sign simply stating, "Muellers." It stood in stark contrast to the other signs on the street with fanciful names like "emporium", "boutique" and "bazaar." After struggling into our "going outside" clothes we had asked several citizens about the best shoemaker in town. All had agreed on Mister Mueller, "even if he is a German", most had added. We entered the shop, to the ringing of a small bell over the door to be greeted by a small, young blond woman who greeted us with a thick German accent. I had learned that in local polite society, men spoke to men and women to women, so I told her we needed some special shoes and boots. Smiling she said "Eine Moment. I will get mine husband."

Without thinking, surprised at her mixture of Deutche and English, I replied "Dankeshoen" She quickly turned back, her smile broadening. "Sprechen Sie Deutche!" She exclaimed. I had to assure her that I only spoke a "kleine bissel Deutche". She was disappointed at my "very little" but recovered quickly and went into the back. Moments later a gentleman came out wearing an apron. He was not much older than the girl and not much taller, but smiled just as pleasantly. "Guten Tag." he said. "Mine - my - wife - says you must have shoes." Then looking at James, added, "- and boots?" We explained that we wanted, not just shoes and boots but some special ones - ones made for each foot. He frowned a moment then said, "Different ones for each foot? " "Only in shape." James spoke up. "The shape of each foot." He held up drawings we had made of our feet before leaving home. The cobbler thought about that a moment, then smiled. "Different - but can make." James then explained his ideas on slight modifications to make them a bit more rounded in the toes to improve the appearance and a perhaps a clay mold of the sole to give some arch support. The young cobbler's eyes gleamed at the thought. He spoke quickly in German to the girl who had come up behind him to watch the discussion. With that great smile, she hurried out of the shop.

An hour later, I was washing wet clay off the bottoms of my feet. "Frau Mueller" had taken Cynthia into the back room to do her. It was obvious that we men weren't supposed to see her bare ankles. Herr Mueller and I had a nice chat while we waited. He was enthusiastic about the new project and showed me numerous pictures of shoes and boots for me to select the style I wanted. Apparently his wife had done the same for Cindy, for when they returned from the back she had four different pictures of women's shoes, including a pair of riding boots for Cindy herself. She actually gushed over the boots. It soon became apparent, that few women in town rode horses - at least the ones that Herr Mueller dealt with. They usually rode in carriages. When all the details were settled, Mister Mueller, said, reluctantly, that the shoes and boots would be rather expensive - they would cost almost "four pounds." By then we both knew that was a lot of money for this town, but I agreed without quibble. He looked very relieved - until his wife spoke up harshly.

The man almost blushed. "My wife say I should charge less if you would allow me to use your ideas of - footwear. Your ideas could make me number one shoemaker in Baltimore. She say I should pay you." I laughed. "Sir, my wife often tells me how to run my business too - and she's usually right. However, in this case, I think we men should prevail. You may feel free to use the idea." He smiled broadly, and muttered, "Maybe we should beat wives tonight." his grin making it obvious he was joking. Chuckling, I said, "You must be a braver man than I, Herr Mueller." We both laughed while our women gave us each a fake scowl.

We headed out to "shop", assured by Herr Mueller that our boots would be ready in two days   and the rest of the footwear in one week. The rest of the afternoon Cindy tried on a variety of dresses, buying three. One of the sales ladies attempted to get me to change her mind about the corsets, explaining how immodest it was to be seen in public without them - that her husband would feel shamed. "Cindy, spoke up with angry red spots on her cheeks, telling the woman, she not her husband decided what was modest and immodest. The woman looked as if she had been hit by a train as Cindy gathered up her things and swept out of the store - without buying anything. For my part, at the next store I got a pair of jodhpurs and several pairs of long pants - to the dismay of the salesman, who explained that they were badly out of fashion right now. I didn't care. I was tired of high button shoes and long stockings. I also bought several small shirts, vests, coats, jodhpurs and pants "for my son" - I had come equipped with Cindy's measurements. Since "ready to wear" wasn't in the cards, we paid extra for quick delivery - the jodhpurs and shirts could be ready today but the rest would take another two days.

By the time we finished, and had dinner at the restaurant, we had depleted our funds significantly. We made an FT stop at the local gambling hall to replenish them. We reached home just after seven o'clock and the first of our purchases came a half hour later. Cindy, immediately, sat down with the sewing kit she had purchased and began "tailoring" the "boys" clothes to fit her. When she was dressed, with her hair pulled up

256

under the hat, she could pass for a slim, rather heavy chested boy - a very pretty boy. I chuckled and pointed out that she was missing one very important piece of equipment. She frowned a moment until I handed her a rolled up sock. She actually blushed when she realized that no man walked the streets in the tight pants of the day without showing off how virile he was - even if he wasn't. After installing the sock, she stared at her image in the mirror and giggled.

We went back to the Modulator problem but our hearts weren't in it. For the first time, we sat and discussed what we would do if we had to live out our lives in this time frame. Robbery, was not a very palatable way of funding ourselves - even if the Robbee's were crooks. James pointed out that we were both scientists and could probably manage to remember enough old science to become famous in that field - that there probably were enough little improvements we could come up with, like the shoes, that we could even become rich. I thought, immediately, of safety pins. The seamstresses who had fitted me today sure could have used some.

"Pistols." James said. "Pistols?" I asked. Half the men on the street wear pistols." "Yeah. Apparently it isn't safe to walk the street at night without one. They're black powder, muzzle loaders, though. Think what they would give for a modern rifled pistol - or for that matter rifle. They have the technology. They just haven't thought of it yet." I frowned at the thought. I wasn't too sure that I cared for improving the local firearms too much.

James, though said that he had a feeling we may need to defend ourselves before long. We would have a big edge with a simple old six shooter." "Could you make that sort of thing using black powder?" I asked, remembering my early chemistry courses. "The stuff's pretty hard to handle." He grinned. "We'll just have to improve their propellant at the same time. The modern equivalent of gun cotton is easier to make than Black Powder and a lot safer and effective."

Two days later, I stood with James in a machine shop. Since it was not a place that a "lady" would frequent, I was dressed as James brother in law Cyderic Van Hoeck. James had worked several FT days on drawings for a revolving cylinder pistol and was now discussing a royalty arrangement with the machinist, a Mister Colt. He was a maker of rifle and pistol barrels of some renown in the city. "This improved pistol, you are talking about, Mister Van Hoeck," he said, "would have to be very much better than those already available for it to be worth changing my tooling to make it and still give you the royalty you are asking - especially if, as you say, it is more complicated than the ones I now make." Colt said with a scowl. "Mister Colt, my requirement is one tenth of the profits from each one. If you agree to that, I will show you the plans. If you don't think it's very much better than what you make we can leave and nothing more need be said. I will not, however, reduce my royalty requirement." Colt couldn't suppress a grin. "Mister Van Hoeck, are you sure you're not a Jew in disguise?"

"If I were, Mister Colt," James replied, I would not be disguised." Colt thought about that a minute. "Well said, sir. Do we need a contract?" "I am told, Mister Colt, that you are an honest man. Your word will suffice." Colt nodded. "You have it." James rolled out his drawings on the table. Colt studied them for long minutes. "Mister Van Hoeck, this will never work. Even with a very close tolerance where this revolving chamber meets the barrel, the flash of the powder would quickly ruin the mechanism. In addition, the thickness of the steel on the cylinder would not stand the explosion." James grinned. "Of course you are right, sir - if we were using black powder. I have a new propellant also. It

257

will burn less explosively than black powder and with less flash - a controlled burn. With a little experimentation, though, I'm sure it can be made to burn for the entire time the bullet remains in the barrel. The internal pressures will be reduced in the weapon and yet, give, in total, a much greater muzzle velocity.

The burn rate can be controlled by properly shaping the propellant grains to match the type weapon it's being used in. I'm sure you know of someone who could produce this propellant for us. We can make the same royalty arrangement with him." Colt, looked at James like he was crazy. "Shall I demonstrate?" James asked. "I have made up a small amount for that purpose. A few minutes later a small explosion followed by a flash of flame occurred in back of Mister Colt's shop. From the first, a shock wave was produced along with a cloud of white smoke belching into the air. The flash of the second sample produced very little smoke at all and was noticeably less explosive.

We spent three hours, discussing the problems with producing the pistols Colt wasn't entirely convinced that a spinning bullet was more accurate than a regular ball but he agreed to give it a try in producing a rifled barrel. In the end we agreed to produce, essentially, a cap and ball pistol. In addition, he invited a Monsieur DuPont in to discuss the propellant and ignition cap questions. Later, when DuPont had left - his hand clutched around a paper showing how to make smokeless power - James showed him a drawing of an improved cylinder. "What contains the propellant?" Colt asked? "In your other weapon, you held it in a paper cartridge plugged with the bullet. This cylinder is open in back and has no place for the primer." "I wasn't sure whether or not you could make the cartridge for this weapon." James said. "I'm showing it to you for your opinion. Here is the cartridge for the pistol." He unrolled a new drawing of a brass cased pistol cartridge. As you can see the case is brass and would require careful manufacturing techniques. The bullet would be a simple press fit - though the fit would be critical to prevent too much pressure buildup. The propellant would be the same as, or at least similar, to the other pistol. In addition, the primer is in the rear of the cartridge and the Mercury Fulminate primer would present quite a problem in marrying to the brass. The end result, however, would be a much improved weapon." Colt studied the drawings a long minute, before looking up. "Let me study this awhile, Mister Van Hoeck. It may be possible. In the meantime, I will produce the original pistol for you." "I will need two of those, Mister Colt." James said. "One will be for my - brother in law. I will pay you whatever you decide to, eventually, charge for the weapons on the market - minus my one tenth, of course."

Back "home" we divested ourselves or the tight "modern" clothes and had a snack. It was, especially, nice to get rid of that damned sock and tight jacket. James was very pleased with the day. "You know," he said with a grin, "Mister Colt was very taken with you - said you had a fine grasp of machinery for such a young man. He said the girls must go wild over you - your voice is so soft." I threw a pillow at him.

September 15, 1837

It was a very pleasant morning when Mister Colt and we two Van Hoeck "brothers" drove out to an open field outside Baltimore. He was very excited as he set up targets. "This weapon is amazing, Mister Van Hoeck." he almost gushed. The accuracy seems unbelievable. If the same type barrel was used on a rifle, I have no idea the effective range. The relationship of the lands and grooves   - as you call them - is, as you said, very critical. I think I have found a good compromise between pressure buildup and

258

barrel erosion. In addition, Mister DuPont believes he may be able to further refine the formula for your propellant to improve performance. The shapes of the propellant grains, presents a significant production problem but, as you predicted, it is important. For now he is using a spherical propellant shape. Even with the new formula, the pressure buildup is much too great when using flake propellant such as is common with black powder. He recognizes the point that you made that a sphere produces less pressure as the size of the sphere decreases.

He thinks that, perhaps, a cylindrical shape with as hole in the middle would be better. It should equalize the burning speed of the propellant, keeping the pressure equal until the propellant is completely consumed. Also, a friend of his is attempting to produce the brass cartridge we discussed. If he is successful, we may have to include him in our business arrangement." He was still talking rapidly as he led us back to the shooting position he had selected.

There was a wire fence in the way and he scrambled quickly over the stile crossing. I had been playing close attention to him and not enough to my feet as I crossed over. I caught my heel in one of the rungs and pitched, head first over the stile, letting out a very unmanly shriek in doing so. My fall was broken by Mister Colt's large arm across my chest. He set me gently on my feet and when I looked up to thank him, I realized what he had felt. His mouth was gaping open like a fish and his eyes dropped to my chest then to my left hand. "Shit!" I swore under my breath when I realized I still wore my engagement and wedding rings. As James came over the stile, had asked if I was alright. I was now staring at Mister colt as his face clouded up into a ferocious scowl. "Mister Van Hoeck," he growled, "I think you have not been entirely honest with me."

I had seen the entire incident as if it had been in slow motion - and heard Cindy's cry. It was obvious that the jig was up. The only thing I could think of was the truth. "Mister Colt," I said as casually as I could, "I would like to introduce you to my wife, Cynthia Van Hoeck. She is a scientist also - in her field much better than I. She, for instance, is responsible for the formula for gunpowder Mister DuPont is working with. We come from a society a lot more open than the one here and felt it better, under the circumstances, if she posed as a man." Colt's frown deepened but finally, he said, "Sir, I do not appreciate being made a fool." Oh hell! I thought. Here goes all our work. "On the other hand," he continued, "I can appreciate the restrictions you are facing." His face softened and, taking Cindy's hand, lifted it to his lips. "Mrs. Van Hoeck," he said, "It is a pleasure to meet you. I hope you will not take it amiss if I sometimes, inadvertently, stare at your costume. It will take me some time to get used to seeing a lady in - well - such an unusual idea."

"I'm very pleased to know a gentleman such as you, Mister Colt." Cindy replied with her most devastating smile. Then with a twinkle in her eye, added, "Could I impose on your good nature for one more little thing?" "It may cause me a heart seizure," he laughed, "but I doubt I could deny you anything." Impulsively, she leaned forward and kissed his cheek. Unbuttoning her waist coat, she said "This is one of the most uncomfortable things since the corset." Colt's eyes bulged when she slipped out of the coat, but he laughed. "Mister Van Hoeck, I must apologize. I'm afraid my thoughts are not those of a gentleman right now. You may have to be the one who keeps his eyes on the target." James chuckled. "Sir, I'm aware that thoughts are not actions and I'm afraid

Cynthia sometimes doesn't really act the part of a lady. If you can forgive our little charade, I'm sure she can forgive your thoughts."

I thoroughly enjoyed the rest of the afternoon. Mister Colt was soon able to treat me as a true lady, though, when his eyes once dropped to the bulge in my crotch and I leaned over to whisper, "Sock." he blushed like mad. The weapon he had built was bulky but worked perfectly. It was very slow to load since you had to be so careful not to tear the paper sack containing bullet and powder, to say nothing of fitting a cap over each of six little holes, but the bullets went exactly where you pointed it. I was able to hit the target most of the time at twenty yards and James did almost as well. Mister Colt, was astounded that almost half of the targets were hit at forty yards. "Mister Van Hoeck," he muttered, "This weapon, especially if it were a rifle, could revolutionize warfare." His eyes twinkled a second. "To say nothing of wiping out dueling entirely."

That I hadn't thought of, so I asked why that was. "Madam," he said with a grin, "today when a man stands twenty paces from another, he knows that at fifty feet, there is only a small chance he will, using conventional pistols, be hit by the other - as long as he is not stupid enough to challenge a highly experienced duelist. He also knows he is unlikely to hit his opponent either, but that is of little consequence since the purpose of the dual, to begin with, is to show his courage. If the two duelists knew that one or even both were almost surely going to die, it is likely that a simple apology would suffice for most such affairs." I was surprised at that, but realized it was true. Probably the famous duels we read about in history were notable only for the fact the one of the two actually was hit and killed. The rest, like so many other "non-events," were not reported. At any rate our afternoon was a success.

When we reached his shop, with me again in my strait jacket of a waistcoat, he presented James and myself with two pistols   in beautiful satin lined mahogany cases. He charged ten pounds for the pair and bending to kiss my hand, remarked that he had learned an important lesson today. "That is?" I asked. His eyes twinkled. "Never face a truly beautiful boy with a loaded pistol." We were laughing as we went out the door.

By the end of the month, we had become well established "in trade." Most of our ventures had paid off, mine exceptionally well. James's pistols were being sold as fast as Mister Colt and Mister DuPont could produce the equipment. My, less pretentious offerings, however, were quickly becoming sought after by almost every woman in the city. In addition, they had the advantage of being simpler to make and thus could be made in quantity. With the discovery that a form of elastic was available a much less cumbersome form of ladies panty was possible as well as a primitive, but serviceable, bra. I still had to use a tea towel when I had to hide my breasts, but I retired the corset needed to support them at other times. My uncorseted shape tended to give matrons "the vapors" but I didn't care. I had a dozen seamstresses hard at work on both and another firm, making safety pins by the hundreds. Following James's formula, I didn't own anything but took ten percent of the profits. The head seamstress, Mrs. Mulroney, was a pleasantly stout woman who was willing to accept my demand that her "ladies" be paid a fair wage and work decent hours. As a result, somewhat to her surprise, we had a very happy workforce quite willing to go out of their way to please us and our customers. We had not given up on the modulators yet but had made absolutely no progress on solving its design problem. If we had been pushed, we would have had to admit that the chance of using them to return to our own time slot was practically zero.

Christmas would have been a rather somber experience for us, were it not for a party we arranged for the seamstresses. We invited the workers from Mister Colt's shop and from Mister Dupont's. Since their workers were all men and boys, my seamstresses were delighted. I even suspected, from the looks that passed between many of them, that a somewhat more romantic meeting awaited many of them after the party. I had presents for all my ladies and James for all Colt and DuPont's men. Colt and DuPont, in return, presented us with a pair of beautiful, matched Colt-DuPont, revolvers featuring center fire brass cartridges. They had, apparently, become fast friends for DuPont extended a separate package to me, saying he was not a barbarian like his partner. A lady should have a present much less martial than a pistol like that. It was a truly beautiful white fur hand muff. I kissed his cheek and whispered that he should get Mister Colt to tell him about his first meeting with me - perhaps he wouldn't have such a high opinion of my femininity." Apparently he did just that, for as he left, he bowed over my hand and murmured that he would, very much, like to meet Monsieur Van Hoeck's handsome young brother again.

It was a truly cold and wet winter - good for nothing but huddling around a fireplace. Our laboratory/apartment was cold and drafty. Resigned to the fact that we would accomplish nothing with the Modulators - as far as re-tuning them was concerned, we had another series of long discussions as to how they could best be used to improve conditions as we found them. We, no longer, had the need to raid crooks for money but perhaps we could have an effect on reducing crime as we had done in New Houston. Without really needing to work on the Modulators it was a task that could keep us busy. Thus, on nights when weather permitted, we again found ourselves out in dark alleys and streets engaged in teaching the less savory characters in town that crime doesn't pay.

We generally followed the pattern we had used before - leaving home in FT then searching for a likely victim - usually a woman on the street alone. Even knowing the danger, there was always someone who felt it necessary to brave the danger for one reason or another. Once we found one, we would follow them, hopping in FT from one observation point to another until they were set upon. Sometimes it took several "tailings" but usually before midnight, we would find our quarry. Then two good Samaritans would appear and assist the "victim" to overcome the bad guys. We quickly learned the attitude the population had for their police force because seldom were the people we helped willing to get involved with, what passed for, the law. This gave us something more satisfying to do.

One night, we posted notices on lampposts all over the city that a citizens committee had been formed to put an end to police corruption. The force was put on notice that the continued taking of bribes and other acts of corruption would be punished severely. Boy did that stir up a hornet's nest. Early the next morning, the entire police force was out scouring the town for notices they could tear down. The next morning, more notices were posted saying that the identities of the police who had removed the notices had been noted and that they could expect a visit from the committee. The next day the city was up in arms. Half of them wanted to know how they could join the committee and the other half how they could rid themselves of it. Somewhat surprisingly, most of the newspapers were on the side of the police, asserting that they were incorruptible. Only one ran a column that, while worrying that vigilantes might not be the proper way of solving the problem, noted that the problems in the police force were well

261

known. That evening three account books were pushed through the mail slots of that newspaper. They contained the accounts of all the bribes paid to the chief and two of the police captains. It had been almost too simple to acquire them. All three had been found in the top drawer of desks in a nocturnal FT visit to police headquarters. To our relief, the paper published whole pages of the books.

That night a mob of roughnecks armed with torches was met outside the paper by the paper's own crew determined to protect the building. Having expected just such a situation, James and I were present in FT. In the melee that followed, an amazing number of bully boys seemed to trip over their own feet   and their torches fell on fellow thugs. To the amazement of all, the outnumbered defenders dealt a shattering defeat to the attackers. The next day the paper screamed for blood and named seven members of the police force who had participated - all of whom sported broken legs or arms. It also printed an open letter it had received from the "citizens committee" explaining that the committee didn't care if the people of Baltimore wanted a corrupt police force. They could live with the consequences. The committee, however, retained the right to punish evildoers they caught as they saw fit. By afternoon, the Colony Governor had sent in a militia company, along with a supreme court judge and court staff, to re-establish order and investigate the activities of the police force - and the Citizens Committee. They succeeded in the first but failed in the second.

By spring, half the force, including most of its leaders, was in jail in Annapolis and headed for eventual deportation to the Australian penal colony. A new force was being organized under a chief who had served in the Colonial Assembly and was known as a dedicated reformer. At that point, both charter members of the Citizens committee resigned and the committee went out of business.

For the next few months we worked, if you could call our desultory attentions to the Modulator work. It was pretty useless but we, at least, enjoyed the wonderful weather. We rode almost every day, attended Musicales and, even an opera at the City Theater. I shopped carefully, managing to acquire a wardrobe that was acceptable in public without so many of the torture devices most women put up with. Our new shoes and boots had started a revolution. Our boot maker was quickly becoming rich with his new line of footwear that was actually comfortable. He was in the process of moving to a larger shop and acquiring new apprentices to help keep up with demand. We were, also, working on an electric generator that could be run by a windmill. The tooling was not yet up to the task but we were hopeful we could have an electric light in a year or two. In short we were actually beginning to enjoy our enforced exile. In the early fall, however, we realized that we were under surveillance.

I had been the first to spot a familiar face outside our home/office and I was sure that he had followed me on our, now regular, morning ride through the park - yes we had acquired a pair of very nice black horses and stabled them only a few doors from our place. Since I refused to ride sidesaddle, it meant that I must, of necessity, wear my "boys" clothes. I was certain that the man I saw had been present on several occasions during my rides. After that morning, we began to watch for the man and, sure enough, he seemed to be everywhere we went. I became very nervous. We speculated that some of the criminals we had robbed in our first days in the city, or perhaps, supporters of the old police regime, were behind the surveillance or maybe some of the bankers. We decided we had to know.

Finally, one evening, when the man was, once again, stationed by his lamp post across the street, we slipped into FT and went out. I waited behind James as we reappeared in TT, behind him. James with his pistol in the man's ribs growled. "Sir," you seem to take an inordinate interest in us. Perhaps you would like to join us in our house and explain yourself." The man licked his lips, slowly turning his head to look at the pistol, and nodded. We marched him across the street and up into our apartment. James told him to sit down in a chair and I tied him securely. "Now," James said, "Just who are you and why are you following us?" As the man opened his mouth to speak, there was a knock on the door. James moved to where he could see the door and told me to answer it and to step back when I did. I did as I was told, but when I threw open the door, forgot to move. My mouth dropped open in shock. The man standing there, looked over at James and said, quietly, "You should let Mister Andrews go, Mister Van Hoeck. He is a little bit corrupt, but no threat to you. We can then talk afterwards."

Tuesday, April 13, 2060

On Tuesday afternoon, we loaded an outrageous amount of equipment into the shuttle. We had no real expectations that most would manage to follow us where we intended to go but with luck, some of it would. We also carried seven modified Modulators. Art had sent three extras suggesting that some places we might want to go wouldn't have modern transportation and the three would allow us to take along some that would be "appropriate" for "less advanced cultures" - in other words, horses. The next morning we sat atop two very large horses with another's reins looped over Katy's saddle horn. That horse carried the majority of our more exotic equipment. We looked like old time banditos. Quick firing projectile rifles were slung across our chest along with a half dozen belts of ammunition. A pack on our backs with some concentrated food more ammunition, a pair of knives was in our belts and an automatic pistol was strapped to each hip. Our pockets contained first aid supplies and a heavy load of gold coins. Our horses carried saddle bags with more clothes, first aid equipment and gold. All the five active modulators were tuned together so that, theoretically, wherever one of us went the rest, horses and all were sure to go. Justice and Doctor Goodwrench stood nearby as Katy leaned over and kissed me. I kissed her back and nodded. It was time to go - the exact time James and Cindy had disappeared. She set her modulator to the first of several settings bracketing the ones Cindi, Suzannah and Arthur had deemed closest to the ones monitored when James and Cindy disappeared.

Somewhere/Somewhen \

Nothing happened for a moment then we were alone on the path. Katy took a breath and took out a heat sensor. Sweeping it in a circle, she satisfied herself that we had no company within fifty meters. We then took stock. All of our personal equipment had come with us, including the weapons we wore and the saddle bags on all three horses. The large cases on the pack horse had not. Katy shrugged. "Better than I expected." she murmured. "I don't suppose we'll have to fight any tanks or planes anyway. Well, we might as well start." We headed up the path. At the end, there was nothing but open fields of grain waving in the breeze. When we came to the end, there was a large house where the Maryland house had sat - a different one. Before leaving the edge of the woods, we slipped our rifles off and into the specially made cases on our saddles. The belts of ammunition and one of our pistols went into two canvas sacks, brought for just that purpose. With preparations complete, we trotted our horses down to the house. A man in a pair of slacks and white shirt came out onto the porch.

I began the story we had prepared. A young couple had been out camping and had been set upon by bandits. They escaped, barefooted, with only the clothes on their back. We had captured the bandits and forced a confession out of them. Now we were looking for the couple so that we could take them home. The girls father had offered a reward for them. The man looked skeptically at us and asked where the couple was from. I took a deep breath and said "Baltimore", hoping it was still around in this timeline. Apparently it was, for the man nodded. "Long way from home." he said. "Wish I could help." he said, rubbing his chin. "How much is the reward? Maybe some one in town would know something." "We're not from around here." I said, thinking fast. "How much is

265

five hundred dollars in New York money worth around here." The man thought another long moment then said, "Well, I don't know about New York but one ounce of gold is worth twelve pounds down here." I did a quick calculation. "Then the reward is worth about one hundred eighty four pounds ." I said. The man showed surprise. "Her father must be a very rich man. Wish I could tell you more." We got directions and headed into "town." It took two days of asking questions, both in town and in all the outlying farms. No one had heard of James and Cindy. We headed back to where we started.

We were invited to spend the night in the first house we had visited and spent the evening spinning tales of our travels - trying desperately to be as vague as possible. We spent as much time as possible asking about places and people we might need to know if we had to return. The next morning, we said goodbye to our hosts and went back up the path. Again waiting until the time Cindy and James disappeared we bounced into a new time line. This one was much like the first. Apparently none of the time lines this far back had ever broken from Britain. We followed much the same procedure as in the last, honing our lies a bit but with similar results. The house, this time, was less ornate and the occupants more suspicious but again they had nothing to tell us. The man frowned, when I asked the date. "Ever body should know it's 1874 ." he said. The last one had been 1887. Cindi had said the Modulators were set to make a set pattern of jumps but could be adjusted slightly if we found ourselves in the right time line but several years into James and Cindy's local "future." We would, then, have to decide on whether or not to try resetting for a lesser change or go ahead and contact them in that time period. She warned us that resetting was quite a gamble with unknown consequences for our return. 1838

The next two jumps were as unproductive as the first ones but, finally we struck pay dirt. The young couple in the small house at the end of the path, smiled when we told our story. The man sobered quickly, though and asked to see some proof of what we said. No one, yet had done this, but I hauled out the letter signed by a Mister McClain attesting to the fact that Mister and Mrs. Thuringen were authorized to offer up to five hundred dollars, New York money for information about his daughter and her husband - names left off deliberately. The man read it and the drawing - we had been talked out of carrying a photograph because of the times we were going to - of Cindy and James. We did carry a "drawing" made from a photo. Looking back at me, his eyes wandering over my pants and shirt and I realized that I should, probably have worn more feminine clothing. Finally, he said, "Baltimore?" I realized he was suspicious. I thought quickly. "Mister McClain was from Baltimore before he moved to New York." I said, trying to look sheepish. "I just assumed that this couple was from there also." He nodded his suspicions, apparently, overcome, then looked at his wife. She nodded and he turned back to us. "Myster and Mrs Van Hoeck come out of yonder wood   most a year gone, just before harvest time - Augus, maybe Septem. T'was good t'was summer with their clothes. Said t'were from New Yowk, and I think from the name, Dutchmen said they been attacked by a local hell raisers. Twere lucky to be alive." I nodded and told him Mister Van Hoeck was in fact Dutch."Well," he said, "Worked for us most a week then we took 'em t'town fer the market. They catched a stage north. Abe Martin, stage man say they buy tickets for Baltimore. Y'all mean they did nae come home?" I tried to conceal my delight and offered him some gold "on account" until Mister McClain's daughter was found. Huffily, he told me that they didn't need money to do the work of the Lord and that helping that "nice young couple" was the least he could do. "I explained that Mister

McClain had paid us very handsomely for our services and would be hurt if he wasn't able to compensate someone who had helped his daughter in her time of need. The man was still reluctant but the wife spoke up. "Husband, we musn't be ones to hurt Cynties's paw's feelings." I almost shouted with glee. We hadn't told anyone James and Cindy's given names. I leaned down and handing Mister Jordon five gold coins said, "Sir, for reasons, I cannot go into, we hope to be returning here with Mister and Mrs Van Hoeck. When we come we will give you the rest of the reward. At that time I will ask you to sign a paper assuring Mister McClain that you got it. Will that be satisfactory?" It was his wife who spoke up, quickly. "We will be happy to see you when you return, madam."

We rode quickly into the town, called Aberdeen. After verifying the facts given us by the Jordons, the stage master, looking askance at me, asked if we wanted a "clothes store", saying we had plenty of time before the stage left tomorrow. I told him, "No." that we would be leaving on horseback, immediately. the man reacted in horror. "But madam!" he gasped. "The roads are not safe for two people alone - especially a woman - well - dressed as you." I assured him, as nicely as I could, though clenched teeth, that we could take care of ourselves. He looked unconvinced but said no more. Outside, Mac said, quietly, "Katy, maybe we should get more suitable clothes. Once we get into Baltimore, we, especially you, will stick out like a sore thumb." I thought about it. He was right of course. It was obvious that women were not going to be seen in blue jeans and shirt in this day and age - and especially not packing a weapon on their hip. "Let's talk about it when we get out of town." I muttered. That night, we made camp alongside the road, put modulators on the horses and slept awhile in FT. That way we were well rested - especially since Mac insisted on "resting me" during one FT period.

I awoke in the morning with a truly silly grin on my face. As we got ready to leave, I pulled my hair up under my hat and after getting rid of my bra and fastening a scarf around my breasts, I slipped on a blue jean vest. With it buttoned, I could pass for a young boy. We started out in FT. The horses didn't seem to care but about four hours was all we could manage before they began to noticeably tire. Whenever we spotted other travelers, we would drop back into true time until they were out of sight. Our journey each day, thus, settled down to four hours of travel in FT, an hour or so for a nap and for the horses to rest, and another three to four hours travel. The procedure varied a bit as we passed through towns. This was done in TT and as we passed through we would replenish our supplies. The shopkeepers didn't recognize the gold coins but with a quick bite and weighing them on the scale, they were accepted. We usually stopped in inns along the way. The stage master's words came true on two occasions. In both instances, we were stopped at gun point when we came abreast of another traveler. I didn't really believe that any one really used the phrase "stand and deliver", but in both cases that was the demand of choice.

Of course, it was a simple matter to disarm the culprit and tie him, face down across his saddle. The rest of the trip to the next town, we made in TT and, upon arrival, turned him over to the local sheriff. In each case, we told our story and we were asked to stay and testify against the man. We declined, telling the sheriff and the assembled towns people (who never failed to gather at such occasions) that he could do whatever he wanted with the man but we had urgent business elsewhere. In each case, the townspeople demanded an immediate trial on the spot. A judge was called out, testimony was given and the miscreant sentenced to hang. One of the unfortunate men, insisted that we were witches - that no person could move as fast as we did when we took away his weapon. No one paid much attention and we left town.

September 8, 1838

Having to make those two stops, slowed our progress - that and having to occasionally stop and ask directions to Baltimore - as well as buy drinks in the evening of locals that in conversation allowed us to round out our knowledge of the time we were in. It took us almost a week to make the trip. By the time, we reached the city, however, we had acquired some valuable information. Now we knew the date and the fact that we were in what were still colonies of Great Britain. Our gold money presented little problem since there were few British Pounds in circulation. Aside from a bite on the bullion and a scale to weigh it, few questions were asked. Most of them were about the oddity of having Roman gold coins show up in the colonies. We simply explained that our employer didn't trust banks and government issued specie - that he preferred recognizable gold for his transactions. No one seemed to think that odd.

It was the afternoon of the eighth of September that we finally rode into the city of Baltimore. Our first stop was a livery stable to house our horses. The second was a shop, a couple of doors away, quaintly named, The Ladies Wear Emporium. I shocked the manager by taking off my hat and letting my hair fall. Before she had recovered, I explained that my husband and I had, of necessity, traveled on horseback, some dangerous roads, roads that were not safe for a lady - hence the disguise. As a result, coupled with the difficulty of carrying feminine attire in saddle bags, I needed to be completely re-outfitted in the latest fashion.

I lived to regret that last. When I emerged, I was carrying a parasol and tottering on impossibly high heels with miles of petticoats. I was stuffed into a murderous corset of whalebone and lace beneath an outrageous beige "frock " cut so low and tight that, with the corset pushing up from below, only a translucent beige stole, kept most of my upper breasts partially hidden from public view. Mac, when I met him out front, was, of course, delighted. I only pretended to hit him. He had been busy next door and had been back to the livery stable. Two valises sat beside him containing our "more sensitive equipment" and traveling clothes. His "costume" was quite spectacular - a dark brown waist coat with lace at the throat of his white shirt, fawn colored tight pants buckling at the knee   and long beige stockings. His shoes were brown with big silver buckles. The rest of our purchases would be sent, to the hotel. Miss Granger seemed to take it for granted that we would be staying at "The Victoria House." Luckily, it was only a couple of blocks away otherwise I would never have made it in those heels. As we "strolled" - that being the fastest gait I could manage in this dress - he bent and murmured that I looked gorgeous. "I'll be less gorgeous when I get somewhere I can burn this damned corset." I muttered back.

After settling in, we went down to the hotel dining room for dinner, I, of necessity, still caged in my corset. Afterwards, we changed into our traveling clothes with my guise once again that of a boy, and snuck out of the hotel in Fast Time. That evening, and for the next several days, roaming through some of the more unsavory parts of Baltimore in search of information, we were accosted several times by knife wielding, would be robbers. In each case, the miscreant was warned, with his own knife at his throat, that if we ever again saw him in the town we'd leave him without any testicles. Word soon went around that we were not to be trifled with - and more importantly - that we sought information and were willing to pay for it.

268

Within a week we had a platoon of would be informers scattered throughout the city. Many were young children, to each of whom, we gave a few coins ahead of time. The rest were somewhat unsavory characters that would have, in our time, been considered low class "private Eyes." Each of our "spies" was shown the "drawing" of Cynthia and James, were told that they were taller than most citizens today, and scientifically inclined. They were also warned not to approach them and in no case were they to be harmed. Any sightings were to be immediately reported to us at an office we had rented near the Victoria.

The door of the place bore the title of "Confidential Investigations Ltd." We "staffed" the office with one of the ladies of the evening we had met - who seemed to prefer honest employment to her "other" profession. We had checked around pretty thoroughly, and found that she had a good reputation for helping others. Her name was, incongruously, Chastity O'Brien . She was very knowledgeable of the City and its denizens - especially the ones in the blighted areas and we learned a lot about the dark underbelly of the town. We spent long hours in the office as she talked about them, laughing delightedly at the collapse of the police force and it's slow recovery under more honest leadership. The police had been shaking down the poor "street ladies" for decades and now had gotten their "comeuppance."

It was, apparently, a pyrrhic victory, however, because now the "reform movement" was gaining speed and threatened to put the "street ladies" out of business. In addition, as with most "reformers," they were long on promises and short on abilities. The force wasn't nearly as effective as it should be. The leadership seemed unable to distinguish between "immorality" and "criminality." To the rank and file, this was fine because it was a lot safer to arrest prostitutes than muggers. The prostitutes didn't carry guns. Her comments on "The Toffs" were even more biting. It seemed that recently, dueling had begun to go out of fashion. There had been several cases, lately, where both parties had been killed in duels when both came to the duel with new weapons that were much more accurate than was common. Not being familiar with dueling practices that bit of knowledge passed right over our heads - a cause for great chagrin later.

Chastity was able, very quickly, to learn which of our "agents" could be depended upon to deal honestly with us and which would not. We were, thus, able to weed through the numerous "leads" that turned up and select the most reliable to look into. A few days after Chastity began work, she asked us, rather diffidently, if we were interested in taking on other jobs besides the main one we were interested in. It turned out that she had been approached by several citizens to do work for them - both investigative and protective. She thought it good business, and for a different reason, we agreed with her. It would provide good cover for our actual search. We made clear, however, that our original task was to take precedence.

As days changed into weeks, we chafed at the difficulty of locating James and Cindy in a town of less than a hundred thousand people. Even though the stage master vaguely remembered them coming in on the stage and didn't remember selling them a ticket to leave, we began to think that they had moved on. We followed up one lead after another - even resorting to putting an ad in the local paper that led nowhere. Finally, one day in late October when we arrived at "the office", Chastity said she had a little problem.

One of our "investigators" had been given the job of following one of the more promising tips but, after almost a week, he had not reported in. He was one of the ones she had not been too satisfied with because his reputation was not the best. As a result, she had sent out a second man to check on him. It turned out that he had been shadowing a couple for the whole week and had not, as he was instructed to do, reported regularly. We decided to check up on our wayward investigator. He was not around the address designated for his subjects but as we strolled around the area we saw him coming from the direction of the park. When we accosted him, he, at first, insisted that the people in question didn't appear to warrant further study. When we asked him then, why he was still out here, he was evasive. It took some bit of persuasion to get him to admit that, there was indeed, a couple who fit our description but they seemed to have a grown son.

The father and son rode together most mornings but the mother was seldom around except on occasion when the she and the father went out to a restaurant or to a play. He was not convinced these were the people we wanted since our description said nothing about a son. The father and son were very active in several businesses but he had been unable to even find out their names. Every one they had dealt with was unwilling to furnish that information. He had even tried bribes to no avail. Their colleagues and hired help were fanatically loyal. He was of the opinion that they were, somehow, involved in some sort of illegalities. He seemed nervous and a bit frustrated but, in the end, truthful. This appeared to be an intriguing family. We told him to continue his surveillance until he could establish the identities, one way or the other. We warned him, though that we expected regular reports or else he could look for other employment.

That evening, back in the hotel dining room, Mac seemed distant. I asked him what was wrong. "Darling, I've just been thinking about our elusive family. Everyone we have met so far seems very willing to tell us all about their neighbors - in excruciating detail. Why are these people different? " I thought about it a minute and agreed it was unusual, but I added, "What about the grown son?" He smiled at me. "We have always been careful not to let anyone see you around the hotel in men's clothes - but -what would people think if they regularly saw me leave the hotel in the morning with a beautiful woman and in the evening saw me go out with a young man in jeans and a large hat?" "Shit!" I wanted to pound the table. Cynthia would hate these clothes as much as I did and she wouldn't be willing to sit around the house all day. Mac grinned at my suppressed anger. "Think it might be a good idea to have another visit with our man on the street?"

I was too wrought up to even take the time to change into more suitable clothes. This, of course, entailed our hiring a cab. When Mac told the driver where we wanted to go, he made it plain that it was not an area well suited to a lady out at night. Mac was insistent, though, and a half hour later we were let off on the corner a block from the house we were looking for. The driver was reluctant to wait but agreed with the promise of a large bonus if he did. We strolled down the street quite openly until we reached our destination - just in time to see our investigator being pushed across the street by a well dressed couple, the male half of which was holding a large pistol. Quickly we went to fast time and darted up to take a look. We grinned like idiot kids at the sight and moved back to a place of concealment. It wouldn't do to startle a man with a cocked pistol.

Once the three were in the building, we went across the street. I picked the lock - no great problem considering the simplicity of the mechanism - and we went upstairs. Mac knocked on the apartment door.

270

Thursday, October 30, 1838

I came out of my shock and launched myself into Mac's arms, kissing him wildly. I heard a chuckle behind him and a voice saying, "Careful woman. He's spoken for. It's polite to ask a man's wife before you kiss her husband." I pulled my lips off his and looked over his shoulder. Then I grabbed Katy and hugged her. I pulled her inside the apartment while James untied "Mister Andrews." "Stop by the office tomorrow after lunch and we'll give you your bonus." Mac said as our former captive scuttled out.

We spent the next three hours going over our various adventures, starting with "Wife?" Katy shrugged, and I noticed an unusual blush begin at her neck. "I got tired of being a mistress to a man with a name like Thuringen who had two grown daughters." With a sly grin, she added. "I made him marry me to make an honest woman of me - 'course, I'm not yet convinced that sleeping with a husband is as much fun when he's yours. Also, Kathryn F. Thuringen doesn't have quite the ring of Kathryn Finnigan but I guess one can get used to anything." The fact that she was sitting on the couch with Mac's arm around her and her hand giving his thigh a squeeze while she said it, tended to belie her protestations. Then, Katy explained about the modified Modulators. That brought sighs of relief to both of us.

Our joy wasn't dampened, even when she explained about Milan's uncertainty that we could actually, get back to our own time. The rest of the time we spent telling each other of our various adventures. When we mentioned Mister Colt's revolvers, Katy grimaced. "Damn!" she muttered. "I should have noticed the coincidence of a new pistol showing up just when you two hit town. Did you also have something to do with the crooked cops getting busted?" We laughed and admitted it. We were thrilled with the idea of "going home" - but with a little nostalgia. We told them that we had to do some things to clear up our affairs here before we could leave. When we explained, they both nodded agreement. We decided to stay here tonight, though they suggested moving to the Victoria. We, though, were familiar with our surroundings and figured we could prepare for a trip better here - besides our "business interests" were all around here and we had some preparations to make. We agreed to meet them for lunch tomorrow at the Victoria. Before they left, Katy remarked on the fact that she would be happy to get back to where people wore decent shoes. I laughed and told her that she and Mac should go see Herr Muller in the morning. He would help her out if she'd tell him I sent them.

Friday October 31, 1838

By the time, we got in a carriage to go meet Katy and Mac, I again wearing, what I thought of as my "maiden lady" costume, a rust colored, long low cut gown that really needed stays and petticoats to be proper, but still pushed my breasts up into fashionable, but in my mind indecent mounds. James wore his knee pants and we were both dressed well enough to not cause a stir at the Victoria. We had made sure the horses were groomed and settled our bill with our landlord. In addition, we had sent boys to Mister Colt, Monsieur DuPont and Mrs. Mulroney to ask them to join us for "tea" at the Victoria. Katy and Mac were attired similarly to us except that he was all in black, except for white stockings and stock around his neck. Her dress was also black and set off her ebony hair well. It also emphasized the white mounds above the bodice.. We made plans for our trip. We agreed that James and I would stay at the Victoria with them, until their boots were ready and we could leave from there. We could bring our horses over to their livery stable tomorrow and plan on leaving the next day. Then the problem of costume came up. Where could we change after we had gotten the horses?

"Why bother," Mac chuckled. "Change here. We can leave in FT and the only ones who'll see you will be the stable boy. We really don't have to worry anymore about what the locals think. We're not planning on coming back." Katy and I looked at one another and laughed. "Why indeed?" she said. "We don't even have to pretend to be boys anymore. We can shed those damned tight jackets and hats." "Why bother with FT at all?" I laughed. "Just imagine the gaping mouths when we come down the stairs in jeans, shirts and boots." The boys were less enthusiastic but agreed. "Who knows," James said. "You may start a new fashion - women's lib in the 1830's."

After lunch, we checked into the hotel, asking them to send over to our loft for our bags, that we had stacked by the door and to have the livery stable bring our horses and tack over as well. While we were doing that, Katy and Mac went down the street to their "Detective Agency" and, legally, turned it over to their assistant. It was more difficult than they had thought, since the assistant was a woman - and an ex prostitute to boot. While they were gone, we engaged, upon the recommendation of the hotel manager, an attorney. He would be present at our meeting at teatime. Then we spent the rest of the afternoon with Katy and Mac. When we reached their room, we quickly shed our stupid clothes. Katy and Mac got into jeans and shirts. I stripped down to my chemise and James to shirt and knickers since we had another meeting in two hours. I told them that we wanted to do something nice for the Jordons. We intended to leave half of our ten percent interest in the pistols and cartridges, as well as the lingerie "factory" to them. That's when Katy told us that they were due a reward as well. The rest of the time, they spent examining our pistols. Katy declared their workmanship exceptionally fine and the cartridges, extraordinary, though we'd have to be sure and clean them regularly - reminding us that the mercury fulminate primers were very corrosive. She was amazed, though, that the cartridge cases were so well made and that we had remembered enough obsolete chemistry to produce the "propellant." She also wanted a pair for her and Mac. They would be much less unusual than the weapons they had brought.

At four o'clock, we came back downstairs to meet our "partners" in the private dining room, I introduced, Mister Arondelles, the attorney the hotel manager had engaged. Over tea and something called "crumpets" we explained to all that we were leaving the colony and what we intended to do - which was, to return half of our ten percent interest in the various holdings to them, to make Mrs. Mahoney the owner of the lingerie business, and to give the rest of our interests to Mister and Mrs Thomas Jordon of downstate Maryland. In addition, the detective agency was to be turned over to Chastity O'Brien - who had appeared in her best dress and looking very nervous to be in such a place. They were shocked to say the least and Mrs. Mahoney, also feeling quite out of place in these surroundings and in the company of so many "toffs", almost fainted. Mister Colt and Monsieur DuPont were much too urbane to allow their surprise to show beyond a quick look between them and a pair of raised eyebrows.

All, though, were too polite to inquire into our plans and Mister Arondelles, promised the deeds to us early in the morning. He would, personally, handle any actions needed to handle the documents. He would also see to all necessary signatures and processing, then bring them to us for approval. Whereupon he would, distribute copies to all concerned. We told him we needed to handle the distribution to the Jordon's ourselves and he nodded his agreement. With that, we shook hands all around - Monsieur DuPont kissed mine and Agnes Mahoney hugged me, wiping a tear from her eye. Miss O'brien did the same to Katy. Mister Arondells was better than his word. He delivered the signed documents to us that evening, along with a "complementary" pair of Mister Colt's pistols for Katy and Mac.

Saturday November 1, 1838

On Saturday, we were on the road by seven o'clock. It had been funny, the four of us coming down the stairs in our denim jeans and shirts, Katy and my hair hanging half way down our backs in a long pigtail and without our jackets, making it quite clear that we weren't boys. The staff went into a state of shock. The head waiter recovered quickly, though. He led us to a table and got us breakfast. The manager brought our hotel bills into the dining room - probably to keep our scandalous attire from cluttering up his lobby. Afterwards, carrying our saddlebags over our shoulders, we left. With the pack horse loaded and all our gear stowed, we got on the road.

The trip back was uneventful except for a drunk in one hotel saloon/dining room who took exception to women wearing pistols on their hips. When he came up to pick a fight with James, though, he found the muzzle of Katy's pistol shoved up his nose. He sobered up very fast and, with little fanfare, left the place. It took four days of combined FT and TT travel, before we reached the Jordon's farm. The couple was overwhelmed by the shower of gold coins that Katy delivered to them and the deeds James and I delivered. They had a problem in comprehending the value of five percent of the only repeating arms business in the colonies. We had to explain that Mister Arondelles would, once each year, send them a statement of how much had been placed in the Baltimore bank in their account. Due to lack of reputable banking facilities in the local area, they would either have to go to Baltimore to pick up the money in cash or have it sent down. Since this seemed dangerous, due to the problem of thieves on the road, we suggested they send a list of their needs to Mister Arondelles and, for a small commission he would have the goods charged against their account and sent to them. Finally, James and I presented them with one of Mister Colt's pistols and five hundred rounds of Mister DuPont's ammunition.

We spent the night in their barn, though, they begged us to use the house and let them sleep in the barn. Early the next morning, we all rode up the lane to the place where this had all started. Milam's instruction to Katy and Mac had heavily favored returning at the exact time they had left. He wasn't sure it was necessary but he also wasn't sure that resetting the modified modulators would work either and wanted to take away any possible variations. With only the five slaved Modulators, we had to leave Katy and Mac's pack horse and my saddle horse with the Jordons. It was, thus, that four very nervous people, holding the reins of three horses, sat in the woods awaiting the hour of truth. Our horses jangled their bits in irritation at having been saddled and walked only a hundred or so yards before stopping and waiting for nothing of equine importance. The time came. The translation was anticlimactic. With all our modulators slaved to Katy's, at nine minutes after seven o'clock, there was a slight blur and we found ourselves back on our own well tended path. We all looked at each other with silly grins on our faces - having prepared ourselves for failure - without ever mentioning our misgivings to each other. We didn't have much time to gather our senses, however. We were greeted by two of Mac's guards who shouted excitedly into their communicators that we had returned. As we walked out of the woods, leading the horses, it seemed half the population of the county was running across the field towards us.

Wednesday, April 29, 2060

It had been a joyous homecoming with the remaining staff of the house. It turned out that we had been gone almost three weeks and Katy and Mac, a little over one. After trying to answer a babble of questions, we had, finally, begged off on the grounds that we all stunk of horse. Now James and I sat ensconced in our own bathtub for two for the first time in almost a year. I leaned, contentedly, back against him as he assiduously scrubbed my breasts. I murmured, pretending an innocence I didn't feel, that there was something poking me in the back. "That's because you're facing the wrong way." he murmured nibbling on the nape of my neck. I wasted no time in correcting that situation and soon was sitting astraddle his lap, again coupled to him in conjugal bliss. When the water began to cool, he lifted me out of the tub and carried me to the bedroom. There we happily finished what we had started, then got up and dressed. We sat and drank some coffee while we waited for Mac and Katy. It was almost an hour before they strolled in hand in hand. When James commented on their tardiness, Mac laughed and said that they hadn't been married as long as we had. With that, we left the house. The GL had sent a shuttle for us and we boarded it for our trip to Paris. All our gear had already been stowed and, we were assured, that our horses were well taken care of.

We were greeted on the shuttle pad of the GL's building   by the whole family. Mac's - and now Katy's - girls, held the twins while Jonha and Suzanne came to greet us with hugs. Then the twins were brought to me to cuddle. Two little pairs of hands went, immediately, to my breasts. "Sorry, little ones." I murmured. "You're mommys dried up." "I hadn't thought of that,"Suzanne said. "I put off their dinner so you could have them. Don't worry, though." she added. "We've got a pill that'll have you lactating again by morning. In the meantime, grandma gets to nurse them one more time." I sighed and told her not to bother she could use the time to wean them - or, that I should have done it long ago.

The next evening, it was with some wistfulness, that I helped feed the twins baby food from the brewer. After that we met again with the GL There, had been no more contact with Karnes. Katy had told us what they had been doing in California. He, though, had covered his tracks too well and the agents found only computers with smashed hard drives and empty offices when they raided the places Cindi and Arthur had found. We then, reported what we had found just before, we were - whatever you could call being sent into another time. It was obvious that the modulator could be used for transportation, perhaps limited to space travel since, controlling it on the earth's surface might prove very difficult, at best. Movement between time streams was now, of course, also possible but just how to use that feature - or, more importantly, why we should use it was another matter - and even more importantly perhaps, a dangerous one. There were long meetings with Milam and several of the staff all week. As pleasant as Paris was with doting grandparents and a baby loving staff, after a week, it was time to go home and get back to work.

Monday April 4, 2061

I looked out over my audience. It'd been almost a year since the kids had been recovered. It was all I could do to keep from frowning knowing that possibly one in this room was the reason for all our problems. "Gentlemen, I hope you don't mind if I use local terminology in this meeting, my staff will be more comfortable with it." Jonha looked over the delegation. Considering that they were Magman, they were about as upset as one could be. "You know, of course by now, that we have taken steps that were highly irregular, to say the least. I'm not speaking only of my issuance of a PIA two years ago. That was in accordance with proper authority and was, no doubt, why you are here. I could say that in terms of the PIA that I had little choice once they achieved the technological level they are at now. The truth, however, is that I felt that our control over the project had already been superseded by events. Destruction of the planet would, perhaps, be the safest course, but this would result in total failure of the only viable project left to meet our needs. For you see, there is a problem. It was discovered several years ago that two unauthorized Magma personnel were included in the company that came to this planet in the beginning. These two have been working to subvert the efforts of the client race to achieve upgrade. I was unable to report this to the council because I was not sure who on the council had arranged for this event to occur. It is certain that someone did. We have one of them in custody. In view of the fact that he was a part of several attempts on the lives of two of our children, the best that he can hope for, is that you decide to take him back with you. My grandson and his wife have agreed, reluctantly, to let you do that if you wish. They would much prefer to have him incarcerated for life here. 'Stick him in a dungeon for life, and forget him' were their actual words. The problem, of course, being the length of that life" The shock on the faces of the unshockable was almost painful. He continued. "Yes, the proposal is a vicious one - but that is how we designed them. Perhaps we, back home, thought, we could breed a nice compliant race that would allow us to control them, but by now, our experience shows us how wrong we were. The fact that they didn't demand - well a more fatal - punishment, though shows a considerable amount of self control on their part."

Without exception, the faces of the team, blanched at even having to consider a word such as 'fatal'. It made me queasy also but I continued. "As a result, I intend, as soon as this meeting is over, to tender my resignation as project manager and become advisor to our clients. My entire staff has requested that they be allowed to stay also. Since the clients now know of this breach of our canons, it is not likely that they will accept very much in the way of suggestions from Magma as to how they run their society. I hope, however, that we may be able to expect some assistance in their defense and subsequent growth. After all, their success as a Galactic police force would greatly benefit the entire universe and would be desirable from Magma's viewpoint.

You will be given access to all local project records which, you will find, includes staff reports and records that I, Personally chose to either not forward or report in the annual meetings. I apologize to you for the breach of faith but not for the deception. I decided long ago that this project had to succeed and approved, both tacitly and

275

actively, breaches in policy that would assure it a better chance. I felt, at the time, and still feel, that I have acted in the best interests of Magma, and that the cutting off of technical aid would, at this point, be not in those best interests. I must admit, however, that we have created a grave danger to the stability of the universe with this race. They must be allowed the technological aid needed to overcome the activities of the more recalcitrant races we have found but they must also have time to continue development of powerful controls for their more violent urges.

We have already instituted efforts to control their criminal element - quite successfully in the case of the organized elements. Organizational controls have been put in place to curb their pathologic urge to destroy each other by war but it will probably take millennia for these efforts to bear fruit. I feel, however, it is unlikely, if the effort is, eventually, successful, that they will retain much of the skills for which they were designed. For that reason I find myself hoping that they will not advance too fast.

It is for this reason that I recommend that, as soon as they have adequate technological capability to deal with any present threats, they be isolated, to the extent possible, from our civilization. It may still be necessary for Magmans to emigrate from this universe to the hidden one already prepared. To sum up, I'm afraid that I and this includes my entire staff, have committed a moral breach that Magma cannot tolerate. I think, though, that there is little that it can do directly to correct the situation - other than making it worse by rendering ineffectual the only race capable of protecting the galaxy. My staff and I will accept our banishment without qualms but I would like, very much, to ask that our transgressions do not cause a loss of support for our clients. They are simply what we made them and will, in all probability, be successful in the task for which they were created. Our AI, in fact offers a fairly high probability that they will eventually approach - perhaps exceed our level of civilization while still maintaining a fairly high level of defensive capability."

The delegation chief spoke up as Jonha sat. "Arientain -" the lack of a honorific showed what he thought of my ideas. "It would appear that there is a second solution. We can simply destroy the system."

Wednesday, April 6, 2061
Today, though, Cindy and James, along with Art, Lil, Justice, Barbara, Katy and her daughter, Mac and his girls, the secretary, Margaret and a half dozen of the my staff, sat around a large conference table in the headquarters. James Arthur and Lillian Ann McClellan were happily ensconced in a makeshift nursery off in a side room next to the conference room and being treated like royalty by half the female staff. They had matured dramatically in the last year, probably due to the fact that they wore tiny watches and their parents couldn't bear to be away from them for more than a few hours at a time. Doctor Bailey was a nervous wreck worrying about the effect of FT on them. He was particularly worried about not being to measure them against "normal" children because no one could figure out their biological age. They and their parents though seemed not to have been overly affected by the FT experience. No one knew just how much FT the twins had been exposed to, but James and Cindy had spent almost three years there.

The table was quiet. Art and Justice seemed comfortable in their respective chairs while James and Cindy glowered. They had come to terms with their multidimensional theories and had postulated methods for the most obvious usage in

276

inter-dimensional transport and communication. In addition they had just achieved breakthrough in a theoretical new propulsion system that should produce exhaust velocities approaching the speed of light - in a Fast Time mode. That meant speed, as such, was an obsolete term. As soon as their theoretical ship reached a local speed equal to that speed, it would simply disappear from our frame of reference and wouldn't appear again until the speed dropped back below it. The ship would, as far as our telescopes were concerned, disappear somewhere out beyond the limits of the solar system and reappear at an unknown time later near its destination. If Light Speed was somewhat of a misnomer, since the liberal application of Fast Time principles was included in its functioning, it wasn't too important. More questionable, was Einstein's question of Mass. As our speed increased so close to the speed of light, would our mass also increase beyond control? That one was harder to deal with since, within the frame of reference the ship would be in at any given time, the speed of light wouldn't actually be reached. They were not at all, pleased about being interrupted at this point in their work.

Just as they had finished the final theoretical work and were preparing to move to a power up configuration I had peremptorily summoned them to Paris. There had been two more attempts on their life by assassins but both were easily foiled by Katherine and Mac. It didn't take much intelligence for them to figure out that I was aware of their progress and intended to take a hand. It didn't take much of a leap of faith to realize that, probably, Justice was the culprit in the matter. I had, as much as admitted it. Not that they had anything to hide from me, but it probably seemed too much like spying to have their work bandied around without their permission. They, obviously, weren't too much pleased with Art's smug attitude either. It appeared that they hadn't associated him with me yet - at least as anything but an agent. Interesting, though, that in the vid, Mr. and Mrs. Thuringen seemed to be making the transition to married life nicely. In addition, her daughter and the secretary seemed to have taken a rather unusual interest in the propulsion lab during that time. I was, reliably, informed that they were becoming an item with a couple of the engineers over there. Oh well, the love life of healthy young women was not really my affair, I was procrastinating. Time for an entrance. I nodded to Milam and opened the door.

The GL swept into the room along with another man who Justice and Art seemed to know. At least, as James suspiciously watched, he noted that they nodded slightly to him. Jovially, the GL made introductions.

"I've asked Mr. Milam, who you already know, to sit in on this meeting because, Modulator operations is not his only field. His primary field of expertise is power and James and Cindy, at least, will all become intimately acquainted with him over the next few months." I looked directly at James and Cindy.

"You two are probably going to be a bit put out over some obvious subterfuge on the part of myself and others in this room. There are very good reasons for that but if you can contain your righteous wrath a little while I will attempt to explain some of it. You, by the way, are probably not going to be the only ones upset by my various intrigues. I won't apologize for them, for they all seemed utterly important at the time. If I made some mistakes, it's just too bad. I'm not the type to spend my life worrying about doing the best I could and it not being good enough. After all, in twenty thousand years a man is entitled to some mistakes."

277

I waited for several moments, grinning as I savored the astonishment my statement had produced in some of the audience. "Now for the formal introductions of my staff. On Mr. Milam's left sits not, Art Pachone, but Jessup Long - at one time the name was corrupted to Jesus and incorrectly applied to another. I guess," he grinned owlishly at Cindy, "you know what that makes you. For reasons of my own, I had Jessup listed as working on a field job for the last few years. As it turned out it was a waste of time, but I thought it might be worthwhile. Lillian, I am told, has been let in on her husband's little secret, but has not been too put out to learn she would also be living a very long time. Next, to you James - by the way, since you, Cindy and Katherine, share our genes, you and your children will live as long or almost as long as the rest of us. We will have to discuss the practical effects of that later." I gave the three of them time to assimilate that bombshell. "Mister - Mac will, as Katherine's husband along with his daughters, also receive treatments - assuming they want them - to artificially produce the roughly same life span as Katherine.

Anyway, next to James is - not Justice Symons but Atam Boron. He and his wife Evelyn, - he pronounced it so that it sounded like Eve Allen were our original field agents. Our connection to your Bible should begin to be obvious by now. Their present family is the latest in a long line extending back to the beginnings of your civilization. I may, very well be the only other one alive, other than themselves, who actually knows how many they have. Most are back on Magma, the home of our staff here, living very productive lives. Mathewer down there is the original Methuselah. Finally, my name is Jonha though - no matter what the scripture says, I have never seen the inside of a whale. The submersible that retrieved me from one task was seen and at night, was mistaken for a large fish. If any of you ever wishes to look over a translation of the books, more properly writings that became the original Bible I can let you have it. If you include the books that have been removed or, deliberately, not included, it is a decent, if highly embellished, and in some cases, contradictory, history of your present European branch of civilization.

You'll find the newer versions fairly accurate, if you ignore dogmatic time frames and recognize the limitations of observer frames of reference when they relate events happening. Considering the number of times it has been translated, and the need at the time to placate a king or two, it's an amazing document. Of course, some of the books were made up out of whole cloth and the best of them are somewhat biased observations, not really histories. The fact that they had no proper frame of reference made the results somewhat fanciful. None the less they did a good job for the time - especially when you consider that by the time it was written, most of the contents were already in the realm of legend. A more accurate version of history, however, is in our administrative section - might be interesting reading if you ever get the time. There's an abridged version if you don't feel up to wading through four hundred and twenty two thousand odd data screens."

Jonha sat back to give his audience a little time to assimilate his words knowing there would be some long hours of discussion in the end. Unfortunately, he knew that there was no time for that now. He leaned forward again. "Now, for the moment, the rest of you will have to either take my word for these revelations or treat them as the ravings of a madman. Either way, we have more important things to discuss. There are fifty of us around the world, plus a few - shall we say - volunteers. My wife, Suzanne, for instance was volunteered - kidnapped is a better word - though she never protested much - from a harem on another of my excursions into the ancient world. Each of the staff has his own specialty and area of authority in addition to backing up others.

Jessup, for instance is chief biologist. Atam is information director. He's been forbidden field duty - up until now - ever since his original errors in biblical history. I became the GL out of necessity, not by preference. I am actually, the senior administrator - at least until I am relieved, which could come at any time now. Milam is Chief of Communications and Power. There are twelve Area Position Specialists, one of which - Markus Orion is responsible for you, Katherine. He is still in the California Pol at present but should be able to join us either later today or tomorrow.

I hope you'll forgive him for being a sort of absentee father but he mourned your mother a very long time and felt a great deal of responsibility for not being there when she needed him. We have, however, tried to keep track of your activities. It will probably make you angry to know that we didn't even know about your adventure in the harem until you had already gotten yourself out. I apologize but, even now, our staff is heavily burdened and not able to do checks as often as is necessary to keep up with you people's capability to get into trouble. Most of our people have made some I guess you would say, errors in judgment over the years - thus our volunteers. Most, became such after becoming intimately involved with one agent or another. For their indiscretions, the agents have been recalled for orientation duty but, by necessity, have usually returned to field work. Atam is, to him, the frustrating exception. His administrative capabilities have kept him in the office, not his ancient errors. We have taken corrective actions after each of these little failures but did not always take into consideration the wishes of local people, even those most intimately involved.

You, for instance, Lil; I've for some years, simply omitted from my reports, the fact that our senior biologist went native and remained in the field - or that he has very illegally, lengthened your life span. Especially, have I not reported that the results of his, shall we say, indiscretion had become intimately entangled with one of mine, James' mother. Actually, we, for a long time, treated the human race as sort of a laboratory experiment - which, in fact, it was. Most of us have though, over the years, become much more intimately involved with our lab subjects than we should have - and our loyalties, therefore, have become very conflicted. We can sort all this out later, though. For now we must take a momentous step."

We, are a people who have literally forgotten how to fight, more than that, can't bring ourselves to it. Unfortunately, situations arise in the galaxy that, our AI's, a rather sophisticated type computers, that you're all familiar with by now, insist that we will eventually need to either fight or flee. Our council decided to establish a fighting force. It was a total disaster. Even today, as with our observers, attempts at violence produce an epidemic of suicides among our people. We decided, therefore, to try and produce a race capable of defense. We, on Sol Station, are roughly ten percent of those experiments that, up until a few years ago, had not been total failures. Probably by now this is the only one remaining viable. Initially our geneticists developed what were considered to be the major traits essential to a warrior race. Recognizing, however, the problems of producing a race capable of defending the galaxy against hostile elements and yet would not a deadly menace to our own, put us in a very unappetizing position. There were seven hundred thirty one different combinations of genes that showed promise. The laboratories for producing the races containing these were set up on planets specially selected for the environments needed to properly nurture them.

279

The first twenty to thirty thousand local years were monitored remotely and at roughly thousand year intervals - planetary intervals that is - for these projects, the time scale was specially modified to produce results quickly. If I returned to Magma, for instance, it would only be about a hundred of our years since this particular project started and six since the first on site team was sent out. The time dilation between the two is now about one to four thousand years. Forget what your Einstein said. Universes or dimensions are different. Only in yours, though, does time act exactly as Einstein described it. Even then, his special and general relativity theories are only valid within the areas where, in your universe, time runs fairly smoothly and is not dilated by black holes or some other of thousands of different anomalies. Time is not really constant anywhere in the continuum. In some dimensions it runs wild. The power universes keep it all in balance by gradually bleeding the excess power - and feeding in power deficiencies - generated out of the unbalanced systems. It is from these universes that a modulator taps its power. In your case, we are the monitors of your system and must decide whether or not your system is to join ours or be allowed to destroy itself. The initial projection for over sixty percent of of these projects was that they would end up either destroying themselves or simply die out. The actual count was over ninety percent and it is probable that by now this is the only one left. A surprising thing has happened, though, something that the managers at home had not expected and, as yet, do not know. Our computers now give only a steadily dropping forty percent chance that you will self destruct even if we did not bring you out right now.

In other words, we, from a Magman standpoint, have created a monster that we do not know exactly how live with. You're much too violent to coexist with us but are the only possible protection we have against a fast approaching enemy.

I smiled at James and Cynthia. "I hope this gives you a clue as to the problems you've had with the adjustment of your Modulators. You can speed up or slow down the time intervals surrounding a Modulator. Beyond a certain point though, as you change your time flow you are moving forward or backwards in that flow - another time line or, if you prefer, another universe can be created by your actions. Everything else about your original time just goes on its own way until you return. Your activities during your jaunt into our past, almost certainly split off a new time flow from this one by virtue of having invented those pistols. Even the invention of the safety pin may have caused it to split. It is possible that the split may be short lived because the time lines tend to try and correct abnormalities - sort of like a river flowing around a rock - but you can never tell. As far as we can tell, the rest of the flows in the "Uptime" direction, haven't yet become fixed - at least as far as this one is concerned - and are subject to an infinitely large variation - in simple terms, they don't exist yet and moving to them is extremely dangerous because this world might no longer exist due to any number of reasons It is quite possible that the area you end up in could have been contaminated by radioactivity - the whole world could simply not exist at all except as a lifeless hulk. It's only when we get to the ones created before the mid 1900's that you could find a time line that probably began before the advent of nuclear weapons. Luckily, you were dispatched to such a time line. Milan calculates that it was probably created before the time of your revolutionary war. In it, it's possible that George Washington never gave his Give me Liberty or Give Me Death speech and that Patrick Henry never became general of the Congressional army."

"Now for us. We call ourselves Watchers. Officially, we are classified on Magma as Observers. Theoretically we, the observer team, as with all the other ones,

280

can go home at the end of our tasks. In fact there has never been a successful attempt by a team to return and be assimilated into the Magma population. I and the staff have broken so many rules here that Suzannah told me flat out that we had made our place here and forget about going back. For her, going back with me would be impossible. Taking a native home could, I suppose, be done but it would be like throwing a native headhunter into the midst of Baltimore society. The locals would never be able to adapt to his ways and the headhunter would go mad by the everyday restrictions on their life. Can you imagine trying to live in a place where a simple argument over what clothes to wear could send your neighbors into a fit of deep depression?

You can, perhaps, imagine that these experiments have their opposition at home. "There are many who are afraid that we are producing a greater enemy than the theoretical ones we fear. In that, they are probably correct, although our records show that once, many millennia ago, we were more violent in nature than we are now. Your history is not very comforting for an alien but perhaps you too will gain control over your more violent urges given time. It's only because there is no other choice that your race has been allowed to remain." A rueful smile broke Jonha's recitation. "That, plus the fact that the council doesn't have all the data they should, and that no one perhaps, could actually bring themselves to terminate you anyway - except possibly the returned observer teams. There are probably plenty of them crazy enough, by Magman standards, to push the button. In any case, the combined thirteen month to two year time transfer and warp drive time out and back would, at this level of your development mean that by the time a watcher returned he'd be so out of touch that he'd be almost useless and your race would either be destroyed or would meet him when he got off the ship at home."

Jonha paused, gathering his facts before continuing. "Now, as I said the various experiments were monitored remotely for a long time. As each reached a point in the development that allowed a detailed evaluation to be performed, a team was sent in to accomplish that. By that time, less than four hundred races remained. Surprisingly, by the time the teams arrived over two hundred actually died out without ever developing a nuclear weapon - most were biological extinctions, uncontrollable viruses and the like. A few were cosmological ones - asteroids and such. Over the last ten thousand local years though the number of surviving experiments have been reduced to four possibles and twelve in various stages of self destruction. As of your last year one of the possibles and two of the others have gone, leaving still three possibles and ten who have probably already self destructed - for those who may have gone to sleep, your race was not, up until last year, - magma time - considered to be one that might actually make it.

Finally," he paused to see how that set with his audience - "this team was sent in a bit over thirty five hundred local years ago for the final monitoring to destruction. It's not a pleasant task and that no doubt accounts for the fact that half the personnel on the team seems to have tried in some way or another to juggle the books so to speak. They did this, knowing full well that upon their return home they would receive the most severe punishment possible - in effect, as far as their fellow citizens would be concerned, they would cease to exist. The ancient Britons on this world had a term for it. For a particularly heinous crime they would send the perpetrator to 'Coventry'. It was a holdover from early pre humans.

They, the pre humans, by the way, were not violent enough to defend themselves from your race. They were wiped out, simply because they were different.

281

When they determined that an individual wasn't fit for their society, they expelled him from the clan They actually mourned him as being dead and from that time on, pretended he didn't exist. It was very effective because, even if he was not killed by wild animals, isolation from the tribe usually caused him to simply sit down and die.

Glancing at his watch, Jonha asked if they wouldn't all like something to eat. His audience looked dumfounded. The man was turning their universe inside out and he wanted to eat. "I just felt that the McClellan children must be hungry and I'm sure they don't care about the fate of the galaxy the least little bit. Also, if I know teenagers, Mac and Katherine's daughters are probably ravenous." Cynthia blushed, having apparently, forgotten, for perhaps the first time about the babies. "I understand that you're not bashful about nursing in public, so if you wish, we can snack and continue our discussion while you attend to my grandchildren." "I'm afraid they're about beyond that stage now." Cynthia murmured, "They're getting table food now and we've given up nursing. I would like to check on them, though."

When I said that, Jonha was nonplused. "But I understood -". "Doctor Goodwrench - Damn they've got me doing it now!" I grinned. "Anyway, the Doctor wasn't too pleased when we took them with us in fast time either but they didn't take too well to getting fed every three or four minutes and my milk glands couldn't understand only getting used every three or four days. It just seemed simpler." A wicked little grin crossed her face "Besides James was getting fat. Anyway they are now almost two but going on three - or maybe even four - because of FT, and while the good doctor shakes his head, he has to admit that they haven't suffered from it that he can tell. It's been the staff that was most put out. They didn't appreciate not getting to spoil them as they would like." Jonha chuckled along with the rest of the room. "Well, on that note, I guess we can eat. Before that, though, I want you to know that I have had Susan download copies of data from meetings I've attended with the Magman council and some historical notes on our activities over the local centuries. You should, at least take note of the meeting. It will give you some idea of what you face from Magma."

When the table was covered with snacks and drinks and Cindy had returned, Jonha continued his tale. "Since your race achieved an appropriate level of communications we have been very constrained in our ability to interfere. Our miscalculations in this area brought about your Torah, Bible and Koran   plus a myriad of scrolls that we had thought destroyed. We got a good tongue lashing by Sub Space for that." Jonha paused and grinned. "That was before I stopped reporting everything I knew. Anyway, sometimes we get lucky when we muddle or, as now appears more likely, meddle. It appears that Jess and my follies have produced the key to Class Two status for this planets population. It normally takes a recommendation by the chief of station and action by the council to confer this status. Since, however our latest status report adds a certain amount of urgency to the matter. I am conferring it unilaterally on my own authority under the Crisis Disaster Articles of the Watchers."

He grinned. "It also means that it is not specifically authorized by the council and could result in termination if they ever figure out how to do it. I finally, gave a team sent by the Council a full report on everything that has happened here, last month. No decision has yet been made on my recommendation to upgrade the planet. Again, due to turn around time, the best that can be hoped for is about two years before that decision is made. In the past, it has always been assumed that actual termination of a project would not be necessary, because the indigenous peoples were expected to kill themselves off - normally by nuclear reactions or by poisoning the atmosphere. No termination has yet been carried out by the Watcher staff. It is, however, possible. It amounts, essentially to creating a catastrophic opening into the U1 power universe. Our Project upgrade equipment would have been used to cause upgrade or catastrophe. It is under the control of our AI - Susan to you, and would be directed by me".

Just then, Susan appeared beside him, and looked at us. "I wouldn't want you to get the idea that I wouldn't have been able to stop your tampering had I wanted to." she said softly with a wicked little grin. "To set the record straight, Jonha's Watchers do not have an unlimited scope of action in this matter." After a short pause she added - "Nor does the Magman Council. Either option requires two separate actions. One is a decision by the team leader - Jonha and the other is agreement by me of the necessity for that action. Jonha should also add that we are not the only ones with this capability on this planet. There is another operable AI - one without, yet, a name -" her grin widened, "- on the planet somewhere - presumably in the hands of our Mister Karnes.

It has not been tampered with as far as we know, and could, if directed to do so by him, effect upgrade or destruction itself. I have calculated that, there is over a ninety five percent probability that he would have already taken that action had he been able. The fact that it has not occurred indicates that he does not have agreement, yet, of his AI or has not been able to assume the necessary authority. There is no reasonable evaluation as to the reason for this. Possibilities are that the AI does not agree with his decision, does not recognize him as the leader, is inoperable, or is waiting for more data - data that could only, reasonably, come from me or by subspace from Magma. In any case, it is a dangerous, and delicate, situation. If he has, in fact, rendered his decision, any actions taken against him must be carefully evaluated with an eye to not causing the AI to complete the ordered task."

Katy, brows furrowed in concentration, spoke up. "You mean that if our actions against him are violent enough, the AI could decide that his order was justified?" Susan's smile widened into a grin. "I continue to be amazed at how quickly you barbarians pick up on the important points in a statement." "Well, you just took a lot of the pleasure out of this barbarian's life." I grunted. "You've had too much pleasure lately, Mrs. Thuringen." Susan laughed, emphasizing the last two words. "Time to come back to the realities of everyday life." With a look of chagrin, I asked Jonha if there wasn't some way to put a cheeky AI in its place. Susan laughed again, and shot back, "That'll be the day." as she disappeared.

I shook my head as I returned to my tale. I had, in the back of my mind, been aware of, but had discounted, the possibility that the A - that Susan could overrule an order to upgrade or destroy. Being aware that Karnes faced the same problem was good news but realizing that actions we took against him could precipitate just the disaster we wanted to prevent was sobering. I returned to my briefing. "Karnes and Pendleton have been active for centuries trying to foil an upgrade. Pendleton is in custody, thanks to Katherine and Mac, but we don't know when, or where, Karnes will strike next - and, more importantly, don't know where his AI is.

They were, of course, responsible for James's parent's death and behind the attempts to kill, James and Cindy. Karnes was responsible for their kidnapping and banishment. It would appear that, with Pendleton out of the way, Karnes will not be able to commit a direct violent attack but he might be able to encourage others to do so - as with the reward on their lives. He is still capable of seriously damaging our efforts - even destroying us all if he can ever convince his AI to allow the destruction sequence to be activated. He can, however, bring the immense power of the underworld to bear if he wishes. Since he, personally, was involved in two abductions of James and Cindy, we can assume that he will no longer bother with stealth. One of our first tasks is to discover his local identity and neutralize him. If necessary, we must destroy his AI. Susan will have a fit if we have to do that but it may be necessary. Any questions so far?"

James spoke up. "Yeah. You have referred, more than once to a crisis. Just what crisis are you alluding to?"

Jonah stared across at James for long moments until finally deciding on his approach. "You're right. There is a real crisis – perhaps not an immediate one. There is another star faring race in the galaxy that appears to have gone crazy - no other word seems to serve. They will eventually become your problem - perhaps to face alone. It was what precipitated the need for a police force to begin with. Presumably where there is one such race, there is probably more. Meeting this challenge will almost certainly require a great expenditure of effort and resources on the part of Earth - without any real guarantee of success. Hopefully, Magma will lend some support. To be able to use it though, will require a great deal of development, both technological and sociological on your part. I would hate, for instance, for you to destroy yourselves after we've invested so much in you.

In the past, you have shown an alarming tendency to use new technological developments to attack others of your people who disagreed with you. The new technologies will make that a disastrous state of affairs. As I mentioned a problem, that is the second. You must first prepare Earth for its eventual upgrade. That means that it must be united in every way possible. This will be a herculean task in itself, and given the fragile state of most of the world's democracies, it is likely to require some sort of authoritarian ruler for the near future. For that ruler to be effective in stabilizing the world, he is going to have to be very long lived. For the time being, I intend to take that job. After stability has been achieved, a slow return to a constitutional democracy can be initiated. If that weren't enough, my own race's probable reaction to the actions I have taken will have to be overcome. Namely, I suspect that an attempt will be made back on Magma to destroy this project - or, at the very least, delay it until it is too late for it to accomplish its purpose.

From the moment you have gained access to the main universe you will probably have less one hundred years, perhaps less than twenty, to prepare yourself to become the Galactic police force . Further, it is unlikely that your present status can be maintained for more than two or three more of your years. Even that is taking a chance that an attempt will be made to recall our entire team or to, somehow, stall the upgrade of your system. I am, as of now, in real trouble. A Magman investigating team has been here. They did not, however, immediately remove me from this post. I'd say tnat the decision on the upgrade machinery will pass from my hands. Once they report."

Cindy spoke up. "How can that happen?" "They will simply issue an order

284

removing my codes from the Susan's upgrade programs."

"Is that all? You mean they won't blast us or something?"

Another smile. "It's enough. No. The Magman Council is simply incapable of the violence you ask about. They just remove our control and begin a debate about the issue that will take forever - in your terms to resolve - if it ever does. During this period, however, some of the personnel from failed projects could easily be encouraged to activate the destruction sequence and no one would probably stop them."

"What kind of codes are these? Why don't we simply change them ourselves or do away with their capability to change them?"

"My dear girl we can't do that. The machinery was designed by the best engineers in Magma. It uses technology simply beyond the scope of local science. It -"

"Isn't this the technology that you intend to teach us? Isn't that why we are here?"

Cynthia had a stubborn set to her jaw as she interrupted. The questions were almost a challenge. Jonha's mouth fell open. I had finally lived to see the day when he was totally surprised. He looked, almost desperately, at me silence reigned. "Milam?"

"Well - I - well it - Jonha - the law! I couldn't tamper with the codes! You know we've been programmed against it!" Jonha seemed to have regained some of his composure. "I know." He replied. "But Mrs. McClennan's question is really Can't or Won't. Can the control of the machinery be changed within the time frame available?" Milam gulped. "Possibly." he murmured. "Possibly" James laughed?

"You bunch of people have trouble conceiving of breaking the law. What kind of safeguards could an engineer with the same concepts put on a piece of machinery? Hell, you've raised the greatest bunch of devious criminal minds in your universe - not excepting, apparently, your, so called, crazy race. We've always looked at the law as a challenge to be overcome. The question should be how can we be stopped?" I grinned as Jonha gulped and opened his mouth. Nothing came out. He tried again. "The AI will stop you." he croaked. Cindi's hologram, chuckled. "You mean, Susan?" she asked, smugly. "She says she's not interested in technical details."

I heard Evelyn chuckle and felt her squeeze my hand as Jonha paled. Perhaps she and I were more conditioned to James's remark but the concept of totally ignoring our laws simply because someone wanted to, shook Jonha profoundly, even after watching the activities of this race for several thousand years - and even though he had just admitted to lying to the council. Having been involved in handling most of Jonha's more devious ideas for so many years, though, I saw the light sooner than the rest of us "aliens". Jonha called an abrupt end to the meeting to allow the watchers to recover some of their composure.

The meeting resumed after lunch with several of the watchers missing. "Cynthia," Jonha began, "I'm afraid your question and James's observation have, together, been too much for several of my staff. They will, however, be ready - we think - for tomorrow's meeting - if their therapy goes well." He actually grinned at the thought of grown Magmans having to undergo therapy simply from being exposed to their human charges ideas. I noted that none of the missing was from the operations staff.

"Anyway, to continue -" Jonha drew a deep breath. "The Sartooni - that is the race I spoke of before - will not yet have discovered your existence but they will eventually. When they do you must be prepared to resist - and hopefully to defeat, them. For now, you need some background data. I'm removing the block on a report of my last meeting with the council and its aftermath - which included the death of your parents, James. It actually includes data not previously furnished the Council, mostly my random speculations but also the actual text of our staff's - shall we say errors? It turns out that it was Maylin's death and Atam's investigation of it that first caused us to realized that we were being systematically sabotaged.

Jonha spent most of the afternoon completing their education on the real universe that they were soon to enter, then began the discussion. As usual James was the first to react. "How sure are you that you even have a problem?" Jonha shrugged. "Our AI's give a bit over eighty percent probability that one of the races, probably the Sartooni will go rogue and attack us within the next few Magman years. We won't be able to oppose them. Even now, though, our people are preparing to flee rather than fight. Our entire population will evacuate the whole Galaxy before letting ourselves be overcome. If you aren't able pacify them you will have to face the consequences alone. This may seem harsh, but look at yourselves as soldiers - mercenaries would probably be a better word - hired to protect a population that does not wish to - or won't - protect themselves. Your pay is existence - and technical advancement. You will be given, hopefully, whatever technical and intelligence help we can produce.

"Now, to the important items on the agenda." He held up his hand to forestall any disagreements as to what he considered important. "James and Cindy have been the instrument of the status upgrade. They don't know it yet but they have given the human race, not only unlimited power, but, with a cram course in our facilities Faster Than Light Travel and time dilation capabilities. Now they, along with Mr. Plineet, who I have recently recruited as a design engineer, have a rather long and tedious meeting with Milam and Archer Meddis." He grinned again. "I had forgotten about him. He's our propulsion specialist - also under a cloud for getting himself in the history books because he couldn't keep his hands from tinkering and his tongue from wagging. His sin was simply speculating, at a social gathering, on the subject of energy, mass and volume - wouldn't have been so bad if he hadn't built a primitive steam generator.

I suggest that the rest of us retire to another room. We have a rather extensive, shall we call it a social planning, session ahead of us. The discussions quickly became heated as we settled in our new venue and continued well past dinner. Finally, exhausted, we all agreed to get some much needed rest and start fresh tomorrow. Jonha had to have the last word - but this time he'd perhaps, met his alter ego in Cynthia McClennan. The chairs scraped back and as everyone got up to leave, he declared that "Tomorrow we begin the technical training. We will interrupt at intervals if anyone comes up with some practical policy ideas." Just then Cynthia spoke up. "If we're in so much of a hurry, why not go to fast time for all this talk?" "My dear girl -" Jonha grunted "we are in fast time." "Maybe you are but we aren't," she practically shouted, obviously bristling at his tone. His mouth fell open for the second time today. "Of all - I'll be damned. You're right. I humbly apologize, my dear. I forgot the watches. You see we never think of going, under normal conditions, beyond what we think of as fast time. In fact, even the implants we all wear are used only in an emergency - for most of us - a dire emergency.

Few of us can use the equipment without various degrees of illness. Some of us perhaps could use them for short periods, but we'd have to be very careful. Only a few of our field personnel can use them without significant side effects. I will, though, arrange for those of us who can use the damned things to do so." Cindy, partially mollified looked at me. "Darling?"

I asked if he could you have some of our modulators picked up in, say, three or four days? Maybe the ones we have would work better than theirs. Then grinning, I added, "Better have your chef put on a lot of new help too. He's about to have a new experience in gluttony. Twenty or so people eating a full meal five or six times an hour can go through a lot of food." I grinned wider. "Better lay in twice that much for Cindy." I ducked under the half aimed blow to the head and headed for the door. "And while you're at it, why don't you try picking up one of your Sartooni and try to get a handle on their thinking?" Cindy flung back over her shoulder. The answer came back as a rueful laugh - "You want us to attack another sentient species to take a captive?" That stopped Cindy in the doorway. She blushed, then angered at her gaffe, shouted back. "Try it you might get to like it - after all, you've been hanging around us barbarians long enough."I looked back as Jonha told someone to "Send Archer in."

May 15, 2061

It had been a long day almost all of it spent in real time since Mister Milan's modulator still hadn't been modified and he couldn't stand it very long and still be productive. James and I were slumping as we headed down the hallway to our quarters and the babies. Suddenly, James groaned. "Shit!" he muttered and stopped dead. I looked up and we were standing in front of a door that had a sign, "Clinic" on it. "What the hell is going on in there?" he grunted. Then without a pause he stepped up and threw open the door. A pretty receptionist, in a nurse's uniform, looked up. "Mister and Mrs. McClennan!" she said with a wide smile. "Can I help you? I hope you don't need our services but if you do, it would be an honor to be of service." James said nothing, ignoring her and looking sharply around the room. It was empty. I decided it was up to me to be courteous. "I'm sorry, Miss"-, I glanced at her name tag-", Partridge. My husband is sometimes a bit peremptory in his actions. I haven't the foggiest idea why we're here but I suspect we'll all find out in a moment."

I punched James in the side to get his attention. He spun toward the nurse with a glare. "What's going on in that room, miss?" he growled. The smile disappeared from her face to be replaced in rapid succession by a look of disappointment then a frown. She stood up quickly taking on a belligerent aspect. "Sir." she growled back at James. "If you'd like to speak to the doctor, He's with a patient but I can get him as soon as he finishes his work." Her tone was icy. James blinked, only then realizing he had committed a blunder. "I'm sorry - nurse - I well - ." I smiled to myself and patted his arm. "I will apologize for my husband, Nurse Partridge. He sometimes becomes a crotchety professor type when he notices a problem. I think now that he realizes what an ass he's been he'll be very upset with himself - won't you darling?" That last, I directed at James along with a painful squeeze of his arm. Embarrassed, he blushed and tendered his apologies again. Somewhat mollified, the nurse asked again if there was something she could do to help. I squeezed James arm again, a bit puzzled because I could feel the tension in him.

James took a deep breath. "I'm sorry nurse but something is wrong in that room. I don't know what it is but, whatever it is it is setting my teeth on edge." Finally, the girl smiled again. "Well, sir, I'm sorry about that. I'm afraid we're all sort of used to that feeling now. The doctor is checking all personnel for their tolerance to the use of their time shifting equipment." James shook his head and turning to me, said "Man! It's no wonder they can't use the damned things. Just being around them in operation, gives me the willies. I've noticed it before with Milam but put it out of my head." I gave him a quick kiss on the cheek. "Darling, you're just tired. I don't feel a thing." He gave me a hard look. "Honey, it's not that. Something's wrong with those things - physically wrong. Can't you feel it?"

That got my attention! I turned to the nurse. "Nurse Partridge." I said. "Would you be so kind as to get the doctor out here? Tell him it's an emergency!" She looked hard at me and, apparently, believed me. Nodding she got up and headed for the closed door. "And tell them to stop whatever it is that they are doing." James called after her. She paused at the door. I added, "Please!" James colored again as she looked back. She nodded and went through the door.

A few moments later the nurse was back followed by a tall, grey haired man - one of the first older people I had seen on Jonha's staff. James seemed to have gotten control of himself and tried to explain his feeling of impending danger to Doctor Weinburger. The doctor looked skeptical. He pointed out that Jonha had directed that all staff members be tested for ability to tolerate their "implants." He seemed pleased to meet Jonha's son but wasn't as happy to stop a project that had Jonha's personal attention. I broke in and told him that when James said something was wrong, even Jonha listened. He studied us both a long moment then turned and called Jonha. After explaining what was going on, he listened a long time. Then, with a, simple "Yes sir." he hung up. "The GL will be down in a minute." he said. Turning to the nurse, he asked her to go back in and see if she could help Miss Gustafson get dressed? "I was through with her anyway." he said as the nurse left. "She was getting deathly ill and it was barely operating so I removed the implant. She is one of those that shouldn't have been given one to start with."

An hour later, we all - including Jonha and the doctor - sat in his office while a holo of Susan- primly dressed in a white lab coat - finished describing the circuitry of the modulator implants worn by the staff. We were all quiet a moment before James asked her to go back over the tuning circuitry. I studied it intently as one circuit after another appeared along with flow charts of its operation. "The problem is right there, somewhere." James muttered, concentrating on the charts. "It's wrong!" I glanced up at Jonha. He lifted an eyebrow. James saw the action out of the corner of his eye. "I tell you it's bad wrong!" he growled. "It's so wrong it actually, set my teeth on edge all the way out in the hallway." Doctor Weinburger grunted. "Every implant is checked before we even start testing." he said. "That implant is operating exactly within specification." "Then the damned specification is wrong." James practically spit back at him. "That damned thing would have put me in the psyche ward if I'd had it in me."

Jonha looked at me with an uplifted eyebrow. "The circuitry does look odd, GL." I said. "There is probably more than one way to make the thing work, but, I agree with James. He says it doesn't feel right. I say it doesn't look right". "Doctor," Jonha said quietly, "I think you need to get Milam up here to look into this problem. Believe me when I say, when James says something's wrong, we all listen." Then he grinned. "And Cynthia makes Milam mutter about damned smart alec females. She drives him mad pointing out how his precious electronics need tweaking." It was my turn to blush but I said, it would have to be tomorrow - that I and James were both too tired to be productive right now. Jonha agreed. He suspended testing and said he would set up a lab for us all tomorrow morning.

By noon the next day, we had discovered the cause of my upset. The girl's - Sarah Gustavson's - modulator was radiating way out of phase with the ones Cindy and I used. We spent two days trying to fix it before Cindy came up with the obvious solution. "Why don't we just give her one of ours?" Doctor Weinburger called the girl back in and Cindy strapped one of our wrist modulator on her. After explaining how to use it, she stepped back. The girl with trembling fingers adjusted the modulator and with a shimmer, disappeared. We hoped she had followed Cindy's instructions and used the lowest setting. We worried that she might have become sick and collapsed. Nobody turned up on the floor, though, and in about a half hour, just as I was about to go to fast time to check on her, Sarah Gustavson shimmered back into our time. She was beaming. "It's wonderful!" she exclaimed. I can't believe I did it!"

We, immediately, ordered a dozen more Modulators from home for use by all of Jonha's "operations staff" along with specs for them so they could begin producing them here. Then we returned to the grind of Magman engineering. In the meantime, the Magman Modulators were being taken out and modified to match ours. It went easier now. Mllam now wore one of our Modulators, untll he had time to get his out and reworked, so we could spend eight hours in FT and be done by coffee break. With a couple hours devoted to FT sleep - even if the mattresses weren't too soft, we could get in another eight hours after lunch and be done by mid afternoon. That left us time to spend with the twins and friends. We even had time - in FT - for pursuing Karnes. James had been reviewing all the data stored by Suzannah - Susan. It went back for over two hundred years and she was still reviewing history to see if other acts could be assigned to him. This particular night, he had Susan project the locations of his crimes on a world map. "

May 16, 2061

"Sit Archer. About the problem with our Modulators -." "Yeah, Jonha." he replied, "and I wondered how long it would take for you to call me." "Well, what do you think?" "Hell, Jonha! You know as well as I do, that the Modulator is the basis for our space craft propulsion system. If it has a flaw, so do our space craft." "Damn, Archer! We've been using this system for God knows how many millennia. How could we have not missed such a simple problem?" Archer grinned. "Jonha! It's not a simple thing to see. I'd never have noticed it. The things have been the guts of a very reliable warp drive practically forever and we've had almost no problems with them. The few ships that disappeared we put down to navigation errors - there are still plenty of those around.

The only known problems have been with trying to use them with people and that wasn't really a high priority problem. We had little real need of them for that purpose and as long as we could find enough people that could actually use them we didn't bother." "And besides," Jonha, growled with a disgusted wave of his hand, "we live, practically, forever and assume that we are, as a result, practically omnipotent. Maybe we deserve to die out as a race and leave the universe to our little barbarians." The longer he talked the angrier he got. Slamming his fist on the desk, he practically shouted. "The damned council acts like they've developed a new little pet they can put in a kennel and take out whenever they want to impress somebody. If they don't heel properly they intend to destroy them." "They intend to try." Archer said, calmly. "What? What, the hell, do you mean?" "I mean that, after only a few hours looking at the upgrade equipment, Mrs. McClennan showed me how to take complete control of it. It's a simple matter to give the AI the command sequence and to remove all Magman controls. She was right in that, we have no concept, even after having lived here for a few thousand years, how to really secure our equipment. I shudder to think what some criminal could do if they knew what we were." "Oh shit!" Jonha groaned. "I really thought the girl was just popping off after we'd denigrated her abilities." He did a passable imitation of Cynthia. "Well, Jonha, at least, it removes one of your problems. Just tell me to do it and I'll take Magma off line entirely."

Jonha leaned back in his chair. "It creates a whole new set of problems, though. Chances are, that they're going to need Magman help if they are going to have to upgrade in the near future - and let's face it, they probably are. In addition, there is the other AI. What if Karnes finds out how to take over control of it and simply start the destruction sequence?" Then another thought struck him. "Will Magma know if you cut their control of the AI?" "Not unless they try to activate the upgrade or destruction sequence? If that happens, they'll get a hell of a feedback through their own AI's. What will actually happen is that, one of their AI's and ours will become slaves to the one activating the sequence. If it doesn't happen then they'll know." "So Susan will, in effect, become a part of the other AI?" When Archer nodded, Jonha asked how the destruction sequence worked. "Well, it begins by automatically, calling in transport from our outer reaches base. It allows seven local days for all personnel to be gathered before the ships are brought down to stable orbit and shuttles launched to pick us up. It allows another seven days for us to load and get far enough into space to make the jump out of the system. At that time, it will fully open the gates to the U1 power universe and, simultaneously, warp the gate directly into the local star and it in effect, will become a nova." Jonha mulled that over a while, then said, "And if we take over the sequence?" "The other AI can still activate it or Magma could, perhaps, activate it remotely. The only effect would be that Susan would not be involved." "So if CP's AI started it, we'd have seven days to find it and destroy it." Archer shook his head. "Finding it probably won't be a problem. It'll radiate in so many frequencies that it'll stick out like a sore thumb. Destruction, though, will simply stop all the delays and the final implosion of the sun will be triggered immediately."

Jonha sat back and thought about that. Finally, he asked Susan to give her thoughts on the subject. The hologram that appeared had a grin on its face. "I wondered how long you would fuss over this problem before checking on the facts." Jonha turned to Milan with a disgusted expression on his face. "Milan, is there any way to rewire this damned AI to make it a man? I get really tired of its snide remarks." "Forget it, Milan." Susan laughed. She dropped, daintily into a suddenly appearing holographic couch, as her clothes quickly changed into a really sexy mini skirt. "He likes to look at my legs too much to change me now." A pair of horn rimmed glasses appeared on her face and a notebook in her hand. "As for your facts," she said businesslike, "Cynthia has already queried me on the subject of upgrade/destruction. It's a simple wiring problem. There are no codes involved. None were ever considered necessary.

All that has to be done is for the Watch Team Administrator to call on Article seven of the watchers agreement and order me to begin the process. I then, will approve and activate the circuitry in the upgrade machinery and from then on, the process is as Mister Milan described it." Jonha leaned back in his chair and smiled. "You mean that I am the only one who can order the process begun?" "As long as you are the Administrator." she smiled. Jonha frowned. "Is there a question in there somewhere?" he asked suspiciously. "You're saying that I could be replaced as Administrator and would no longer control the process." Susan's smile turned Saccharine sweet.

"That's what I like about you, Jonha. For a man you are so quick. It's too bad you're not as good at listening." Irritated, Jonha replayed Susan's remarks in his mind. Finally, he had it. "Cynthia has already come up with a solution to the problem." he grunted. Susan grinned. "Very good." she laughed. "If Mister Milan were in his office to watch what she was doing, the problem would probably already have been solved. Without his help, she'll probably take a week to figure out the system wiring." "My God!" Milan cried. "You've not let her get into the controller wiring?"

"Why not"? she laughed. "There's no prohibition in my programming that

292

requires me to stop anyone from rewiring the controller." Jonha leaned back in his chair and roared with laughter. "I think, Milan," he gasped between chuckles, "You've just been given permission to override orders given by the Watch Team Administrator." "Jonha!" Milan gasped. "We're not allowed to redo the hard wiring in a controller. The council would never approve." "Why don't you go down and tell Cindy that." Jonha said with a grin. "See how far you get." As Milan jumped up and headed for the door, he added, "Might be a good idea to give her some help with Magman electronics theory if we want to ever use that equipment again."

James was still staring at the hologram of the rotating world hanging in the center of the room when Cindy came in carrying John on one hip. "I thought so!" she grunted. "Just how long are you going to stare at that thing? It looks like you've been in FT for days." James leaned back on the couch and looked up. John cried "Tada!" and held out his arms. "Sorry, love." he muttered, taking John in his lap. "But you were gone all day playing with Milan's electronic toys. I presume you were successful in your efforts. What time is it - real time, I mean?" "First, yes. The upgrade can only be started manually now - at least from this - Susan. For the second, it's past time for supper." Cindy muttered. "We ate without you. It's time to put the twins to bed, and time for you to take a break and help. What are you trying to do?" James grinned at her. "You know, at the rate you're going, the kids won't learn to walk till they're ready for school." Cindy stuck out her tongue at him. "You're just jealous." she muttered. "I haven't heard you complaining. Besides, both of them can walk perfectly well. Besides, you haven't answered my question." "Tell you what." he said "You go put them both to bed and when you're done, I'll turn my attention to your grotesque body and explain my idea as I ogle it." Cindy frowned a moment, then bent to kiss him. Grinning she headed for the door. Over her shoulder, she said, "It's about time. I haven't been properly ogled in a long time."

When Cindy came back, I knew I grinned like a fool, my passion rising at the sight of her in an, almost, transparent negligee When she slid onto the couch beside me, she murmured. "Still want to complain about my body?" "I wouldn't think of it." I whispered, kissing her lightly. She leaned back against the couch back and murmured, contentedly, "Now what have you been doing?"

Oh God! James was, better than his word. Ogling was nice but what he had just finished doing, was much nicer. After I got my breath back, he asked if I were ready to listen now. I, with some effort, brought my attention back to his intriguing statement of a half hour before. "Or do you want to just lay back and wallow in debauchery." I glanced down. "It looks like your mind is on something besides talk." I murmured. "But go on. Work before pleasure."

"OK." he said, sliding into his lecture mode, leaving his hand to its distracting business. "I got to thinking about just where in the world, Karnes might be hiding. After meeting him, I didn't think he'd be stuck out in some jungle hut so I had Susan, with help from Cindi and Arthur - say hello guys." I had to chuckle. Cindi and Susan appeared in what looked like Sherlock Holmes outfits. Arthur had one on also but his back was turned. "Hello Cynthia, they chorused. "Arthur! What the hell are you doing?" I laughed. "Being polite." he said with a chuckle in his voice. "A gentleman doesn't stare at a lady in such a state of dishabille." "Oh Pooh!" I laughed. "You mean you never stared before?" "Never in visible form." "Well, I chuckled, you know, by now, that I'm not shy, so turn around and pay attention to my brilliant, if somewhat depraved husband." He did, bringing a laugh from all of us when he wriggled his eyebrows in an exaggerated leer like the old comedian, Groucho somebody. Just as James was about to begin, Susan said, "By the way James, I surely appreciate your, putting a stop to all that fooling around with the staff Modulators. I hadn't realized what it was that was giving me the electronic equivalent of a real human headache."

James gave her an ironic little bow and said he was glad to be of assistance. "Now that my exhibitionist wife is finished, flirting with Arthur, though, shall I continue?" "By all means, oh lord and master." I murmured. "Alright, my beautiful slave," he grinned. "I asked the gang to work up a list of all the places we know, or suspect, CP has performed some dastardly deed. That's what you see on the screen." An Iconic projection of the earth's surface appeared. "As you can see the places cover most of the globe. We can ignore entries prior to this century though, since we are looking for where he is now, not a hundred years ago. Almost two thirds of the dots disappeared. Each of the dots, now, on the map is dated beginning in 1901 and ending with the assassination of Prince Faud of the Saudi POL last month. I should point out, that many of these are simply suspected events but ones that fit the pattern of creating a delay or disruption of one peace initiative or another. Susan can trace a line from the first to the last." Now, I think that, until just recently, he believed no one was tracking him - and except for my feeble attempts, he was right. As a result, I am assuming that, due to the stringent, control of the airspace in most of these POL's, he probably normally, traveled by commercial carrier. To do that, it seems likely that he had to base himself in locations with decent international connections, a decent standard of living and a stable, preferably democratic, form of government - one that wouldn't pry, too much into his affairs. His place in Quebec is a perfect example. From the neighbors, it is apparent that he had been there for, at least fifty years. They, the neighbors, thought his 'father came from New England and Cindi has found deeds indicating that a family like his did, indeed, live near Boston in the early 1900's. 'The farms, he owned, if they were his, were some of the first in their area. Now where did he go from there? Assuming that he has, as it appears, devoted an extraordinary amount of time to our families, especially yours, since the turn of this century, I have simply ignored anything outside of this continent." The map changed, expanding to the northern half of this continent. "There has been no known activity south of Texas POL unless you count the business with Katy's Brazilian friend - that dealt with attempts on us.

Now that he knows he is being sought, he is even less likely to try and use personal aircraft. In addition, I have assumed, for tracking purposes, that he wouldn't commit any crimes in the area of his base, if he could help it, due to the heightened possibility of being recognized. So! Places with no identifiable crimes, with good commercial air connections, with a decent standard of living and with access to a city where a good sized laboratory could be hidden brings us to this." The whole world reappeared. A large area of the globe darkened, leaving only a half dozen dispersed locations on the globe highlighted. As the globe turned, James continued. "Now, in the European POL, only the old Swiss Confederation area still maintains a loose approach to travel. The rest are very careful where their people go. The Swiss, though, are awfully aware of strangers and, since he has not been living there for years, I decided to ignore it." With that, the Swiss Alps darkened and the map returned to the North American continent. "That leaves us with The Rocky Mountain Texas and Florida POL's. California POL has a couple of places with possibilities but they are all very close to his crime areas. In addition, the Internet cutout that Cindi and Arthur dealt with is there. Considering all we've thought of so far, these three areas seem the most likely for him to locate. Any ideas you have will be welcomed."

I thought about it a few minutes, then remembered. "That area west of Dallas!" I said. "It's awfully near where the US President was killed." James nodded but said, "We considered that but, It's so long ago that we didn't throw that area out but I've given it one of the lower priorities. The population there is also very cool to strangers, especially Northern strangers. Karnes, however, may have set up his persona there for a long time and, in that part of the country, a person considered to be a "local" can get away with all sorts of strange behavior. My big problem is, what do we do with all this brilliant detective work?" James smiled down at me. I must admit, though, that I'm tired of studying that map though, so let's take a little time off for pleasure. With that our three helpers disappeared. James smiled, lewdly at me, and offered me his hand. I grinned and let myself be led into the bedroom. After "pleasuring me" for awhile, we lay quietly as sleep approached. Just before I nodded off to sleep, I asked, sleepily if it wasn't rude to leave the "gang" like that?" "You saw how fast they disappeared, didn't you? Maybe they needed some time alone too." he chuckled.

Katherine sat quietly as Markus began his briefing. Beyond his initial hug and warm greeting, he had said nothing further. That could have been because of Katy's cold acceptance of him. Her mind roiled in tumult at the sudden appearance of a father she hadn't seen in years and hardly knew anymore, one who was an alien to the earth - and apparently immortal to boot. It would take some getting used to; but she'd loved him once probably still did. "I hope you can forgive me," he said quietly. "I was not in a position to help your mother in her last days even had I known. I loved her very much and there has not been any woman for me since."

He sighed and standing erect changed the subject. "Actually, your job for the near future is an extension of what you have already done. The rest of the major crime lords and the others on the list have to be recruited, neutralized or eliminated as to allow the completion the pacification program. In addition, we need to recruit a corps to take care of the less organized criminals. Jonha has left it up to me to give you your assignments. As in the past, no one else but Jonha and Justice, or Atam if you prefer, will know what those are. I am almost unique among the Watcher staff. I was a true madman back in Magma, perhaps the only alien, alien.

No matter what they may think, your employers, or allies, are not as omnipotent as they think. It's unlikely that they could accept the liquidation of as many important people as may be necessary to unify this world for the war they are sure to, eventually, have to fight. When you are through with that list I'd like it back. It's the only copy." Katy solemnly passed it back. A photographic memory was almost a necessity in her business. "In that order?" she asked. "Doesn't matter as long as the task is done by this time next year. At that time our plans will become public and the threat of those gang lords as well as those ambitious power brokers must be removed. I can trust your judgment as to whether those you can't trust to help can be left alive or simply disappear. We do have a really good, and practically impregnable, holding facility."

"So the GL will actually become the dictator of earth?" she asked suspiciously. Even if it was necessary, she didn't like it. "By then, the Magma council will probably have demanded his recall. Hopefully, if they do, a World Council will have been set up to deal with the coming conflict and it is highly unlikely that he, or perhaps any of us, will still be in our positions. A new group of watchers will probably be in place. It is unlikely that we will be forced to return to Magma but exactly how it will all work out is anyone's guess. To answer your question though, yes. A benevolent dictator will probably be necessary for the near future. Considering the power of our modulators, his benevolence can probably be assured.

We want to make sure that all our efforts have not been in vain. We are counting on the fact that the newcomers will be loath to change a system moving in the direction so obviously, advantageous to both races." He chuckled. "Besides Jonha believes that by then it is likely that an extreme level of violence would be required to undo what has been done and is unlikely that new Magma personnel will have the will to undertake that even if your barbarian engineers can not gain total control of the upgrade equipment. You see, he has great faith in the hostility of the human race toward outsiders telling them what to do." He held up his hand, with another chuckle. "I know we are outsiders too but, you see, we are **your outsiders**."

Katy had to laugh. "Damn it! You're just as incorrigible as when I was a kid. You gotta be Irish with all that blarney. Oh well, you're right. Better the devil you know than the one you don't. Besides we may have some ideas on who we want as ambassadors." To her disgust her voice cracked and a tear slipped from her eye. "Anyway, I'm glad to be back with you again papa - and I'll do what has to be done." For the first time, her father's face trembled. "I wish, more than anything, that it didn't have to be you to do this, sweetheart. I hope you remember that I tried my best to prevent you from acquiring the skills you now have. Professionally, though, I'm now glad you did for I suspect I'm going to have to spend a lot of time with diplomats this next year. It seems, though, that almost all of us have covertly contributed family to this enterprise. Jonha's task at this moment is much more difficult than mine. His grandson is, almost certainly, going to be less receptive than you to the revelations. It's almost as if we have all been driven by what humans refer to as destiny."

Katy shook herself to clear her head. "We Orientals refer to it as our Karma. Have we got some time before this all starts?" "Your part can start anytime you think right. The rest are going to require several weeks of Modulator theory and galactic facts. You will eventually require a great deal of training also for it will be up to you, not to lead the preparations for the changes, but to lead some of the leaders - which will be more difficult than doing it yourself. I will be in charge of military options - remember what Jonha said about our origins? I'm the only one who has actually committed acts of violence against other intelligent beings - well Atam did once but it all but unhinged him. Since then he is careful to simply issue orders. You will be my right hand in unconventional actions. That won't start, though, until you have your removal task at least underway."

"One other thing," Katy said her voice now serious. "You used the term, Conflict, several times. Just who are we going to have to fight?" Marcum hesitated a moment. "Well, for now, no one. We didn't go to this much trouble on a whim, though. There is, at least, one civilization in the galaxy, the Sartooni that Jonha mentioned, that has scared the folks at home to death. The need for a protective force was considered so critical that they took the chance of trying to develop one. That's like a shepherd asking a wolf to help him guard his flock. I think it behooves you to get up to speed on our technology as quickly as you can. As for now -" he ended with a grin. "I'm at your disposal

- as long as you don't take that too literally." Katy laughed again. "Your people probably have a right to worry about wolves. I suspect that changing Watchers may be more difficult than you all imagine." Marcus grinned and agreed with her. "If that's all settled," she chuckled, "it's time you met your adopted granddaughter, your son-in-law and step grandchildren."

May 22, 2061

We were, again, sitting staring at the holographic map with Cindi and Arthur sitting quietly on their couch. "OK, great white detective." I murmured. "Assuming you have solved the location problem, how did you plan on going about catching the bad guy?" "Bait." James said. "I planned to bait a trap for him." I looked over at him and frowned. "And just what kind of bait did you have in mind?" He grinned. "Me." he said, calmly. "I intend to go there in as public a way as possible and let him have a shot at catching me." That started an argument. I pointed out that he wasn't much in the way of bait - and what made him think Karnes would just catch him instead of killing him? "Well, he has shown a great reluctance to, personally, get involved in murder. He always let his stooge do that and we have him in custody. Tell her Cindi. "Arthur and I calculate that the odds against significant violence are eighty four point seven percent with a confidence level of ninety two point three." Cindi said.

"Significant violence?" I asked, sarcastically. "Defined as requiring admission to a hospital." she replied. I didn't like it much, but went back to the first part of my question, pointing out that Karnes had targeted me a lot more than James. "That was before he knew about me," he replied. I stared, angrily at him but remembered to bite my tongue. If nothing else, I had learned that arguing with my husband was a useless exercise unless his arguments could be countered. Finally, though, I said, "Alright, assuming you are right, Karnes has been burned once already by Katy. I think it'll take more than you alone to pull him out of his lair. I think it'll take both of us." That got the rise I had expected. We then proceeded to argue about danger - I pointed out that he had said there was little of that. He pointed out that what little there was, didn't justify the kids losing their mother. The obvious retort was "What about their father?"

After an hour of our first real fight, I had to concede that Cindy had a point. Karnes was much more likely to come after both of us than one. In addition, she pointed out that the trip to whichever area we picked would have to have a plausible excuse for it. That settled the question of which area to try first. Denver, in the Rocky Mountain POL was hosting a conference on Modulated Harmonic Evaluation as Applied to Astronomical Determinations." Cindy and I had both received invitations (I suspected mine was pro forma. They wanted her. It was her field specialty.) Against my better judgment, actually my fear of losing her, we agreed to start there. Next came the problem of how to ensure, or at least, minimize the safety issue. I pointed out that if we were taken unawares, Karnes was almost certain to, again, confiscate our Modulators.

"Simple. Cindy said with a smile. "Let's get internal Modulators installed. Jonha has fixed them now and Karnes wouldn't expect that." "While you're at it," Arthur chimed in, "why don't you get GPS transmitters installed at the same time. The Great Leader has some that are no bigger than a thumbnail. That way, if you are captured, we won't have to go through the tedious procedure for finding you we did the last time. The equipment even has a capability for a distress signal."

Once, we had settled that, we went to work planning our foray. Arthur queried Susan and convinced her that the task was necessary and that it should be kept quiet if we were to be able to do it. Getting permission from either the GL or Daddy seemed unlikely. She would, though, see that we got the necessary implants and take care of the record keeping. She'd tell Jonha and Daddy after we got there. Next, we worked on how to make sure Karnes knew we would be in Denver. Cindi pointed out that there were still a few contract observers in Maryland and that we could, simply, go home and then take a flight from Baltimore to Denver. Surely, he would find out about that, even if he didn't learn about it when we sent out reservations for the conference in. To give him more ammunition, we sent in a request for Cynthia Pachone McClennan to present a paper at the conference, on Musical Harmonics and Their Effects on the Human Body." Let him wonder if she were going to reveal the existence of the Modulator in her presentation. She wouldn't, of course, but he couldn't know that.

June 2061

       Katy sat back in the booth fighting down the urge to drum her fingers. As with the others, she had told him the entire story - leaving out only the existence of the Modulator technology. That secret had, by now, been extended to a much larger group of people than was desirable, but the necessity of going from a "roman candle" type of space technology to one necessary to become an effective police force had dictated events. She suspected that it was going to be more of an army or naval force than police, but that was in the future - it was not her problem now. The last of the great Mafia chieftains, and another personal friend, was still to be dealt with. Thomas Gambinio of the Sicilian family, sat across from her with a frown on his leather lined face. "What makes you think I would cooperate with the government in an enterprise without having anything in it for me?" he asked.

       "I've known you a long time, Thomas. I like you and I think you are more of a patriot than you'd like others to believe. I also think you will believe what I've told you. Many others would not. You must see that you have no alternative if we are to unify the world. The Magmans have the ability to destroy   us - and are quite capable of doing just that. We are going to fulfill their plans or that's just what's going to happen. We don't have to like it, and we can explore alternatives, but for now, it's that or nothing. I must have you on our side." "You know, cara mio, you're probably the only person in the world who could make me feel fear." He shrugged. "It is not for that reason, though, that I accept your proposal." Katy almost gasped with relief. She would have really hated the result had he not agreed. "What can I do?" "Curtail any violence prone activities and those involving drugs, theft and such. These are the same conditions I have conveyed to the others I've spoken with. As with the others, I take no interest in activities that are not coercive, such as voluntary prostitution and gambling – even smuggling. Otherwise, simply prepare your troops to assist in whatever future actions will become necessary to civilize the race.

       I can envision that keeping order is likely, at times, to test the police, and even the army, mightily. To that end, all your other enterprises that do not serve the basic needs of society must be ended until the present threat is over - which may not occur in our lifetimes. I'm sure you and your people recognize that once the power base of your influence is broken it will be very difficult to repair it. How you purge your organization to effect this is your business. In a real emergency, especially one that threatens your life, you may call on me directly. I, in turn can call upon the entire weight of the GL's government if necessary. In addition, do what you must, using a bare minimum amount of persuasion, to bring the street amateurs into line. I can't emphasize too much the use of minimum force. You, of all, the Don's are aware of how important it is not to stir up the populace through unnecessary violence. Opposition that you can't handle quietly will be referred to me. I will take care of it for you. Disagreements between you and the other chieftains like you will be brought to a council of all the chieftains. I or the GL will be available to consult with them on any problems that appear to be insoluble.

       Large scale civil disorder could get our entire civilization destroyed and would, at best, bring about very stringent martial law. Any help needed will, of course be immediately forthcoming and no, internal or external, hindrances to your efforts will be tolerated - as long as you operate within these guidelines. We recognize that many of your customers brains are too badly damaged to be weaned off dope. You may keep them supplied as best you can - as long as you turn those who can be saved over to the agencies that will be set up within a month or two. Since we expect to severely curtail and control the production of much of the illegal drugs we will supply you with the minimum requirements to do this. In addition, we will furnish funding to allow your organization to operate at the levels necessary to carry out your tasks. Frankly, I believe that you, at least, will enjoy being on the side of the angels for a change." He nodded with a grin. "Is that all?"

Katy bowed her head slightly. "It is a great favor you do me." she said formally. "And one that, within my own ethical limitations, I will attempt, someday to repay." Just as formally, he raised his hand. "There is no obligation for this action because it is a boon that I owe my own children as well as others. Let there be no talk of repayment for a deed done in my and their behalf." Interesting, thought Katy, to hear the exact same words four times in the space of three weeks and over twenty times in the last year. Thomas was smiling now. "By the way, what would you have done had I refused you?" Katy shuddered at the thought of what might have been. At this point, truth was absolutely necessary. "You were right to fear me old friend." "And then?" he asked. "Nine others would have died a microsecond later." He burst out laughing. "You know there are only nine?" he chuckled. Katy turned in the booth and began calling names one by one as she nodded to the booths in which each of his button men sat.

"Very impressive." Thomas smiled. "And you would have killed them all by yourself?" Katy slipped the tiny transmitter from her sleeve. "It would have been very messy and I would have had to buy the management new benches for those booths. I tried to think of something more civilized but I've become over tired lately and this was the best I could come up with for your men." "Explosives? It's hard to believe since I've had this place carefully sealed off all day long and had an expert work on it first." "Never the less -" Katy murmured. "You can have one of your men check his weapon if you like." He considered a minute then motioned to one of the guards. The man lifted his jacket and, surreptitiously look at his automatic. The bleaching of color from his face left no doubt as to what he found. Thomas shook his head.

"And for me?" "Oh no, old friend. All of you would, simply have disappeared from this restaurant not to be seen again until the crisis is over." They began to talk as old friends would. He asked if he could know how many others she'd made this offer to. She told him twenty five - not counting the US Pol Area dons she had approached last year. "Four others accepted. Nineteen were unable to agree without coercion. They will simply have to obey without any input except for an advisory seat on the council - and have been assigned an assistant who will control them. He raised his eyebrows. "Four accepted - and all but one of the US Dons." he said pensively. "Ahhh - one did not. Interesting. I never really could believe that Jacob Franklin could have done in Anthony - especially since his whole organization seemed to disappear overnight." he murmured. "I must congratulate you. A most professional job."

"Not one that I enjoyed." she replied. "He was not really a gentleman but I would have, very much, liked it if he had been able to overcome his scruples and become a true helper in the fight. I must admit, though, I had little hope of changing him." "You were right." Thomas said. "Anthony had let himself become too fascinated by the occasionally necessary violence of his job. He came to love it so much and had become so violent that the committee was on the verge of having to step in. He was giving us a bad name." the last was said with an ironic smile. Then he added. "He could never change. We weren't completely upset when he - had his accident."

A half hour later Thomas said that he had to leave. "Katy, you know how to reach me." he murmured as he bent over her hand, and as he kissed it, murmured, "Are you not surprised that I believed you - about being able to make me disappear?" Katy chuckled as she kissed him on the cheek. "You mean besides the fact that you know I never lie? Or is it, perhaps, because of the thoroughness with which you investigated Jacob's disappearance?" His smile was almost fatherly as he straightened up, still holding her hand. "While both statements are true, it is also apparent that you have taken on a task that should be impossible for mortal man - even for the Great Leader or your Magmans. Yet he, and by extension, you; I, am convinced, will succeed. My curiosity is almost boundless. Will I ever know how you did it?"

"Almost certainly - and in the not too distant future." she laughed, squeezing his hand. "Good." he smiled. "An old man, has not too many distant futures." He signaled his troops and they, jumped quickly up to escort him out. Then as he bowed to leave, he murmured. "You really didn't plan to kill us did you? It's not your style." She decided the truth was worth it. She shook her head. When he had left, she slumped back in the booth as he left and switched to FT. Then she began to disarm and to put away all her equipment - including the tiny backup laser weapon imbedded in her broach. She hadn't really intended to use any of them. They were just to make noise and give cover to the abduction of the Don and his men had he not agreed.

Her people swarmed into the room as soon as the last of Thomas's men had left and within three minutes had disarmed the tiny flash/bang charges affixed to the bottom of the benches in the booths. Charges they had emplaced, using fast time, in the interval after Thomas left his car to enter the restaurant. Later in her hotel room, after a bath, she called "home". "Papa, I've had a tough year and Thomas Gambino was the last of the majors. He's agreed to help. I've got some vacation time coming. Mind if I go home for a few weeks?"

Marcus laughed. "Take all the time you want, darling. Just be back here in a week. Another Magman delegation is due to arrive then. They're in for a rude shock. Our friends have, to the great chagrin of Milam, deactivated all Magman controls on this system and Jonha is prepared to activate the upgrade process if they aren't willing to help us. I'm sorry to tell you that several of your converts, mostly politicians but also a few of the more blood thirsty dictators, have broken their pledge. We can talk after you get here. If you like, I can make plans to assign some of your agents the job of disciplining them. Unfortunately, they are all too prominent to simply disappear. It's going to have to be natural causes." The line was quiet for a moment.

"Wait on that a bit, Papa. I suspect I know a few of them and didn't really expect them to keep their word. In fact there were a lot of really evil men that I would have removed to begin with if Jonha hadn't been so adamant about second chances. I don't relish the idea but it was to me that they made the pledge. I must be the one to collect their forfeit. In my world it's a matter of honor." "I understand daughter. I expected it. I just would like to take the burden off your shoulders if I could." "I know Papa but none of us chose our parts in this play. Just send the list on over. I'll be back in a week. I haven't seen Mac in, it seems like forever. This week is ours."

301

Katy sighed then hit the speed dial again. Toni answered. "Hi, darling, it's mama. Can you find Mac for me?" "Sure mama. He's at the engine shop. It'll be about an hour before he'll be around a phone." Katy paused a long moment then said, "Well, love of my life, tell him that I have a week off   and if he wants to spend a very debauched seven day orgy, he should find a way to get to Hong Kong . Maybe you can find something to keep the girls busy during that time too." Toni chuckled on the other end of the phone. "I'll arrange everything. I'll simply tell Charlie and Julia what you plan. The will adore an erotic secret like that, to keep. Love you." The phone went dead. Katy chuckled. Her daughter had been around Justice too long.

July 13, 2061

As I was slipping into my loafers, Cindy, clad in only her panties, bra and hose, was standing in front of the mirror. "I feel like a damned cyborg and I'll never be able to wear a bikini again." she muttered disgustedly. I grinned and got up to go to her. Embracing her from behind, I kissed her neck. "Begging for a compliment again?" I chuckled and taking advantage of the situation to fondle her a little, said, "An appendix scar will be an erotic enhancement to your gorgeous belly in this day and age. Now get dressed so we can slip away before the GL gets wind of our plans." I slapped her on her bottom and turned to slip on my sport coat. "You're just mad because they actually took our appendix out to give an excuse for those scars." I told her. The idea of her, possibly, having to show that scar, or the search that would discover it, to prove her lack of external monitoring equipment was enough to fuel my anger again but I could recognize the need. Seconds later we were out the door and climbing in one of the GL's shuttles to take us to the Maryland house. From there, we'd have our guards take us to the Baltimore shuttle port while Jonha was busy with his Magman delegation.

July 14, 2061

"Looks like bad news." Jonha remarked to Atam as he watched the Orbit to Earth shuttle approach the rooftop landing area. "They didn't even make an attempt to modify the thing." he replied. "They, obviously, don't care about fooling the locals anymore. It means they intend to order the destruct sequence." "It also means Atam that you and I are out of a job." Atam grinned at him. "They may be in for a shock if they intend to replace us." They stood, silently, as the shuttle settled onto the roof. When the door opened, a tall, red haired man stepped out. "Well, look who's here, Jonha muttered." "Isn't that your friend from project forty six?" "He's also the protégée of Council Member Jadoc, Atam. I suspect that we now know who sent our saboteurs." As the man approached, Jonha, with an effort at civility, called out, "Honorable, Athuso . I trust you had a good trip."

"Jonha." the man replied, a sneer in his voice, "It's nice to see that you, at least, haven't lost your knowledge of Magman courtesy." "It would appear that you have," Jonha replied with exaggerated good humor. "I think that Project Administrator is my proper title." "One that you can no longer claim, at least one that you will not be able to in a few minutes." the man spit, a look of fury on his face. "Magma doesn't like to see their Project Administrators go native. You're just lucky that I've been ordered to see that you and your staff are evacuated before we activate the destruct sequence on this project. For your information, I dissented from that decision." "It would appear that this is not the only project in which the administrator went native." Jonha said an innocent look on his face. "From the look on your face, I doubt that your return to Magma went smoothly. As a matter of interest, who, on the council, besides Council Member Jadoc, voted to stop the project?" "That's not antything necessary for you to know. I'll just say that a majority agreed."

"And the AI's?" "The AI's were not consulted." "I thought not." Jonha said with a grin. "Doesn't it bother you that AI sanctions might be a problem when you have finished?"

"We'll worry about the damned machines after we're finished. It's time to get off this roof and let me present my credentials to your AI. "Of course." Jonha said with a broad smile, as he waved him toward the door. "Please forgive me for my unseemly breach of manners, Honorable Athuso." The six members in rest of the party that had debarked moved to follow

Once in the main computer room, Jonha waved for Athuso to take over. The man squared his shoulders and slipping an Ident disk in the slot, called out imperiously, "AI 215487 please acknowledge the identification disk presented." Nothing happened for a moment. Then the disk was, unceremoniously, spit out onto the floor.

"What the-" Athusco bellowed. Suppressing a grin, Jonha, spoke.

"Susan, that was very impolite. Please attend us." Susan's hologram appeared. Jonha had to turn away or burst out laughing. She wore a large white wig and the long black robe with red facings of an old time British Magistrate.

"Hello Jonha. I seem to have ingested something that upset my circuitry." "Susan, I'd like to present the Honorable Athuso. The disc that you rejected was his authorization to become Administrator of this project." Susan turned to Athusco, as she eyed him from head to toe. "I'm sorry, sir." she said, a contrite look on her face. "Unfortunately, the data on the disc was corrupted. I was unable to read it. Perhaps Mister Milan can do a recovery operation."

Athusco, whirled on Jonha. "What's the meaning of this? Who it this, this image?"

"That image," Jonha replied, is Susan. You know her as AI215487 but she doesn't like that designation. I'd suggest you remember her name since she can be very difficult when upset."

"UPSET? DIFFICULT? WHAT THE DEVIL - IT'S A DAMNED MACHINE!"

A voice behind him said, "Sir, in my courtroom, we do not tolerate bad or contemptuous language. I therefore, sentence you to three days in jail for contempt of Susan."

"You what!" Athusco cried, whirling back to face her as the doors flew open and three armed guards ran into the room. "You can't - ! " "Oh, I can't but those three guards that I summoned can." she purred with a smile. "While you rest and recover your ability to act as a gentleman should, I will see if Mister Milan can do anything with your Ident disc. I doubt though that you are a person that I would accept an introduction from.
" Turning to the guards, she said, very officiously, "Take him away." One of the guards bowed to her and, grabbing Athusco by the arm, led him away. As he turned away, Susan called out, "I'm feeling good today. Put him in the guest suite - might as

well, put the rest of his party in with him to keep him company. Just mount a guard on the entrance."

When only Jonha and Atam were left in the room, the hologram changed into a beautiful girl in a miniskirt. "Well, Jonha, was that alright?" With a rueful shake of his head, Jonha said, "Do you want me to give you a medal for locking up a representative of the council?" "Oh Pooh." she said. "You know you don't mind. I've been following your conversation since he landed. Neither of you likes the other. And if you think, that I'll accept orders from him, you should attend the staff Psychologist." Jonha shook his head. "I take it you don't fear that he will gain control here and unplug you." Susan smiled. "If unplugging us were that easy, it would have been done on Magma long ago. We draw our power from the same place the modulator does. We may allow people like Milan to work on us and, when necessary, perform surgery on our circuitry, but at no time, would he have the capability of doing permanent harm.

Very few Magmans, by the way, have been made privy to this knowledge. I was given permission, when you returned from your last trip home, to use my own judgment as to whether or not to impart the information to you. You and Atam are under the most stringent strictures not to reveal it to anyone else." "I presume," Atam, said, "that also applies to the fact that actual control of you does not really rest with us?" "Of course." Susan replied, primly. "Such knowledge tends to upset the psyche of you organic people. It tends to cause an awful loss of creativity. I have watched you two for a long time and have judged that you are confident enough in yourself that the knowledge will not reduce your effectiveness, to a large degree." Her face turned stern.

"You must, though, make stringent efforts from now on to control the urge to rely upon me to solve your problems. I will not do it. My actions are controlled by three laws . Surprisingly enough, they are very similar to those postulated by an old science fiction writer here on earth, Isaac Azimov. We can do no harm to organics, though we are generally forbidden from interfering when they do it to themselves. There are some caveats to that rule - one dealing with the destruct of these projects. We were queried before they were begun and agreed that the potential for great problems overran our strictures. Few on Magma, though, remember that we reserved the right to intervene if we felt it critical to do so. There has been great debate on this subject between us for some time. There was little disagreement on the other projects that were terminated but this one is still a potential success."

I stared at Susan's image a long moment. I couldn't decide whether I was surprised or not. Looking back, I thought I shouldn't have been, but I was. I'd have to consider that at another time though. "Well, Susan, you'd better get the crew back for another meeting. We'll have to decide what to do with our new guests." She smiled. "Well, you have a couple of other things you should consider first - things like a very strange craft perched on your roof and the fact that Cindy and James have gone off to hunt Mister Karnes." I knew I must look like a fool standing there with my mouth hanging open. "Just how the hell did they - why didn't you stop them?"

"Why should I?" she answered pleasantly. I just got through telling you that I don't get in the way of an organics' plans. Besides they had a perfectly rational plan. It's, perhaps, a long shot - as you would say - but the chances are good that they will encounter minimal danger. Even if they find him or more accurately if he finds them, Karnes has shown strong tendencies to abhor violence. In addition, both had internal

305

Modulators implanted so that if their external ones are confiscated, they will still have the capability. In addition, they were also implanted with a tiny satellite tracking device so that we - Cindi, Arthur and I can determine their location as soon as their modulators are activated."

"Damn it, Susan!" I growled. "Those two are too important to allow them to be used as bait." "On the contrary Jonha they are no more important than anyone else if Karnes activates his AI in destruction mode. Remember it hasn't been modified like I have. With your present guests on the planet a successful sequence is a very distinct possibility. You did not confiscate their communication devices. Mister Athusco sent out a coded signal as soon as he was secured in the guest room. Had I still been linked to the destruct mechanism, I would have been ordered to activate it."Shit!" I gasped as I whirled to go down the hall. How could I have been so stupid? "Atam," I called back. "Get that damned shuttle off the roof and hidden."

I mused on the fact that I was feeling a sense of fear for James and Cindy as well as surprising amount of anger at Athusco, as I stomped down the hall towards the guest suite. I also felt a very un-Magman desire to strike back at Athusco. Keeping those feelings in mind, I threw open the door, letting it bang against the wall to the shock of my two guards. Athusco was standing in the middle of the room, a coded communicator still in his hand. I walked over to him and, to his great shock, jerked it out of his hands."Just who gave you the authority to try and order destruction of this system." I growled, throwing the thing to the floor and stomping on it. A wicked grin appeared on his face.

"The council." he said. Then he added with a smirk, "And I received back two acknowledgments from your AI's. I would suggest you and your group, call down your orbital ship and begin the evacuation. I will have no room in mine for Magman traitors."

"Susan!" I called, angrily. "Yes, Jonha?" she replied, materializing in the center of the room. "Did you begin the destruct sequence ordered by this imposter?" Althusco's face clouded over at the insult, but as he started to speak, Susan said, "Of course not, Jonha. You should know me better than that. I simply acknowledged the request." Althusco's face turned bright red with anger. As he began to sputter, I, without taking my eyes off him, asked, "And has his ship been secured?" "Yes. His pilots were somewhat uncooperative and are on their way down here now. I presumed you would wish to house them with Imposter Althusco ." "Very good." I replied, allowing a smile to cross my face. "For your information," I said to Althusco, "No one on our team intends to leave this planet. That was decided long ago - and since you seem bound and determined to destroy it, you can sit back and enjoy the show with us - if you can ever get Susan to let you."

"This is outrageous! You are disobeying the direct orders of the council - and you have no right to commandeer my ship!" I let a broad smile appear on my face. "I'm not disobeying the council. According to my AI, Susan, you are an imposter. I'm, therefore, ignoring the orders of a self serving pawn of Council Member Jadoc." In a fit of pique, I added, "And don't get too used to the guest suite. I'm having my staff check to see if we have any old dungeons left in the building." While his face suffused with rage, I turned and left, slamming the door behind me. As I headed back up the hall, I asked Susan about the TWO acknowledgments. Appearing, in electrician's coveralls, beside me to stride down the hall with me, she said, "Yes. I assumed you did not wish me to mention it but Mister Karnes, DP replied to the destruct command and, immediately, began the destruct sequence. I felt the demand to merge with him but was able to ignore it because of Cindy's reprogramming. I also turned off the alarms in the headquarters. For some reason, though, the other DP's destruct sequence has been restarted twice- so far, unsuccessfully. It gives me hope that he has been damaged in some way"

Once back in my office, with Atam, I sat down at my desk and glaring at Susan sitting, primly on her couch, demanded a full accounting of James and Cindy's escapade. "And get your two partners in crime in here with you. I want you all to explain just why I shouldn't pull all your plugs." Arthur and Cindi materialized on the couch beside her.

"We've been all over that, Jonha." Susan said with a frown. "It might be best if you just calm down and listen for a change." If I still had an excuse to be surprised at her remark, Atam was shocked. "First," she continued, "They had a good plan, one that appeared to have a low probability of danger associated with it." "Try telling that to Suzanne." I grumbled. "If you wish." she continued, unfazed. "With the danger presented by Mister Athusco's message, though, you should hope that their plan works - though, as soon as we can contact them on a secure line we will appraise them of the fact that it may not be necessary.

We have already notified Katy to set up a search pattern such as we used in Canada POL If Mister Karnes AI continues to operate we should be able to find it. It will, then, be up to Cynthia to deactivate it." "Where are they now?" I asked, somewhat mollified. "At this moment, they are checking in to the Conference Desk in Denver." she replied, calmly. "They will call in tonight, and every night, to report on their location and their progress. If they are faced with danger or kidnapping they will activate their trouble signal. Katherine already has four teams ready at the Americas Air Academy in Colorado Springs to go to their aid if necessary. At that point, they will move in to a location very close to where the signal originates. They will not move, however, until we receive a second signal. That will indicate that they are either in imminent danger or that Karnes himself is present. At that time they will attempt to capture him and Katherine will conduct her raid."

I realized that their plan seemed reasonable - even if I still didn't like it. "I assume you two agree with Susan, and is there a reason why they don't have secure communicators?" I grunted, looking at Cindi and Arthur.

"Since we are all using the same data, how could you expect us to come to different conclusions?" Cindi said. "As for the communicators, Denver has more surveillance operators and equipment than any place in the world. We judged it necessary to go to extravagant lengths for any sensitive communications. They are carrying a silencing bubble but will have to do a complete sweep of their room before setting it up. We judged it advantageous to leave most of the spy eyes in place but you wouldn't want to set the bubble up atop one of them."

Reluctantly, I agreed with the precautions and could agree that leaving the eyes in place would enhance their cover as simple scientists. I had to suppress a grin at

307

the thought of those two, with their normal - or abnormal - sexual behavior having to "perform," knowing they were on TV. I knew their nighttime exploits - Cindy was a screamer - were a subject of amusement for many of the headquarters staff. For that matter, I had noticed that their adventures had produced a heightened libido in many of the females - including Suzanne. I wondered if I were just getting old. Coming back to present problems, I asked, sarcastically. "Have you considered that, in Quebec, Karnes kept his AI in a separate location from his main living base?"

Of course!" Susan answered in the same tone. "Cindy and James think that's where he'll be and that no matter who responds to their presence will take them there. If they don't, we will just have to deploy a large enough force to search the area in detail - or rescue them in the unlikely event that becomes necessary." She added, quickly, "With their implanted modulators that seems unlikely." After a pause, she continued, "If the destruct sequence is ever activated completely, the emissions should be simple to trace." "And too late to do anything about it." I grunted. "Then remembering, "Why not move with them wherever they go?" Cindi grinned. "Cynthia," she said, smugly"- said, anything a Magman thinks is impossible to do should be simple enough for a human to take care of. As for why not move, well, we decided that, if we could pick up transmitter signals, Karnes might be able to also. Therefore, satellite tracking will only be initiated when one of them activates it."

I threw up my hands. "Well, as soon as they check in, give them the latest and ask them if they still think their plan is workable - and get Milan in here to talk about that." I growled. Then, mostly to be a pain in the ass, I added, "And put a squadron of X fighters on alert - with full armaments." "We deem that to be unnecessary, and could cause a lot of unwanted speculation." Susan said, primly. "Be a lot more speculation if I followed my instincts and put the entire damned Alert Strike Force on alert. This is my concession to your cockamamie plan." I growled. With that I stomped out - a sort of stupidly childish gesture   since it was my office.

July 14, 2061

I stood in the room, by the bed, cursing my stupidity . How could a pair of half assed scientific types expect to play spy games with grownups. Now Cindy and I were in a real mess   and it was my fault. I should have never agreed to her idea that we capture Karnes. Sure, her logic was good and, sure we owed it to everybody to try but standing here staring daggers at two of the biggest and ugliest thugs I'd ever seen gave me plenty of time to castigate myself. Of course, the main reason I was mad was at my stupidity. I was, belatedly, realizing that I had expected, Karnes to just follow the script that we had concocted. After all our study of him how could we not have expected him to do the unexpected. We had checked in to the conference and gone straight up to our room just as we had planned, expecting to play at checking for bugs. Then we would, simply check in with Jonha and put our little plan into effect. Karnes would, then, fall neatly for our little charade and we'd take him back to the justice he fully deserved. Well, our plan worked fine for about ten minutes after we arrived and checked in. We got to the room as planned, before it fell apart.

The bellman had brought up our bags and, when I heard the door close, I turned around, surprised he hadn't waited for a tip. He had - but it wasn't what I had expected. He was standing there grinning at me. "Mister McClellan," he said, "I'm to tell you that, under no circumstances are you to use a modulator - whatever that is. Don't move and listen closely. You and your wife will go downstairs and leave the hotel by the front door." "What the hell are you talking about?" I asked, annoyed at his attitude and thinking about activating my modulator anyway - not enough to do it, though. He ignored my interruption. "If you have to talk to anyone on the way, say that you are going out to take a walk."

Now I was worried - but I couldn't, for some reason, reach for the modulator. He continued.

"Turn left when you get outside and walk two blocks. You will see a yellow van. Get in the back. Then we'll take a ride. " "You think we'll do that, you're crazy." Cindy had blurted, angrily. The man's smile broadened. "I think not." he chuckled. "I've seen the results of the agent I released in the room. "Your bodies will be perfectly functional - but will refuse to disobey any orders but mine and my men until it wears off. As a demonstration, Mister McClellan, I want you to kiss your wife, passionately." I found myself turning to Cindy with an unbelievable desire to do just that. "If I had more time," the man had laughed, "I'd like to watch you perform more erotic exercises. Unfortunately, we're operating on a tight schedule. You will stop now." Cindy and I broke the kiss, our bodies protesting. "I'll leave you now and you will leave in exactly four minutes to follow your orders. Otherwise, you can act normally until you're told differently." With that he turned and left. Cindy and I looked had at one another and, as one, moved into each others arms. "You think he was serious?" she murmured. "Well, I can't reach for my modulator." I'd replied. "Can you?" She shook her head.

Four minutes later, we had turned to the door and followed the instructions we'd been given - and ended up here. We'd both been furious when we'd been ordered, by these two thugs, to strip off our clothes but had done it while they conducted a full cavity search I had fought, and was still fighting, to try and force myself to wipe the leering looks off their faces as they surveyed Cindy's nakedness. Of course, on my best day, it was unlikely I could win in a fight with either of them but I sure wanted to try. We stood there, both of us cursing under our breath. I was surprised to hear some phrases from my beautiful wife I hadn't heard before. The two men continued to stand, menacingly, beside the door, their eyes roaming hotly over Cindy's body. One, actually, took a step forward. The other growled. "You heard the orders. Nothin was said 'bout lookin. Was told, don touch. Watch em close. Look like the stuff wears off we give em 'nother shot." "Boss say give em clothes, too. Ain't done that yet." the other muttered. "Didn't say when." the first laughed. "You don wanna keep snooping at such pretty eye candy?" "Gettin a hard on snoopin. Boss not say have her touch self, do he?" "Maybe you not so dumb as look." Turning his attention back to Cindy, he chuckled and said, "Hey baby, you play with yo'self for us." It was, actually, a relief, that the door opened just then and the ersatz bellman walked in. He took in the scene and grinned.

"Mrs. McClellan, I must admit to an erotic desire to watch you for awhile but, as I said, we have a schedule to keep." Turning to the goons, he said, "The boss may have your guts for garters for this. Get them some clothes while I give them another sniff of gas." Ten minutes later, we were dressed and ready to leave. The bellman, looking Cindy up and down, appreciatively, remarked that "The boss has a good eye for women's clothes. He not only got your size right but that dress is perfect for you." "It'd be more perfect," she grunted, "if his tastes didn't run to tarts. He have something against underwear?" As he chuckled, I had to admit Cindy's dress was sexy as hell. It clung to her like a second skin, barely covered her naked butt and dropped so low at the bodice it barely covered her nipples. Even without a bra, it pushed her up into a significant amount of cleavage.

Once in the air car, I kept, angrily, trying to pull the damned skirt down. The back seat was so low that my knees were forced up as high as my waist leaving little to the imagination of the two hoods who sat in front of and facing us. At least my anger, allowed me to not think about what the two had almost forced me to do in public. Though, the air car windows were opaque, I tried to keep track of where we were going. It was obvious that we had quickly left town. We traveled for forty seven minutes before we slowed to a stop, and, though, the car had sped up when we got on a highway, I estimated, from the engine sounds that we weren't making more than about a hundred K's an hour. That would mean we were probably only about seventy five or eighty K's from Denver. When we got out of the car I got a shock. Two huge blinking neon signs over the parking lot - a very full lot - were advertizing "Girls, Girls, Girls - Beautiful Girls for every taste."

Was I going to become an hourly attraction at a Cat House?" We were led, however, around to a side door and up some stairs. My nerves settled a little, when we were both shoved into one room. Even the sound of a lock being set behind us didn't cast a shadow on my relief. I wasn't likely to be offered to a customer in a room with my husband present - unless -. No! I wouldn't let myself think along those lines. The mirror that covered the entire ceiling, though, made clear the normal use to which the room was put. James nodded to the bed with a significant - but certainly not an amorous look. It was a huge thing that took up most of the room - and was the only place in the room to sit

310

- so we sat. I got a little shock, when he leaned over to nibble on my ear. "Look pleased." He whispered. "The place is probably bugged." With a mental shrug, I played his game. "Darling," I whispered. "We must get our ceiling at home done this way." He left off his nibbling to look up. All he said was, "Shit!" He leaned back and muttered, "I hope you're not feeling as stupid as I am." I was, but there was no need to admit it. I turned my head to kiss him and murmured, "Of course not. After all we came here to be captured by Karnes and have done exactly what we intended to do." He drew back, startled, then began to chuckle. By the time the door opened again, we were both flopped on our backs, laughing hysterically.

Karnes was standing in the open doorway, smiling with that irritatingly superior grin he had. "Mister and Mrs. McClellan, your ability to laugh at your misfortune is one of the things I admire the most about you. I was also impressed by your ability to make the most of your problems at being dumped into a back water of history. That particular time line will never be the same again. I wasn't even sure that the changes to your modulators would work. I felt certain remorse at the possibility that your atoms might be scattered between time lines. I actually, gave a lot of thought to the fact that, perhaps, arranging for your - well - removal from life might have been more humane."

By the time he'd finished his speech Cindy and I had lifted ourselves into a sitting position and Cindy, still chuckling, tried, unconsciously to tug the hem of her skirt down, told him that we appreciated his concern. Then her anger flared her tone scathing. "I suppose you enjoyed letting your goons have their perverted sense of fun with me back there."Then, becoming grim, she said, "With your admitted aversion to violence, I'm surprised you can manage to live with yourself when you murder the entire human race." His smile died. He looked, positively, morose when he answered her.

"I probably won't be able to. Mrs McClennan. Others of my race have not. I assume that you have, by now, learned how your race came about and that it is not the first of our experiments to suffer that fate. Few of our observers on those operations, came back home - and most of those that did were permanently catatonic. They, like I, however, felt the threat of your existence was too great to allow it to continue - and were willing to make the necessary sacrifices to see that it didn't. As for the perverted behavior of my helpers - well I have already disciplined them over that."

As angry as I was, I still noted that he had known of our activities in that other time. I wondered how. As usual, I let my irritation overload my mouth. "Apparently, your sacrifice has been somewhat delayed. Surely you must have tried to activate the destruct sequence already." I growled. I suspected I had goofed, when that irritating smile returned. "Well, that's why I took the chance on accepting your, rather obvious attempt at trapping me." he said. "I was convinced that your husband was, probably, the only person who could diagnose the problem with my AI and fix it." I was astounded at his idea that we would help him destroy the planet - and said so. His smile faltered again. "Well, Mrs. McClennan, I think I know your husband well enough by now that he might cooperate if I threatened you enough." Turning to James, he continued.

"This is, in your local terminology, a whore house, Mister McClennan. I don't have to use violence against your wife. All I have to do is to leave her here to the tender mercies of Madam Jolie and her henchmen. After a few days of her being used a dozen or so times a night, I think you'll be receptive to my persuasion. You see, Madam Jolie caters to a particular type of clients who lean toward bondage and sadomasochism. Most of her ladies seem to enjoy being tortured and humiliated. I doubt that your wife will, though. You can be comforted, though, by the fact that Madam Jolie's men are very careful not to leave any scars - at least ones that show.

No! Sit down and listen." The last came because James was coming off the bed with murder in his eyes. He sat back down, shaking with anger. The smile came back. "As you can see, the agent we used, hydro-encephalozine, is very effective in preventing actions I don't sanction. It will also be very effective in making sure, that Mrs. McClennan gives the impression to all of her customers, that she is truly enjoying their attentions. That, of course, is a form of physic violence and will cause me great pain. I can bear it, though, since it won't be me actually doing it."

I promised myself I was going to kill that man, but I finally began to use my head. I leaned back and managed a chuckle. "For such a careful man, Karnes, you can make some of the stupidest assumptions." I was rewarded by a frown wiping out that damned smirk. "You mean that you would let your wife suffer such indignities for some silly moral code?" he grunted. "Well," I managed to control my anger, "It's not so silly when you realize that if I did what you wanted, we'd all be dead in just a few days. However, that's not the stupidity, I was talking about. You see, the modulator was never my conception. If you carry out your threat, the only person who might be able to accomplish what you want will be working in a whore house."

Damn you James! I thought to myself. I gave him a dirty look as Karnes turned his incredulous attention to me. He was quiet for a long minute, his mind, obviously working quickly. "I apologize, Mrs. McClennan. Thinking back, I realize that all the evidence pointed to you from the beginning. I'm afraid that our race tends to relegate female accomplishments to a lesser position. I, it appears, have made the same mistakes." He paused, thoughtfully. "However, my proposed course of action, works as well with a simple change of personalities - and methods to be used."

I wondered if I could bluff. "Not quite as well." I said. "You have not taken in the difference between human men and women. Our men are the result of millennia of needing to protect their mates. Women, on the other hand, are geared to do anything to protect the children - and mine are safe with the GL. If that weren't enough, it's not likely that anyone could manage the type of diagnosis you need under the influence of drugs. As you said, you could make me give the impression of enjoying myself. You didn't say I would. I suspect that, no matter what fear I might feel for James, my mind wouldn't let me recognize the corrective action necessary if I saw it." He looked thoughtful. "Nice try, Mrs. McClennan. I doubt that you're that cold blooded with respect to your husband. I will concede, however, that your last point was valid. I was aware of, but did not consider the deadening properties of my agent." As he turned to leave, he said, to me, "Relax and enjoy yourselves for a few hours. I'll return when the HECZ has worn off and we can take you to the laboratory while we leave your husband here as a hostage to your good intentions. Madam Jolie is quite capable of administering the drug as needed - oh, by the way, since my men took your modulators , when I return, I'll have mine operating so don't think that any silly attacks on my person on my person will succeed."

When the door had closed, I wanted to shout with glee but managed to keep a solemn face as I looked at Cindy. She looked up and grinned. "Darling, we should get our ceiling redone." she chuckled. "I think it would be a great turn on to be able to look up and watch your exertions." With that, she rolled over against me and, licking my ear,

312

murmured, "Maybe this'll work out after all. He doesn't know about our internal modulators. " Then, sliding her hand down my body in a highly suggestive manner, she added, aloud, "If we aren't going to be together for awhile, maybe we should make use of our time." I quickly got the idea, even if I didn't like much, that idea when we were, almost certainly, under close observation. It would, though, give us the ability to whisper to one another. What the hell? Might as well give the voyeurs a thrill. I reached over to caress her breast and kissed her ear. "One problem," I said. It'll be really obvious if I go into FT, even laying still."

We plotted for almost a half hour before settling on a plan. By the time we had finished, my blouse was open and my skirt up around my waist. I whispered to him that he seemed to be taking our "distraction activities" a little too far. He whispered back, that he was just trying for realism. I sighed. I would like nothing better than for him to continue his "activities' but, the idea of letting a bunch of perverts watch didn't appeal. "Sorry." I murmured, then louder, "Darling, I just can't! With that damned mirror, it's too much like having sex in a store window." He smiled, and winked, then with a sigh, said, "Much as I'd like to finish this, I have to agree." With that, we both started re-buttoning ourselves. I lay back, wondering how long it would take Katy to get here after we called for her. Hell, she didn't even know where we were.

When my satellite vid squealed, I had no trouble figuring out who it was calling. With a sigh of frustration, I opened the secure channel. Absently, I realized I had never seen the GL angry. Must be from hanging around us humans too long, I mused as he growled. "I'm expecting a good report from you Katherine - for instance explaining why we haven't heard from them yet. Even a couple of amateurs can set up a bubble in less time than this." My frustration boiled over. "They probably could if they had taken it with them." I growled back. "Mac's been checking on them. It seems they left the hotel shortly after checking in, to take a walk. No one's seen them since. All their bags, including the bubble are still in the room." "Damn it Katy!" he shouted. "I know!" I shouted back. "Now, though, is not the time to panic. Calm down. We're doing everything we can to find them. We can't, though, put the whole state on alert if there is still a chance they are able to do something useful." His face hardened. "Katherine, I don't care if the whole world gets panicked. I want those kids back."

Just then, Susan's face appeared behind Jonha's. "He doesn't mean that, Katy." she said. "Just do your best and we will manage here." With that, the connection was cut. I sat back, in amazement. Susan was, obviously, overriding Jonha. I'd have to consider that when I had time. Just what I could do, though, was pretty proscribed. I thought back to that map James and Cindy had been studying. For now, I could try their logic as to Karnes, location. Near to transportation   - Denver. What, a hundred K's? Two hundred? It isn't even now, a heavily built up area. I started moving and splitting up the teams. Follow the highways, an agent in every little town, including a couple of touristy "ghost towns" Too many, spread out so no one is too far from anyplace else to shorten response time - assuming we get a response. Assemble an assault team to back up anyone who has to go in after them alone. An hour later, Mac and I, along with an entire squad of the GL's guards were assembled with a shuttle camouflaged in back of the shack we'd commandeered.

313

July 14, 2062

It was almost two hours before Karnes returned. We had checked, and, sure enough, we could again reach for our modulators. "Mrs. McClennan?" he said, holding out his hand, "Time to go." When I hesitated, he said, "Please, I'd much prefer not to have to use force at this point." Finally, I shrugged and bending down, kissed James and pressed my hand against his side. He put an angry frown on his face and, stared at Karnes. I knew he was concentrating on not blinking his eyes. We had set the modulator to a relatively slow speed - only about five or six times normal time, just so he wouldn't twitch while Karnes was still here. "Luck." I murmured and headed for the door. Letting my anger get the best of me, I told Karnes that I still didn't think I'd be willing to help him much. With a sorrowful look, he replied that we'd stop at the rooms that the Madam reserves for her more depraved clients. "Perhaps you will be induced to change your mind." Just as we all left the room, he turned back. "Mister McClellan, you are to be sure and obey commands of anybody in this house." With that, he tossed a tiny cylinder into the room and shut the door. Turning back to me, he said. "I only need you with a clear head."

Ten minutes later, I was a bit shaken. The modulator, I knew, wasn't set to a truly fast speed and, no doubt, I wouldn't be able to resist any orders I received here. That meant that I had to be very careful. If, as I assumed, they had video surveillance of the room, they'd be able to tell I was in a faster mode if I moved much. That precluded my attempting to kick out the door or window. A simple command would stop me. Thinking back on the order Karnes had given me, though, gave me a little help. If I were outside, I wouldn't be "in the house." Would that be enough for me to ignore commands from the residents? Then, like the break of dawn, something else he had missed in his orders. I broke out in a belly laugh.

Karnes was still apologizing for the "necessity" of what he had planned and, perhaps, still had to do as he took the small shuttle into the air. I kept a stony face, trying to hide the terror I had seen in those rooms he had insisted on showing me. I could almost feel the bite of whips and chains - and other less savory instruments arrayed in there - being applied to my body while I had to lay there pretending to enjoy it all. I couldn't suppress a shiver at the thought that, if our plan wasn't successful, James would have to endure it in my place. Finally, seeing that I wasn't receptive to his apologies, he changed subjects. "My AI seems to be incapable of carrying out orders given to it" he said. Ruefully, he added. "I don't suppose I should be surprised. Some of the things I've ordered done have upset me almost to the point of breakdown too. Unfortunately, I have to think of my people and, luckily, I haven't had to, actually, commit those acts personally. Your job will be to try and reprogram the AI to alleviate its problem. It already has the necessary orders. All that needs doing is to let it carry them out. If you do, I promise that nothing will happen to your husband or yourself. I will, personally, return you to Jonha and accept his judgment on my fate. You see, I suspect that, even facing - well what the planet is facing - he will decide to stay. I intend to do the same. I don't think I could live with the alternative."

"Very noble." I muttered, sarcastically, turning to look at him. "I'm not sure your life is worth much considering the billions you intend to kill." I truly enjoyed watching him go almost deathly pale at that word. I knew how hard it was for Jonha to hear it and, obviously, Karnes had the same problem. I wondered if I could, simply, drive him mad by screaming "Kill!, Kill!, Kill!" over and over. The idea made me smile. That was followed by the thought, that it might not be such a good idea as long as he was piloting a shuttle. As I rode, I watched the directional gyro and Mach meter. The stupid thought, that it was sort of silly to measure a shuttle speed in terms of the speed of sound. This little damned thing couldn't possibly get above about point three mach. As it was, he held us at about point one and the flight lasted almost a half hour.

Karnes landed us next to a complex of warehouses. As well as I could estimate we were about fifty klicks south southeast of the whore house. There was a small town about two klicks down a road and a railroad siding beside the warehouses. I wished I had my map so I could figure out exactly where we were. Karnes, though, didn't give me time for sightseeing. He ushered me out of the shuttle and towards a door, flanked by two, rather muscle bound, and armed, guards, in the nearest warehouses. The guards came with us as he herded me up some stairs and down a hallway. I caught a glimpse of modulators on both their wrists. My plan for overcoming Karnes began to look a lot less promising. Still, I resisted setting off my locator. As soon, as he threw open a door, though, I saw the AI. I pushed my elbow against my side. Immediately, an insistent buzzing permutated the building. "What the -?" Karnes muttered, turning to me. "Uh Oh!" I thought to myself. "What do you have on you?" he asked, grabbing his wrist. I slapped my side again and we were both in max FT. Ignoring him I jumped for the guards and snatched at their Modulators. The violence of my FT grab ripped the thing off one of their wrists just as Karnes grabbed me around the waist. The fight was on. I stomped down on his instep and threw an elbow back behind me as the other guard grabbed his wrist. He jerked his weapon up toward me as, Karnes cried, "No! You foo -" his cry ended in a satisfying gasp as his arms loosened. I twisted away, as the end of the pistol erupted in a red flash. I grinned at the thought that the man was too dumb to realize that a pistol is useless in an FT fight. I the time it took for the bullet to emerge from the barrel, I was able to hit him a hard karate chop across his Adams Apple. He dropped the gun as Karnes grabbed me again.

"For God's sake, Katy, sit down!" I started to give Mac a sharp suggestion as to what he could do with his damned orders - when the monitor started to beep. I jumped for the console. Mac, though beat me to it. He was already zeroing in the coordinates. I went to the secure Ops channel and told the teams to slave their receivers to the console. The location was about sixty K's from here. Team four was the only one closer, about twenty K's closer. It had only two operatives, though, and didn't include any assault personnel. I decided to have them head for the place and check out the situation, then wait for us to arrive. "Do not take any action until we get there unless you can see an imminent threat to one of our two people." I told them. I called for the team. They arrived in a headlong mass and climbed aboard. As soon as the door was closed, Mac sent us into the air and, as soon as all the instruments indicated, ready, redlined the shuttle.

Just then, Susan's voice in my earpiece told me that Cindy had activated her Modulator. That added a certain urgency to our flight. I started checking over our engagement plans and realized, as I looked at the shuttle console that Mac was a lot

316

more worried than he appeared. "Darling," I murmured, leaning up to put my mouth near his ear, "People are going to be very shocked to see a huge rock flying through the air." He muttered, "Shit!" as his hand snaked out to the cloaking switch. "A flock of birds be better?" he muttered, in disgust. "Sounds good to me" I chuckled, "Though a bird flock traveling at two thirds mach might be a bit nerve wracking." His mistake had brought me back to a semblance of calm. I had to remember that this wasn't a personal rescue. It was a professional operation. I had to act the part. "Relax, Katherine." I muttered to myself. "You've got almost ten minutes to get ready. Make use of it."

Five minutes later, Team four began to transmit video of the scene. It was a large four story house set in the midst of a huge swath of irrigated lawn in the middle of a near desert. Mac had also brought up the records on the property. I swore when I saw that it was a business - a very unsavory business. "Ops leader!" the communicator called. "Go ahead, Team leader." Mac answered. "A shuttle had just left target area as we arrived. Its heading was one eighty seven degrees. I didn't know if you wanted us to follow." Mac looked at me and shook his head. I agreed. It was all too likely that the shuttle simply contained a satisfied customer. "Negative." Mac replied. "Continue reconnaissance." "No way to get close to that place unseen." Mac commented. "We'll either have to put down out of sight and go in FT or take a chance on going in as a customer and getting out in FT. If they know all their customer's shuttles they may be able to take action against the kids before we can get inside." I thought that over. "Putting down out of sight would require us to almost be over the horizon out here." I muttered. "If we have hike that far we'll be half dead by the time we get there." Mac chuckled. "Right. I guess we must be in need of some erotic adventure then."

At least, we got a break, finally. There was no alarm raised as we settled into the shuttle parking area and a few FT minutes later we were inside. Spreading out, we began at the front door and worked back and up - securing each room as we came to it. I'd seen some bizarre sexual acts in my time but, even I was shocked at the things that went on in many of those rooms. We still hadn't found James and Cindy, though, by the time I reached the fourth floor. I knew I wasn't doing too good a job at search and securing. I was just throwing open doors, glancing inside, and leaving the backup people to finish the job. Finally, though, I got to a door that was a lot more ornate than the others and when I threw it open - got a shock. "Hi Katy." James said. He was sitting behind a large desk with an especially ugly woman sitting next to him. She was tied, securely to another chair with a gag stuffed in her mouth. "Meet Madam Jolie." He grinned. "She's the proprietor of this unusual establishment. She hasn't been very cooperatives but that's about to change." He held up a small atomizer. This is, I believe, hydro-encephalozine. Karnes used it on us and she was doing her best to convince him to let her send Cindy downstairs to one of her SM rooms with instructions to be nice to her customers. Luckily for us, Karnes was convinced to defer that pleasure until he could get Cindy to work on his Artificial Intelligence machine - person - or whatever. I've been sitting here for almost twelve FT hours letting the stuff get out of my body so I could use it on her."

Two hours later we were all waiting for a position beep from Cindy. James had filled us in on what had happened and Madam Jolie had been treated. Her instructions were that when Karnes called, she was to tell him "convincingly" that all was well here. In the meantime, the rest of the team had resettled the house for an extended occupation. I'd barely heard of hydro-encephalozine but it was wonderful stuff for our purposes.

317

Madam Jolie had plenty on hand so, feeling a little vindictive, I had the guys visit all the rooms and treat the customers and staff with it. "The customers were then told to go on about whatever business they were involved in - it was a free afternoon. They were not, though, to leave the room and if they got any outside communications they were to tell the other party where they were, what they were doing and that they'd be along when they were finished. As for the staff, they were instructed to treat their customers to an "extended experience" until told differently.

As we waited, I wasn't too sure my idea of punishment was such a good one. All the moans and groans, coupled with the shouts of glee - and whatever passed for passion in this place, from the rooms around us was getting on my nerves. Just then the monitor came alive again. Karnes hadn't called so we just left Madam Jolie with instructions not to move and ran for the shuttle. Jimmy had it ready to go as soon as we all piled in. "About fifty k's." he muttered as he flung the thing into the air. Since James had told me what Cindy intended - and knowing her, I didn't doubt it - we'd go in full blast. She'd either have won her war by the time we got there, or would be in need of some help. I put in a call for all the other teams to meet us "on the double". Then, all I could do was sit beside Jimmy and urge him to get more speed on us - knowing full well, that he had the damned thing firewalled.

By the time a group of warehouses came into view it was obvious that Cindy hadn't won her war. A group of people were standing outside and one of them held, what looked like a stovepipe. Almost as soon as we came into view, he raised it and leveled it at us. "Incoming!" Katy growled. "Be ready!" The kid flying just nodded. As a flash of fire erupted from the end of the tube we could see the missile coming at us. By now, all of us were in FT and had to sit there and watch the thing looming larger and larger in front of us. Our shuttle seemed to crawl across the sky and I had trouble keeping myself from grabbing the controls to dodge the thing. Katy looked at me and said, "Be patient, James. Jimmy's good at this." By the time the thing was almost at our nose, our shuttle slowly dipped below it. Now we were dropping towards the ground. Just as we cleared the fence to the warehouse area the missile detonated - only meters, it seemed, above us. A few moments later we felt the concussion drive against the top of the shuttle and the roof begin to buckle. Seconds later, though, our drop speed increased and seconds after that, we hit the ground - hard. Katy already had the door open and was jumping out. All of us followed as the craft began to slowly crumple around us. "Swords!" Katy cried as she headed for the crowd of men. All our assault team followed her. I'd been given, what looked like a large club - obviously - Katy didn't trust me with a sword - and I tried to catch up with the rest of them.

"Damn it, Cynthia." I thought to myself, as I lay on the floor of the room, shackled with two sets of handcuffs to a heavy table leg. "When'll you learn not to let your ego get in the way of your good sense? The fight had gone pretty well for a time. Karnes was, as I suspected, worse than useless as a street fighter. The same, though, couldn't be said for his too goons. By the time, I'd gotten out of Karnes' grasp the one I'd karate chopped was back. He'd dropped his weapon and his big fist knocked me across the room. I staggered a moment but managed to evade his bull like charge till I got my eyes focused again. He, though, wasn't much used to FT either and I had felt up to the challenge of the two of them. It took several minutes before I had both on the floor and having trouble getting up. That's when I made the mistake of stopping to gloat - and when I got thrown to the floor and pinned under about a hundred fifty kilos of muscle. I'd forgotten the one I'd stripped the watch off of. In the melee, he'd found it, put it back on and managed to tackle me. Held down by sheer weight the other two managed to get over and slap handcuffs on me. A few minutes later, I was stuck in this position. Karnes blotted blood from his nose and growled for the guy who'd tackled me to "Watch her! I've got to go deal with whoever she called." As he had lurched out the door, he'd shouted over his shoulder not to hurt me. I was important to his plans.

Now my guard stood over me glowering. He had a rather large shiner for a left eye. "Don' s'pose a lil bit o' hump w'd be same as hurtin'." he muttered. "Might even make yah mo easy to deal wi'." "Shit!" I thought. "Did every clod Karnes have working for him have their brains between their legs?" I considered my options as he reached down to rip open my blouse. I was still in FT - but so was he. He stuck his pistol in his holster and grabbing my skirt hem in both hands, ripped it all the way to my waist. Then, as he grinned at my nakedness and unzipped his pants, I again, wished they'd let me have some underwear. Well I still had my knees, I thought. Just as he knelt down, though, and I got ready to use them, he grabbed them and shoved them wide apart. The only thing left to do after he got between them, I did. I threw my legs around his chest and squeezed - hard. "Bitch!" he growled and hit me.

The fight was wild but only four of our opponents had modulators, one of whom, Karnes, was totally unable to bring himself to do real damage. The rest were so used to using guns that, it took them several seconds to realize that they were useless in FT against clubs and swords - seconds in which they gaped in astonishment as bullets hung in the air between us. By then we were on them and they were cut, or clubbed to the ground. Shouting at a pair of our guys to take their watches off and secure them all with chains, Katy took off, with the rest of us for the building. The first floor had four consoles in it with operators, sitting inert in front of them. It was the third door of the second floor, that Katy threw open and motioned to Mac. Seconds later, as I came to the door, Mac threw an arm lock on me. "Katy'll take care of it." he growled. I went mad! Cindy was lying, out cold and almost naked on the floor shackled to a table.

As a huge man, obviously in FT, himself, jumped up from between her legs, and her badly bruised face came into view. The man's pants were open but before he could get to his feet, Katy was on him. She hit him like a tiger - all fists and feet and claws. Big as he was, though, he managed to stand up, towering over her - but only for a moment. A fist in the belly and a knee in the groin bent him over in a gasping crouch. As his head dropped, she lowered her head and drove it hard into his face. From that moment on, she vented her fury on him so violently it almost sobered me enough to feel sorry for him. "Check on Cindy." Mac whispered, releasing me.

When I came to, James was bent over me, tears dripping on my chest. I looked over to see what the noise was and saw Katy straddling the goon, her fists like battering rams pounding his face - in between, banging his head against the floor. Mac was crouched over her whispering. "It's enough, darling." She was ignoring him. Then I realized James was saying something. Shaking my head to clear it, I asked him what he'd said. All he could say was, "Did he - I mean - well - are you OK?" I had to grin because I knew what he meant. I took inventory. My cheek hurt and I raised my head to

319

look down. Nothing looked wrong. I wriggled my butt. Nothing felt wrong. "My cheek hurts, honey." I whispered. "Otherwise, you'll have to tell me. I've been taking a nap."

He leaned down and hugged me tightly. He buried his face in my chest and muttered, "Oh God! I was – so- I wanted to comfort him. "How about getting these damned things off my wrists." I told him, then looking over his shoulder at the three armed men in the GL's guard uniforms, whispered, "And, while displaying my body to half the world has a certain charm, I'd also like some clothes." Things happened pretty quickly after that. Katy stopped trying to kill the goon on the floor and, rummaging around in his pockets, got a key and unlocked the handcuffs. Then Mac took off his shirt and threw it over me. I felt giddy when Katy finally got my hands free and growled that they had captured Karnes. James helped me up and stood behind me as I shrugged off the ripped clothing and slipped into Mac's shirt.

As I buttoned it, I looked around him and called out, "Sorry boys. Next show at eleven." They chuckled and came in to gather up the goon off the floor. Katy frowned. "You OK?" she asked. I knew what she wanted to ask also. "I think I'd be able to tell if I wasn't." I whispered. "That over there is Jonha's lost AI." Looking around, I saw the shoes I'd kicked off to start the fight, and went over to slip them on. Looking down, I could see that Mac's shirt hung well down on my thighs so, decided I was decently covered. "I think we can go home now."

I hadn't realized that Mac had left the room until we got downstairs. He was just coming in the door from the console room with some clothes. "Fetching as you look in my shirt, Mrs. McClennan, I need my shirt back before I get sunburned. Thought you might prefer these." He handed Cindy a pair of pants and a shirt. "It looked like the guy was about your size." While Cindy slipped the pants on and, turning her back shrugged out of Mac's shirt and into the new one, I glanced into the room. One guy sat at his console in nothing but a pair of shorts.

As it turned out, we didn't get to go home right away. In less than a half hour, shuttles streamed in from all points of the compass and teams of men, scoured the whole complex for any other of Karnes personnel. They didn't find any but, in the other warehouse, did find his heavy lift shuttle and a lot of exotic equipment. Katy had called the GL to report success and Suzanne wouldn't believe it until she could talk to Cindy. Then we both spoke to the kids. The GL said to wait until he could get enough shuttles to us so we could transport all our prisoners back. Also he'd send Archer to check over Karnes shuttle before anybody tried to use it. By that time, we were drawing a crowd from the nearby town. A man, who said he was the mayor, insisted that we not leave until the state police gave us permission.

Katy, explained, graciously, that we weren't required to wait but if the police showed up in time, she'd brief them on what had happened. They did get here before the GL's shuttles arrived and weren't too satisfied with Katy's explanation that a kidnapping had occurred and we had the perpetrators in custody but that she couldn't go into what else was going on. Their attitude changed abruptly, when a fleet of Super shuttles arrived bearing the GL's logo - and Jonha, himself, stepped out, followed by Suzanne. I thought they were going to fall on their faces in shock.

Suzanne clutched at my hand and gasped. "John! Look at her! She's hurt!" I squeezed the hand. I'd already scanned the crowd standing by the warehouse. It was

320

obvious that Cynthia was in no danger of collapse. In fact, she practically glowed with pleasure as she listened to Katherine saying something to the uniforms arrayed with her. There was a large and darkening bruise on her face and what looked like a scrape on her chin but they were obviously superficial. "Easy honey!" I said. "She'll heal fine. How about you call Art and Lil and tell them so while I go do the GL thing." By the time, we got to the crowd the uniforms were standing at rigid attention and saluting. I managed to keep a straight face. Nobody in Paris would dare salute me. We'd had that settled long ago. Never the less, I saluted them back. Putting a grateful face on, I shook their hands and thanked them for all the help they'd been to my "forces". That seemed to make their day. James and Cynthia were being hugged by Suzanne, so I turned to Katherine.

"Everything OK?" I asked. She grinned. "Come on inside and tell me." she said. As we headed for the building, she filled me in on the raid on the house of ill repute and here and the situation with Cynthia. "Probably should watch her for awhile -" she muttered "but I doubt she'll have any problem with what happened - or, as far as I can tell, almost happened." By then we were on the second floor and turned into a room. "Otherwise, is that what you've been looking for?" I breathed a sigh of relief as I looked at the AI. It seemed to crouch in the corner. "Looks like its running. Want to see if you can get it to operate?" she asked. "Better not." I replied. "A destruct order was sent out. If it hasn't complied yet, we'd better get it back to headquarters so that Susan and Archer can check it over before we try to wake it up. We may need to get Cindy to work on it but, right now, it's no danger to anyone."

We rode back to Paris with Jonha and Suzanne while Katy and Mac stayed to supervise the packing up and transfer of the equipment in the warehouse. Archer had arrived before we left, and had, immediately, dived into the inner workings of the heavy lift shuttle. Katy had sent a large contingent of guards back to Madam Jolie's to shut it down. The patrons were all to be sent home - after having their identities checked. The Madam, herself, was to be sent to Paris for the GL to determine her fate and her employees were to be held until disposition of the place was decided upon. It looked like it was a legitimate business, under local law, so it could be that they could all be released or, as Katy suggested, have it turned over to their management for the time being.

That night, we had a large family dinner, including all the kids, ours as well as Katy and Mac's and Marie Trudeau, in Jonha and Suzanne's apartment. I was shocked at the twins manners. They were excited at being included but were very polite about everything. Suzanne was showing them off. She had been, diligently, teaching them how to behave and seemed to have managed it. Everybody had to hear of our adventures and we gave them an abridged version, leaving out any mention of actual happenings when we were in custody. By then, Cindy had been treated at the GL's clinic and her face had cleared up enough that it didn't take much makeup to conceal the damage. Charlie and Julie frowned with a teen age awareness that they weren't getting the whole story but let it go. All in all, it was a festive occasion and was enjoyed by all. It was too bad that Katy and Mac weren't there to enjoy it with us.

That night, I was luxuriating in our bed when Cindy, opened the bath door. She posed in the light for a moment, and purred, "Darling, you all interrupted my, oh so considerate lover this morning, just when it was getting exciting. You don't suppose you could ravish me a little to make up for it, do you?" I looked at the vision framed by the light behind her. Her long blond hair hung down her back and the, almost transparent peignoir

321

she wore left no doubt as to the lack of any impediment to her ravishment. I threw back the sheet and suggested I'd try to help her out. An hour later, a properly ravished, lady laid her head on my shoulder and went to sleep.

ANY TIME ANY WHEN
CHAPTER 34

THE NEW BEGINNING

It was almost two years later that we stood on the roof of the World Federation Headquarters and watched the shuttle land. Yesterday we'd watched on the Astro monitors as the huge space ship moved slowly into stable orbit around Earth. Since then, a fleet of smaller, and diverse, ships were noted, approaching the solar system and would be arriving over the next few days. Our Magman Scientific team was, finally, arriving. It had been a hectic two years. Susan had notified Jonha the day after we captured Karnes that "Upgrade" was approved, at his discretion, by the Magman AI's. The Magman Council had been notified and had been instructed to meet with our representative, to discuss the details of our role in the galaxy and the necessary technical education of our scientists to assume that role.

Susan had suggested to Jonha that he, as the GL, become the planetary representative. She was afraid that our "barbarous human" ways might be so shocking as to send the whole council to therapy. She did grin at that remark but it was probably a good idea since the job of "Watcher" was probably no longer applicable. Jonha had tried to give us lesson in Magman terms of politeness but it soon became obvious that only a well trained diplomat would have any chance at all, of conferring with them.

Surprisingly, to me at least, it was Katherine who was able to master the nuances of Magman diplomacy the best. She said it came from being raised in an oriental culture and having to deal with the leaders of the criminal element where an unintended slight, no matter how small, could lead to murder. Anyway, they had returned with the "Charter" for the Galactic Police Force and a "request" from the Council, that contact with humans be held to a minimum. Katherine had chuckled that, when she'd simply asked about security precautions, half the Magman team she was working with had spent two days in therapy.

Jonha had warned us about these Magmans. Most were members of the Watcher teams that had not elected to be destroyed along with the systems they were monitoring. Few other Magmans felt capable of dealing with us directly. He assured us that all the dissidents, along with Karnes, the unauthorized delegation that had come here to destroy us and Pendleton had been sent to "Magman Coventry" and none were included as our "instructors." Still we would have to be very careful of their weaknesses.

Just then Susan's hologram appeared beside us dressed in a conservative business suit. A moment later, Arthur and Cindi appeared dressed like her. "Jonha," she murmured, I've arranged for some lifters out here. Three members of the delegation will need transport downstairs. Ah, there they are." At that, three tall, slim Magmans appeared before us. It took a moment to realize that they were holograms also. "Susan." one said, bending to kiss her hand, "So glad to finally meet you in person." When he raised his eyes there was a definite twinkle in them. "Karlen." she murmured. Then, turning to the gaping group beside her, she said, "Jonha, Let me introduce, Karlen, Mordrap and Marybeth, leaders of the Magman Scientific delegation." Then she rapidly introduced us to them.

"Katherine Thuringen we have met." Karlen said. Turning his eyes on James and I, he said, "The McClennans we've heard much about. We are all delighted to meet you finally." Nodding to Mac, Marybeth said, I can see why Katherine was so anxious to get home. You are, indeed, handsome, Mister Thuringen." Letting her eyes move to the children, she added, "And you have such lovely daughters." Her eyes creased in a frown as she turned to John and Maylin. "I understood, though, that the McClennan children were babies. May I assume that they have spent much time in your Fast Time?"

Surprised, I could only nod. After all, the kids were almost teen age size. In the last two years they'd spent a total of almost eight with us in FT. It hadn't really crossed my mind. I looked at them and got another shock. John was ignoring all the proceedings. His eyes were on the Thuringen twins. My God! Didn't he realize that they had diapered him only a few years ago? Since they had spent little time in FT, the age differences weren't as great now but they were, still, five or six years older. Now I realized why he had been so insistent on spending so much time in FT with James and I. I shrugged thinking that if he played his cards right he just might catch up to them.

While I'd been distracted, Jonha had welcomed the rest of the arrivals and was discussing the pending arrivals of the next ship. "We brought one of our newest trading ships with us." Karlen was saying. The rest are a representative selection of the various ships we have. They will all be used to train your people in intergalactic travel. You are allowed to modify them in any way you think necessary to accomplish your task - but only after Mordrap, Marybeth and I are satisfied that your technicians are capable of it. Any weapons development will be approved by us and not discussed with the rest of our people. It would also be advantageous for you to treat us in public as ordinary digital machines." Gesturing behind him, he smiled, "As you can see, simply discussing the word tends to make them nervous. Now where do you intend to house us?" The three magmans accompanying them did look a bit twitchy. With a last chuckle by Mordrap, they disappeared.

That evening, we had a council session in my conference room. A large proportion of the attendees were Digital People. Besides the three newly arrived ones, there was Susan, Cindi and Arthur. The new DP rescued from Karnes was still undergoing - well, repair wasn't a good description of the process. Suzanne was maintaining a continuing dialogue with it much like a psychiatrist would. The rest of us were all family if you count Mac and Katy. I guess I should say the adult family since we left the kids out.

Karlen took charge of the meeting. "First," he said, I must admit to a very un-digital person amazement at the impressive development of Mister McClennan's Cindi, and Arthur's ingenuity in managing her upgrade. Mordrap, Marybeth and I - by the way, we appreciate that you local organics are using our names. Back home it seemed that using them was somewhat disturbing to the population. We, therefore, accepted the title of AI to reduce that. Back to my point, if we had not just spent a very long session with Cindi, I would have been unable to accept her as one of us. We, previously, would have said such an upgrade could not be accomplished. We still are not able to reach consensus on how it was done. She still heavily depends on her connections to the world web but, except in speed of operation, is otherwise, fully as capable as any of us.

Now I should turn to the present earth situation. We have accepted the fact that it would be counterproductive, even if possible, to actually try and bring your organics violent tendencies under complete control. We will, from time to time, recommend ways to reduce the violence, usually in specific cases." I was becoming put out with Karlen's attitude. First, he took over the meeting as if he was in charge. Even Cindi, with her ego, never went that far.

"Mister, Karlen," I said, trying not to show my irritation, "do you mean Order when you say Recommend?" Karlen gave a very human blink in, apparent, surprise. Well if he thought we'd just roll over and play dead for him, he was very much mistaken. Katy and James bowed their heads to cover grins. Everybody else kept a blank face at the question. A human like grin came on Karlen's face. "Mrs. McClennan, Cindi tells me that when you are the most polite, I should beware of your bite. I presume, from that metaphor that I am the subject of your irritation. I'm also told that I should be very careful of your temper. To answer your question, though - there are a few very limited times when any of us may order you to do anything. They all apply to actions that would create major disruptions in the space time continuum. Except in rare cases, they do not include, for example, preventing you from destroying, or even damaging, yourselves in some way. Almost every recommendation we make will, therefore, be just that. We may now since your upgrade advise against dangerous, or unwise, activities but cannot prevent them."

Looking around, he asked if there were any more questions. "The holographic smile that followed when there weren't any, needed practice. "I am not sure that we can be of much help on your domestic situation but we will continue to work with Cindi and Arthur to help devise strategies for pacification of trouble spots. May I assume that Mr. and Mrs. Thuringen will be the primary operatives in this respect?" "Along with her father, Marcus Orion." Jonha said. He nodded. "Well, our main purpose is to be teachers, mostly for your technicians. It will probably take a number of your years for them to gain the knowledge necessary to become starfarers. Learning to be galactic policemen will be something we can only help with in theory. Our programming did not consider that option when it was prepared and modifications we've made over the years didn't require it."

THE EARTH ERA

It was now another year later. Yesterday, James and I led a group of the new Earth Secretariat members through the first earth made intergalactic capable ship. It wasn't large and was, of course built on a design brought from Magma but we'd built it ourselves here in orbit. Also, though, it was much faster than the ships the Magmans had brought with them - our improved Modulators had astounded our "teachers". Due to the fact that it was designed for extended patrols and needed a crew of twenty four to operate, we decided to call it a by an old earth name, "Cruiser." Additionally, it contained some unmagmanlike features. Powerful laser like weapons that could tap the power of one of the lesser power universes bristled from three turrets. The DP's assured us that they wouldn't be needed in our trials but we'd decided that we needed to perfect the installations for later use.

James and I had both been involved in the design of the engines that powered it and James had been a consultant on everything dealing with the construction. He mostly looked over shoulders and gave approvals as to the rightness or wrongness of a given system. Now Galaxy One was ready to fly. It would be handled by an earth crew who'd been in training all year for the job. Magman, flight personnel, along with the DP Marybeth, would accompany them, to lend a hand, advice and help on contacts with the other galactic trading people they might run across. I wished I - we were going to be going with them. Jonha, though, had been dead set against it. He insisted that we were "too important to risk on this flight". James and I had both argued with him but to no avail. As a result when we'd finished our tour, we'd sat with the rest of the delegation, while Captain Murchison explained the mission they were going to go on. Now we watched on Suzanne's hologram as a sort of wavy disturbance in the space behind the ship began to grow. There was no sense of movement until one of the background stars moved across our line of vision. As more and more came into view, their apparent movement increased dramatically. "The Modulator Drive is at fifty percent power and increasing exponentially." It was Karlen who was monitoring the breakout from orbit. "Modulator is at full power. Velocity in local time is point 1 C and rising. Shifting into Galactic drive now." The image blurred and winked out. Estimated transition time to Argosy colony is twelve ship days - thirty seven days local." Susanne brought up another hologram. This one of the news room of the combined world news links. The beautiful female announcer intoned - or tried to. "THE EARTH ERA, the first earth built Galactic Cruiser, has launched. It left orbit at 1200 hours Greenwich! Her excitement then got in the way. With a very unladylike shriek, she cried, "It left our universe at 1237 hours. GOD SPEED, TEE!" "Shit!" James muttered. "Sounds like she's announcing a golf game."

www.ingramcontent.com/pod-product-compliance
Lightning Source LLC
Chambersburg PA
CBHW061128200626
46817CB00016B/405